Changeling Dream

Dani Harper

BRAVA

KENSINGTON PUBLISHING CORP.

www.kensingtonbooks.com

BRAVA BOOKS are published by

Kensington Publishing Corp.
119 West 40th Street
New York, NY 10018

ISBN-13: 978-0-7582-6516-6
ISBN-10: 0-7582-6516-6

First Kensington Trade Paperback Printing: July 2011

10   9   8   7   6   5   4   3   2   1

Printed in the United States of America

Changeling
Dream

Sometimes we raise our kids and sometimes our kids raise us. This story is for Jordan, Jaime, Abby and Sam, who continue to be very good parents to their mom.

Love will find a way through paths where wolves fear to prey.
—LORD BYRON

Prologue

September 30, 1981

Tendrils of smoke rose ghostly white against the night sky like escaping spirits. Two days had passed and the house had collapsed to one side in a heap of charred beams and ash. No human could have survived such devastation.

James Macleod was not human.

Far beneath the blackened beams, he lay burned, bleeding, and broken. Close to death but as yet unable to embrace it. Now and then, he broke the surface of unconsciousness, only to be dragged under again by relentless agony and despair.

The waning moon hid its face as James opened his eyes at last. For a fleeting moment he thought he was blind, then realized night had fallen, although which night it was he had no idea and didn't care. He was still alive—barely—and didn't care about that either. His broken ribs screamed at him as he began to cough up more blood and soot, but this time oblivion stubbornly refused to take him back.

Evelyn. He couldn't see her beneath the debris, but he could just reach her delicate fingertips. They were cold and unyielding. He felt again the slash of agony in his heart that was far greater than the pain in his body. She had been human. Vulnerable, both she and the child within her, *his* child. He had failed them both, failed to protect them, failed even to discern any danger to them. He had been moving the cattle to summer pasture in the deep coulees along the river when a calf blundered into the fast-moving water. Saving the young animal and regrouping the herd had set him back an hour, then two. Just two scant hours in which all that was dear to him was left defenseless.

He'd known at once. James had barely turned his truck for home when cold terror suddenly clawed his heart and his wife's voice echoed briefly in his mind. Gunning the old pickup, he'd kept it on the rough dirt road by sheer force of will. Faster, *faster*, heedless of the rugged terrain. He had to get home, *had* to reach her. When an axle broke, James left the crippled truck and raced flat out, first on two legs, then on four.

The house had been strangely dark when he reached the yard. Evelyn always left a light on for him. Always. And then he had spotted the smoke churning from an upstairs window. He caught no stranger's scent as he ran into the burning house, as he shifted his shape and shouted for his wife. He had smelled blood, however, mixed with the thickening smoke. He followed the metallic tang of it straight to the dining room, knowing and not wanting to know that it was her blood. And that there was far too much of it. *Dear God.* James had squeezed his eyes shut against the ugly gunshot wounds that had stolen her life even as he cradled her small body against him. She was gone. Their child within her, already loved, was gone as well.

It was his fault, all his fault, although James had no idea who had done this. Few people could even find his ranch. It was remote, all but hidden, with the nearest neighbor miles away. He knew no enemies in this country, yet in his shattered heart he also knew it was no random act that had taken his loved ones from him. He should have known better. *He should have known.* His family's entire sept of Clan Macleod had been forced to leave Scotland more than two centuries earlier, when fear of Changelings caused all wolves to be slaughtered to extinction there. Why had he thought it would be better here, safer now? Why had he assumed humans were any more civilized now, any less driven by fear and hatred of those who were different? But then there had been Evelyn, and she was wholly, completely human. Evelyn, who embodied all that was good about humanity, who knew what he was and accepted him, who loved him with a heart that was bigger than she was. Evelyn who had just paid for that love with her all-too-human life.

Already half-mad with pain and grief, his own human side wanted nothing more than to follow his loved ones. Changelings were long-lived and tough, gifted and powerful. But they were not immortal. And not immune to bullets even if they weren't silver. Evelyn's killer had still been in the house, waiting for James, and James hadn't known. Perhaps he hadn't cared then either. The last thing he saw was his whole world in his arms—then nothing.

Left for dead. Now, his Changeling nature was automatically trying to heal the horrendous wounds, weakly attempting to regenerate burned skin and tendon, repair and replace broken bone. But with so much damage and so little energy left, the process was winding down before it had really begun. Soon it would stop altogether and he would get his wish.

For one clear moment that wish coalesced in his mind—a soul-deep desire for death. James embraced it without reservation, forgetting that his inner wolf was driven by a powerful and primitive instinct to survive. Without warning, fresh agony slammed into him from every direction. His heart was being squeezed through his ribs, his very bones felt as if they were exploding. The animal within had gone completely wild. Unbidden, it frantically clawed its way to the surface.

Dark clouds diffused the moon, hid the massive wolf that crawled out from under the charred wreckage, veiled the singed white fur in shadow. Sides heaving, the creature limped on three legs to the edge of the clearing and collapsed. James lay there for a long time and regarded the wreckage. Fists of sorrow beat inside him, but his lupine eyes could not weep. Instead, a cry of anguish was ripped from his throat, gaining in strength as it sliced through the silence. It rose and became an ululating lament echoing over the ruins of his home, his heart, his life.

As he howled out his grief, the sky cleared. The moon was far from full but still it blanketed him with pale silvery light, lent him its peculiar strength that only Changelings knew. James stood. So his wolf nature wanted to survive? Then it could damn well do it without him. He would set it free and never walk upright again.

The wind picked up. Although only three legs would obey him, the white wolf began to run. Run, to outpace the agony that could rip and tear a human heart. Run, to outdistance the human grief that could not be borne. Run, to be as the moon, a swift white shape gleaming in the night. Run, to be a wolf and only a wolf.

As he raced away into the welcoming arms of the night, James was only fleetingly aware that he had just buried his human self alongside Evelyn. And then he was aware of nothing.

Chapter One

March 31, 2011

The wolf dream again.

Jillian Descharme rolled over on the lumpy folding couch that doubled as her bed and squinted to read the alarm clock. *3:29 A.M.* She didn't need to reach for the light—the dream was no nightmare. Far from it. Fifteen years ago, a great white wolf had emerged from the darkness and saved her life.

Her counselor, Marjorie, had favored other theories. She felt that the white wolf was something Jillian's mind created to protect itself, to protect her very sanity from a trauma that couldn't be borne, from a brutality beyond imagining. "The wolf is a symbol your mind has adopted," Marjorie said. "And in the study of dream images, a white wolf in particular symbolizes both valor and victory, plus the ability to see light in the darkest hours. It's an extremely powerful and positive image."

Marjorie was a skilled counselor, as well as a kind and loving person. She had helped Jillian work through a great deal of pain, and Jillian knew she owed her a lot. That was why she always felt a little bit guilty. Because although she stopped insisting the wolf was real, she never quite stopped believing it.

And she didn't stop dreaming of it. Jillian dreamed of the white wolf when she moved away from home, when she entered veterinary college, when she wrote exams, when she applied for jobs, when she competed in martial arts tournaments—pretty much any time she was nervous, stressed, or even lonely. Okay, *especially* when she was lonely.

Not alone. Here with you, the wolf always said to her. She didn't hear the words so much as felt them in her mind. *Not alone.* And in the presence of the wolf, she could believe it. Jillian always felt soothed, comforted, safe. Between them was a connection that defied description. A sense of wholeness she had never conceived possible.

"Nothing like being codependent on an imaginary friend." Jillian got up for a drink of water, realized that wasn't enough to get rid of the fuzzy taste in her mouth, and decided to brush her teeth.

Popping open the tube of toothpaste seemed to jog a memory at the same time. Jillian always welcomed the wolf dream and the calm it brought her whenever there were changes in her life. But in the past few years she'd noticed a new pattern—the wolf dream also seemed to show up just *before* something in her life changed. And this was the third night in a row she'd had the dream.

That had never happened before. Back in bed, she lay with her eyes open, wondering what the dream meant, wondering what was coming. She hoped it wouldn't be the bank calling about her student loans again. That thought was enough to keep her awake for the next hour. When her alarm went off at six, however, there was nothing unusual about the morning except that it took three cups of coffee to jumpstart her brain instead of one. There was nothing different about the weather. It was the same as it had been for weeks, just another humid scorcher in southern Ontario. There was nothing different at work. There were no new animals at the environmental center, and no unusual visitors. She accidentally sat on her lunch bag, but except for being squished, her peanut butter and honey sandwich tasted exactly the same.

Later, at the post office, she had nothing but bulk mail in her box. She dropped the flyers and ads into the trash by the door as she left. At least there weren't any bills. But there was no winning envelope from Publishers Clearing House either. She attended the last of her weekly Tae Kwon Do classes—she couldn't afford any more—but there were no breakthroughs there. She had yet to master all 29 movements of the *hyung*, the complicated practice sequence that would allow her to progress to the next level.

The feeling of letdown was heavy by the time Jillian opened the door to her tiny rented room. It was silly, it was childish, but she couldn't deny she was disappointed that not a single out-of-the-ordinary thing had occurred that day. On top of that, she was tired to the point of being downright cranky. *Maybe the stupid dream didn't mean anything this time. Maybe it isn't* supposed *to mean anything. Maybe Marjorie was right and this whole wolf thing really is a figment of my—*

The phone rang, making her jump, and she snatched up the receiver with a growl. With any luck it might be a telemarketer and she could unload a little of her frustration. Petty, she knew, but it would be something. She promised herself to feel guilty later. "Yes?"

"Is this Dr. Jillian Descharme?"

"What are you selling?"

The caller didn't even pause. "A job. I'd like you to come work for me. My practice is running me ragged, and I need a hand. If you're as good as your instructors say you are, it could turn into a partnership. That is, if you like northern Alberta."

She fumbled with the receiver then, certain that reality had taken a complete holiday. "What?" Her brain finally kicked in. "Wait a minute. I forgot what day it is—this is a stupid April Fool's joke, isn't it?" Jillian wracked her brain to figure out who might pull such a prank. A coworker? A former classmate? "Of all the mean, rotten—"

"No, it's no joke, honest. Hey, if I'd realized what day it was, I would have waited until tomorrow to call you. I promise you, this is a real call about a real job. Look, it's calving season and I haven't slept in two days, so if I sound desperate, I am. Will you come?"

"I don't know you from Adam. And you haven't even met me. You haven't seen my résumé. I haven't even applied for the job yet. I didn't even know there *was* a job." She certainly hadn't looked for anything that far away, had never been to that part of the country. Mentally she pictured a map of Canada and visualized Alberta. It was one of the largest provinces, stretching from the American border all the way up to the Arctic Circle. Just how far north was this clinic? Was there still snow on the ground there?

"I've been friends with a couple of your instructors for a long time. That's where I got your name. They both said you're good, and that's good enough for me." He rattled off their names and enough personal details to prove he was telling the truth. Or that he'd really done his research. He seemed to read her mind then. "Call them up. Ask them about Connor Macleod, and they'll tell you I'm not a nutcase or a stalker."

"But I *have* a job."

"I heard. I also heard your present position's temporary. I

happen to know the director of the place—he thinks you're extremely talented too, by the way. Says he'll even let you go early, if you decide you want the job here."

She sighed and swore, forgetting that the man could hear her through the receiver. She ran a hand through her choppy blond hair, causing it to stand straight up in places. It was all too true that her job at the environmental center was up at the end of the month. She'd tried hard to find another opportunity to work with wildlife, especially wolves, but most positions these days were filled by volunteers. Those that weren't were largely government-funded—and that funding had dried up considerably after the last election.

Tapping the phone against her chin, Jillian figured that this Macleod guy really must be flat-out desperate. Why else would he call someone on the other side of the country for God's sake? It was on the tip of her tongue to say *no*, to tell him she'd rather patch up coyotes and feed orphan skunks than work with livestock and pets. Not only were they more interesting to her, but coyotes and skunks didn't have owners to deal with. She wasn't as good with people as she was with animals. Okay, she could be downright lousy with people, especially ones that didn't take care of their animals.

But she couldn't make herself say no, especially when Macleod told her that living quarters were part of the deal.

Jillian hadn't been out of veterinary college very long. She desperately needed a full-time position, any position that would give her a chance to pay off her massive student loans and get on her financial feet. She might have a DVM after her name now, but that was all she had to her name. No cash, no savings, no car, no furniture, no apartment. No family that could help her out either, not since an accident had claimed her parents when she was in college. She didn't even have her textbooks anymore—she'd been forced to sell them last month to keep her small room near the environmental center.

"Hello? Hey, are you still there?"

She realized she'd left the man hanging. "Sorry, just thinking things through. It's a big move. You're just about on the other side of the country."

"Let me make it easier then. Commit to giving us six months, and I'll pay your way here. If you really hate us after that, or we can't stand you, no harm done. I'd pay your way home, too."

She could do six months. That wasn't a long time. She could keep her temper, make nice with clients for six months. Probably. Macleod likely ran a cramped, shoestring operation in the middle of nowhere, but the guy was offering good pay and a place to live. And surely there must be wildlife rehabs she could look into while she was there. Maybe she could work for Macleod's clinic for a while and then move on to what she really wanted to do with her career. Besides, how bad could it be? Making a mental note to check this guy out with her instructors and maybe even the RCMP before she actually packed any suitcases, she said yes.

And remembered the wolf dream as she hung up the phone.

The full moon called and the Pack answered. The lights of the town of Dunvegan were left behind as seven creatures ran silently, effortlessly, mile after mile. Nothing could cover distance as efficiently as a wolf's perfect form. Charcoal and tawny, gray and silver, gold and black, the wolves were a diverse group, yet they moved as one with the smooth grace of long practice. Eventually a white wolf joined them, easing into the band without a ripple.

The Pack loped along the game trails at the very tops of the coulees, high above the Peace River valley. The wolves' path seemed almost suspended between sky and water, moon above and moon reflected below. Joy, fierce and bright, was all around.

Stars wheeled overhead, revealing the constellations of the early morning as the Pack leader turned toward Elk Point. There, she slowed at last and picked her way along the rocky promontory until the trees parted to reveal a sweeping view. Tongues lolling, sides heaving, the wolves flopped down on the stone plateau just as a wind gusted up from the valley. Dry leaves swirled into a lazy vortex around the group. The air crackled, flashed here and there with tiny sparks, as static electricity began to collect. The power built until the ground thrummed with it, until the very rocks vibrated.

Sudden silence burst as loud as a thunderclap. Human laughter and human words flowed in quickly to fill the vacuum. The breeze died away, the leaves fell to earth. Where eight wolves had been, there was now only one. A lone white wolf and seven human beings.

Connor Macleod automatically reached out a hand and ruffled the thick soft fur. His older brother was not just the only one in the family with such a snowy pelt, but the only Changeling that Connor had ever seen with that coloration—not an albino but a true white. Their father had often called James a *winter wolf*, but there was always a touch of sadness in his voice when he did so. Connor had pressed him for an explanation once. *It's a verra long journey until spring for a winter wolf, lad. A verra long journey.* Connor had been too young to attach any meaning to his father's words. Now he saw that they had been all too prophetic.

He spoke to his older brother in his mind. All of them had that ability; it was part and parcel of being Changeling. *Good to see you, bro. Have you eaten tonight?*

Old moose, lame. Easy hunting. Full now.

James's words were always clear in Connor's mind, but they were few and labored, as if it were a strain to use human words at all. As if running as a wolf for thirty years made it difficult to even remember the language. Seven words in a row nearly counted as a speech.

It might have given Connor a tiny glimmer of hope, but he hadn't allowed himself that luxury in many years. His hand fell away from the thick white pelt as he automatically blocked the rest of his thoughts from his brother. What possible good could it do to tell James how much he missed him, ached to talk with him, to joke and laugh with him, hell, even to fight with him? How the whole family grieved for James, as if he was dead. And he *was* dead to them. Even as a wolf he very seldom ran with the Pack or came near any of them except Connor on occasion. James had forsaken his human self entirely, and it was unclear if he was bound to the Macleods by remembered human ties or merely a wolf instinct to be part of a Pack.

But not one of us blames him for it. Good Christ, how could we? We weren't there. We were too far away, all of us too damn far away. He shook his head. By the time they'd arrived at James's farm, the house was a heap of blackened beams and cold ashes. *Too damn late to do anything but bury poor Evelyn.* It had nearly been too late for James as well. The Pack had tracked him through deep wilderness for two days, unable to catch up with him until he finally collapsed from his horrific wounds. Over thirty years had passed and still

Connor shivered at *that* memory. He had barely recognized the blackened and battered creature that once was the white wolf. Changeling or not, it was a miracle James had lived.

But the miracle was incomplete. The wolf came back to them, but not the man. Connor glanced over at his brother. The massive white creature was stretched out on the ground beside him as if relaxed, but the vivid blue eyes flicked from person to person. Alert. Ready, Connor knew, to disappear. Everyone else knew too. Connor noticed that each member of the Pack, family and friend alike, would glance over at James and then quickly turn away, not knowing what to do or say. Fearing to break some unknown spell, fearing that the white wolf would leave them even sooner than he usually did.

It's hard on James but it's hard on all of us too. Your older brother has lost his balance, his ability to be comfortable in both worlds.

Jessie Watson's voice was warm and strong in Connor's mind. He knew the Pack leader was focusing her speech so only he could hear it. He did the same. *I don't know how to help him.*

You're doing all you can. James is doing all he can, too. He's chosen to stay here, for one thing. He wanders but always returns. He still feels a connection to this land that your family claimed and settled, a bond to something that symbolizes roots. And he responds to you, Connor. Cares for you as a brother, not just a Pack-mate, even guards you. Haven't you sensed him on some level when you've been working late at the clinic?

Connor looked across the fire, saw it brush golden highlights over Jessie's dark skin. There was always something regal about her, a sense of power. She was a small woman, downright tiny when standing next to her husband Bill.

Yet she possessed a formidable blend of courage and wisdom, as well as more exotic gifts. Including magic. He didn't doubt her, but the news came as a surprise. *James has been at the clinic?*

Many times. Perhaps you haven't noticed his physical presence because thoughts of James are always in your mind. Take a walk tomorrow and use your Changeling senses to check the stand of trees behind the building. Scent the air, the ground. Watch for hairs in the hay bales in the compound, prints along the fences in the corrals. He watches over you, Connor. He watches over the others too.

Well, then he should be fired—he didn't make sure everyone was dressed tonight. Connor tried to lighten the subject, a little uncomfortable with the notion that the older brother he worried so much about was guarding him. He turned his attention to where his younger brother Devlin was mercilessly teasing his twin Culley about missing shoes and socks. Anything—clothing, objects, tools—that touched a Changeling's body as it shifted to wolf was automatically suspended in a another dimension until human form was resumed. What or where that dimension was exactly, Connor didn't know, only that the current theory favored the existence of many more dimensions than the four that Einstein declared. That was Devlin's passion, exploring the physics associated with Changeling life. Culley, however, couldn't care less. Always in a hurry, he often Changed without checking to make sure he was fully clothed.

It wasn't a problem unless they had to shift back to human form unexpectedly. Explaining why their youngest brother was barefoot in the middle of the night could be tricky. Culley had no jacket either, only a light T-shirt, but a Changeling's ambient body temperature was much higher than that of a human. Connor shook his head, nearly smiled. *That boy would be comfortable if he was buck-naked in a snowstorm.* Then he saw Culley steal a wistful glance at the white wolf and the heavyheartedness returned full-force.

They think he avoids them, Jessie. And he does, he steers clear of everyone. Except me, Connor thought. *And he doesn't exactly hang around much with me either.* They were just a year apart in age, and they'd been inseparable when they were growing up. Even when Evelyn entered James's life, they'd remained close. Close before everything went to hell. *I miss him, Jessie. It drives me crazy, wishing I could help him.*

You are *helping him. You're there for him. How many months was it before James even attempted to communicate? Yet he speaks to you now in your mind. How many years before he would venture near the Pack? Yet he often runs with us now, ran with us tonight. Progress is slow and subtle, very hard to see when it's happening—but James has been opening the door a little at a time. He doesn't know it, but he is ready to be healed. And because of this, the healer will come.*

What healer? Who?

I don't know. I haven't seen that. I just know that the Universe reaches out to us when we make an effort, when we show we are ready. James is ready. The healer will come. She broke the connection then, turning her attention to something Bill was saying.

Connor looked down to find the white wolf gone. *Good Christ, I didn't sense a thing.* James was like a damn ghost at times. His brother might be talking—well, technically, using mind speech—a little more, but if he was making any real progress, Connor couldn't see it. He couldn't imagine who or what could possibly heal his brother's shattered soul. Still, Jessie's words gave him a little actual hope. He let himself feel it this time, savor it. Hope that James could find his way back to his human self, hope that he would find a reason to want to come back. And stay.

Douglas Harrison heard the song of wolves in the distance and shivered as he sat by his father's bedside. The old man had been dreaming again, and thrashed the blankets and sheets into a twisted wad. He took his father's hand from where it clawed the air, clasped it, and remembered how that hand had once seemed so large, so powerful. The fingers were always cold now, the tough calluses covered with the velvet-soft skin of age. His dad's grip was still strong, but not nearly as strong as it once was. The old man licked dry lips and whispered fiercely, "It's here, son. We didn't kill it. It's still here, walking among us. I *know* it's here. Get your gun, Dougie, we gotta get it, gotta finish it off."

A chill zipped down Douglas's spine, tingled like ice-cold electricity. He tried to keep his voice calm, level. "We took care of that bear, Dad. Made a big rug out of it, re-member?"

"You know what I mean, boy." His father's eyes fastened on him, angry and a little wild. His voice was hoarse but rapidly gained in volume. "The werewolf, the white one. The one you didn't shoot when I told you to shoot. You stood there and bawled like a damn baby until I had to drag you out of there."

Oh God, not that again. Douglas was thankful that none of the caregivers who came to their home believed his father's stories, but he found himself checking behind him just the same to see if anyone was listening. "Dad, I—"

"I told you. I *told* you we had to finish him. He's alive, and he'll be tracking us, hunting us both unless we hunt him down first. Get my .338 out of the truck, boy, the one I use for bear."

It took an hour this time to get his father settled. When he left the room, Douglas felt wrung out and apprehensive, even though he knew that the old man was unlikely to remember any of this in the morning. Wisps of an Alzheimer's fog had settled over Roderick Harrison's mind in recent years. More and more, the past mingled with the present. Including a part of the past his son would much rather forget.

It had to be the full moon. His father was always worse during the full moon. Last month during this lunar phase, Roderick had been found halfway down the lane in his pajamas, carrying a broom like a rifle, determined to destroy the creature that filled his dreams.

Douglas had gathered up all the hunting rifles after that incident and sent them over to the ranch manager's house for safekeeping. A decision about a nursing home needed to be made soon—but he didn't feel like making it right now. He couldn't picture his father in such a place, away from the ranch he had ruled with such fervor. Knew too that in his dad's lucid moments he would feel betrayed by his son.

A small voice within mocked him. *What about that long ago betrayal by your father? What about that night your dear old dad took his young son along to help him commit murder? Face it, Dougie-boy, you don't want to put your father in a nursing home because you're too afraid someone might start listening to his stories, that somebody might* believe. . . .

Douglas tucked his father in and decided against going back to bed himself. Instead, he headed downstairs to the bar for a drink. Maybe several drinks. As many as it would take to make that small inner voice shut up.

Chapter Two

Despite the fact that it was still April, despite the early morning hour and Jillian's fervent wishes to the contrary, it was already hot and humid in the city of Guelph, Ontario. She got on a crowded Greyhound, praying that its air conditioning could handle the unseasonable heat wave that had plagued eastern Canada all month.

Dr. Macleod had wired enough money for a first-class plane ticket and some extra besides, but the cash she saved by choosing the bus had paid off the rest of her rent, the balance on her phone bill, plus her tab at the little corner grocery store. No loose ends, she thought with some satisfaction. Nothing left behind, either. Everything she owned was in a battered knapsack and three large boxes held shut with duct tape. Fifty-seven hours and twenty-one minutes later, she arrived at the little northern town of Dunvegan, Alberta, with only the knapsack, a pounding headache, and a determination to strangle, then sue, every bus line employee she could find.

The clerks at the small terminal—which apparently doubled as a dry cleaning establishment—never knew their danger. They were spared the moment Jillian stepped down off the bus. She caught only a glimpse of a white-haired woman in a citrus-green suit before she was swept into a bone-crunching hug.

"You made it. You must be exhausted, dear." The woman stepped back, still holding on to Jillian's arms, and looked her up and down with hawk-bright eyes. "Name's Birkie Peterson. I'm officially the receptionist at the clinic and unofficially the glue that holds the place together, and I, for one, am *damn* glad to see you. Been trying to tell the bossman he needs another pair of hands for years now. Welcome to the north."

"Um. Thanks. Thank you." Feeling a little off base, Jillian noticed that the woman's white hair was elegantly styled, her suit tailored and crisp. Tasteful gold jewelry gleamed at her ears and throat. And those shoes, those lovely little slings, looked like real leather. Next to Birkie's cool and polished exterior, Jillian felt like a rumpled, sweaty mess wrapped in rags. Fashion had never been her top priority, but she was dead certain that a homeless person would possess more style than she did at that moment.

Birkie didn't seem to notice. If she did, she didn't think a thing of it. "Let's get you out of this heat, hon. At least you've left the humidity behind you. We're dry as the proverbial bone here, and I've got a cold beer with your name on it, or a cola if you'd rather. Connor would have been here himself, but he got called to a foaling out at Van-derkerke's not half an hour ago, and they're two hours north of here in Eureka. We'll be lucky to see the bossman before tomorrow. How much luggage did you lose?"

"What? Some boxes. How did you know?"

"Honey, hardly anyone comes off that bus with all of their possessions. It's almost a tradition around here— things tend to get rerouted over to Spirit River or up to

Fort St. John. I'll give them a call, get them to track down
your stuff. Should get it back in a couple days at the most.
Truck's this way."

Jillian let herself be steered by the arm and found that
Birkie was as good as her word. There was an ice-filled
cooler with an assortment of drinks, but after the lengthy
bus trip, it was the beer that appealed to her the most. The
air conditioning in the bright red pickup felt delicious. Jillian took her first deep breath since Winnipeg and began
to unwind a little. She thought the older woman was a bit
of a puzzle, but a friendly and interesting one. With such an
impeccable appearance, Birkie might look more at home
in the back of a limousine, yet she handled the big truck as
if she'd been born behind the wheel. And her earthy
humor made the grand tour of the town a memorable experience.

"That's Kinney's. If you want a good deal on furniture,
you go to them, but you won't need anything right away.
Apartment's fully furnished, you know. And make sure you
see Greg Kinney, not Bob. Bob wouldn't give his own
mother a good deal on the time of day. Besides, he farts
something awful.

"That apartment of yours, by the way, is right inside the
clinic. Northwest wing, down the hall from the lunchroom. Good location for getting to work on time, not so
good for getting a break from your work. You'll want to
watch that.

"Have to go to Macklin's down the street here if you
want any sporting goods. Do you fish? I like to go for trout
on the weekends, sometimes get a few perch to fry up.
Sergeant Fitzpatrick, now, he likes to fish for sturgeon. I see
him on the river quite a bit. When he's not fishing, he
heads the RCMP Detachment in these parts, and if he asks

you for a date, say yes. He's a good man. Connor is too, but he's taken. Mind you, his younger brothers are still available and all the Macleod men are easy on the eyes."

Jillian goggled, not certain how to respond to such bluntness.

Birkie peered sideways at her and grinned. "Just letting you know how things are. By the way, Connor's wife, Zoey, runs the newspaper here. You'll like her. And she likes you already just because she'll finally get to see more of her husband now that you're here to hold the fort. Zoey's in Vancouver at a publishers conference right now but she'll be back next week. In fact, she'll probably contact you for an interview first thing."

"Whatever for?"

"Not from a small town, are you? New people are *news* around here. Everyone will be wondering who you are and where you're from and so forth. Probably put your picture right on the front page."

Alarm must have shown on Jillian's face because the older woman suddenly burst out laughing and thumped the steering wheel.

"Don't you worry, Zoey's very kind. She won't print a thing you're not comfortable with, and she doesn't ask embarrassing questions. If there are any skeletons in your closet that brought you all the way up north, she won't rattle them."

"No skeletons here—it's my empty bank account that rattles. I have student loans to pay."

Birkie nodded. "Tough to get ahead these days. No one makes a fortune in the veterinary business but you'll do all right here. Heaven knows there's no lack of work to do." She waved to a man with wild gray hair who was just leaving a drugstore. "That's our lawyer, Herb Salisbury. He's the only lawyer in town, but a good man and honest. Damned unusual for someone in his profession, it seems.

"On that corner is Chez Mavis. It's a sandwich shop, belongs to Mavis Williams. She's got a hot bacon salad that'll put you in heaven right before the cholesterol kills you.

"But you want the *best* food in town, you go to the Finer Diner. Bill and Jessie Watson own that operation. I'll take you to lunch there in a day or so when you're settled. Although you can sample plenty of their wares in the lunchroom at the clinic—they keep the staff fridge stocked for us. Probably the only reason Connor hasn't starved to death with the hours he puts in. Now that you're around, maybe he won't work himself to death either."

Birkie continued to rattle off facts about everything and everyone and Jillian's frame of mind improved with each block they passed. Dunvegan might be remote, but it looked both friendly and prosperous, not the tiny rundown village she had feared it would be. And there were definitely no igloos or dogsleds anywhere—so much for the northern stereotype. Slowly she relaxed and forgot her headache. Forgot her missing boxes. And nearly forgot her own name when she caught sight of the clinic. The North Star Animal Hospital was a sprawling modern building, and inside it turned out to be as well-equipped as the college labs had been.

Agitated, the white wolf paced the shadows in the trees just behind the clinic. The massive creature didn't know why he was here, only that he needed to be. He had been here countless times on numberless nights, watching, guarding when Connor stayed late. But his brother wasn't here. None of the family, none of the Pack, was here. Yet *something* had tugged him away from the hunt, drawn him from the tall forests along the steep coulees, pulled him away from the deep shadows and bright starlight. Even the newly full moon couldn't compete with this urge. He couldn't ignore it, didn't want to resist it. The wolf had felt this sense, this *something* before, followed it before. . . .

Not something but some*one*.

Scents lingered around the outside of the building, on the pavement, in the yard, in the corrals. Hours old, days old, even weeks old. Many animals had been here. Many humans. And Changelings. He could identify every smell—except one.

The massive wolf stopped in his tracks. His nostrils flared, taking in the subtle traces. Human. A woman. It was her scent that lingered here and there in the corrals, in the doorway, in the yard. She was somewhere in the building now. He inhaled deeply, drawing the tiny molecules over the delicate olfactory tissues, seeking information. The scent was fresh, and it was not one that he had ever encountered here. He snorted and inhaled again. There was something vaguely familiar—and important—about this strange woman. But the wolf could not discern what it was and whined softly in frustration.

Not a wolf.

The sudden thought jarred him. Intruded on his senses, confused him. The thought came again, stronger this time. *I am not a wolf.* It felt dangerous, threatening in some way. The white wolf growled low in his throat and crouched as if to leap at an enemy. Suddenly another awareness stirred, deep inside. It reached out to the creature, calmed it. And for the first time in years, took control.

James Macleod blinked. Still in wolf form, he was fully awake as he hadn't been in a very long time. Aware. Cocooned in the body of a wolf, James didn't have to think unless he wanted to, could sink down beneath the surface of the animal, enough so that human thoughts and human emotions were dulled, or he could sink even deeper and silence them altogether. So that the raw edges of grief and pain couldn't slice at him, couldn't even find him. So that he could breathe, could keep on breathing.

Aware. His human self was no longer submerged beneath the wolf, and after all this time it was strange, almost alien to him. He turned his head slowly, taking in his surroundings with this new and foreign perspective. Dawn was burning a thin bright line along the eastern horizon. It was a color; there was a word for it. Red. The sky was *red*. He pondered that for a moment, had no idea what to feel about it.

I'm not a wolf. He didn't know how he felt about that either. But he did know that whatever—*who*ever—had drawn him here, coaxed him back to full awareness, was inside Connor's clinic. Animal instincts warned James that he was far from the forest with daylight almost upon him. The urge to head for cover was strong. But the man within the wolf wanted to see this woman, learn what she was to him . . . and was surprised at how powerful the desire was.

James wavered for a few moments until a pair of headlights appeared on the road beyond. He slipped smoothly back beneath the animal persona. The wolf shook himself hard, then wheeled away and raced across the open fields to the trees beyond, a white streak in the morning mist.

Chapter Three

Closing time at last. While Birkie was putting the sign on the waiting room door and drawing the blinds, Jillian leaned against the counter in the lunchroom and wiped her face with a paper towel. Frowned at the dirt that appeared on it. Technically only eight hours had passed, but it felt a lot more like twelve. So far, each day of her first week at the North Star Animal Hospital had felt about the same and today was Day Five. Or was it Day Six? Thursday? Friday? Or later? Lack of sleep was definitely fogging her brain. She had expected the wolf dreams to stop once she got to Dunvegan. Instead, she was now being awakened by them every single night. They were good dreams, but there was no getting back to sleep afterward. Too restless to read, she'd begun practicing her *hyung* in the open area of the livestock wing before the sun rose. At least she was remembering the 29 moves more easily now. Or perhaps she was too tired to notice when she missed any.

Jillian rubbed her eyes and refilled the coffee machine. Connor hadn't been exaggerating when he'd told her his practice was busy. She had served practicums at many busy clinics before graduating—but those practices boasted several veterinarians each and a brigade of animal health technicians to support them. Still, she wouldn't dream of complaining. After all, according to Birkie, Dr. Macleod—who preferred to be called *Connor,* even by the clients—had been practicing pretty much solo for the past ten years. How he'd managed it was a mystery to Jillian, at least logistically. There was no doubt in her mind that the man had enough talent for three vets, maybe four.

Pretty easy on the eyes too, as Birkie so bluntly put it. Connor was one of the tallest men Jillian had ever met, yet his lean frame was packed with muscle almost as if he bench-pressed cows for fun. He was dark-haired but fair, with pale gray eyes that were startling in their intensity. Nope, looking at him was no hardship at all.

Not that she had much time to look at Connor. The busy practice consisted mostly of a constant parade of cows and horses, cats and dogs. But to Jillian's delight, that parade was also punctuated by wildlife. A young deer, an injured fox, two fledgling owls, and a hawk with a sprained wing. And yesterday, a trio of honest-to-god beaver kits. She was going to gain some experience with wild animals after all. Caroline—a levelheaded and competent assistant who freely admitted to having a crush on Connor—had mentioned that a wolf cub had been brought in last fall. Jillian couldn't help but hope that might happen again.

She studied every printed word on *canis lupus* she could find and surfed the Internet for more studies, more data, but there was just no substitute for observing the real thing. Only one had ever passed through the wildlife center Jillian had worked for, a young black female with a permanently lame front leg. The wolf had been checked over by the head vet and sent on to a zoo, but not before Jillian got to examine the beautiful animal thoroughly. She was determined to someday specialize in these creatures. Closing her eyes, she envisioned a future where she was the director of her own wildlife center. Pictured herself giving lectures, imagined someone introducing her: *Dr. Jillian Descharme, world-renowned authority on wolves.*

The picture in her mind blurred, shifted. The lecture theatre became a forest. Instead of standing at a podium, she was seated on a large flat rock—and the white wolf sat beside her. Without hesitation she leaned into the massive creature's fur, felt the warmth that radiated from its muscled body even as she sensed the warm presence in her mind.

"They say you shouldn't wake sleepwalkers, but I'm just not sure what to do about sleep*standers*."

Jillian's whole being felt jolted as she snapped into the here and now to find herself leaning against Connor. "What? Oh, jeez." Awkwardly, she tried to sidestep away from him—until she realized that he had a firm hold on her arm, holding her up. "I'm okay, I'm fine, thanks."

He nodded and steered her neatly to a chair. She sank into it gratefully, feeling disoriented and slightly ridiculous. "I'm sorry," she stammered as she rubbed her hands over her face. "I must have drifted off. I haven't been sleeping well, and I guess it caught up with me."

"I'm not surprised. You've had a lot thrown at you in a single week. It's not usually this busy around here. I'm out on farm calls a lot, and when I'm gone, most small pet owners take their animals over to the clinic in Spirit River." He placed a cup of coffee in front of Jillian, took a long sip from one himself. "But the word's gotten around that we've got another vet here, and now everyone wants to check you out."

"Great. They'll be really impressed if they find me asleep standing up."

"Hasn't been bad for business so far. It's the busiest Saturday we've had in years."

"Saturday. It's Saturday already?"

"Oh, you *have* had a long week." Connor grinned at her. "Trust me, it'll get better. Wait till the novelty wears off. Business will settle down to its normal manic pace."

She drank the entire cup of coffee and half of the next one he poured for her. It cleared her head and revived her somewhat, although she knew it wouldn't last. "Guess I'm going to bed early tonight. I just have to check on Poodle—"

"Damn! I forgot all about Poodle. Look, I can come in and do that. You don't have to get up."

"That makes no sense. I'm right here, and Birkie says you live several miles out of town. I promise I'll have a nice long nap before supper, and then I'll be just fine. I can check Poodle a couple times during the night and go right back to bed."

He looked unconvinced. "I just don't want to wear you out completely in your first week," he said. "Are you sure?"

"Absolutely certain. And I'm the one that worked on him, so I really want to follow up and make sure he's okay."

Connor nodded. "I get that. I'd feel the same way. At least you can sleep late tomorrow."

"I can?"

"Just because we started working you the second you got off the bus doesn't mean you're a slave." He laughed. "You've got two whole days off, Sunday and Monday."

"What about you?"

"I'm on call tomorrow, and I've got surgeries scheduled for Monday. So I'll be holding the fort." Before she could protest, he raised a warning finger. "Next weekend, *you* can be on call and do Monday morning surgeries. For now, just take a breath and get settled in. There must be dozens of things you've been waiting to do."

"Explore," Jillian said at once. "Hike probably, maybe along the river. See the countryside, take some photos. Are there any good trails around here?"

"Plenty but if you're into photography, I think Elk Point will be your best choice. You can see lots from there. I'll draw you a map before I go home."

The moon sailed across the night sky, full and bright, the Huntress in her silver chariot. Behind her she drew the tides, tugged at the night breezes, lured the creatures that roamed the other side of day. Normally she pulled at the white wolf too, demanded he follow the hunt. But not now. Something else was drawing him, calling him. Not a sound or a scent but a nameless sense as tangible as the migration season which called the geese, and as powerful as the instinct for survival. A restlessness teased at his consciousness during the night, the same one that had whispered in his wolfen dreams during the day.

Finally he could no longer resist. It was almost summer, a time of warmth and plenty, but the white wolf was compelled to leave the forest. He glided through the moonlit fields like an icy shadow, passed ghost-like over roads and ditches, skirted sleeping farms and approached the town itself. Unseen, unheard, he unerringly made his way through dim and darkened streets to the far outskirts of Dunvegan. To the North Star Animal Hospital.

The building was dark. Silent. Animal senses told him that the woman was within, and other senses surfaced in response. James took control more easily this time, and his human self studied the clinic for options. He paced slowly, thoughtfully, circling the building once. Then he suddenly bounded up the hay bales that were stacked outside, leapt a span that would have been impossible for an ordinary wolf, and landed in the loft above the stable area. And discovered that the loft was not only open to the outside, but opened to the clinic within as well.

Dr. Jillian Descharme blindly reached for the alarm, slapped it into snooze mode, and lay in the dark until her eyes focused. Three in the morning was traditionally known as *the midnight of the soul*. It was actually four in the morning, and she had no idea what *that* might be called, only that it was too damn early. Groaning, she scrambled out of the bed that took up half of the room in her tiny apartment within the North Star Animal Hospital. It was time to check on Poodle again.

She winced as she realized the name sounded just as ridiculous in the middle of the night—or perhaps even more so—than it did in broad daylight. Throwing a threadbare pink robe over her pajamas, Jillian headed down the hallway under a series of skylights. The pale moonlight silvered everything it touched and deepened the shadows, like walking through an old black and white movie. The clinic seemed larger than ever, stretching off into darkness in all directions. It was quiet. Peaceful. And the tiled floor was a lot colder than she expected. Her bare feet were starting to cramp by the time she padded by the X-ray lab. She made it past the pharmacy, cursing aloud, but finally had to stop for a few moments. The mat in front of Connor's office was like a tiny island in an icy sea.

Jillian balanced on one foot and placed the sole of the other against her calf muscle in an instinctive attempt to warm it. She stood like a flamingo for a while, squinting at the collection of comic strips and articles that almost completely covered the door. Birkie had said there were "enough letters after the bossman's name to start a whole new alphabet." On a whim, Jillian lifted a sheaf of papers to read the nameplate: *Head Janitor*. She grinned and shook her head—no one would ever accuse Connor of taking himself too seriously.

When her feet felt warm enough to brave the tiled floor again, she padded quickly through the staff kitchen where a low wattage bulb acted as a nightlight. Made a left at the examining room, zipped through the small animal surgery and came to a halt in front of a stainless steel kennel. A faint raspy mew sounded from the depths of the big wool blanket within.

"Hey, Poodle. There now, Poodle, it's okay. It's good to see you awake." Jillian reached in and stroked the velvety fur of a Siamese cat of indeterminate age. "Mrs. Malkinson must be missing you a lot." The animal was the constant companion of Mrs. Enid Malkinson, also of indeterminate age. All Jillian could figure out was that both of them were exceedingly old for their respective species, both a thin collection of angles and sharp points, yet with a curious dignity. It was difficult to accord them that dignity with a straight face however when both had watery blue eyes that were crossed just enough to be comical. If ever there was a case study for pets and their owners looking alike, this was it.

They didn't act alike, however. Enid was best described as a classic worrywart, fearful and cautious, while Poodle seemed to thrive on finding trouble. This time trouble had come in the form of a rhinestone earring—a heavy vintage piece with the screw-on backing and flashy stones of its era—that had lodged in Poodle's throat. Why the cat insisted on trying to swallow it in the first place, Jillian had no idea, but she'd spent over an hour in surgery to remove the stubborn piece of jewelry.

Jillian trailed her fingers through the water dish and dripped a little onto the cat's tongue, which hung out the side of his mouth. "Come on, Poodle, you must be pretty dry. There now, doesn't that feel better?" A rusted-out purr threatened to shake the bony body apart. How he managed to manufacture the sound so soon after throat surgery, Jillian couldn't imagine, but the sound vibrated up her arm as she petted him. Forgetting her cold feet, she spent a long time gently running her hand over the cream and sable fur, until the old feline fell back asleep with his tongue still hanging out. Jillian smothered a laugh and gently poked the errant tongue back into the mouth where it belonged.

Satisfied that Poodle was fine, she closed the door and wandered back through the halls toward her apartment. Shadows draped in the corners, pooled on the floor. Deep and black. Except one. One was *white*.

Jillian stopped dead, her heart seeming to stop as well, as the white shadow suddenly stood and shook itself, resolving into an immense specimen of an impossible animal. *Canis lupus.* A wolf.

She couldn't form a single thought. Couldn't move, couldn't breathe. Could only stare as the creature turned its massive head in her direction, stared back at her for a long moment with strange blue eyes that seemed lit from within. Then it vanished. The abruptness of the disappearance shook her from her paralysis.

"No." Jillian lunged forward, ran to the spot where her mind had insisted a white wolf had stood. "Wait! Wait, don't go! Please! You can't go!"

* * *

Connor had understated this place. The view was nothing short of astonishing. It had taken much of the day for Jillian to make her way to this rocky spot, but a view like this was worth every bug bite, every scratch from a wild rosebush and every stretch of muscle it took to climb the steep grade. She emerged from the brush, sank onto a sandstone boulder, and took a long draw from her last water bottle. She drank in the view too. Numberless coulees converged into the valley floor far below. Forests of spruce and groves of poplar, chalky cliffs and fertile floodplains, tumbled-down cabins and tidy farms—all were linked together by the broad Peace River. The sweeping S-curves of flowing water glistened in the sunlight of the late afternoon.

She regarded her old 35mm camera affectionately. It was too late in the season to capture images of prairie crocuses in the grass, but Indian Paintbrush and other wildflowers were just coming into bloom. She had photographed an old riverboat that was beached near the bridge, then veered off the tourist's graveled path in favor of following some of the game trails that led up and down the hills, to and from the river. The detour had paid off with the sighting of a female moose with twin calves foraging for cattail bulbs at the edge of a pond. Jillian hoped her shots would turn out, wondered if she should have taken more to make certain. If she ever got out of debt, she was *so* getting a professional grade digital camera, one with every lens attachment known to man and extra memory cards. Back east, she'd drooled many times over just such a camera in the electronics store down the street from the bus stop.

She might be able to afford a camera like that if she stayed. And she had to admit she might do that, might stay more than the six months she had committed to. The hours were long at the clinic, but the pay was pretty good, especially with a place to live thrown in. Jillian had initially regarded the job as a necessary evil, something to cover the bills until she could land a job working with wildlife. She hadn't planned on actually *liking* the clinic. And Birkie, Caroline, and Connor already seemed like family. Some of the clients did as well. The food was a real surprise too— the fridge and freezer in the lunchroom were always well stocked with microwavable foods but not from any grocery store shelves. The savory array of single-serving soups, casseroles, and meat pies came directly from the Finer Diner. Birkie affirmed that Bill and Jessie Watson replenished the food every week. Jillian had never seen anything like it, almost a miniature catering service, all for their friend Connor. And anyone lucky enough to work for him. Jillian's tiny apartment had kitchen facilities, but she didn't have to use them much, thanks to the unusual job perk. A person might be willing to work for free just to be fed so well.

Of course, finding time to eat was a challenge. The clinic was a busy place, which was just the way Jillian liked it. But she had to admit she'd like it better if she could get some uninterrupted sleep. A dream of the white wolf had awakened her every single night since her arrival. And last night the dream had occurred not once but several times, waking her even more often than the alarm clock she had set so she could check on her patient. Small wonder she'd had such a realistic vision last night. And small wonder that she had actually gone from room to room to hunt for a live wolf. Of course, it seemed pretty silly in the light of day. *As if a live wolf is going to get inside the clinic with all the doors locked.*

Still, it was disconcerting to be dreaming about the wolf

at all. The dream had certainly warned her of impending changes to her life before Connor offered her this job. But now that she was here, shouldn't the dream disappear?

Even the rugged beauty she encountered during her hike couldn't shake the thoughts from her mind. Why was she still having the wolf dream? And why so frequently? As she sat gazing out at the river valley below, Jillian wondered if she should call up her old counselor, then dismissed the notion with a snort. It had been years, *years* for God's sake, and Marjorie was probably not even there anymore. And what would she say to the woman? *Help me, I've had a few dreams? Actually, they're really good dreams, it's just that there's a lot of them and. . . .*

"Okay, maybe not," she said aloud. "Let's save the counseling for someone with scarier problems." But maybe thinking of Marjorie could be helpful just the same. What would she say about all this? "She'd probably tell me to consider anything that's different in my life." Well, that was a no-brainer—only everything. New job, new digs, new town, even a new part of the country. New people, new boss. New equals change equals s-t-r-e-s-s. No matter how positive all these new things were, they still caused stress.

"Simple." Jillian felt much better. Now she had something tangible she could point to. "It would be amazing if I *wasn't* having dreams." Just ordinary stress, pure and simple, due to a huge list of new things to get used to all at once. And that meant that as she became accustomed to her new life, the dreams would stop.

So why didn't that explanation satisfy her? Truth be told, she'd miss the white wolf, even if he was only a dream. His appearance brought her a feeling like no other, a powerful peace. Warmth radiated from the enormous wolf as if from a banked fire, a warmth that relaxed and replenished.

Jillian sighed and turned her attention back to her camera to shoot several frames of the stunning landscape. The light was slanted now, tingeing the shadows with gold and gilding the river. Her stomach tried to remind her that she hadn't eaten since breakfast, but she didn't want to reach for her energy bars right now. All she wanted was to get some photos and head back down the hillside before dark. The scolding of a red squirrel made her start and turn around. "What?" she laughed. "What's the matter, am I too close to. . . ." Jillian's thoughts trailed off as the evening sunlight suddenly illuminated a stony plateau behind her. "How did I miss this? It's almost as beautiful as the view." She must have bypassed it when she came through the brush and trees on the west side, focused only on gaining a vantage point of the valley below. Jillian rose and slowly made her way around the wide, flat-topped boulders that formed a rough circle, a circle with a floor not of earth or stone but soft reddish sand, a testament to ancient seas. Tall spruce marched right up to the edges of the stony ring but did not enter it, only stood as sentinels around it. No brush grew in the center of the plateau, only the occasional wisp of grass. A few charred bits of wood suggested there had been a recent campfire in the sand.

What a wonderful place to practice Tae Kwon Do. She could picture herself in this peaceful setting, her energies balanced, her timing perfect, as she performed every block, strike, and stance of the *hyung* without flaw. Heck, she might even get the order right at last.

Jillian hopped up to sit on one of the bigger rocks, and swung her feet like a first-grader on a grown-up's chair. The stone was warm beneath her hands, tempting her to stretch out on it. Maybe she could find not only balance here but uninterrupted sleep. Unfortunately, the sky was deepening to amber, and she knew she ought to leave while she could still find her way back.

She packed her camera away and hefted her backpack. She'd taken no more than a step when one of her water bottles came loose, bouncing and rolling off among the rocks. Swearing, she chased it down and reached to retrieve it, but her hand froze in mid-air. Prints. Three perfect paw prints in the sand and several partials. Large. Deep. Dog-like yet elongated. *Wolf.*

Chapter Four

Jillian sat on her heels and gazed at her find for a long time. Wolf prints. There were honest-to-God wolves living here. Giddiness and a bone-deep reverence mixed chaotically within her as she unpacked her camera and strained to find an angle that would give enough contrast. Only after she'd shot several frames did her excitement allow her to realize something unusual about these prints. The sand sparkled slightly as Jillian traced the outline of one print with her finger in wonder. It was more than merely *large*. Including the claws, it was as big as her entire hand. Nothing she had ever read, nothing she had ever seen, prepared her for the sheer size of the animal. Jillian knew some Alaskan wolves could top 175 pounds. But *this* creature? The hair on the back of her neck prickled as she found a quarter in one of her pockets, set it by one of the untouched paw prints as a size reference, and shot the last of her film.

Jillian scanned the ground around the rocks and quickly discovered dozens more prints. All were on the large side, but there were enough variations in size to indicate several wolves, likely a pack. The sand revealed plenty of shoe prints too, also of varying sizes. She identified no less than five distinctive treads, from assorted sneakers to hiking boots. Somebody had been barefoot too. But the prints were all mixed together, and she was unable to discern which had come to this spot first, the humans or the wolves.

Probably the humans, she thought. If they had a fire, they probably had food. And if there had been food, perhaps the wolves had simply followed their noses and checked it out after the humans left. Jillian's stomach reminded her once more that it was empty. She straightened, blinked, and realized she'd been squinting at the prints. The light had faded considerably. It was past time to leave.

She put the camera away quickly, fastened the errant water bottle to her pack, and set off down the hill the way she had come. As much as she wanted to hurry, the thick brush wouldn't permit it. The game trail was narrow, criss-crossed with other narrow trails and fallen trees. Nothing looked familiar in the fading light and she had to concentrate to choose the right direction, focus to place her feet carefully. One wrong step along this steep, rugged path and she would have a lot more to worry about than the dark.

What kind of woman runs after a wolf?

James was no closer to answering that question than he had been many hours before when he had paused in the clinic loft, two bounds away from the open window, and listened to the human calling after the white wolf. He had been startled to find the woman up and around so close to dawn, but more surprised by her reaction when she spotted him. She should have been terrified, should have been screaming. Instead she had stopped still, remaining quiet until he melted back into the darkness—then had plunged forward in a vain attempt to follow him. She acted as if she knew the wolf, but how could that be? There was something else too; something in her voice had almost compelled him to—what? Answer her? Reveal himself? He didn't know. The woman had gone from room to room then, switching on every light, searching.

He wasn't surprised when she didn't check the loft. After all, it was fifteen feet above the ground floor and accessible only by a vertical ladder. A wolf couldn't climb it, and she had no way of knowing that what she pursued was not a wolf and that the ladder was no impediment to him at all. The stack of bales outside, from which he had initially leapt, was more than thirty feet from the loading door of the loft. Only a very large tiger might cross such a span. Or a Changeling.

James felt a strange disappointment tugging at his senses, almost a regret that the woman had not found him. *Who are you? Why do I know you?* Within his lupine body, James chuffed out a breath in frustration. *And why do I care?* The angle of the fading light told him it was time to hunt, that deer would be on the move. Weary of human thoughts and human concerns, he relaxed into his wolf nature and disappeared beneath it.

"What a tourist I am!" Jillian berated herself for not bringing a cell phone, for not paying more attention to the time, for traveling in the bush alone, for not packing at least a chocolate bar. Two chocolate bars. Maybe three. The energy bars she'd brought tasted like wet cardboard. She made a long mental list of the things she was going to do to be more prepared for the next hike, because as difficult as the trail was, she simply had to go back to that rocky plateau, had to see if the wolves would return. Was it part of their territory or were they just passing through?

The sun was long gone. Stars were pinning a deep indigo sky, and a full moon was floating just above the horizon. It had climbed enough to glimmer through the trees and lay a broad swath of light over the surface of the river when Jillian finally found the marked hiking trail. Compared to the goat path she'd been traveling, the graveled corridor was like a wide paved highway, level and free of overhanging brush and fallen logs. It promised easier, faster travel in spite of the darkness. She was still two and a half, maybe three, miles from the truck she had borrowed from the clinic, but at least now she had a direct route.

The flashback broadsided her without warning.

It might have been the crunch of gravel beneath her feet, the rustle of leaves in the trees, or the scent of the river, but whatever the trigger, she was suddenly on another trail by another river. Phantom images, sounds, even smells burst vividly upon her senses. Jillian stumbled forward and fell to her knees, skinning them both right through her jeans. She rolled and sat, but clasped her hands to her head rather than to her wounds. "Don't close your eyes, don't close your eyes. You're not there, it's not real, it's over. Jesus, it's over, it's over and you're okay. You're okay." She spoke slowly, deliberately, coaching herself until the shaking stopped. "It's a different place and a different time. I'm not back there, I'm here. I'm here and I'm okay." *I'm okay, I'm okay.*

But she wasn't, not yet. She rocked back and forth in the gravel. "My name is Jillian Descharme and I'm a licensed veterinarian and I'm okay. I'm thirty-two years old and I'm in Dunvegan, Alberta, and I'm okay. Nothing is threatening me, nothing is wrong, I'm okay." She drew a long shaky breath and rubbed her runny nose with her sleeve like a child. "I'm okay. Jeez! Jeez goddamn Louise!" She was cold, freezing cold, her clothes soaked with sweat and her skin clammy, but the fear had her by the throat and she couldn't move. She had to think of something fast, something to help her break away from this terror, break out of this inertia or she'd be here all night. And then it came. The image of the white wolf—the memory, the dream, flowed into her, warmed her like brandy. Jillian clung to that mental picture like a life preserver in rough seas, let the wolf's unspoken words fill her mind and calm it. *Not alone. Here with you.*

She rose at last on trembling legs and cursed as her knees made their condition known. The sharp stinging cleared the last of the flashback from her head however, banished the nausea from her stomach. She stood for several moments, hugging herself, rubbing her hands over her upper arms. She sucked in great lungfuls of the cool moist air until she felt steady again, and took a few tentative steps along the dark path—but had to resist the impulse to run. If she ran, she might never stop.

"Think of the white wolf, think of the white wolf." Calm, she had to be calm. Take big breaths. "Walk like a normal person. It's okay to walk fast because I'm busy, got things to do, places to go, people to see, but I don't have to run. I can walk because nothing's wrong, I'm okay." She was in control, she would stay in control. As she walked, however, she couldn't stop her senses from being on hyper-alert. Jillian's eyes flicked rapidly from side to side, searching the darkness, her ears straining to hear any rustle of leaf or snap of twig. She noticed the tiny brown bats that dipped and whirled in the air above her. She noted the calls of night birds, of loons settling and owls hunting. A mouse hurried in front of her, crossing and recrossing the path. A few moments later, a weasel followed it, in a slinky rolling motion. Jillian was keenly aware of everything—the blood pounding in her ears, the sound of her footsteps in the gravel, the liquid sounds of the nearby river—but not the tree root bulging up through the path.

She yelled in surprise, then in pain as her knees hit the gravel again. She rolled to a sitting position, cursing the sharp stinging and her own clumsiness—hadn't she *just* successfully negotiated a rugged game trail down a steep hillside for heaven's sake? She couldn't see much even with the moon's light, but a quick examination showed both knees were bleeding, her jeans in shreds. She cursed even more as she picked out a few obvious shards of gravel, but cleaning and bandaging were just going to have to wait until she reached the truck. At least it wasn't anything worse. Annoying, damn painful and embarrassing, but not a broken ankle or snakebite. Her eyes strayed to the under-brush in spite of herself—there weren't any poisonous snakes this far north, were there? "Good grief!" Jillian yanked her mind firmly away from *that* train of thought and was pondering whether it was possible to stand with-out bending her knees when she heard the howl.

She sat bolt upright as if an electric current had suddenly passed through her, every hair on end, every sense alert. The call came again, closer. Deep, primal, long and low. Drawn out and out and out, an ancient song, mournful yet somehow sweet. When it fell silent, Jillian felt as if time it-self had stopped. And she found herself straining to hear the song again, fascinated, even as her brain told her to run and instinct told her to freeze.

The moon was higher now. The pale light filtered down through the trees and laid a dappled carpet of silver on the stony path. There was no wind, no breeze. Jillian held her breath, listening, watching, but all was still. Her heart was pounding hard with both excitement and fear. Normally she would have loved to get a glimpse of a wolf in the wild, but the idea was a lot less attractive when she was alone in the dark. There were few recorded incidents of wolves attacking or killing humans, but all the data in the world wasn't very reassuring when she was sitting there bleeding. Immediately she wished she hadn't thought of that. It was just a little blood, but she struggled to get the image of a wounded fish in a shark tank out of her head.

A movement at the edge of the path beyond seized her attention. A pale shape emerged from the shadows, seemed to coalesce in the moonlight and grow larger until it was a vivid white creature of impossible size. Jillian's heart stuck in her throat as the great wolf slowly turned its massive head and stared directly at her.

Oh, Jesus. She had studied wolves more than any other wildlife, but only from books and captive specimens. Wolves don't attack humans, she reminded herself. Wolves don't attack humans—but there had been cases in Alaska. She gritted her teeth and sat perfectly still, afraid to breathe as the wolf began to slowly move in her direction. The creature approached within ten feet, then abruptly sat on its haunches and stared at her.

It was enormous. She swallowed hard, realizing if the wolf attacked there would be nothing she could do. Nothing. She wouldn't even manage a scream before it was on her. Not one bit of her martial arts training would help, especially when she was sitting on the ground. Nevertheless she scanned the ground with her peripheral vision for anything she might use as a weapon. Her fingers inched toward a rock, closed around it as the wolf rose, took a slow step toward her, into a pool of moonlight. Instantly its snowy fur gleamed and its eyes were . . . its eyes were. . . .

Blue.

Jillian felt as if the air had been knocked from her body.

The rock rolled out of her palm. Trembling, shaking, she reached a tentative hand toward the animal. "You. It's you," she choked out. "Oh, my God, it's you, isn't it? You're real."

The wolf closed the gap between them and licked her outstretched fingers. *Omigod, omigod.* She couldn't move at first, both enthralled and terrified—until the animal nudged its head under her hand like a dog asking to be petted. Jillian moved her fingers lightly across the broad skull, scratching hesitantly at first. Then fear fell away, and she worked both hands behind the sensitive ears, into the glossy ruff. The wolf stood panting mildly, the immense jaws slack and the great pink tongue lolling out in apparent pleasure. Jillian had no illusions about the animal's power—it might behave like a big dog but those jaws could easily crack the leg bones of a moose, those teeth could tear out the throat of a bull elk in full flight. And as surely as she knew those facts, she knew the wolf would not hurt her. It wasn't sensible, it wasn't logical, but the certainty was core-deep. Instinct? Intuition? Insanity? She didn't know and didn't care. The wolf held steady as Jillian wrapped her arms around its great neck and buried her face in its thick white fur. "I thought I dreamed you. You came to me. You came when no one would come, but they all told me I dreamed you because no one saw you but me. And I looked and looked for you, but I couldn't find you."

Here now. Found you.

The voice in her mind was real. The fur beneath her hands and face was real. The heat radiating from the wolf's body was real. Her voice hitched as joy overwhelmed her. "You're in my dreams all the time. I'm so glad that you're here, that you exist." *And that I am not crazy.* Although her rational brain told her there was certainly something crazy about being in the forest at night, hugging a giant wolf.

But she couldn't think about that right now; she had this moment in time and she had things to say. "I owe you a lot; you don't know how much you've done. You saved my life all those years ago, but you saved my sanity too. When things were hard and horrible, and I didn't want to face them, I thought of you and it helped me get through. I got through the hospital and the counseling and the therapy and came out on the other side, because of you." She wiped her cheek on the soft fur, but couldn't stop the tears. "I thought I was done then, I really did. But after a while I felt like it wasn't enough to be alive, that I hadn't really survived until I started living my life again. And you helped me do that too. I thought about what to do with my life and it was so plain to me—I wanted to work with animals, work with wolves. Because of you, I found that dream inside me. You did that for me, and I can't tell you how thankful I am, how grateful I am that you were there for me. Even now, just handling ordinary life, I feel like I'm never really alone."

Not alone. Here with you. The wolf nuzzled and licked at her hair, then lay down beside her. Gradually the tears subsided, and Jillian tumbled into an exhausted sleep with her arms still around the wolf's neck.

He couldn't remember who she was. Within the body of the wolf, James struggled to understand how her scent could be so familiar yet her identity elude him. All he knew was that she was important. Vitally important. In her presence, both his wolf and human natures were strangely in accord, balanced. Almost at peace. As she slept, he had nudged her to softer ground by the side of the trail as he would do for a cub. He had even felt compelled to try to heal her injured knees as he would do for a Pack-mate. Yet she was neither cub nor Pack-mate. Not a stranger. What was she?

As he had lapped the dirt from her torn skin, he was shocked to discover that he had tasted this blood before. *Her* blood. But he had no idea where or why. James eased himself away from the woman and sat up on his haunches, but remained close enough to share his warmth with her. He knew he had done that before too. Last night her words had resonated with truth and deep emotion, but they had shed no light on the mystery. He wished she had said more—not only in hopes of learning more about her, but because he liked the sound of her voice.

The sun had almost topped the horizon when James slipped away into the forest. He paused and looked back at the small figure in the brush by the side of the trail. For a split second he saw another trail, another forest. Saw the woman much younger, barely a teenager, lying just off the path and looking more like a discarded doll than a human being. Her blond hair was long and matted with blood. But her eyes were open. Green. Sea green. And infinitely sad as she observed the wolf—and waited for it to kill her. As she grieved not for the ending of her life, but for being alone.

James shook himself hard, looked again, and there was only the woman sleeping peacefully as before, full-grown and uninjured except for her skinned knees. Her hair was short, and tufts of it stuck out in odd directions as if it had a mind of its own.

What the hell had he just seen? A vision? A memory? An hallucination? Was it confirmation that the white wolf had encountered her before? Come to her aid, even comforted her? And last night he had certainly comforted her again. Even though his human self was controlling the wolf this time, he had *wanted* to comfort this woman. He wished he knew why. Why being near her somehow comforted *him*, why he didn't want to leave. . . .

The wolf was licking her face again. Jillian was reluctant to awaken from the best sleep of her life and shoved at the creature's soft muzzle, mumbled at it to stop, but it persisted. An excited whine had her fluttering her eyelids, wondering what on earth was—

"Hey!" Her shout caused the young Labrador to bounce back and fall over its own big feet, but it was too friendly to stay away. Jillian sat up hurriedly, trying to keep the silly black creature from licking her face again.

"Good God, are you all right? I'm really sorry, ma'am. Buster, get down! Get off her!"

Jillian looked up to see a stranger trying to offer her a hand and shoo the dog away at the same time. The man was dressed like most of the farmers who came into the clinic, including a baseball cap advertising the local grain buyers. Auburn hair curled out from under the cap, amber freckles dusted the strong face but his eyes were an unexpected golden brown. And far older than the rest of him, as if he had seen too much. He would have been handsome— very much so—if he'd smiled, but something told her that happened rarely, if at all.

"I'm all right, I'm fine. Really. Don't worry about the dog." She tried to wave him away but instead he grabbed her hand and pulled her to her feet as if she were weightless. "Ouch!"

"Oh, Christ, are you hurt? Damn dog. He just gets so excited. I'm sorry he knocked you down. Jesus, just look at your jeans."

Luckily he was trying to put a leash on an unwilling Buster and was too distracted to notice the faces Jillian made as she gingerly flexed her legs. Her knees were stiff and sore, although not as bad as she had expected. They didn't look too bad either, but she'd better get some peroxide on them soon. The wolf—

"Where's the wolf?" Panic grabbed her by the throat. Jillian looked frantically over the spot where she'd been lying, looked off into the woods, scanned the brush in every direction. "Where is he?"

The man came back with the now-captive dog, frowning. "What's wrong? Did you lose something?"

"The wolf, he was right here. He was here with me and I don't know what happened to him." She whipped around and grasped the man's shirt, causing him to back up a step. "Did you see a white wolf? Maybe you just saw part of something, a big white animal, maybe you thought it was a dog or a—a calf or something."

"No. No, nothing." He backed up further, pushing her hands from his shirt. His face had paled and his eyes darted about. "There's no wolves around here, lady."

She stared at him. "Of course there are. I saw prints all over Elk Point yesterday, big ones. And there was a *white* wolf right here—"

Jillian realized suddenly how bizarre she sounded. The dog's owner was glancing down the trail, sidling away from her and giving every sign of wanting to be gone. The morning air was cool, but she could swear the guy was sweating. Small wonder. She was probably coming across as a little deranged. The guy must think he had a crazy woman on his hands. She ran her hands through her untidy hair, straightened her jacket and decided to make light of her outburst. "Well, I guess I must have seen something else and made a mistake. City girl, you know. Maybe this is how those Sasquatch stories get started," she chuckled, expecting him to laugh along. He didn't. She tried something different. "Say, I work at the North Star Animal Hospital. Buster's a great-looking dog. Has he had his shots?"

"What? Oh, yeah. A couple months ago when Dr. Taku was at our place doing a herd check."

She leaned down and petted the ecstatic canine straining to reach her even as his owner was moving slowly in the other direction. "George Taku? Guess you must go over to the Spirit River clinic then. Well, I guess I won't see much of you, Buster." She looked up at the man. He didn't look receptive to shaking her hand so she didn't offer it. "I'm Jillian by the way. Thanks again for stopping. And you are?"

There was the slightest hesitation before he answered. "Douglas. Douglas Harrison. See you, ma'am." He turned and walked quickly down the trail, with the reluctant dog in tow. He called loudly over his shoulder, "You be careful in these woods now."

She shook her head as she watched him disappear around a bend. *Too late. I've already spent the night with a wolf. Even Red Riding Hood didn't do that.*

Chapter Five

The day promised to be a hot one. There was no dew on the fields, and only a few birds were singing from the roadside brush as Dr. Connor Macleod struggled to drive, stay awake, and keep tabs on the bundle on the seat beside him. He'd been called out of bed to deliver twin calves and discovered there were actually three in the tangle. Two were already dead and it had taken the better part of the night to make sure the lone survivor wouldn't join them. The first-time mother had completely refused to bond with the undersized calf. Now it was wrapped in a blanket on the front seat, another orphan to be nursed at the North Star Animal Hospital. At least the weather was good—cattle producers in the Peace region tended to calve their herds in either January or May. If he had to get up in the middle of the night to attend a calving, Connor certainly preferred it to be at *this* time of year.

Thank God for Birkie. He was going to be late for his surgeries but at least the North Star Animal Hospital was in capable hands. The receptionist's efficiency bordered on the superhuman. By now, Birkie would have opened the clinic, noticed his absence, checked his whereabouts with dispatch—and formulated a battle plan. Anything that didn't require a licensed veterinarian would be passed to Caroline. Anything that did would be rescheduled.

And next weekend Connor wouldn't have a single qualm about directing their dispatch service to call the new vet instead of him. He was pleased with how well Jillian had fit into the practice in such a short time. She was highly skilled, passionate about her work, and eager to learn more. A potent combination in his books. He'd just have to keep an eye on her to make sure she didn't work herself into the ground.

Meanwhile, it would be a real treat not to work *himself* into the ground. Before he'd married Zoey, Birkie had often been on his case about putting all his passion into his practice. It had been hard not to. The work he did absorbed him; he lived and breathed it. He still did, to a degree, but he had to admit he'd rather spend time with Zoey whenever possible. She was busy too, and loved her newspaper as much as he loved animals, but nothing else existed when they were together at the end of the day. Sometimes they just collapsed on the couch like any hard-working couple. Most of the time, they called the Change and chased each other all over the farm and throughout the river valley.

To run as a wolf was freedom and joy and a tremendous sense of wholeness wrapped together. And it was all the more so now that Zoey was by his side. He'd lived a very long time, but nothing he'd experienced held a candle to the wonders of having a mate.

Like all of the Macleods, Connor was far older than he appeared, would live beyond several human lifetimes, but there were few Changelings left in the world. Most of his kind built relationships with humans. Fortunately, a human could become a Changeling too, could share in the gifts. Just like in the old werewolf tales, anyone bitten by a Changeling would become one. Their saliva contained a unique peptide. A single bite could inject enough of the substance into the bloodstream to activate a gene, one that existed in every human being. Not all human partners chose this path, but most did.

There were success stories all around him. The Pack leader, Jessie Watson, had Changed her human mate, Bill. Within his own family, Connor's mother had done the same for his father half a millennia ago. Both had been well prepared and welcomed the gift of the wolf with joy. It had been different for Connor's wife, Zoey. The gift was forced on her by a Changeling gone rogue, before she even knew that such creatures existed. Despite such a rough beginning, however, Zoey loved her new life. She'd not only adapted well but displayed a talent for shapeshifting beyond Connor's own abilities.

James and Evelyn had discussed the Change many times, but then she became pregnant and they had decided to wait until after the baby came. Connor had wondered for years if Evelyn might have been able to save herself if she had been able to call forth the Change. Did James wonder that as well? Was it one more weight added to an already unbearable burden? Connor questioned anew if his brother was ever going to return to his human self. Would he ever even want to after losing so much? Jessie seemed so certain that James was improving but Connor just couldn't see it.

Come to think of it, he was probably too tired to see anything. Even Changelings had to rest sometime. He'd been out on farm calls almost every night this week, and the second calving season of the year had barely begun.

The tall vet left off thinking about his brother and focused instead on hopes of hot coffee and a hot shower as he pulled into the bay at the back of the North Star Animal Hospital. He tucked the blanket more securely around the tiny calf and carried it inside—and suddenly every wolfen sense flared to attention. A Changeling had been inside the clinic in wolf form. And it wasn't just any member of the Pack. There was no mistaking the white wolf's scent. It hung in the air, as three-dimensional as a holographic image to Connor's lupine senses. *What the hell?*

He blinked and found that Caroline had already taken the undersized calf from him, and was asking something about an IV. He rubbed a quick hand over his face and found his voice. "Sorry, I'm not all here. Yeah, an IV would be good. And I milked out some colostrum from the mother—I almost forgot. Thanks." He pulled the quart jar from a deep jacket pocket, thankful that he'd remembered it before he broke the damn thing, and handed it to her. "It's not much. I left the owner milking out the rest. He'll bring it by in an hour or so."

Calf and assistant disappeared from his sight and his mind. Connor inhaled carefully, certain that thoughts of his brother must have influenced his senses. But there was no mistake. He walked slowly forward, following the airborne traces to the large livestock area . . . the stack of bales . . . the hallway. What on earth had brought James inside the clinic? He had no answer for that.

A noise from down the hall signaled the arrival of another truck in the bay. A moment later Jillian came through the doorway with her knapsack and something else. The scent of the white wolf enveloped her, swirled around her and preceded her down the hall like a live thing. A human could never have detected it, but to Connor it was as powerful as a punch to the head. He found he couldn't say a word or form a thought, only stare at her.

"Hey there," she said as she approached. "I'm a little messy, but I don't look that scary do I?"

Connor shook himself mentally and found his voice. "No, not at all. I mean, you look a little tired maybe." The scent of the wolf was overwhelming, the scents of the forest strong as well. Connor could have named the places she'd been right down to the plants she'd touched. "Did you get to see Elk Point?" He knew full well she had.

"Sure did. It was great, even better than you described. I'll have to bore you with my thousands of photos one day. Say, do you know that a wolf pack has been in that area?"

"Really?" Good Christ, there was white hair all over her jacket. Had James lost his mind?

"Tons of prints everywhere."

Connor nodded, tried to act casual. Normal. Anything other than how he felt. "You're a pretty good tracker for a city girl. Maybe you'll get to see more. I know you're interested in wolves." And one of them seemed to be interested in *her* for some reason. How the hell did she get so damn close to him? And why did he let her? There were a hundred questions Connor was dying to ask the young vet and no plausible way to do so. What on earth could he say? *Hey, did you see my brother the wolf?*

She didn't give him any more information either. Instead she studied him intently. "Are you sure you don't need me today? It's barely Monday, and you look exhausted."

"No, you go ahead and enjoy your day. In this business, you take your time off when you can get it. I'm looking forward to having the next weekend when my wife will be home." Connor realized Jillian was looking at his stained coveralls. He probably looked like he'd delivered a dozen calves. "I was just on my way to get cleaned up."

"Okay, well, I've got some errands to run downtown. Thanks again for the use of the truck."

"You're going to use it often enough when you're called out to a farm. Might as well get some enjoyment out of it as well." She smiled at that, then continued on past him down the hallway and into her apartment. When her door clicked, Connor leaned on the wall for support and rubbed both hands over his face, hard.

"Jesus. Sweet Jesus Christ." He knew he wasn't going to get much more information out of Jillian, not without raising her suspicion. That was okay. He would Change tonight and go looking for his older brother himself. James Macleod had a hell of a lot of explaining to do.

Douglas sat in the kitchen and poured a double shot of Jack Daniels into his coffee. Drank it down. Tried to reassure himself that it didn't mean a thing when Jillian had said there were wolves. Of course wolves lived around here, just like bears and cougars did. Good God, he had even hunted wolves, ordinary wolves, when he was just a kid.

But the woman had been looking for a white wolf. *White.* Maybe he didn't hear her right. Maybe she was mistaken completely, maybe she saw just what she suggested— a dog or a calf or who knows? But he knew who she must be. He'd heard about the clinic's new lady vet and figured that anyone who made it through seven years of veterinary college wasn't stupid or prone to seeing things. If she thought she saw a white wolf, she likely did.

"But so what?" He refilled his cup with more Jack Daniels than coffee and pondered the question. So what if she saw a white wolf? Wolves were known to come in a wide variety of colors, and white wasn't uncommon. Hell, most of the wolves in the arctic were white for Christ's sake. And none of them lived for thirty fucking years either. It wasn't the same creature, it couldn't be. It just wasn't possible.

But then he hadn't thought it possible for werewolves to exist. And he wished for the millionth time that he had never seen one.

Wished he hadn't heard the back door close just after midnight. Wished he hadn't been so fucking nosy, wished he hadn't crept outside to find his father loading the Remington 12-gauge as if to go hunting—and hunting for something big too. Jesus, he'd all but begged to go along. After all, they'd stalked deer and moose since the boy was old enough to walk, sometimes even bear or wolf. Maybe the old man was going for the cougar their neighbor had spotted recently. His father had hesitated at first, tried to make him go inside. Then he relented—and told him a story that made his young blood chill. He'd grown up thinking his mom had simply left them. His sister, Rosa, was old enough to remember their mother, and said she had run away when he was still a baby. His father had never said anything at all. Roderick had refused to talk about her or answer any questions, had refused to even let the subject be mentioned. But now his father was telling him that his mother hadn't run away at all, that she'd been killed, and not by anything ordinary. By *werewolves*. Holy fucking crap, werewolves for real, just like in the movies and the comics. It was terrifying and exciting at the same time. *No way* could Douglas stay home.

But when they'd made their way to the Macleod farm, it wasn't what he expected, not at all.

"Dad, she don't look like a wolf," he had dared to say at last. He didn't look at the crumpled figure in the middle of the bloody floor but saw it all too clearly in his mind. Douglas had owned a rifle since he'd been large enough to carry one, gone on countless hunting trips and had never once been squeamish. But this was *different* and his stomach felt like it had crawled into his throat. "Isn't she supposed to turn into a wolf after she's dead?"

"That's an old wives' tale. They don't change unless they want to. Don't need a full moon either, but they're stronger at the full moon. That's why we had to come tonight, when the moon's getting small."

"But she . . . she looks like Rosa. She looks like Rosa and you shot her anyways." Dougie's voice quavered in spite of himself. Rosa was married now and expecting his niece or nephew any day now. At fourteen, he thought it was going to be really cool to be an uncle.

His father turned on him at once, shoved him hard into the wall and gripped the front of his shirt. The old man's voice was a whip. "Don't you go feeling sorry for these damned creatures. That's how they fool you, by looking like us. You get it through your head that they're predators, deceivers and predators through and through." He gave the boy a sharp shake to underscore the words, then tossed him back to slam against the wall again. "Once a pair starts breeding like this, we'll be hip deep in the bastards before you can blink. You want that, Dougie? You want them going after our livestock? Maybe going after Rosa like they did your mother?"

"No, no, I didn't mean—"

"You watch, boy, you just stay right here and watch. You haven't seen these animals like I have. That's why you can't believe. You wait. And then you'll see and you'll know. We've taken care of one and now her mate will *have* to come here. He'll be drawn here and we'll be waiting for him." The man stood in the shadows of the darkened house, the pump action shotgun resting across his arm, watching both the front and the side windows.

An hour went by in silence, then two. Finally his father spat in disgust. "It's been too goddamn long. I don't know where the son of a bitch is, but I'm not waiting any longer to destroy the den. We'll have to go after the male another night." He gathered up the gas cans and headed for the stairs. "You stay here and keep watching, hear me? I don't want any of those bastards sneaking up on us."

The boy turned to the window again, feeling both older than his fourteen years and much, much younger. He was grateful that the smell of the gas covered up the stink of blood in the air, glad for the beginning crackle of flames above that almost drowned out the thoughts whirling in his head. His dad was nuts, completely and totally a nut case, shooting some poor lady thinking she was a werewolf. Using a shotgun of all things like she was dangerous, like in some movie. He should have stopped him, should have made his dad stop—but he hadn't stopped him, oh Jesus, he hadn't even realized what the old man was going to do before it was done . . . and neither had she.

The boy welcomed the waft of smoke that stung his eyes, gave him an excuse for the tears that filled them. He rubbed them and tried to focus on the line of trees beyond the barn. The moon's light was weak and the forest looked black and ominous. Suddenly there was a flash of white and a great silvery shape sprang from the darkness, running hard.

"Hey—hey, there it is. I see it!" He stared at it, terrified and fascinated at the same time. "Holy shit! It's big, it's fuckin' huge."

His father was beside him at once. Thick smoke was now hovering near the ceiling and there were loud popping and crackling noises as flames consumed the rooms above them, but the old man was determined to finish what he'd started. "Get back behind the wall over there. Let him come all the way through the door, then pull the trigger. Got it? Aim for the head if you can."

"But the fire—" It was getting hard to breathe.

"There's time, we can get him. We *gotta* get him. Listen to what I tell you." The old man ducked back to the other corner of the dining room.

Seconds later the front door burst inward as it was struck by the massive animal. Dougie flinched at the explosive noise of shattering wood and nearly dropped the gun. He swallowed and forced himself to peer around the corner, his heart pounding so hard it hurt his chest. A great white wolf stood in the doorway, nearly filling half of it. Then abruptly, instantly, it became a tall, blond man. It was almost more than the boy could do to remember to breathe and yet keep from gasping aloud. His throat constricted with the effort. *Holy Jesus. Dad was right. He was fuckin' right!* The teen pressed his back to the dining room wall and gripped the rifle in one shaking hand and his crotch in the other, praying he wouldn't piss his pants like a baby. That's when he heard the sound—not a sound he'd ever heard in his life and not one he ever wanted to hear again. A wild keening of terrible grief, unendurable pain. The unearthly howl pierced his head, stabbed at his heart. He couldn't stop himself from peering around the corner again. The blond man was kneeling on the bloody floor, cradling the woman's body, rocking back and forth.

Without warning the old man sprang out and fired twice in deafening succession. The son stepped away from the wall as well, but his .22 was slack in his nerveless hands. He watched as their quarry slumped to the floor in a strange kind of slow motion. Even dead, the man seemed to curl himself protectively around the woman.

Dougie's father shouted at him, urged him to shoot, shoot *now*, but the boy could only stand and stare through the thickening smoke with helpless tears running down his face.

Suddenly an ominous crash sounded right above them and a great shower of sparks and wood collapsed into the stairway. His father grabbed his arm and hustled him out the back door, both of them coughing and choking. Dougie nearly fell twice as they ran across the backyard and into the forest beyond where the truck was hidden. And all the way home he could still hear that terrible out-cry of grief in his head.

Thirty years later, Douglas Harrison still heard that howl in his dreams. Still woke up sweating, sometimes in tears like the boy he had been. Tears were running down his cheeks now, as he held his coffee cup in front of him with both hands as if in supplication, praying for forgetfulness.

Chapter Six

Connor had every intention of hunting down his brother for an explanation. But when night came, the tall vet was tied up for hours with an emergency surgery on a boxer that had been struck by a car. By midnight, the anxious owners had gone home, and the dog was recovering from the anesthetic in a kennel. By one a.m., Connor was sure the dog would live, but he was less certain that *he* would. He didn't dare try to Change, not until he had eaten and slept and eaten again. Changing burned up an ungodly number of calories. Add a rapid metabolism to that, and the need for rest and nutrition became paramount. Two things he hadn't had enough of in well over a week. The hunt for James would have to wait.

It didn't prevent him from thinking about his brother, however. As Connor drove home, he wondered how on earth Jillian had encountered the white wolf. She would never hurt the wolf, of course, that wasn't the danger. But was James being deliberately careless? It shouldn't be possible for Jillian to find James by accident. Even the Pack couldn't find James if he didn't want to be found—the white wolf simply seemed to melt into the forest and disappear. Connor wasn't completely certain he could find his brother either.

Why would James reveal himself to a human? He was still mulling that question when he climbed into bed and fell into a dreamless sleep.

Far on the other side of Dunvegan, James was wondering the same thing. He had submerged himself beneath the animal persona from the time he left the woman on the trail. He didn't want to think about her, didn't intend to see her again. He resolved to stay away from the clinic, the trails, anywhere he might encounter her. It was safer that way. He was unconcerned about possible danger to himself. But he was all too aware that he could bring danger to this woman. Associating with Changelings had proved perilous to humans throughout history. They had nothing to fear from the Changelings—it was forbidden among them to harm humans—but everything to fear from their fellows. James was certain that death had visited Evelyn, had taken her because she was married to *him*, and someone had known what he was. Humans as a whole tended to be suspicious of those who were different, fearful of anyone not like themselves, and their fears sometimes erupted into violence.

Yet the wolf resisted James, refused to take shelter in the deeper forest even though it was broad daylight. Refused to do anything but lie barely hidden under a spruce canopy, head on its paws, facing in the direction of the town. James began to wonder if he had finally lost his mind. He *was* the wolf; how could he be so at odds with *himself*? It felt uncomfortably like the wolf was becoming a separate entity and surely that way lay madness.

Maybe if he figured out who the woman was, he could solve the puzzle and be able to leave it alone. If he could just get some answers, maybe then he could stop struggling with his animal self and slip comfortably into oblivion again.

*   *   *

Jillian signed up for a post office box, transferred her eastern bank account to a local branch, and explored a few shops, but was unable to achieve any kind of distraction. There was a poster for a new wolf stamp at the post office. Wolves ran along the front of her complimentary wildlife-themed checkbook cover. The faces of wolves stared out from greeting cards, puzzles, T-shirts and framed wildlife pictures. A poster in a DVD rental outlet advertised a movie with wolves. A child in a stroller held a stuffed wolf—okay, it was supposed to be a husky, but it had blue eyes for God's sake.

Jillian knew that on any other day, she would barely have noticed these things. Okay, maybe she might have noticed *some* of them because she liked wolves. But last night she had met a real wolf, *her* wolf. And there was just no way to rationalize away that experience even if she'd wanted to. When she'd undressed to shower, she'd discovered white hairs on her clothes—a few black ones from the enthusiastic Buster but dozens upon dozens of pure white hairs. Evidence that she had not only seen a white wolf, but touched and even hugged a white wolf. *And it had permitted the contact.* The whole idea was exhilarating and terrifying at the same time. By some accident of fate, she'd somehow stepped outside the bounds of normalcy and made a connection with the unknown for the second time in her life.

There was no proof, of course, that the wolf had communicated with her, had spoken in her mind. She would allow that she might have imagined that in the grip of emotion. But all the rest was absolutely, completely true.

Her brain was churning as she walked along Dunvegan's red brick sidewalks. Maybe a little research was in order. Jillian stopped at the public library and signed up for an hour on the Internet. Three hours later, she was still there. There were still no wolves over 175 pounds on record anywhere in the world. Her wolf was far bigger than any canine she'd come across, and she'd had experiences in college with very large dog breeds such as the St. Bernard and Great Pyrenees, both of which easily topped 200 pounds. Plus, there were the eyes . . . Wolf eye color typically ranged from yellow to brown, occasionally green. But not blue. Not clear, brilliant blue. Conclusion One, she thought, was that the wolf was physically unusual, unique among its kind.

The wolf had appeared on two similar occasions, both times when she was alone on a trail at night and was injured in some way. Okay, that first time she had been near death. The skinned knees barely counted as an injury by comparison, but still it seemed too much of a coincidence. How had the wolf known that she was in trouble? Why had it come to her? And how about the fact that the first time had been in eastern Ontario, while this latest visitation was nearly two thousand miles west of that province? How had the wolf known where she was? And just what would motivate a wolf to travel so far? Conclusion Two, she decided, was that the wolf possessed unusual abilities, could do things that couldn't be explained by normal means.

Those conclusions led her to expand her fields of research. She found articles and stories suggesting that the wolf could be a metaphysical being, a totem animal, a spirit guide, even an Irish pooka. But it didn't seem likely that such a mystical creature would leave hair on her clothes.

She looked at the facts again and decided to scratch Conclusions One *and* Two. Wolves simply didn't live that long, not in the wild. She had been attacked, what, fourteen years ago? Fifteen? The white wolf that had driven off her assailants had been unquestionably full-grown at the time. Although zoos reported wolves living close to twenty years in captivity, a wild wolf typically had a lifespan of only five or six years. Ten to thirteen at most. And an aged animal wasn't difficult to spot. Its muscle mass would be diminishing, its coat dull, its teeth worn. There was a look, a feel to the body that no veterinarian could miss. And the wolf she had just encountered on the trail seemed to be very much in its prime.

So which was more far-fetched, that it was the same wolf that saved her years ago, or that there were two completely identical wolves, and both of them seemed determined to protect her?

Jillian had a pounding headache and not a single answer by the time she headed home. She had a stack of books beside her on the seat of the truck, but there was no way she was going to open them tonight. Instead, she picked up a container of chocolate pecan fudge ice cream and resolved to eat it in front of the TV until she forgot all about wolves for a while.

Within the wolf, James padded silently through the shadowed clinic. Dogs and cats slept in kennels, a cow and two horses dozed in the livestock wing. None stirred as the Changeling passed by them in the darkness. He wasn't hunting *them*. Instead, he inhaled deeply, drinking in the woman's unique scent, and followed it unerringly. Doors presented no impediment. Every door in the clinic had levered handles that were easily pawed open. Connor had done that on purpose, no doubt. *Bet he didn't expect* me *to use them.* Within minutes, the white wolf stood outside the room where a small, blond woman thrashed in the grip of restless dreams.

James could sense the tension as he pawed open the door. Was she having a nightmare? Operating with both wolfen instinct and human caution, he moved silently until he stood by her bed, his nose nearly touching her arm. Her blankets were tangled, her skin shiny with perspiration. She moaned, then suddenly went still as if on some level she sensed the wolf's presence. Her eyes didn't open, but her fingers coaxed him closer, her lips murmuring soundlessly. To his surprise, her thoughts shone clearly in his mind. *I missed you. I'm so glad you came back.* She stroked the great animal's head, buried her hands in the snowy ruff. *The doctors tried to tell me you were just a hallucination, but I knew you were real. I knew it inside. I hung onto that, knew I wasn't alone. I knew you'd come.*

She smiled broadly, her eyes still closed, relaxed and drifting down into a deep and peaceful sleep. James watched her for a long time, puzzled by this new development. He shouldn't be able to hear her thoughts. Changelings could usually only hear the thoughts of other Changelings. And he was confused by the feelings she stirred in him, confused even to *have* feelings. He had spent so many years buffered from emotions. As a wolf, he instinctively wanted to guard her, protect her. Not like a cub or even a member of its Pack. More than that. It was important to keep her safe, if only from her dreams. But deep within the wolf, James himself was restless. He wanted something else, something more, something he didn't recognize.

And then suddenly he did. With the blinding intensity of a lightning flash, James suddenly understood exactly what it was that he wanted. *Needed.* To see her with a man's eyes. To touch her with a man's hands. To puzzle out the connection between them as a *man.* The unexpected urge to

resume his human form was so powerful that he ached
with it—and was nearly overwhelmed by it. The white
wolf jumped back from the bed as if it was on fire, and
James fought to stay in control. He wanted nothing more
than to bolt down the hallway and out of the building, to
race for the forest. But there would be no sanctuary there
as long as the riddle of who this woman was—and who she
was to him—remained unsolved.

Maybe if he slipped out of the wolf's skin . . . if he was
in his human form just for a moment . . . maybe then he
could remember her.

A sudden breeze stirred the air in the room although
there was no window open. A flurry of blue sparks eddied
about the wolf as static electricity built. The animal vanished. A tall, powerful man stood in its place—and abruptly
sat down hard on the floor.

Ow! Jesus! His teeth had snapped together with enough
force to make his head ring. Luckily his tongue hadn't
been in the way, and thank God he hadn't made too much
noise. James's skin prickled as a new awareness stole over
him. He was different. Human skin. He'd forgotten how it
felt, wasn't sure that he liked it. And everything else seemed
different too. Not only was his outward form changed, but
his senses had shifted, altered. Almost dulled. In human
form, Changelings possessed stronger senses of sight and
smell and hearing than real humans—yet not nearly as
powerful as what they experienced as wolves. The sudden
difference was confusing, almost frightening. James held his
hands out as if for balance, in spite of the fact he was still
sitting down. He glanced over and marveled that he *had*
hands, waggled the fingers on one, then the other. He had
forgotten what that was like too. Had it been so long?

His heart hammered against his ribs. Emotions assailed

him and were beaten back as James struggled to stay in control, to orient himself to this new state of affairs. He tried to breathe normally, succeeded mostly. Awkwardly he pushed his hair away from his face, glanced down quickly, and was relieved to find clothes. They felt odd—they just didn't move with him the way that fur did—but thank God he was dressed. It hadn't even crossed his mind when he called the Change. The woman was certain to be upset if she awakened to find a stranger in her room. A naked stranger would likely have her screaming the place down.

He looked over at the bed. Didn't intend to wake her, of course, didn't want her to be frightened. But he needed to know, he *had* to know who she was.

James rose shakily to his feet, feeling as coordinated as a newborn giraffe, and sat carefully on the edge of the bed. He looked, really looked, at the woman for the very first time. She lay on her back with an arm curled above her head, the other arm outflung. She had a childlike appearance at first glance, her pajamas covered with silly cartoon frogs, but the rumpled material clung to soft curves, rounded breasts, things the wolf wouldn't notice but the man did. Her short blond hair was a pleasing riot of cowlicks, but it looked wrong somehow. It should be long. Somehow he remembered that her hair had been long. But when? Where? James tried to will the memories to return, frustrated that there were only baffling fragments that meant little. He had been so certain that as soon as he resumed human form, the hazy picture in his mind would clear and the troubling puzzle would be solved. The disappointment was almost tangible.

The woman beside him was breathing deep, still oblivious to his presence. His *human* presence anyway. He turned his attention to carefully studying her features. There were faint, fine scars along the cheekbone, the underside of the jaw, tiny irregularities that Changeling eyesight perceived, but ordinary human eyes would never know. What had happened to her? He felt he should know, that it was important. It meant something. The woman—*J-something, her name begins with J*—certainly meant something to the wolf. Did his wolf side know things that his human side did not? *J, Jane, Jennifer, Julia, Ji—Ji—Jill, Jill,* Jillian. It was a small triumph to remember her name, although he suspected the wolf had supplied it. He whispered it softly, conscious of how his human mouth formed each syllable. "*Jil-li-an.* Jill-*i-an.*" Repeated it until it didn't feel so damned awkward, as if his lips were out of shape or something. He had a name now but it didn't prompt any further memories. He wondered if she knew *him,* then realized it was far more likely that she knew not the man but the wolf, had seen the animal somewhere. She probably wouldn't recognize James at all. Disappointment poked again at his insides, and he swore softly, then got up and paced silently about the room.

A hefty pile of mail and newspapers occupied a small table by the door and he fanned out the top few envelopes. *Dr. Jillian Descharme, DVM.* He was strangely relieved to have remembered her first name before the address labels revealed it to him—yet her last name was unfamiliar. It looked like it might be French, maybe French-Canadian, but he had no idea how to pronounce it. She was a veterinarian, and that struck no particular chord either, except to explain why she was living at the clinic. She obviously worked with his brother. For a fleeting moment James considered asking Connor about the woman—but dismissed it quickly. He didn't want to involve his brother unless he had to, would far rather figure things out for himself.

James replaced the mail, trying to arrange it the way it had been, when he happened to glance up. A calendar was on the wall, and he stared at the year in disbelief. It was a joke, had to be. His attention snapped back to the mail and he pawed through it now, seeking postmarks, rifling through the newspapers for a date. Each time he found one, he'd toss it to the floor and find another. And another. *Jesus Murphy, that can't be right. There has to be a mistake.* The year looked bizarre, like science fiction. Could the century have turned without his knowing?

When he got to the bottom of the pile, he leaned against the wall and stood there for a very long time. His mind fought to accept that he'd been running as a wolf for more than thirty years. Dear God, it hadn't felt like that long. A wolf's concept of time was limited. It was aware of the moon and the seasons—but it didn't count them. His human side had paid no attention at all, preferring to give up all awareness in favor of the wolf. Finally James blew out a breath and straightened. It didn't matter. It couldn't matter. One year or thirty or a hundred, he was damn well going to run as a wolf again, just as soon as he solved this particular puzzle.

He sat on the bed and studied the woman, noticed things that he hadn't as a wolf. Her features combined to create a unique beauty—the wild cap of hair, the fine sharp angles of her face, the tiny frown between her brows. She looked like a bad-tempered faerie. And she smelled good, a little different through human nostrils, but the scent was still distinct, still tantalizing. He knew the scent because the wolf knew her scent—but her face, however appealing, told him nothing at all. His frustration mounted. Why couldn't he remember her? Why did he know her name, her smell? She was completely human, but he had heard her thoughts in his mind as clearly as if she was a Changeling too.

James thought of the strange vision he'd had on the trail, the momentary sight of a much younger Jillian, injured and anticipating death. What had happened to her? She said the wolf saved her life but how? When? The questions beat at his brain as hopelessly as the moths against the bedroom window. James glanced over at it, noted the graying of the night sky along the eastern horizon. He almost sighed, although whether it was in relief or resignation, he'd be hard-pressed to say.

He fully intended to leave. Was going to get up and walk out the door. Instead his hand went to Jillian's face, brushed the wisps of hair away with a tenderness he didn't know he was capable of. Her fair skin was soft, so soft . . . and it hit him hard that he hadn't felt a woman's skin, hadn't *wanted* to feel a woman's skin, in fact, hadn't so much as *thought* of it for a long, long time. He brushed his fingertips lightly over her cheek, felt something electric along his own skin. A connection pulsed between them. . . .

"Who are you, Jillian?" he whispered. As if in response, she sighed and turned a little toward him. It distracted him just long enough for a snake-quick hand to seize his wrist in a surprisingly strong grip.

James found himself staring into furious green eyes. Mentally, he flailed for the appropriate words, realized there weren't very damn many for a situation like this. *Shit.* He cursed himself for being a complete idiot even as he tried to paste on what he hoped was a friendly expression—he'd had no time to practice. "Don't be afraid. It's . . . it's not what you think."

Chapter Seven

Jillian had all kinds of things she intended to say to this nervy intruder, right before she pounded the creep into next week. At least that was her plan. The words stuck in her throat when she opened her eyes and saw an enormous Viking looming over her—or so her mind tried to tell her. The strong intelligent face, the warrior build, the white-blond hair, those blue, blue eyes . . .

On some level she couldn't help noticing the stranger had a warrior's voice too. Low and quiet, almost a growl with steel underneath it. And familiar somehow.

She didn't indulge the odd thoughts, just continued to glare murderously at him while maintaining her grip on his wrist. Tried to ignore the fact that her fingers couldn't even reach halfway around that powerful wrist. Tried to ignore the fear that clawed at her throat, the terror of a nightmarish past repeating itself. "What the hell am I *supposed* to think?"

"You were dreaming—" He caught the fist with his free hand, stopping it just under his chin, held it. He frowned and shook his head.

Jillian was certain that instead of stopping her attacker, she'd just made him mad. That furrowed brow brought a frightening ferocity to his features. And although he wasn't exerting any pressure on her fist, it was effectively caged in his iron hand. Oh Jesus, what now? She tried to think. Could she bring a leg up, kick him in the head? Let go of his wrist with her free hand and arrow her fingers into his throat? All her martial arts training seemed to desert her as she looked up into that harsh yet handsome face.

"You should have done that first, you know," he said, surprising her. "Should have decked me just as you opened your eyes, doc." His words were slightly halting, as if unfamiliar with the language. "It would have been a hell of a lot more effective than grabbing my wrist, would have used the surprise to better advantage." He continued to hold her fist, held it close enough to his chin that she could feel his close-cropped beard against her knuckles. Never taking those blue, blue eyes from hers, he quickly turned the wrist she held in her other hand, neatly freeing it and seizing *her* wrist instead. "See? Bad choice for you. Want to try it again?"

She goggled at him now. Was this some kind of a sick game? "Try what?"

In answer he released both her hands and sat back. Jillian didn't hesitate. She snapped her body into a roll that took her out of the opposite side of the bed. She landed on her feet, sprinted for the corner of the small apartment that served as a kitchen. Dove behind the tiny island, ripped out one drawer after another in search of a knife. Found one at last—a pathetically blunt paring knife, not the long-bladed one she'd hoped for—and whirled to face her attacker.

Except she wasn't being attacked. The stranger was gone. The door was closed. On shaky legs Jillian came out from behind the island, holding the knife in front of her, eyes flicking everywhere. Cautiously she sidled along the wall until she could slap on the light switch. There was no sign of the blond man anywhere. She checked the door handle, found it locked. She lowered the knife. Suddenly she sensed rather than heard something and whipped around. Gaped. The white wolf was sprawled on her couch. At least she thought her couch was under it—the massive white creature dwarfed it. The wolf let out a very puppy-like yip and wagged its great plume of a tail. Reality tilted crazily as the floor came up and hit her.

Jillian's hair had a mind of its own and shoving her hand through it—as she did frequently—made it even more unruly. She didn't notice, wouldn't have given a damn if she had. It was the end of her second week in Dunvegan, her second week of work at the North Star Animal Hospital. And every night since her arrival, she had been awakened in the night by vivid dreams of the wolf. They were good dreams, pleasant dreams to be sure, but the constant interruptions to her sleep were sapping her energy.

And what was she to think about Monday night's dream, the bizarre one about the big blond man? Waking up on the floor the next morning had weirded her out. She didn't have a habit of sleepwalking, yet there were three kitchen drawers thrown on the floor, the contents scattered across the linoleum. Just how did she sleep through *that*? She'd had her hand on the phone to call the cops and report an intruder—then realized that the white wolf had been there too. Just as the creature had shown up in her dreams every other night. *Yes, officer, there was a man in my room but the wolf on my couch must have chased him away.* Nope, not a good plan. Maybe she'd run into a real wolf on the trail, but there was no way she was going to convince anyone, even herself, that a wolf had actually been in her apartment.

Come to think of it, how about the guy's clothes? They

were shredded as if he'd been in an explosion—there was barely anything left of that shirt. But his body looked completely fine. Way more than fine. She thought of his powerful chest, the smooth muscled abs, all plainly visible through the gaping holes in the material. She rubbed her hand over her face to rid herself of the goofy smile that popped up. *Okay, okay, so the guy's built. Really, really built. But those clothes just aren't normal.* In fact, she was reminded of that old Marvel comic book, *The Incredible Hulk*, that her cousin used to collect. Every time the big green guy turned back into his alter ego, Bruce Banner, his clothing hung in tatters. The comic had never mentioned how Banner managed to afford a new outfit every day.

She yanked at her hair with one hand as if to jerk herself back to reality. The whole thing was just silly, way too ridiculous for words. Obviously no one would deliberately dress like that unless they were on a movie set. She'd been having a stupid dream, no doubt brought on by eating chocolate ice cream before bed. Jillian supposed the dream should rightfully be classed as a nightmare, but it was tough to do when the blond man was just so damn sexy. Talk about something worth dreaming about. Did that signify some kind of progress, that she was now dreaming about good-looking guys as well as wolves? There hadn't been much time for dating in the past few years, but she wasn't dead. She wondered if she was lonely, if that was why her mind had conjured the man. She certainly had a much better imagination than she'd thought. It was annoying, however, to find herself hoping to dream of the big Viking again. So far, though, only the white wolf had appeared.

"I've got to get some real sleep. Now I'm missing a man who doesn't exist."

It was just past five when Jillian stripped off her gloves

and gown and headed for the pot of coffee in the staff lunchroom. She hadn't had breakfast, missed lunch, prayed that maybe she could get just a minute or two to eat something now. And rolled her eyes when her mouth automatically started to water. The Watson's sublime food should carry warning labels, she decided. *Caution, tasting may lead to addiction.* She selected a plump little pie enticingly labeled "Rosemary Chicken" and popped it into the microwave. Stood there with her hands on the counter . . .

"That must be some daydream you're having, hon."

Jillian blinked to see Birkie waggling her perfectly shaped eyebrows at her. The scent of rosemary filled the air, and the woman waved her over to the table where the pie was waiting.

"You'd better get some food into you. I imagine it's been a long day in a long week for you."

"Yes, yes it has, thanks." Jillian bit into the pie gratefully. The exquisite flavor was heightened by her hunger, and when the pastry had disappeared completely, she closed her eyes in bliss and sighed deeply.

"You'll be glad to know the "Closed" sign is on the door, and I'm about to take the really good coffee out of the vault to make a fresh pot."

"That's a good thing on both counts." Jillian noticed the older woman's clothes. She knew, *knew*, Birkie had just hosed blood off the concrete floor in the large animal wing. A lot of blood, due to a pair of steers being dehorned. Yet the older woman looked as fresh and put together as she had at the beginning of the day. The suit, a turquoise blue one today, was wrinkle-free, spot free. It even looked *hair*-free, a near impossibility in this business. Jillian had been forced to change her scrubs at noon, but even the fresh ones were now wrinkled, blood-spattered, covered with fur from three species, plus one knee was torn. She restrained a sigh, not the satisfied one of a few moments before but the sheer resignation of knowing she'd never be able to match Birkie's level of tidiness. Instead, she settled for running both hands through her unruly hair.

"By the way, you'll want to watch out for the dead parakeet over by the cups. The bossman ran out to a farm call, left the bird on the counter for Caroline to package up when she gets back from the feed store."

"Dina Monroe's bird? The fat blue one?" Jillian walked over to inspect the unfortunate creature in its clear plastic baggie. It looked like a cartoon, the way it was sprawled on its back with wings askew, legs in the air and feet curled tight. Classic heart attack pose for budgerigars.

"Yup. Dina insists on having it sent out to the lab. She's certain the creature perished from some new and fascinating disease instead of from eating too much buttered toast from her husband's fingers. If its poor heart had held out a few more months, they could have eaten that bird for Thanksgiving."

Jillian couldn't help smiling at that. "What do you stuff a parakeet with? A crouton? My God, it's truly frightening how people manage to give their pets the same health conditions and bad habits they have. Both the Monroes are pretty economy-sized themselves."

"Wait till you meet Ed Barnes's donkey. He likes cigars." Birkie finished filling the coffee machine and pressed the button before turning to the young vet. "Look, honey, I've been meaning to ask you, is something wrong? You look like you've been dragged through a keyhole backward. There're shadows under your eyes, and I swear a zombie would have more color in its cheeks."

Jillian blinked at the blunt description, then laughed. "That bad, huh? I'm just not sleeping well right now. It's probably the time difference, or maybe sleeping in a different bed. Lots of changes, you know. I'm sure it's just temporary." To her surprise, her friend simply took her arm and nudged her into a chair. "What?"

"We need more than mere gourmet coffee here, if we're going to have serious gal talk." Birkie nimbly climbed a chair to reach an antique tin of horse liniment from a high shelf. The yellowed, peeling label claimed the contents "excellent for all ailments." The fragrance was anything but medicinal as Birkie tugged off the lid and offered it to Jillian. The young woman's eyes widened. A dozen bars of dark chocolate gleamed in gold foil wrappers. "My emergency stash," explained Birkie. "Go ahead, pick one."

Jillian didn't hesitate. A moment later she was biting into an almond-filled delight. She rolled her eyes in ecstasy as it melted on her tongue. "Omigod, this is fantastic. You may have just saved my life."

"My Gram was a healer, almost what you might call a naturopath today. She taught me everything she knew about herbs and such. But I find that chocolate is pretty damn fine first aid at times and it's got nothing to do with *antioxidants*." Birkie broke off a square from her own bar and nibbled it delicately. "Now, tell me what else is going on besides not getting enough sleep. You're not just tired, you're worried. I hope it's not about your job, hon, because Connor and I both think you're the best thing since sliced bread."

Jillian paused. She'd known Birkie only a short time, but she instinctively counted her as a friend. Maybe it would be good to tell someone about her dreams. If she collapsed in the middle of a pet spay or something, at least someone would know what was the matter with her. "No, nothing about the job. I love my job. It's just that I've been having these dreams . . ."

"Still? I know you said something about having an awful lot of dreams earlier this week. Bad dreams, strange dreams, nightmares?"

"I wouldn't call them nightmares. They're actually pretty good dreams except that I wake up every time I have one and can't get back to sleep. And I've had one every night since I got here, after not having them for years and years."

"You've had these particular dreams before then. My Gram was a great believer in dreams, and I have to say I pay attention to them as well. We can learn a lot from what goes on in our heads at night. How about you? Do *you* think the dreams mean anything?"

Jillian had told very few people about her experiences. Enough time had passed, however, that it wasn't so much difficult as awkward. "Well, I'm not sure I can explain it without giving you some ancient history. Are you sure you have time for this?"

Birkie just crossed her legs and settled more firmly into the chair. "Honey, I have all the time in the world for you. You've reminded me of one of my own daughters since you got off that bus. And nothing you say is going to leave this room, so no worries about that. I talk about people all the time, but I never betray a confidence."

"It started with something that happened a long time ago. When I was seventeen, they opened a trail system along the river valley that ran through our city. There were miles of different trails winding through the thick cotton-wood trees, and I was trying to walk them all one day. By myself, but when you're seventeen, you think you're invincible."

"Turns out I wasn't invincible." Jillian measured out the words. "Five guys attacked me, raped and beat me. They were going to kill me. But this wolf—I know how crazy it sounds, but a huge white wolf suddenly came out of nowhere and chased them all away. And then it stayed with me, like it was guarding me, like it cared about me. It stayed all night until someone found me." She waited for the older woman's reaction, waited for the look of shock and disbelief, the pulling back, the pulling away—but Birkie, bless her, didn't even blink. Instead she reached forward across the table and grabbed Jillian's hand, held it firmly.

Warmed by the encouragement, Jillian continued. "The first year or so, I'd dream every single night about the wolf. You can't imagine how much it helped me. I felt so much peace and comfort, my dreams were almost like a sanctuary for me. But then, with time and counseling, I learned to let myself feel the emotional pain and the anger over the attack, acknowledge it and let it go, in small increments. After a while, the dreams didn't come so often. And now it's been years."

"You've healed very well." Birkie nodded approvingly. "That's a mighty terrible thing to go through, and an awful thing to have to remember. Most people would have curled up in a ball, let it cripple them. But you've shown real courage in going on with your life. There you are with a veterinarian's degree and the guts to take a job, sight unseen, clear across the country. Well done, girl."

"Sometimes I wanted to curl up in a ball. A lot, at first. But those men had taken so much from me, I didn't want them to steal the rest of my life too, didn't want them to steal *who I was*. It took a long time, though, just to make myself go outside, or go to the store. Go to school. Took even longer to go back into the woods, to hike the trails, be outdoors again. But I wanted the things that I loved back. I wanted myself back. And I think the wolf helped a lot. I didn't see him again, but I thought about him every time things were tough. Something wonderful had stepped in and saved my life. So I had to try to save my life too."

Birkie kept her hand where it was. Her expression showed nothing but acceptance and support. "And you've done a damn fine job of it. Did you ever tell anyone about the wolf? I'll bet some people tried to tell you he wasn't real."

"Of course no one believed me," Jillian snorted. "And I can't blame them. A wolf in the middle of an eastern city? Sure, the occasional deer ran through the river valley park area where I was walking, but a *wolf*? The police said I'd probably seen a big dog, perhaps a coyote—if anything. My counselor thought the white wolf was something my mind made up to protect itself. I went along with that, but I was never quite convinced, or maybe I just liked the idea that somewhere out there was this wonderful creature watching out for me. You know, the way some people like to believe they have a guardian angel.

"But then, last weekend, I—" She glanced at Birkie. She hadn't planned to say a word about the encounter, but she hadn't realized how much she needed to tell someone. She was tired of puzzling through this on her own. "Look, I'm taking a chance that you're really going to think I'm crazy, but I met the wolf again. Here—well, actually I was hiking on the trail below Elk Point. It sounds nuts but I know it wasn't a dream. There were white hairs all over my clothing when I woke up the next morning."

"Do you think it was the same animal, or could it be a different one?" Birkie asked, as easily if they were discussing cows.

"No mistake. It was huge and it had the most amazing blue eyes. I recognized it right—" Jillian gaped at her. "You believe me. I'm telling you I not only had a close encounter but a fond reunion with a real live wolf—which sounds ludicrous even to me when I say it out loud—and you believe me."

"Why shouldn't I? As Shakespeare put it, there are more things in heaven and earth, Horatio . . ." Birkie waved a square of chocolate in the air. "My Gram saw a lot of things in her long life, things that can't be explained. I've lived long enough to see a few things myself, to know for a fact that truth is often a lot stranger than fiction, honey. So you saw this white wolf, and it was the same wolf that helped you. Did the wolf recognize you too?"

"Yes, yes it did." Jillian had read somewhere that the greatest luxury was to be understood, and as she grasped what that really felt like, she found herself blinking tears away. "Look, I just can't tell you how much it means to be able to tell somebody. I haven't known what to think about the whole thing, and it's . . . it's. . . ."

"It's kind of lonely trying to figure out extraordinary experiences on your own," Birkie finished and smiled at her. "And it gets mighty heavy carrying things like that around. Maybe it will help you get some sleep tonight, now that you've gotten it off your chest."

"Maybe it will. Thank you so much for listening to me—and for believing. I know this whole thing sounds so bizarre, and especially meeting up with the wolf again, of all things."

"I should think that it would be wonderfully affirming to encounter the wolf a second time, to know that it's real. You won't be questioning your sanity at least."

"You're right, I am glad it happened." Jillian finished the

chocolate, then laughed a little. "The wolf dreams are okay too. Like I said, they're good dreams. It's just that I can't get back to sleep after I have one." She almost told Birkie about the blond man who had visited her dreams too, but decided not to. There was something more personal about that, maybe because she often found herself fantasizing about him. Besides, she had only dreamed about the man once. It didn't mean anything.

The older woman finished her chocolate and tossed the crumpled foil neatly into the wastebasket without looking. "Tell you what, dear, I think you'd better come on over to my house for supper. It'll be late, but you definitely need a break from this place, and besides, I have satellite TV with nineteen movie channels. Zoey's going to come over for a while too, and you can get to know her a bit."

"Oh that sounds great, but I'm on call—"

"The dispatch service can find you just as easily at my place as yours. Take the clinic truck, and you'll be equipped to respond from wherever you are. You'll find, though, that Friday night seems to be the one time that no one calls you. Connor and I figure it's either because the farmers are out for a beer or the cows are."

Jillian chuckled at that. "Well, I'd love to come over then, thanks."

"Good. Seven-thirty's when I usually eat. Hope you like pizza. The address is in the book."

Chapter Eight

The days were steadily lengthening toward full summer. The sun took its time settling into the west, and for a while, day and night held hands in an orange glow. Finally darkness fell over the North Star Animal Hospital, but to James's surprise, the woman wasn't there. The white wolf paced around the building, casting for her scent. He placed his paws on the windowsill of her apartment and pressed his nose to the screen. *Probably got called out; she's a vet, she could be delivering a calf or something.* Still, he was disappointed—and angry with himself for feeling that way. *It shouldn't matter.* But it did. Especially when he hadn't intended to come here, wasn't going to go anywhere near Jillian Descharme ever again.

The wolf had other ideas, however, resisting that plan every step of the way until James seriously feared for his sanity. He'd tried to submerge himself beneath the animal persona soon after leaving Jillian's apartment, but it wouldn't work. Days later it still wouldn't work. James was stuck with his human thoughts and human feelings in a lupine body. And it was getting damned uncomfortable. There was no respite from the tumult in his head and the memories that sliced his heart and twisted his gut. Even sleep didn't bring him any peace. With human awareness came human dreams. His dreams were filled with nightmare images of Evelyn calling to him for help, of Evelyn dying, of Evelyn dead. Then Evelyn's face would be replaced with Jillian's. Wounded and dying because of him. His fault, all his fault.

In his waking hours, he was trying to figure out the peculiar tie he had to Jillian. The only thing he was sure of was that whatever connection she had with him was with the wolf, not the man. That was made plain the night he was in her room. Had some part of him wanted her to wake up, to see him, see his human self? There'd been no recognition in her eyes, however. It had disappointed him, when he didn't want to care at all, and later it had kindled a hot anger within, as if he was jealous of his own wolf nature. Still, it looked like he wasn't going to get an ounce of peace until he resolved this issue. Was there something he needed to know? Something he needed to do? Something she could do for him? He had no inkling, none at all. And so here he was, and here he would wait until the woman came back. What then, he didn't know—but he sure didn't have any other ideas.

The bales were still stacked in the side yard. The white wolf had no trouble making his way up them and leaping into the loft. He would wait here. It was quiet, and he would spend the time thinking. Trying to remember something, anything. As if he hadn't already spent most of the entire week doing exactly that.

Hours passed. No memories came to him, no new information sprang to mind, but one single thought did occur—when he was in human form in Jillian's apartment he had remembered her name. Would he remember more, then, if he were human? Would his wolfen side ration out a little more information to him? Maybe that was the key.

James called the Change. Standing on two legs didn't feel quite so awkward this time—at least he didn't fall on his ass—but he sat quickly on a bale just in case. For a long while he simply watched the moon climb across the sky, reach the highest point of its arched path, then begin its downward slide. His eyelids drooped. Human form brought human needs. Changing used a great deal of energy, and James had had very little sleep in days. It wouldn't hurt to catch a quick nap. He was confident that his lupine senses would wake him the moment Jillian drove up. Wading through the sweet-smelling straw, he found a particularly thick pile and stretched out on it. But he didn't glide into the light sleep of the wolf. Instead, James fell headlong into slumber as only a human can, slept deep as a man sleeps, and dreamed as a man dreams.

Century-old spruce trees rose black against a deep blue velvet sky. Stars circled in a slow dance overhead. The white wolf padded along a game trail, high along the ridge of dark hills to the west. An old elk had been through here just an hour ago, but the musky scent failed to hold the predator's interest. Something was wrong. *Something.* Suddenly the wolf stopped and lifted his head, looked down over the sweep of land below, where a silvered river wound its way to a distant cluster of lights that looked like numberless stars piled on the ground. There. It was there. Something wrong, close to the river. *Something.*

The wolf hesitated a moment. It went against every instinct. He never wandered near human settlements, certainly never close to a city. But there was a need, an urgency to head for the river valley in the very heart of all those lights. *Now.* It was important. Vital. *Now, now, now.* And so he ran. Built for speed, the wolf's body ate up the miles, yet it wasn't fast enough, he knew it wasn't fast enough. He pushed himself to the limits then, to speeds that only Changelings could attain.

The city rose glittering on either side of the river, the buildings towering over the tallest trees of this forested valley. The white wolf followed the riverbank into a maze of mulched walking trails that wound through dense brush. The sharpness of fear and the reek of violence were on the breeze. And the metallic tang of blood, human blood. Without a pause, the wolf wheeled onto one trail in particular and ran full out. And found a group of men standing over the fallen figure of a small blond woman. One was raising a metal pipe high over his head. . . .

Jillian fully expected to enjoy having supper with Birkie and Zoey, and she wasn't disappointed. Birkie's bright and blunt personality would add spice to any meal, and Zoey's tales of local news reporting gone awry had them in stitches frequently. But it was a flat-out surprise to all of them when they stayed up almost all night, talking and laughing like high school students, making popcorn and watching the silliest movies they could find.

There were other surprises too. After Zoey had finally pleaded exhaustion and left, Birkie had led Jillian to the enclosed porch off the kitchen to show off her hobby. There, rows upon rows of pots under greenhouse lights held a myriad of plants and vines. The air was thick with their fragrance. Bunches of herbs hung upside-down, drying in the dining room. An entire wall boasted shelves of carefully labeled jars, while another wall held a vast collection of books on plants and herbs. Jillian was astounded.

"Learned this stuff from my grandmother," said Birkie. "Been studying everything and anything I could get my

hands on ever since. Gotten pretty damn good at it too."
The woman deftly put together a selection of teas and cap-
sules for the young vet. "All natural, I promise. About as
harmful as the basil on your pizza. These are to help you
relax, help you sleep, and help you *stay* asleep. These ones
here are to build up the blood—you're looking downright
peaked, girl. I'll jot it all down for you so you remember
what to take when. But this thing here is to keep away bad
dreams."

Jillian glanced over at the carefully crafted circle of
rawhide and feathers on the seat of the truck next to her.
Birkie seemed to put as much stock in the dream catcher as
in the supplements, and instructed her to hang it over her
bed. "I know you can find these things at just about every
craft sale in the country these days. Even saw some Asian
knockoffs at the Bargain Mart the other day. But this one is
different—been working on it all week, ever since you first
mentioned having dreams and since I noticed you looking
so tired. Made it out of natural materials, added some particular crystals and stones so it's full of positive energies. It's
designed especially for you, hon, that's why it's bound to
work for you." Jillian wasn't sure about that, but it was
pretty to look at. She didn't have any decorations in her
apartment yet, and she was touched that Birkie would go
to so much trouble for her. She accepted the gift with a
thankful hug.

Jillian yawned as she pressed the automatic door opener
in the truck and drove into the clinic's back bay. She
yawned again as she parked and gathered up her treasures.
She was intent on heading to her apartment when a movement high above her, a small flicker of something pale,
caught her eye. She stared up at the loft. Of course its door
was open—the air was welcome in the clinic at this time of

year—but Jillian couldn't see a thing beyond the yawning doorframe. It was 'black as the inside of a cow,' an apt phrase she'd picked up from the local farmers. She strained to listen but could detect no sound.

An owl? Or maybe a bat. Whatever it was, she'd probably disturbed it when the lights went on. She crossed the concrete floor, slapped off the light switch, paused in the darkness, and waited for her eyes to get used to it. She was tired but owls were her favorite bird. Maybe she'd get a rare peek at one if she could be quiet enough. It was too late in the season for a Snowy, so perhaps it was a Great Gray. Or even a Horned. Excited by the possibilities, Jillian set her things on the floor and carefully climbed the ladder into the loft.

She had to stand still for a while until her eyes adjusted again. There was light coming in the far end from the open window, a mixed palette of cold white light from the waxing moon, warm yellow light from the sodium lamps in the parking lot, and the pale watery light of the eastern horizon. Shadows resolved themselves into shapes, the sharp-edged blocks of neatly stacked bales and vast heaps and hills of loose straw and hay. Wisps were stirred by a warm breeze from the window, bringing the scent of sun-dried fields to her senses.

A movement beside her caught her eye, and she jumped in spite of herself. She realized it was just an old lab coat hung on a nail, watched as the air billowed it slightly, and was disappointed. Was that what she had spotted from downstairs? She began wading carefully through the deep straw as she searched the rafters above for any sign of life.

She was nearly to the window when she stumbled over something solid. She flung her hands out to save herself and came in contact with warm skin. There was no time to jump back. A large man, powerfully muscled and bare-chested, burst up from the straw and grabbed her. With a yell worthy of an Amazon, Jillian Descharme fought like a woman possessed.

"Jesus! Hey!" James was trying not to hurt her, but he would deflect one punch only to have her small fist drill him somewhere else. One blow landed sharply between his ribs, distracted him long enough for her to knee him solidly. His breath exploded out of his lungs, but he wasn't as disabled as a human would have been. In one rapid movement, James wrapped his arms around his assailant and rolled on top of her.

"Let me up, let me go!" Jillian found herself completely pinned. His arms were like massive cables, and she couldn't do a damn thing against the combination of his weight and muscle. Not from this position. She couldn't even head-butt him. Flashback images pounded in her head, terror that her worst nightmare was happening all over again. Heart hammering, her voice rose in pitch in spite of her efforts to sound authoritative. "Let go of me this minute!"

He ignored her as he tried to orient himself, calm his animal nature—and give his balls a chance to quit throbbing. "Be *quiet* for a minute. Let me wake up." He took a few breaths, then rolled to one side to look at her.

As she felt his body weight shift, she gathered herself to fight or flee—but froze instead when she saw the Viking eyes, vivid blue even in the pale half light. "You! It's you! You're . . . but you can't be." She fell silent, confused and scared. *Really* scared now. Reality had just taken an abrupt holiday.

James had no trouble reading the expression on her face. "Goddammit, quit looking at me like that. I'm not going to hurt you. And you're not crazy, so you can quit wondering about that too." It couldn't possibly be a good idea, but he felt he had to give her the truth, felt she deserved that. "Yeah, I was the guy in your room that night. Easy, there. I *said* you're safe." Mostly safe. She was struggling again and the feel of her lithe body beneath his gave him ideas he'd rather not have right now. . . .

Jillian could neither free herself nor punch him again and was forced to relent. It was too much like trying to budge a tree. "Bastard!" she spat out at last, frustrated and furious in spite of her terror. "You bastard! What do you want?"

"Not a damn thing. As soon as you quit trying to kill me, I'm going to let go of you."

"But . . . but you were in my room."

"It seemed like a good idea at the time. You were having a bad dream, and I came into your room to see if I could help." Okay, not exactly but close enough. And he'd just leave out that little part about Changing from wolf to man. And the fact that he had been in the clinic before. There were limits to the good that honesty could do. "I probably ended up scaring you worse than the nightmare you were having. If it's any consolation, you scared the hell out of me just now, so we're even."

Scared *him*? "You grabbed me."

"Reflex. I was sound asleep and you fell on me." He could scarcely believe he'd been that deeply asleep, surprised that he had slept at all. Why hadn't his wolfen senses warned him of her approach?

Indignation flashed like heat lightning across her features. "Why the hell are you sleeping up here—what are you, homeless or drunk or something? Does Connor know about this? Are you on drugs? Just who the hell are you?"

He nearly winced at the onslaught of questions. "I don't

happen to have a place of my own just now. And yes, Connor knows I'm here." Against his better judgment, he admitted, "I'm his brother, James."

Connor's brother? She knew her mouth was open but couldn't seem to close it. She thought her boss had only *two* brothers—Culley and Devlin. The twins stopped by the clinic often. Like Connor, they were tall, wide-shouldered. All three had thick wavy hair that was nearly black. Connor's eyes were pale gray. The twins' hazel eyes wavered between gray, blue, and green. She stared at the man who loomed over her. Studied the angles of his face, the strong jaw that was accented rather than hidden by the close beard, the line of his brow. Tried to look at the shape of the eyes instead of their hue. And finally saw through the warrior image and the fair coloring to the family resemblance beneath. It was there, powerful and plain. He was a Macleod.

And he was true to his word. James Macleod released her carefully and sat back. She jumped to her feet, muscles bunched to sprint to the door—but something about him made her pause. Something in his eyes that she recognized, as like recognizes like. This man knew a lot about pain. "So, are you okay up here?" she heard herself say. "Do you need anything?"

It was his turn to be surprised. "I'm fine." He remembered his human manners, dusted them off and added, "Thanks."

"Well, I imagine you already know the staff kitchen's pretty well stocked. The Watsons just filled the fridge yesterday or the day before." She looked around, wondered if he needed a blanket or something. Her eyes kept coming back to his broad chest, his muscled arms. There was something wild about him, primal. Adding to that impression was the fact that his ragged shirt had taken the worst of the struggle and much of it was hanging in tatters. So why the hell was she standing here worrying about a weird stranger instead of running for her life? "I guess Connor's already told you he has spare clothes in his office and probably anything else you need."

He nodded as if that were true. Actually he didn't have a clue what was in Connor's office and didn't care, but he couldn't say that.

"I'll see you around then."

No, you won't. "Sure, doc. See you." He watched her leave and was surprised that he didn't really want her to go. He'd like to hear her voice some more, watch her face, see the flashes in those sea-green eyes. And he'd like to touch her again, hold her again—not out of surprise or reflex this time, but deliberately. Awake and aware, to just pull her body, warm and supple, against his, to run his hands gently over those soft curves . . . and maybe feel her arms slide around him, hold *him*. . . .

Great, just great. Jesus Murphy! He rubbed his hands over his face and swore again. His human form had gained him no new information at all. Instead it had brought him a brand new problem. He was seriously attracted to Dr. Jillian Descharme.

Chapter Nine

Sleeping was hopeless. It was five in the morning when Jillian entered her apartment, but her brain was racing like a hamster in a wire wheel. She could still feel those iron muscles, hard and tough under skin that was lightly dusted with crisp blond hair. Those intense eyes, that strong face . . . it added up to quite a delicious package, and it stirred her more than she cared to admit. Still, she made a point of locking the door and angling a chair under the handle. Stacked pots and pans on the seat of it. Every dish she owned was plastic, so she gathered glass jars until she had a double row of everything from cold cream to peanut butter marching along the window ledge. James Macleod wouldn't be entering her apartment again without giving her plenty of warning. She checked the phone beside her bed, made sure she had 911 on speed dial. And tomorrow she would have some words with Connor. He really should have given her some sort of heads up that his brother might be staying in the building. In fact, it would have been more polite to introduce her to James, not to mention a whole lot less scary.

Satisfied, she looked at the clock. Six A.M. The clinic was open every weekday but only every other Saturday—and this wasn't one of them. She didn't have to get up unless

someone called in with a problem, so she should really try
to get some sleep.

Sleep? *Oh crap!* She shoved the chair full of pots aside,
dashed out the door, and returned a moment later with the
bag of herbs and the dream catcher she'd forgotten by the
loft ladder. Jillian hunted through drawers until she found a
large pushpin and hung the dream catcher as her new
friend had instructed, on the wall above the head of the
bed. She stood back and admired it, enjoyed the way the
feathers cascaded down from it like a soft waterfall. The
early morning sun caught the tiny crystals in the webbing
and along the quills of the feathers, making them glint and
gleam. Rose quartz, fluorite, and citrine—she remembered
those three. And there was some turquoise and some
amethyst too. The rest she'd have to ask Birkie about again.

It was all of 6:20 A.M. and Jillian couldn't think of anything else to do. She'd barricaded the door again, lined up
the bottles of herbs on the kitchen counter. Her eyes kept
returning to the dream catcher, fascinated with it as the
pale morning light played across it. She decided to lie
down for a while, but she wanted to be able to see Birkie's
beautiful creation, so she arranged her pillows at the foot of
the bed instead.

She yawned hugely as she got into her favorite flannel
pajama pants and topped them with a soft cami. The mattress yielded comfortably beneath her, the blankets were
soft and warm. The sun dappled the wall but wasn't bright
enough to bother her. Instead it lent a pleasant golden haze
to the room. Slowly her eyelids fluttered down.

James's lips descended over hers, barely making contact,
but she could feel the heat of them. He brushed the corners of her mouth, then back over her lips, again and again.
He touched nothing else, yet every inch of her skin seemed

electrified, abuzz with sensation and want. Her fingers ached to knot themselves in his hair, pull his mouth to hers, but her wrists were willing prisoners in his grasp.

Slowly, lazily, James nuzzled her face and took possession of her mouth, cradling her head in one of his large strong hands. Heat. Much more heat. Jillian had kissed a date once right after he'd taken a swallow of hot coffee. But this was far hotter, this was *living* heat. Not the parched dryness of a fever, but the radiant warmth of an inner fire. She melted into the kiss, felt her own lips become pliant, supple. She feasted on each hot breath, drawing it into her lungs as if from some sultry tropical night. His tongue explored softly, lapped at her lips and slid gently alongside hers . . . and she had a sudden mental image of dolphins mating in a heated lagoon. Her own tongue dared to skim his lips and dart swiftly just inside. She inhaled sharply as he caught it in gentle teeth. Held it there until she let out her breath in a long slow exhale. She could have pulled away but instead permitted him to suckle her tongue softly, shivered as he drew it carefully into his hot, wet mouth. Then realized she couldn't pull away, not with that strong hand cradling her head, holding her in place. But the tiny quiver of fear only heightened the delicious sensations.

James drew her tongue in and out of his mouth with painstaking slowness, released it and lapped at her lips, occasionally pressing the point of his tongue at each corner of her mouth. She took his bottom lip in her teeth and tugged softly. Wanted, wanted something, wanted anything. Accepted his tongue eagerly when it plunged deep.

Jillian had never imagined a man making love with only his mouth. Her hands were free, but she could think of nothing but touching his face, cupping his powerful jaw beneath the close-cropped beard, and tracing his strong features as he kissed her long and deep and slow and hot. Again and again. And as he kissed her, James began to stroke her throat from chin to collarbone with a heated hand.

Her body had relaxed, gone lithe and supple. She exulted as her cami was skimmed away, leaving her naked to the waist, and the warmth of his body blazed into her skin right through his clothing as he lay beside her. Her heart skidded and skipped as she realized she could feel his erection, hot and straining within his jeans. Her hip was pressed tightly against the thickness of it.

Suddenly he cupped her breast, engulfed it in heat. He broke off kissing her and leaned over to taste her nipple, lapping at it with a hot, wet tongue. *Oh!* Her breasts felt tight, the nipples hard and seeming to strain toward him. Deep within her core she could feel the sudden hard clenching of her womb, the spread of warmth and moisture between her thighs. Dear God, she wanted this man.

His eyes never left hers as he slowly opened his mouth and drew her nipple into the moist warmth there. He suckled gently at first, letting the reaction of her body guide him. Then James paused for just a moment to breathe deeply, to inhale as if to pull her scent into his lungs, as a lion or a wolf might savor the subtleties of pheromones newly released. And to her chagrin, Jillian whimpered a little, missing him already. He bent his head to suckle once more at her breast, harder this time, faster, as if it were the most delicious thing on earth.

Jillian held his head to her, almost shaking with the excitement he was creating in her. His hand rubbed softly, steadily over her pajamas, up and down, up and down the thighs—then dipped insistently between her legs until she parted them, moaning for more. He palmed her then, pressing firmly against those sensitive parts until she arched and pushed back, until the flannel was soaked through. And then the pajama pants disappeared. One moment they were on and the next there was only cool air against her quivering skin. She supposed she should feel vulnerable, completely naked now while he was still fully clothed. Instead, it simply added to her arousal.

His hand slid down and rubbed her flat belly. She was surprised at how exciting that felt, how intimate. She jumped a little as his fingers moved further down to barely brush the soft curling hair.

James! Her hands tightened their grip in his hair. She felt nearly wild with wanting him to go on, to reach further, touch her *there*. He lifted his head and sought her lips again, his tongue darting in and out, in and out, wet and hot. Then without warning he ran his fingers up the insides of her thighs and stroked lightly across the soft moist folds that enclosed her most sensitive places.

Jillian was certain her heart had stopped. James's light touch electrified her, fanned tiny embers into flame. In a split second she had forgotten all, forgotten everything she had ever known except that she wanted James's touch, needed, *craved* his hands, strong and gentle, hot and soothing, on every part of her body.

His fingers brushed her downy folds a second time. A third. He smiled against her breast—funny how those harsh warrior features were lightened by that smile—and ran his tongue over her other nipple, as his fingers parted her folds and dipped into the moisture there. Her breath hitched as he began to stroke her intimately.

James! Oh God, James! Don't stop, please don't stop. I'm—

There was a ringing in her ears, then a ringing in the room. A doorbell. An alarm. No, a phone. *A phone!* The dream vanished like a soap bubble. Jillian's eyes shot open and she lay there stunned. Awake. Wide, wide awake—and very unsatisfied.

"Jeez goddamn Louise!" She kicked the blankets off in a fury and got to her feet, wanting to punch something. Cursed herself, cursed whoever was on the phone (which was still ringing and damned if she was going to answer it) and most of all, cursed James Macleod. It was bad enough that the man had occupied her waking thoughts far too often—and that was before she knew he was real. It was downright unfair for him to start taking over her dreams as well.

She glared at the dream catcher on the wall and pointed an accusing finger at it. "You! Why did you let a dream like *that* in here?"

Jillian plunked down on the edge of the bed, her body abuzz with an unfamiliar pressure. Got up hurriedly when she realized James had once sat on that very spot. "Good God, there's no hope for me. I need a cold shower. Something. Anything to stop thinking about him."

Coffee was a good antidote for almost anything. Making it in such a distracted state proved difficult. She spilled the entire package of coffee filters when she caught herself wishing James had turned around just once so she could catch a glimpse of his behind. It just proves I'm not dead, she reasoned. That's all. And that's what she told herself again in the shower when her skin felt over-sensitive to the water spray. "Hormones. All hormones. And I'm dead tired. Don't they use sleep deprivation to brainwash people?" She leaned against the tiled wall, was tempted to bang her head against it. "Look at me, I'm drooling like a brainless idiot over some strange guy I just met. Talk about mind control."

Two cups of strong coffee later, her brain kicked in enough that she wasn't thinking about his body. Well, not constantly. She was wondering about the look in his eyes. That haunted expression, the one that had stopped her in her tracks when she was about to run out of the loft screaming. What had happened to James Macleod?

I should be asking what happened to his clothes. Maybe he's not quite right in the head or something. Although you'd think Connor would have warned me. She shoved those thoughts away as she poured coffee into a travel mug, checked her watch, and headed out the door. If she hurried, she could still go yard-saling with Birkie. Maybe she could even find something useful for her apartment. Like a baseball bat to keep by the bed.

James badly wanted to Change. He had had his fill of being in his human form, of feeling human emotions and thinking human thoughts. But not a damn thing had been resolved. And now there were even more things to think about. For instance, there was that little detail about the date. He was still in shock from *that* discovery. He knew instinctively that he had been a wolf for a long time. Knew Evelyn had been gone for a long time—he could feel a distance. But thirty years?

And the dream—he couldn't even remember the last time he'd dreamed like that. *Like a human.* When he was a wolf, there were only brief pleasant dreams of the hunt, the chase, forgotten within seconds of awakening. This dream was different. Not only did he recall every detail, it felt more like a memory than a dream. Had he been remembering something? James thought carefully, recalled the sight of the blond woman on the ground. The picture matched the odd vision he'd had when he left her sleeping on the trail below Elk Point. It had to mean something. And if it was a memory, then there was more to remember. Would he dream again?

As he paced the loft, he caught sight of something from the corner of his eye. The bit of fluttering plaid turned out to be a hanging strip of his sleeve. Closer inspection of his clothes—or what was left of them—revealed that he wasn't as dressed as he'd first thought. No wonder Jillian thought he was homeless.

Annoyed, he seized his shirt in both hands and yanked. It came away with no resistance, and he held the shirt up to look at it. The material was not just torn, but the edges looked charred, and the entire left shoulder was missing. James stared, then touched a tentative hand to his own shoulder. Changelings didn't scar, but there had been a wound there, no, two of them. Shot. How had he forgotten that? There was no blood on the shirt of course—the Change had taken care of that, converted it into energy as it did with most organic substances. But he *had* been shot. By whom he didn't know, only that it had happened as he knelt over Evelyn. *Jesus. Jesus Christ.*

The urge to Change was strong. He didn't want to think about any of this stuff, didn't want to think about anything at all for that matter. Except now there were practical concerns to be dealt with. Even if he was planning to be a wolf, there was always the chance he'd have to switch to human form, even briefly. Who knew what situation would come up? He'd certainly never expected the situation he was in now. And Jillian's reaction to what he was wearing—which was little better than nothing—proved that he didn't have a hope of blending in with other humans. Instead he would attract attention, something that went against every natural instinct. *Shit.* He'd have to follow her advice and raid Connor's office, find something to wear, something to last the next thirty frickin' years. It was definitely going to take him a while to adjust to that date.

In the end, he remained as a human and sat in the loft to wait. He watched Jillian drive away in one of the clinic trucks, saw traffic on the road beyond the clinic. One car turned in a little later, with a young girl behind the wheel. James could hear the keys in her hand as she unlocked the front door, heard excited barks in the kennel room and sounds in the livestock areas that told him she was looking after the animals. The girl left. The traffic slowed to a trickle. Shadows grew smaller, then nonexistent as the sun reached its midday peak. And still James sat staring out the window.

As a man. A man who was highly attracted to Jillian Descharme, whether he wanted to be or not. He still couldn't remember what the connection was between them—between her and the wolf, he corrected—but he knew there was one. He could feel it. More than that, to his surprise he wanted to feel the connection, but James shoved that notion away every time it surfaced. It was only attraction. Nothing more. If he hadn't Changed to human form, if he wasn't in human form now, he wouldn't be having these feelings at all. He felt guilty for having them, as if he was being disloyal, even unfaithful to Evelyn. It added to the burden of guilt that he carried over her death. He had brought that danger to her.

Just like he was putting Jillian Descharme in danger every moment that he lingered. He should leave right now and never go near her again. But what about the wolf? If he returned to lupine form, submerged the human fully within the animal, would Jillian be safe then or would his animal nature continue to seek her out? Hell, the wolf seemed drawn to her as the tide was drawn by the moon. What on earth was the attraction *there*?

Suddenly his heart stuttered as the animal within stirred. *Mate. Mine.*

James clapped a hand to his chest. Fiery pain exploded there as the wolf within tried to force the Change, tried to claw its way out, snarling and snapping. *Mate. Mine.*

Long moments passed before James was able to regain the reins of control. When it was over, he was kneeling in the straw, sweating profusely. The blood was pounding loudly in his ears, and his ribs felt like they'd been kicked repeatedly. "Jesus. Jesus Murphy. What in the goddamn hell was that?" The wolf was part of him, was him. It didn't have a mind of its own. Did it? Had he finally snapped? Had he been a wolf too long?

He drew a long shaky breath. *Mate*, the wolf had declared. That was ridiculous. It couldn't be that, it wasn't possible. Some Changelings were said to be able to recognize their future mates, but he didn't know any personally. There were stories in Changeling history about it, but he had always figured they were myths, the lupine equivalent of the human 'love at first sight' theme. Hollywood had always made money with that story line, probably still did. The uneasy thought that he had no idea if Hollywood was still around crossed his mind.

Besides all that, he didn't need a mate. He'd had a mate, had chosen her and loved her with all his heart, and because she had loved him back, she was dead. He wasn't going to let that happen again, had already resolved to live a solitary life. Yet the wolf continued to be focused on Jillian. Even obsessed. Had he slipped over the edge without knowing it, splintered into two personalities, the man and the wolf?

A truck pulled into the laneway and around to the bay. Connor. James had a momentary impulse to escape out the window but was instantly ashamed. His younger brother was a Changeling too, with all the senses and gifts that entailed. The moment he opened the door, he would be all too aware that James had been there. Undoubtedly Connor already knew that James had been here before. *Better to be up-front about it, let Connor find me here.* But he would find the wolf, not the man. James didn't plan on staying in human form one minute more than he had to. He sure didn't want his brother or anyone else to get used to seeing him in two-legged form.

"Aha, just as I thought." Birkie dug between layers of stained melamine bowls and chipped glass ashtrays until she had a small dish in her hand. "I think this little treasure should go home with us."

Jillian squinted at it in the dim light. The garage ceiling was low, with only a single bulb hanging from it, giving the whole place a cave-like atmosphere. The dish in her friend's hand was shaped like a scallop shell, but there were lots of shell-shaped dishes in the world. Except for the fact that it was much dirtier than anything else in the garage— earth was crusted inside as if it had been used under a plant pot and there was even a dead fly stuck rakishly on the rim—she could see nothing special about it. "Um. It's interesting. . . ."

"Much more than interesting, hon." Birkie held it up and used a manicured thumbnail to gently scratch away the grime that obscured the mark on the bottom. *Limoges, France.*

Jillian's jaw dropped. "Is that what I think it is? How on earth did you know? You must have X-ray vision." She gestured helplessly at the cluttered stacks of mismatched dishes that covered every square inch of an eight-foot table. She felt like an archaeologist on a dig. No, more like the archaeologist's bumbling assistant who didn't have a clue what to look for. Birkie had already plucked an Austrian crystal candy dish from under a stack of plastic fast-food cups. She'd mined similar treasures from the other yard sales they'd visited that morning, all of which were lined up like trophies on the backseat of the truck. With them were Jillian's spoils—a couple of paperback books she knew she'd probably never get around to reading, a set of four glasses with cows on them, some extra spoons, and a TV table. She'd found a baseball bat at the last sale but conceded it to a little boy and his mom.

The older woman smiled. "It just takes practice, hon, and the love of a good bargain. So, back to your adventure with James. You were saying you just left him in the loft?"

"What else was I supposed to do? He's a grown-up. And if he wants to sleep in the hay, I can understand how that might be pleasant. Short-term, anyway. Although I don't understand why he's not staying with one of his brothers. I wondered if maybe he was a little, well, *off* or something, especially with the condition of his clothes."

"Were you afraid of him? You *were* eyeing that baseball bat."

"Yes . . . no . . . well, when he surprised me, I was scared shitless. But after that, no, I wasn't afraid. There's just something about him."

"Well, there's the fact that he's tall, blond, and handsome as sin. Could sure help a gal to overlook a lot." Birkie deliberately fluttered her lashes as her friend rolled her eyes. "Those Macleods always *were* a good-looking bunch."

Jillian latched onto that. "So, you've lived in this area a long time. You must have known James pretty much his whole life."

There was a pause as Birkie circled a couple of ads. "Not his *whole* life but quite a while, you could say. Say, aren't those eyes of his something else? You have to admit he has great eyes. Just like a—"

"Like a Viking? That's what *I* thought when I first saw him."

"I like that. Yes, he certainly would make a great Viking. All those muscles, and him so tall too. I can just picture him on the deck of one of those dragon boats."

Suddenly Jillian could picture that too. James dressed in leather, his belted tunic open to the waist so his muscled chest was clearly visible. His arms bare except for ornate bronze bands circling his thick biceps. Below the tunic would be powerful legs. She imagined they would have the same dusting of blond hair as his chest. And as for what was under the tunic . . . Jillian started and blinked to find her friend fanning her with an old calendar.

"Takes a girl's breath right away, doesn't he?"

"Oh, all right. I admit it, he's hot. Scorching, have-a-fire-extinguisher-with-you-at-all-times *hot*. Connor's gorgeous too, but for some reason it's not the same. I don't daydream about him. And I did find myself wishing James would turn around for just a moment."

"What for?"

"So I could see if his butt matched the rest of him."

They both burst into helpless giggles then, and when other yard-sale enthusiasts turned to stare, giggled even harder. Still laughing, they staggered out into the sunshine, clutching each other's arms for support. Jillian finally had put her hand over her mouth to stifle herself while her friend counted out dollars to an elderly man basking in a lawn chair.

Back in Birkie's red pickup, Jillian asked, "So is something wrong with him?"

"With who?" Her friend was scanning the classifieds for their next yard sale.

"James. Is something wrong with him? Mentally, I mean."

Birkie looked up quickly. "Good heavens, no. Not at all. In fact, James Macleod is as smart as they come. Believe me, the brains match the brawn in this case."

"And?" Jillian pressed. "Oh, come on, you have to give me *some* details. I'm the one who nearly had a heart attack over an intruder in my apartment. I'm the one who had years taken off her life when a man grabbed me in the loft. I deserve a little description here. If you have any compassion at all, you'll spill whatever juicy information you know."

"Well, I'm not sure that I remember very much. My memory—"

"*Birkie!*"

"Sorry dear, you're just so much fun to tease. Let's see now. James is an independent soul, very hardworking. Talented too—not many people have the knack for farming that he does. Crops or animals, doesn't matter. He's amazing at both. My Gram used to travel out to his ranch sometimes. They'd talk plants and herbs for hours."

"He has a ranch?"

"He and his wife did, on the other side of the valley. Near Spirit River actually. But it was sold a few years back. He's . . . well, James has been away for some years now, hon."

"His *wife*? He's married?"

"Was." Birkie pointed to the newspaper. "Look at that! Enid Malkinson has herself a little sale going on. We've just got to say hi to her and Poodle before we grab a late lunch."

Jillian had to leave off fumbling with her seat belt and grab the handle on the dash for balance as the red truck sped away from the curb and headed down the street. She liked the elderly Siamese cat and his owner, but right now they seemed to provide Birkie with a convenient diversion from her questions. So James was married once. Well, that happened to a lot of people. Not everyone stayed together. But she couldn't help wondering why any woman would want to let him go. Did he snore? Did he squeeze the toothpaste tube wrong? Gamble? Drink? Womanize? James had seemed gruff, almost grouchy. Had he always been like that?

Birkie was still talking a mile a minute about Enid Malkinson. Jillian sighed inwardly and put her questions on a back burner. For now.

Chapter Ten

Connor clung to the top of the ladder, staring into the loft. Changelings had keen eyesight, but it was still a struggle to adjust to the late afternoon sunlight glaring hotly in the far window. He shaded his eyes, realized they still had that gritty ache of not enough sleep, even though he'd slept like the dead last night. It was sheer luxury having someone else on call instead of him, but he had been up at dawn just the same, tending to things on his own farm. Now he was in the middle of a very long list of errands, and picking up some udder balm and antibiotics from the clinic was one of them. Still, despite the distractions, the moment he'd crossed the threshold of the building, he had scented his brother.

James? James, what the hell are you doing up here? He spoke by thought, even though there was no one to overhear him.

Good hiding place. No hunters. There was a movement to Connor's left, and a white wolf raised its massive head, shook the straw from its face, and regarded Connor with its vivid blue eyes.

Connor climbed the rest of the way into the loft and sat beside the wolf, even as he frowned over James's words. Wolves weren't a protected species here, but the forests surrounding Dunvegan were more likely to be filled with berry pickers than hunters at this time of year. *Sounds like bullshit, James. Since when do you give a rat's ass about hunters? They'd never get close to you and we both know it.*

The white wolf turned its head to the window.

Look, bro, don't get me wrong, you're welcome here—but why are you here? And for that matter, why did my brand new vet come in this week smelling like you and covered in white wolf hair? She's crazy about wolves so I'm sure it gave her a thrill to see you up close and personal, but it's not like you to run around revealing yourself to humans. What the hell's going on with you?

Don't know.

What do you mean, you don't know? Connor stopped himself then. Took a deep breath, then another. Sat down in the straw, shoving the great wolf over a little to make room. *Let me try that again, James. It scared the living hell out of me to find out that a human has not only seen you, but gotten close enough to touch you. You're usually so careful that even the Pack can't find you unless you want them to. I'm lucky to be able to find you—you're like smoke. I was thinking about trying it, though, because I wanted to make sure you're okay.*

The creature unexpectedly laid its massive head on Connor's leg and gave a very human-like sigh. *I don't know what the hell's going on. The wolf knows her, remembers her from somewhere, but I don't. There's this strange connection. The wolf knew when Jillian came to town. It couldn't know, but it did. It knew when she was here in the clinic, and it knew the moment she set foot in the forest.*

Connor sat very still, his hand frozen in the thick white ruff. James was talking to him. Not in spare and stilted words but really talking, like . . . like a human being, like *James.* It brought a tidal wave of emotion rolling up into his throat, but he swallowed it back hard, blinked away the moisture that sprang to his eyes. He tried to focus on what his brother was saying, but it was damn hard. The words didn't quite make sense either. *The wolf? What wolf?*

The wolf, my wolf, has a goddamn mind of its own. I know how crazy that sounds but I swear it's acting on its own.

"Your wolf—" Connor was stunned, forgetting all about mind speech. For a Changeling, wolf and human were simply different facets of the same being, the same personality. But James had been a wolf for over three decades. Had that skewed some internal balance, maybe made the animal side stronger than the human? "I guess your wolf side is used to protecting you, doing things for you. But taking over and making decisions for you?" He suppressed a shiver. It was downright creepy to discuss the lupine persona as if it was a separate entity. "The wolf is still you, right? Deep down, it has to be."

I'm not certain anymore. Everything changed when Jillian showed up. The wolf is obsessed with her.

"I don't like the sound of that. First you tell me you're not in control of your wolf side, and then you tell me it's zeroed in on my new vet. And you still didn't explain how she got your hair all over her. Tell me your alter ego didn't attack her or some damn thing."

I followed her when she was hiking, just wanted to see who she was, why the wolf was so aware of her. I hadn't planned to approach her but the wolf deliberately stepped out in front of her. It wanted to be seen. By her.

"Good Christ, that must have scared her to death."

No—that's the weird part. Turns out that she recognizes the wolf, she knows the wolf. She's not afraid of it, thinks of it as a friend. Says it helped her or something.

"And you don't remember doing a thing like *that*?"

I got this strange flashback, just for a second, where she was a lot younger and hurt somehow, hurt bad. But I can't remember anything else. And the wolf won't tell me—

"What do you mean 'it won't tell you'? Look, bro, the way you're talking about your wolf side is really weirding me out."

How do you think I feel? Like Dr. Jekyll and goddamn Hyde. Tell me how the wolf knows things about her that I don't. It even knew her name, Connor. Damn wolf didn't bother telling me until a few days ago. And you know what else is strange? I can hear her. I can hear her in my mind just like I can hear you.

Connor gave a low whistle. "Holy-o shit. That doesn't happen very often."

I don't know what it means.

"It means that in addition to being the best damn vet I've seen in years, Jillian may have a few other talents too. Telepathy is rare in humans but it's not unheard of. Most of them don't even know they have it. It doesn't necessarily mean anything." Connor didn't quite believe that however. Not in light of everything else he was hearing. He scrubbed a hand over his face and pressed the heel of his palm to his forehead. What he really wanted to do was to throw his arms around his brother, punch him, wrestle with him, laugh, cry, and ask a million and one questions. But it sure didn't seem like the right time. The situation his brother had described was too disturbing on a number of levels. "So what are you doing here in the loft?"

Just trying to figure out why the wolf wants to be near Jillian. Guess I'm hoping Jillian will say something, do something that will trigger my memory.

"And when you remember, if you remember . . . do you think that will fix things for your wolf?"

I don't know. Maybe not. At least I'll know what the wolf has in mind, what it wants.

"And what if you don't agree with the wolf? What if it can't have whatever the hell it wants? What if it just wants to follow Jillian around like a big dog forever and a day? That could be dangerous for both of you."

No! No, I won't do that. I won't endanger her. The massive creature stood and shook himself. *I've already drawn that line, and the wolf won't cross it. I won't let it.*

Considering the strange conversation they'd just had, Connor wasn't convinced that his brother could effectively leash his wolf nature, but resisted saying so. "Okay. For now, we'll play it your way. You know that my home is your home, and Zoey feels the very same way. Likewise with the clinic. If it helps you to come here, fine, great. But I'm trusting you to be careful, damn careful, to stay out of sight. Understand?" Connor glanced at his watch and swore under his breath. "Look, I don't want to go, but I gotta get back and treat one of my cows. She's been climbing through the neighbor's wire fence to get into his clover field and picked up some nasty scratches on her belly and udders."

Best get them before they're infected. Is it one of your Angus cattle or the little Jersey heifer?

Connor felt a lump the size of a basketball rise in his throat. Of course his brother had seen his farm, observed his livestock and made note of them, even if he was a wolf. Connor had nearly forgotten how gifted James had been as a farmer and rancher. Their father, Ronan, had often declared that his oldest son talked to the earth and its creatures, charmed and persuaded them to produce uncommon quality and yield for him. Connor knew the gift lay in James's ability to read the land and work with it. Whether it was crops or livestock, he understood the needs and strengths of both and wasn't satisfied until there was balance and harmony. James had loved that life. Did he ever miss it? Did he ever even think about it? Not trusting his voice, Connor switched back to mind speech. *Before I go,*

I'll throw some bales so no one will have to climb up here for a while, but for God's sake, keep your head down, okay?

Head down. The wolf nosed his hand. *Careful. Thanks, bro.*

Connor didn't feel as reassured as he would have liked, but he tossed the bales down into the livestock area anyway. Timothy and alfalfa hay for feed, oat straw for bedding. More than the clinic could possibly use in a month. He climbed down after them and stacked them against a wall. "Later, James," he called out and got an answering yip from the loft. He drove off to attend to the rest of his errands with a lot more on his mind than when he'd started. His brother had spoken, really talked to him, and the years had simply fallen away. It was James and they were close again, as they had always been. *I should be ecstatic. I should be doing cartwheels.* Instead, he felt uneasy, as if he was missing something.

It wasn't until Connor was driving home that he identified the real source of the niggling disquiet he felt—*ozone.*

His eyebrows shot up, and he had to pull the truck to the side of the road for a few minutes to collect himself. Human to wolf or wolf to human, there was always a gathering of static electricity in the air during a Change, and with it came a faint telltale trace of ozone. The same scent that heralded thunderstorms, the same signature left behind by lightning. Had the white wolf tried to Change? Succeeded? Failed? And what did it mean? Connor didn't know, couldn't even guess. But he knew what he wanted to believe, what he hoped for. *If you're trying to be human, James, don't stop. Don't give up. Fight for it, fight your way back to us.*

"My father and I built this operation from nothing, did it all with our bare hands." Roderick Harrison never let anyone forget that, least of all his son. It was the one thing he didn't forget even when the Alzheimer's was especially bad. There were times when the old man either talked to Douglas as if he were five years old again or mistook him for a ranch hand. But he always knew what the Pine Point Ranch was and that it was his.

Knowing the speech by heart, Douglas tuned his father out and headed for the door. Old Varley, the ranch manager, had called down from the horse barn to let him know the Dunvegan vet was just finishing up. It was too damn bad that George was away. Dr. George Taku of Spirit River had been looking after their animals since Douglas was nine or ten. In fact the Harrisons did all of their business in that community. It made sense. Their ranch was several miles closer to the town of Spirit River but Douglas knew full well he'd personally avoided Dunvegan since hearing that one Connor Macleod had set up a practice there. *Admit it, Dougie. You're afraid Macleod might resemble the man your father killed. Afraid he'll look at you and know you were there, know you didn't stop it.* He slapped the thoughts away. He didn't know if this Macleod was even related to that long-ago family, and even if it turned out he was, Douglas was determined not to give in to his fears. So determined, in fact, that he was the one who told the manager to call the North Star Animal Hospital when one of the logging horses turned up lame. Just being sensible, he told himself. There was no other vet within two hundred miles, and the horse needed attention. Just plain sensible. Although it had taken several shots of Jack Daniels to help him make that *sensible* decision.

But it wasn't Dr. Macleod kneeling beside the horse. Instead, Douglas saw the strange woman from the river trail, and despite his earlier determinations, an icy thread of fear coiled through his belly. Sweat sprang at the base of his spine, fear-sweat, although Dr. Jillian Descharme didn't *look* particularly frightening. In fact, she appeared rather child-like at the moment. On her knees, her head barely reached the belly of the Percheron mare whose leg she was wrapping. But she had been searching for a white wolf when he saw her last. For a moment he considered letting the ranch manager handle the whole affair, but just then she turned her head and spotted him. Was that embarrassment that made her cheeks redden?

"Afternoon, doctor." Douglas composed himself and tried to remember her name. It started with *D*, he thought. Something French-sounding. *Hell.* "Good of you to come out on such short notice, especially coming so far."

"No problem. It's my job. And I've got another farm call to go to that I can catch on the way back to Dunvegan, so it all works out." She finished the bandage and gathered up her materials. "Where's Buster today?"

"In the house. We don't let him around the horse barn yet. He's still a pup, doesn't have the sense not to nip at their feet."

"Probably a good thing. This gal's foot certainly doesn't need any more irritation. I found a rusted piece of wire jammed into the frog of the hoof."

"Shit. We thought it looked infected, but we couldn't see anything in it."

"The swelling was hiding it. I had to pour a stain over it to get the puncture to show up. Took me a while to get the wire out, and then a ton of pus drained out too." Jillian turned to the horse, talked to it as she patted its massive black shoulder. "What a brave girl you were. I'll bet that foot feels a whole lot better already, doesn't it?" The animal nosed her as if it agreed, and the vet turned her attention back to Douglas. "The foot's still hot and swollen. It needs to be soaked twice a day, and she'll need a course of antibiotics. I gave the instructions to your manager."

"That's just fine. We'll make sure the instructions get followed." He nodded. "Sheila's a good horse, so we sure appreciate that you came out."

"It's a treat to get to work on a draft horse. There's not many around anymore. In fact, I'm surprised at how many horses you have."

"You're not from Alberta, then, are you? There's more horses here than anywhere in the country. We use them."

She looked surprised. "I thought farms and ranches used ATVs and trucks."

"We've got our share of ATVs all right, but a quarter horse is still the best when it comes to working cattle." He warmed to the subject. "ATVs don't have the maneuverability, and they don't have the natural cow sense, the ability to anticipate, that a good working horse does."

"Does Sheila work cattle too?"

"Nope, she has different talents. We do selective logging on the hillsides and coulees, and we have horses like her to pull the logs out of the brush. Heavy equipment would just mow down half the forest."

It was going well. They were actually having a conversation. Maybe that whole wolf thing had been imagination—hers, his, somebody's. Douglas felt himself relax as he walked the vet to her truck. She was actually kind of a pretty thing with those green eyes. He wondered if she had a boyfriend.

"Get away from her! Jesus God, Dougie, you oughta know better." Roderick Harrison was standing at the top of the porch, a plaid flannel work-shirt flapping open over pinstriped pajama bottoms. His feet were bare. "Get the hell away from her. Can't you see she's been near one of *them*?"

Dammit! Where the hell was that nurse? As his father made his way down the stairs, Douglas turned quickly to the vet. "Please excuse my dad. Alzheimer's has him pretty confused these days. Just mail me the bill, okay?"

"No problem. Birkie'll send out an invoice on Monday." Dr. Descharme started the truck and leaned out the window. "Look, let me know right away if you don't think the horse is improving, okay? Don't let it go more than a day. There's a lot of infection in that foot."

His reply was cut short as his father seized his arm with unexpected strength. The old man's voice was shrill in his ear, reminding him anew that his father remained taller than he was. Easy to forget that when the man was in bed half the time. "Get back from there! Can't you see it on her? That goddamn werewolf has marked her as his own. It's all over her, blue as its demon eyes. I told you we had to kill that big white devil, Dougie, I told you and you wouldn't listen."

Jesus H. Christ, not this stuff again, thought Douglas, frantic to hush his father, to hustle him away from the truck. But Roderick gripped Jillian's arm as well and leaned into her face with wild eyes. "You still got time, girl. You still got time to run before they get you, make you into a wolf like them. Run, you hear me? While you still got only two legs."

No longer interested in being gentle, Douglas pried his father's fingers from the vet's arm and forcibly wedged his body between the old man and the truck. All he could manage was a quick glance at Jillian and a jerk of his head, but thank God she got the message and put the truck in gear. His father continued to yell at the vet over Douglas's shoulder even as she drove away. "Run! Run while you can!"

Chapter Eleven

James sat in the loft for a long time after Connor left. As a man.

He couldn't say what had prompted him to Change again. Maybe it was the pique of having his younger brother tell him to be careful. James snorted at that. Humans would never find him unless he wanted them to. Years of life as a wolf had honed his forest skills to an uncanny degree, even for a Changeling. He moved as a ghost—unseen, unheard, and without trail. Then he remembered with no small chagrin that Jillian had made it all the way into the loft and actually tripped over him before he was aware of her presence. What was hell was that, another mysterious gift of hers? Suddenly something much more ominous occurred to him. What if the wolf had been aware all along that Jillian was there—and deliberately did not inform his alter ego? *Great. Now I get to be paranoid on top of having a goddamn split personality.*

James decided to risk venturing downstairs. He felt a little clumsy on the ladder, but at least walking was coming easier. And he had to walk through the whole building. The absence of names on the doors forced him to look in almost every room. Finally he spotted a door thickly papered with cartoons and articles.

Bull's-eye. There was no doubt it was Connor's office. His brother's scent was concentrated here, almost tangible. Connor's jacket was hanging among a motley group of lab coats and surgical scrubs. An oversize couch sagged along one wall, with an accumulation of mail and newspapers covering torn cushions. An enormous desk was groaning under stacks of papers and books. In the far corner, an open door revealed a bathroom with bedraggled towels hanging everywhere and clothes on the floor. It looked just like Connor's half of the room they'd shared as kids. A sharp pang struck his heart as James recalled living at home with his brothers and sisters. He suddenly wondered how his mother and father were and where they might be—and ruthlessly cut off that line of thinking. It didn't matter, it couldn't matter. He wasn't going to be around. It wasn't like he was going to go visit his folks for Sunday dinner or some damn thing. He was going to get the damn clothes, turn into a damn wolf, and hit the damn road.

James made his way through the clutter to where a dresser was burping out socks. He was reaching for the top drawer when he caught sight of the mirror above the dresser. Instantly he froze in a confusion of instincts—then shook it off. He was not a wolf, not in wolfen form. The human in the mirror was him.

James ran his hand over his beard, a little surprised that it hadn't grown out. It was as he had always worn it, just as his hair was its usual length. He had often heard it said that a Changeling's human body didn't age or alter while the wolf form was being used. But had anyone ever tested it for this long? In fact, he didn't look any different than he remembered. Not physically. Something in his eyes, however, *had* changed. They seemed almost ancient compared to the rest of him.

He turned away, both from the mirror and that line of thought. James shucked his tattered clothing and got stuck only once when he had to fiddle with the button on the waistband of his jeans. He might be walking just fine, but his fingers were frustratingly out of practice. He yanked open the top drawer of the dresser and ended up catching it just before it hit the floor. Obviously he was out of practice with a lot of things. He'd have to remember to temper his Changeling strength before he broke something.

Why the hell were there so many socks? He wasn't used to making these kinds of decisions. Finally he pulled out a likely-looking candidate, only to find it single. He pawed through the drawer and discovered they were all singles. Most had holes, big holes. James cursed his brother soundly as he dug around for a mate to the one in his hand.

"James August Macleod!"

Both hands still full of socks, James whirled to find Birkie Peterson grinning at him from the open doorway. *Ah, damn.* Out of annoyance at being caught in human form, his voice was rougher than he intended it to be. "I thought the place was closed down. If you're looking for Connor, he's not here."

"Nope, I was looking for *you*, James," said Birkie. "Been feeling your presence around here for days now, and Jillian mentioned she'd run into you. So I stopped by in hopes of seeing you too." She waved a hand toward him. "And what I'm seeing is that you're in human skin."

He scowled. "Well, keep it to yourself. I'm not planning to stay in it."

"Now that's just a shame. It's a damn fine skin." Her chuckle was deep and rich.

Awareness dawned. James snatched a shirt from the closet and held it in front of him. "God, I'm sorry. I didn't think." And he hadn't, he realized. He was busy getting clothes in case of a possible future need for, well, camouflage. Was he so accustomed to his wolf skin that he couldn't even notice when he was bare-assed naked?

"Oh, don't spoil it by apologizing, James. My pleasure actually. An old bird like me doesn't get such a pleasant view very often. Tell you what, why don't you get yourself together and meet me in the lunchroom? We can talk over a meal." She disappeared without waiting for an answer.

Goddammit. He didn't want to sit down and visit, and definitely not with this woman, as much as he liked and respected her. She wasn't a Changeling, but the power she could wield made both Jessie, the Pack leader, and his father, Ronan, look like amateurs. Yet it wasn't her magic that bothered him.

He wasn't surprised she had detected him, either. He should have thought of that. She was more than able to discern a Changeling at a hundred yards even if it wasn't in lupine form. Birkie had always claimed it was the aura that gave Changelings away, noting that wolfen beings had a halo of light around them that was distinctly blue. But that didn't bother him either.

No, he was ill at ease because she was Evelyn's great aunt. She'd been a frequent and favorite visitor to their home, and Evelyn adored her. He'd enjoyed her immensely too. But he wasn't interested in a trip down memory lane, definitely didn't want to talk about Evelyn. The fact was, she'd been alive the last time he'd spoken with Birkie.

Yet he couldn't see any way to say no. It would be, it would be . . . *rude.* That was the word. And worse, it would hurt her feelings. He sank heavily onto the couch with a pair of socks and wondered at this turn of events. Yesterday he'd been a wolf minding his own wolf business. Today he was a human negotiating a maze of human considerations. He'd ignored his instincts to leave and ended up having a full-scale human conversation with Connor, who would now expect it from him. Human convention dictated that James find suitable clothing for his human form, and it had delayed him long enough to get caught in that form. Now he'd been seen. *Really* seen, he amended, noting that human social mores also had him covering himself—belatedly—in the presence of a woman. Human manners plus human emotion now boxed him in, prevented him from turning down Birkie's invitation to visit over lunch.

If he could ever get the damn clothes on.

James frowned and cursed as he fought to put on socks. It required fine motor skills, a challenge for hands that had been paws for decades. He counted himself lucky that the first pair of jeans he found had fit him, and that he'd managed the button and zipper a little better this time. Shirts were another story. James had always been broader across the shoulders and chest than Connor and it took several frantic minutes to locate something large enough. He soon gave up on trying to put anything back on a hanger and simply left the discards in a pile on the floor. Given the state of the room, Connor was unlikely to notice.

The buttons were a nightmare and finally he just left the shirt open. Had to settle for sneakers to replace his boots. Luckily he and his brother wore the same size in that department, but no way in hell was James going to attempt those laces. He tucked the loose ends in roughly and made his way across the room. Ended up having to almost slide his feet to avoid losing the shoes.

God, he missed being a wolf.

Although he'd found the kitchen earlier and would have been able to locate it again by memory, this time it was easier to simply follow his nose. The scent of food, human food, was almost overpowering. And very nearly foreign. Not only was it laden with spices, but the food was *cooked*. It enticed and repelled at the same time.

Birkie had just added a bag of warmed buns to a table already laden with food. She waved a hand at him to sit. James pulled out a chair, feeling awkward as he slid into it. There was a plate in front of him, a knife and fork. A glass. He eyed them warily.

"I remember you used to like lasagna quite a bit, so I set this aside for you when the Watsons filled the fridge this week. It's Bill's own recipe. Everything they bring is packaged in individual servings of course, but the portions are large. Have to be, to feed Connor."

James took the steaming dish from her, sniffed it carefully. The spices were heady, nearly overwhelming, but he could identify all the ingredients, pick them out from one another. Suddenly a huge and ravenous hunger made itself known, and he almost dropped the dish. Only a supreme effort kept him from burying his face in it. Quickly, James dumped the pasta on his plate and shoved his hands in his lap where Birkie wouldn't see them clenching.

"By the way, you can relax while you're here, son. Connor's at his farm with Zoey. Jillian's out on a call. She's all the way over by Spirit River, and she's got another call after that. We're not going to be interrupted anytime soon."

"Jillian—she's okay?"

"She's just fine. Why wouldn't she be?"

"I scared her, that's all. Not on purpose," he added quickly at the woman's questioning glance. "Figured she might be mad or upset or something."

"You startled her," corrected Birkie. "You'll find that Jillian Descharme doesn't scare easily, and while she's capable of a real good mad, she doesn't hold onto it like some people. Interestingly, she was concerned about you." She poured milk into both of their glasses, took something else out of the microwave. "Usually we eat off paper plates around here, but I thought you might find those a bit flimsy to practice on. So these are stoneware. Solid but not breakable." Birkie winked at him. "Human coordination probably takes a little getting used to."

He didn't dare look at the lasagna on his plate, but the smell was driving him wild. He concentrated on Birkie's words even as he began to sweat. "You always were very perceptive. And considerate." James' voice sounded strained even to him. He needed to eat. He had to eat. A wolf wouldn't wait, but a human must. Would the woman ever sit down?

"And *you* were always very independent. You could have asked for a little help with the buttons and the shoelaces, you know." She laughed at his scowl. "I have to say, it's good to see you again. I've missed you, boy." She gave him an airy wave with one hand while she slipped into her chair and picked up her fork. "Of course I don't expect you to have missed me, James. Or anyone else for that matter. Being a wolf surely precludes a lot of emotions. I imagine that's why you've been one for so long."

There didn't seem to be anything he could say to that, so he grabbed a fork too. The sensation of holding a slim metal object, the concept of using it as a tool, seemed bizarre and that annoyed him. It wasn't as if he'd never been human before. Gritting his teeth, James gave the lasagna an experimental poke. Birkie cleared her throat, and he glanced up to see her cut the stacked pasta neatly with the side of her fork. He tried it, succeeded in dragging the first layer off his lasagna instead. On the second try, he managed to cut a forkful but it ended up on his bare chest. Finally a bite made it to his mouth.

The meal continued like that, with Birkie making conversation and James making a mess. She didn't turn a hair when half of his milk landed in his lap, the result of accidentally trying to lap from a glass. And she completely ignored his curses and noises of supreme frustration.

James was determined to eat like a human being, to remember how. And gradually, he did. Mostly. But there was no holding back his non-human appetite. He quickly worked his way through most of the Watson's menu. Birkie simply talked while he ate, occasionally warming up more food and placing it on the table, clearing away empty containers. She seemed to deliberately stay away from any mention of the distant past, and instead brought him up to speed on the everyday workings of the clinic, the growth of the town, the latest issues that were making headlines in the *Dunvegan Herald Weekly*. And gradually she segued into the daily lives of his brothers and sisters. Their human lives. Connor's marriage, Culley's business, Devlin's books, Kenzie's studies, Carlene's children. Things he knew nothing about, and it bothered him suddenly that he didn't.

"You know, I think you've gotten the hang of it, son," Birkie said at last, as the last bun disappeared from the bag. "And I must say, you're a lot neater at it than Connor, and believe me, I've seen him pack away food after a Change. I don't know what it's like to shapeshift, but I imagine it uses up a truckload of calories."

James nodded. The truth was, he'd completely forgotten about that little detail. For years, he'd lived with only a wolf's natural appetite. He was unprepared for his stomach to turn into a snarling bottomless pit, a black hole with an appetite for entire galaxies, but knew he should have expected it. Too many Changes, not enough chow. He blamed his wolf side for that. If it had just cooperated, paid attention to wolf business instead of trailing after Jillian, then he would have hunted this week. "I guess I'd better thank you for lunch. Looks like I needed it more than I knew."

"Don't worry about it. I'm used to Connor's habits. He gets so involved in his work that he often forgets about eating until he's desperate. Bill and Jessie noticed that about him years ago, that's why they fill the fridge here every week. Then if he perishes from starvation, it won't be on their conscience. But even with the food right here, I still have to remind him from time to time."

James chuckled at that and startled himself. Both the sound and the ticklish sensation it gave the back of his throat were strange. When was the last time he'd laughed or smiled or done anything of the sort? When was the last time he sat at the table with a friend? He tried to fend off those thoughts and caught only the tail end of something Birkie was saying.

". . . and besides, all this practice will come in handy when you ask Jillian to go to dinner with you."

A fork clattered to the floor, and he stared at her. "What?"

"Oh, don't look at me like that. You like her, don't you?"

"Dammit, Birkie—" he began, but she raised a hand.

"First off, let me assume you're embarrassed and uncomfortable because I'm Evelyn's great aunt. Don't be. I loved Evie like a daughter. More importantly, I know that you loved her. My dear boy, no one could have seen you with her and not known that. We all grieved when she died and her baby with her, grieved when we thought we lost you as well. But you survived. What about *your* life?"

"My life is fine." His words were tight, almost bitten off.

"Your *wolf's* life is fine, hon," she corrected. "Your own is a little lopsided."

"It's the way it has to be."

"It's the way you *think* it has to be."

"I said I'm fine."

She rolled her eyes then. "There's no point in being defensive with me, James. You know I see far too much for that."

He knew, all right, and scowled at the truth of it. Birkie could see his human skin, and likely every single thought that lay beneath it as well. There just had to be some way out of this conversation. "Look, I really don't want to talk about it right now." *Or ever.*

"I'm certain that you don't, and normally I wouldn't press you. But there's more than just you involved. I happen to like Jillian very much, and I'm concerned for her as well."

"I'm not interested in Jillian," he roared.

She didn't even blink at his outburst. "And that's why you've been following her around? Because you're not interested?"

"You don't understand. The goddamn wolf is following Jillian. And I don't know why. I don't know what it wants, so now I'm following her too, hoping to figure it out." He scrubbed a hand over his face and suddenly felt very tired. "And that sounded crazy even to me."

"You've met Jillian before."

"Yes—at least I think so—but I can't remember her exactly and the wolf won't tell me a damn thing. And if you need more details on that situation, ask Connor. I'm not up to explaining it all over again."

The older woman sat back then, folded her arms in front

of her and studied him intently for a long moment. "Maybe your wolf will explain it."

"What—" The hair on the back of James's neck prickled, as the atmosphere in the room shifted, changed. A phantom taste burst on his tongue and the scent of it filled his senses: evergreen, wild rose, buffalo berry, bindweed, milk thistle, a bouquet from the very heart of the forest. Deep within him, the wolf stirred, restless and alert.

Birkie spoke then—he could see her lips moving—yet as much as he strained, he could hear nothing. It took some moments before he realized the wolf was responding to her, while he himself had been firmly shut out of the conversation. James struggled to regain control, his frustration escalating until finally his temper exploded. He shoved the wolf out of the way, shoved it deep into some inner compartment and slammed the door.

Birkie found herself face-to-face with a very angry man.

Chapter Twelve

"What the hell are you doing?" James growled at Birkie. Sparks of iridescent green flashed in his blue eyes, a sure sign of an enraged Changeling. "Why are you talking to the damn wolf instead of me?"

She didn't flinch, didn't flicker an eyelash, but regarded him gravely. "You heard nothing?"

"Not a goddamn word and you know it."

"No." She shook her head, surprise evident in her face. "I didn't know it. I knew there was some schism between you and your inner wolf, but I didn't know it was like this. I've never seen this before, and I've studied Changelings for a very long time."

He clenched and unclenched his fists, trying to regain control of himself. "I've had enough of the wolf taking over whenever the hell it feels like it."

"I imagine so. And I have an idea as to what the problem may be. A Changeling's human side is in control no matter what form he's in. That's the rule. But you know from Changeling history that there are a couple of exceptions to that rule. *Important* exceptions."

The anger began to ebb. James took a deep breath, then another. Considered. The wolf could rise involuntarily in any Changeling to ensure their survival. The wolf might also come out to defend a mate. "I don't get it. Those situations don't apply to me, not now."

"I'll bet they do, just not the way you might think. Believe it or not, the wolf is on your side. It's looking out for you, protecting you. Ensuring your survival."

"But that makes no sense. I'm not in any danger. I *have* survived."

"Depends on how you define survival. How a wolf defines survival."

James shook his head. "I'm not sure what you're getting at."

"Evelyn died. It was horrible, it was unfair, it was wrong, but it happened. You were mortally wounded. What was your first impulse when you realized she was gone?"

He was silent, though he knew it would do him no good.

"You wanted to follow her, didn't you? Of course you did, that's a natural impulse. But what did the wolf do?"

Ah, damn. James sat heavily and stared at the floor. "It took over."

"It had to, to save your life. Believe me, I know. When the Pack found you, Jessie called me to come and help if I could. I saw what had happened to you, James. You were hit by a shotgun, twice, at fairly close range." Her voice was grim, but she stood beside him, put a gentle hand on his shoulder, the shoulder that had been wounded. "It's a miracle you didn't die outright. And if you'd remained in human form, you would have died for sure. Your wolf knew that.

"Changing in that condition could have killed you too, of course, but your wolf is very strong, *you're* very strong. You got through it and the shift stopped a lot of the bleeding, bought you some time until we could work on you."

He sat quietly for several moments, staring off into the past and absently running his fingers over the places where the wounds had been. Finally, he looked up at her. "I didn't know that. I don't remember much after the Change, but I guess I should say thanks." He sighed. "But I'm not wounded, and I'm not in danger now. I'm trying to see it, Birkie, but I just can't make any connection between that situation and this."

"You're not thinking like a wild wolf, a real wolf, especially an alpha wolf. What does a wild alpha wolf do if it loses its mate? Does it spend the rest of its life alone?"

Apprehension prickled the hair on the back of his neck. "It's not the same, Birkie."

"The wolf will mourn his mate, but then he'll go on with his life. Survival means going on with your life *in all ways*."

"It doesn't apply here." Suddenly he realized where she was going with this, and his voice took on a warning note. "Birkie—"

She ignored him. "The wolf finds another mate because he isn't designed to be alone. Your wolf has found one. I should say *you've* found one, but only your lupine side seems to have recognized her."

"No." He got up, backed up, knocked over the chair. Pointed at her and shook his head. "No. Don't tell me that, goddammit! You've got it all wrong." Dishes clattered noisily to the floor as he backed into the counter.

"Why do you think the wolf is so focused on Jillian? Why do you think it took steps to find her and ensure her survival years ago, just as it's working to ensure yours now?"

"Jesus Murphy, Birkie!" Was the woman deaf? "How many times do I have to say I'm not interested in Jillian?

And I'm especially not interested in having my wolf side pick out women for me."

"You're not interested or you don't want to be interested?"

"I can't be interested, goddammit!"

"Son." She caught his gaze and held it. "I know you miss Evelyn, and part of you is always going to miss her. But surely you know that she wouldn't want you to spend your entire life mourning her and never moving on."

Her eyes were unwavering, the soul within them ancient. He felt like an unruly child and it pissed him off even further. Still, he fought to stay in control, to be civil. "I know you're trying to help, Birkie," he said through gritted teeth, "but you don't understand."

"What I understand, son, is that you've already spent thirty years alone. And I understand that you fully intend to spend the next thirty like that too."

He moved toward the door but she was in front of it. "You don't get it. I can't be with anyone. Not Jillian, not anybody. I can't do that to someone again."

"Do what, James?" she asked quietly.

Pain hoarsened his voice, wrenched the words from him. "Evelyn's dead because of me. Didn't you know that, Birkie, didn't you see that in your goddamn crystal ball? It's my fault. Some bastard killed her because she married a Changeling."

"You don't know that."

He took a step toward her, then another. Leaned down until he was nose to nose with her. Although his words were quiet and deliberate, there was a terrible certainty to them that struck like a hammer blow. "Instinct tells me that. My gut tells me that. I *do* know it and I know I brought that to her. It's my fault she's dead. I won't do that to someone again. Not to Jillian. Not to anyone."

James pushed past her then. He could hear Birkie calling after him, but he ignored it. Rude or not, he had had enough of human concerns and human manners and human emotions and human goddamn everything. He had the necessary clothes, he'd had enough conversation to last him years, and he'd had more than enough of his wolf dictating his life. He was done with it all and especially with Jillian Descharme. He was going to do what he should have done on Day One, which was the right thing, the best thing, the safest thing for her. Get out of her life.

He strode quickly, purposefully down the hall, intent on reaching the back door. It was still light outside, but he knew he could duck into the thick stand of trees near the building. There would be enough cover there to Change and—

He ran straight into Jillian.

Jillian rubbed the back of her head where it had struck the floor and looked around for the bus that had hit her. Instead she saw James Macleod. For a moment he just stared back, then knelt quickly beside her.

"Did I hurt you? Are you all right? Christ, I'm sorry."

"I'm fine I think. Hey, don't you know the local speed limit is 25?" She sat up and reached for the papers that had spewed out of the folder she was carrying, but he was already gathering them—or trying to. For every one he managed to pick up, two flew farther away.

"I didn't see you. I said I was sorry." He looked at her hard, as if daring her to disagree.

"You don't look sorry, you look angry." The intensity of

his eyes was like a physical punch, almost making her dizzy. Still, she could swear there was something behind them, something that pulled at her. "Is something wrong?"

"No. Nothing."

She saw it then. Like twin lightning flashes, sadness and deep pain played across his rugged face. Then the fierce frown returned.

He seized the last of the papers and stuffed them into the folder, handed it to her. "I'm just in a hurry, that's all."

"Well, hell, don't let me keep you." She reached over to the wall, intending to stand. Then powerful hands gently caged her waist. She was lifted up and set on her feet as if she weighed exactly nothing. The hands lingered. She could feel the strength behind them, yet sensed also that the immense force was deliberately tempered, carefully reined. James was close, so close that she could feel the heat from his body and suddenly she couldn't breathe, couldn't speak, could only look up into his face.

He released her so abruptly that Jillian lost her balance and landed on her butt, hard. Every individual vertebra from stem to stern protested the jolt. She swore, but it was at empty air. James was gone. Just gone. All she saw was the door swinging shut at the far end of the building.

She was still sitting there, dumbfounded and staring at the door, when Birkie rushed up behind her. "My heavens, girl, are you hurt? What happened?"

"I'm fine, I'm okay," she said as Birkie insisted on helping her up. "I've just had another close encounter of the James kind."

"Swept you right off your feet, I see."

"Ha. Dumped me on my ass is more like it." She went to straighten her clothes and realized she was still in her dirty coveralls. Rubbed the back of her head and discovered a sizable lump had developed where she had banged it on the floor. *Shit!* "You think that's strange, you should have been with me on my last call. Why are men so damn weird?"

"They can't help it. They're wired that way." Birkie stepped back, hands on hips and surveyed Jillian. "How long will it take you to shower and change?"

"For a good cause, fifteen minutes or less. Finer Diner?"

"Frankly, I was thinking the Jersey Pub. I need a cold beer, hon. And I'm betting you could use one too."

"God, yes! And a plate of nachos to go with it. I'll be ready in ten." She hurried down the hallway to her apartment, paused halfway in the door. "You know, if I had to guess, I'd think that James has a split personality. He can be so nice sometimes but other times, he's got to be the strangest man I've ever met in my life." She disappeared into her apartment.

Birkie shook her head. "Honey, you don't know the half of it."

Chapter Thirteen

The wolf emerged from trees near the clinic at a dead run. Its belly was low to the ground, its limbs reached long and pistoned hard as it crossed the fields to the far forest, a sleek white comet tinged with the gold of the fading sun.

Nature had designed the wolf's body for running, and an ordinary wolf could cover sixty miles in a single day, a Changeling, many more. James raced flat out for hours, through narrow game trails in the dense forest, along the very tops of the coulees high above the river, until amber twilight gave way to deep velvet night. Still he ran, swift as white water through a spillway, devouring the miles. The moon rose, its glow revealing a silvery shape arrowing through forests, across fields. James ran on until flecks of bloodied foam flew from his drawn lips, until his throat nearly closed for want of water. And still he could not outrun the pain in his heart, or the dilemma of his dual nature.

Dawn was not far off when James slowed at last and splashed into the river's edge to drink, flanks heaving, lungs burning for air. He stretched out on the bank, heedless of the mud, and gave in to exhaustion and the blessed oblivion it promised. The promise proved false, however, as oblivion dissolved into a dream, the very same dream James had begun in the loft.

Deep in the river valley that divided the city, the air was thick with the metallic tang of human blood. The white wolf discovered five men standing over the fallen figure of a small blonde woman. One was raising a thick metal pipe over his head.

A deep-throated growl was sufficient to make the men turn, their prey forgotten. The sound vibrated along their nerves, resonated in their bellies. Five pairs of eyes gleamed wide as a monstrous nightmare stalked stiff-legged from the cover of the trees. The moon touched its white coat, rimmed it with unearthly silver. The creature's lips were drawn back to expose long deadly teeth; its eyes glowed with green fire. Suddenly there was shouting, screaming, a mad scramble to escape. The man with the metal pipe flung it at the giant wolf but the pipe fell wide of its target as he fled down the trail.

The wolf howled once, short and sharp, a hunting call to panic the men further. The urge to chase the men was powerful. But another instinct was stronger, drawing the wolf away from its quarry. The woman needed help and quickly. And so the white wolf went to her.

Still dreaming, James struggled deep within the wolf, seeking a path to the surface, to awareness within the dream. He recognized now that this dream was a window to the past, knew his only hope of understanding his situation was to somehow see this vision as a man. He wrestled with his wolf nature but could not subdue it completely. Instead, with a sudden rush of clarity, he became both wolf and man at the same time, saw Jillian through eyes that were now both animal and human. And as he watched, the present slipped away and his dual nature became fully immersed in the past.

Her blond hair was long and matted with blood. The fine angles of her faery face had been battered by ruthless fists; her features were swollen and bruised. His heart twisted at the sight even as fury glowed white-hot within him. Until her eyes opened. Green. Sea green. And infinitely sad as she waited to be killed by the wolf. As she grieved not for what had been done to her, but for being alone. That had jolted him, temporarily doused his rage. He could hear her thoughts. James suddenly felt himself struggling for words. It had been so long, so very long, since he had used any.

Not alone. Here with you. Carefully, tenderly, he lapped the blood and tears from her face. There was little or no danger that his saliva would carry the Change into her bloodstream, not with her wounds bleeding so freely. Only a deep bite could accomplish that. He concentrated on cleaning the abrasions as he listened to the outpouring of grief and pain in her mind and heart. Learned that her name was Jillian. Sent her calming, soothing thoughts and laid his powerful body close beside her broken one, radiated Changeling heat to warm and to heal. Yet instinct told him it wasn't enough. Finally, as the sky blushed with dawn, he gave her of his own life energy. A transference from aura to aura. To save her.

Hours passed before the morning sun was high enough to give her its own warmth. It was then that his wolf hearing detected a small truck laboring up the trail. Only then did he leave the girl's side. He watched with narrowed eyes from the nearby cover of bushes as the park maintenance workers found her, as they covered her with their coats, called for help on their radio. And as the wolf kept careful watch, James talked to her in her mind, reassured and comforted her until an ambulance came and took her away.

The white wolf slipped away when the police began to search the trail. He didn't go far—he didn't have to. With so much cover it was easy to keep from being discovered by humans, and no dog would willingly follow a Changeling's scent. And when they left the area after dark, he began to hunt. Not elk this time but human prey—the brutal men who had raped and beaten Jillian. The wolf had memorized each and every scent from her damaged body. The five would have gone to ground by now, hidden themselves in the concrete warrens of the human city, but it would not be enough to elude nature's swift justice.

It was Sunday. Wonderful, glorious Sunday. Jillian rolled over and slapped off the alarm, snuggled back into the deliciously soft quilts. She was still on call. But the clinic was closed today, and she had a second chance to laze in bed until someone phoned her with a problem. And that could be hours from now. Maybe not at all. Instead of falling back asleep, however, Jillian found herself staring up at the white ceiling and recalling yesterday's visit to Pine Point Ranch.

Werewolf. That was the term Douglas's father had used. *Good grief.* The poor man was obviously not in his right mind, but he'd spoken of a big white devil with blue demon eyes. What else could it be but her wolf? Birkie had said it only made sense that Jillian wasn't the only person to encounter it. Although that thought caused a tiny finger of disappointment to poke at her. After all, she was used to thinking of it as *her* wolf. Her imaginary friend and real-life hero. Logically, though, she had to agree with Birkie. And if Harrison Senior had seen the wolf somewhere, maybe *werewolf* seemed a reasonable explanation to him for the existence of such an enormous and unusual creature. After all, she'd been trying to define the wolf herself, even started reading lupine myths and legends. Who was she to say that *werewolf* sounded weird?

She'd recognized her cue to leave and driven away from the ranch, but not before seeing something in Douglas's face as he struggled with his father. Fear. It seemed out of place on such a strong intelligent face, but it was there nonetheless. Was he afraid for his father, afraid of what she might think, or was he afraid of something else altogether? Come to think of it, he had looked pretty spooked on the trail when she'd asked him about the white wolf . . . but that was before she knew what he was dealing with at home. Maybe he had always thought his dad was imagining the white wolf, and it was scary to hear about it from someone who didn't have Alzheimer's. Although she had probably come across as a complete loon at the time.

Jillian yawned and stretched. Last night she'd nursed a single beer over a giant plate of nachos and chili, then said goodbye to Birkie at about nine. She loved the older woman's company, but Jillian simply had to lie down. It had been a very long week. And to her surprise she not only fell asleep right away, she stayed asleep. Of course, it might be due to the bump on the back of her head. She reached around to feel it and winced at the touch.

What was it with James, anyway? Every encounter she'd had with him seemed like something out of a TV show, but she couldn't decide if it was a drama or a sitcom. She'd been scared shitless to find him in her apartment, he'd surprised her in the loft—and that had been scary too—and then he'd run over her in the hallway. At least she hadn't been afraid that time. It had happened too fast.

What would it be like to just meet him on the street like

a normal person? Or better yet, why couldn't he have shown up in the Jersey Pub last night and asked if he could buy her a beer, sat and talked with her, maybe asked her to dance?

A slow dance. That painted a delicious picture in her mind. In the loft, she'd been held captive by James's powerful arms, had felt his rock-hard body pinning her. But in the clinic hallway she'd felt those same muscles held carefully in check, those hands filled with a heart-melting gentleness. It had mesmerized her in spite of herself. In fact, she could still feel James's hands on her waist, and it wasn't hard to imagine being surrounded by his tempered strength on the dance floor.

Mmmmm. Jillian half-closed her eyes and smiled, held out her arms as if holding a partner. She'd only circled the room twice, enjoying the fantasy in spite of feeling a little foolish, when a brand new thought struck, one that doused her passions more thoroughly than a bucket of ice water could have. She lowered her arms, her uneasiness laced with prickles of fear.

James was a real man. A little on the strange side maybe, but living, breathing real. He had admitted to being in her apartment. But up till then she'd concluded that whole first episode was a dream because she had seen the white wolf on the couch. *How could I have been awake to see James and then suddenly asleep to dream of the wolf?* No, that made no sense at all to her. For heaven's sake, she'd been throwing out drawers in search of a knife to defend herself with. Surely no one could fall asleep after that.

Had she fainted out of some bizarre sense of relief when she saw James was gone? Had she gotten the sequence of events mixed up? Maybe she passed out and *then* saw the wolf on the couch. *Okay, maybe. I don't like it, but maybe.* Jillian didn't really think she was the fainting type—but she *had* awakened on the floor the next day. So, as wussy as it made her feel, it was a given that she must have been asleep or passed out. She knew why James had been there, or at least why he said he'd been there. So there were plenty of explanations for everything—except for why a giant wolf was hanging around in her apartment.

Maybe she had been hallucinating? Maybe she needed to feel safe, so her mind obligingly produced the white wolf, just as Marjorie had said all along. *Wait a minute. I can't suddenly go along with her theory* now. *I met the wolf, and he's as real as James is.* Of course, just because the wolf was real didn't mean she'd stopped dreaming about him. For that matter she'd had some pretty explicit dreams about James. She swore in frustration as a tingle ran through her body as if on cue. She gritted her teeth and focused. It had to have been a dream, because a real wolf couldn't get into her apartment. But James wasn't supposed to be there either. Had he left a door open somewhere and inadvertently let in the wolf? Was that possible? And even if it was, why on earth would a wolf be waiting outside, looking for an opportunity to get in? The prickling feeling on the back of her neck made her shiver. And pushed her to walk to the couch on the far side of the room. Gingerly she picked up the newspapers she'd tossed there from the past few days. The opened mail. Books. Like peeling back the layers of an onion, she removed everything that hadn't been there before that night.

Suddenly her blood chilled, and she had to struggle to draw a breath. There were white hairs, many white hairs, clinging to the worn fabric of the couch.

Chapter Fourteen

Jillian sealed white hairs into sample bags. It had taken an hour, with gloves and tweezers, to gather enough—labs preferred to have at least fifty strands to work with—and to make sure they were of decent quality. She'd had to view the strands under the microscope in the lab to make certain there were roots attached to the hairs so that DNA could be extracted.

It looked like ordinary dog hair, ordinary everyday white dog hair. Which it probably was, she told herself, probably fell off her clothing. After all, a collie had been boarding in the clinic kennel that was mostly white except for the black patches over its eyes and ears. A snowy Samoyed had come in to have its teeth cleaned. There was no lack of sources for white canine hair at the clinic, no lack of possible explanations for its presence in her apartment. But not in such quantities and not on her damn couch. She seldom sat on the couch, and although she was hard-pressed to keep it from becoming a catchall for books and papers, she seldom tossed her clothes there.

Thorough by nature, Jillian had already gone through the books from the library, studied everything they contained on wolf legend and lore. She probably would have skipped the parts about werewolves—after all, *some* things were just too farfetched—but thanks to that little incident at the Pine Point Ranch, she read those too. She didn't believe anything she read, yet she felt a need to cover all bases.

Now, however, it was time to get serious and let science have its say. She had a few—very few—facts to work with, but they were rock-solid. One was her firsthand knowledge that the white wolf was a real animal (hence the hair). However, she also believed that it wasn't an ordinary wolf. There were too many obvious physical and behavioral differences. It had occurred to her that perhaps it was a brand new subspecies—and wouldn't it be exciting to be its discoverer?

Of course, there were other, more mundane, possibilities. Because dogs and wolves could interbreed, her wolf could be either an accidental or deliberate hybrid. *Canis Lupus* meets *Canis Familiaris.* Jillian figured it might be possible to combine, say, the heavily muscled body and white coloration of a Great Pyrenees with the lush coat and blue eyes of an Alaskan Malamute, then mix them with a large breed of wolf. It might even explain the creature's curiously benevolent attitude, its unusual desire to protect humans. Or at least one human, anyway.

She reminded herself of the white wolf's apparent benevolence frequently. Jillian was grateful that the massive animal had saved her life years ago, was glad to have met up with the wolf again and know that it wasn't just a dream. But now she was, well, nervous. "It's all fun and games until you find a wolf in your apartment," she muttered.

So here she was, packaging bagged samples into an envelope. Wolves and dogs were so closely related that there was less than a one percent difference in their genetic material—but there *was* a difference. And if the animal was a hybrid, tests existed that would show genetic input from a wolf, although not necessarily how much or when it had occurred in the animal's family tree.

Jillian stripped off her gloves and prepared a mailing label. The samples would go out by priority mail the next day to a lab owned by her genetics instructor from veterinary college, Ian Craddock. She'd told Craddock that the animal had turned up in her practice, and that she was naturally curious due to her interest in wolves. Plausible. Sane. At least saner than saying she'd found it in her apartment.

The DNA tests would take about six weeks to complete. And the price of the testing would take most of her next paycheck. As much as she needed the money for other things—and her hopes of that really nice digital camera just fizzled—it was well worth it if a state-of-the-art laboratory could help her solve this puzzle. Besides, if she was going to be a lunatic, then she was at least going to do it up right.

For now, maybe she needed a change of scenery. Birkie was planting some of her outdoor garden today—maybe she could use an extra hand. Jillian knew she'd feel a lot better just being around someone.

Immediately her thoughts jumped to James. After the mid-hallway collision yesterday, she'd noticed that he had finally changed his clothes. That blue denim shirt looked great on him, even if it wasn't done up. Okay, maybe *especially* since it wasn't done up.

Where had he been going last night? Why such a hurry? And why so damn rude? It was hard to conjure much indignation, however. She was too busy wondering what might have happened if they'd stood there, together, another moment or two. Because she had the oddest feeling he'd been about to kiss her.

Something inside her did a flip-flop at the thought of kissing James. Down, girl, she chided herself. It was just plain old-fashioned physical attraction and nothing more. "He doesn't even know me. I don't know him. We don't have a relationship, just a very bizarre hit-and-run acquaintanceship." And still she wondered what it would be like to kiss him.

"That's enough!" Jillian pulled at her hair with both hands. "I'm not hanging around here with my raging hormones. I'm going to dig in the dirt at Birkie's." And if that didn't cool her thoughts about James Macleod, she could always throw herself into Birkie's fishpond.

The dream had long since faded, but James couldn't seem to wake up. Instead, he drifted slowly toward full consciousness like a diver rising in measured stages from the depths of some dark ocean. The wolf was there too, with him and part of him at the same time. Despite the strange duality, James knew he wasn't dreaming anymore. And he found himself able to ponder the meaning of the dream. *Memory. It wasn't a dream, it was a memory.* And if it was a memory, that meant he had killed Jillian's attackers. Even though he had never taken human life before, even though it was forbidden to do so by Changeling law, he had no regrets. Not only was he certain the men would have preyed on others if left alive, the protection of another Changeling or a pack member was a higher law. Protection of a mate superseded all.

A mate. Why did that cross his mind?

The wolf stirred within. *Mate. Mine. Ours.*

Not that again. Look, hanging around with Jillian is going to put her in danger—

Protect her. Mate. Ours.

Stop saying that. We need to leave her alone, do you hear me?
Alone, danger. Together, safe. Mate. Ours.
Goddamn it, since when do you know how to talk? I can't believe I'm arguing with—

James woke at last, but the wolf was gone. At least his awareness of the wolf was gone; he could no longer be certain that the damn wolf ever really left. Exasperated, he rolled over and opened his eyes—and froze as he realized two things simultaneously. One, he was in the hayloft at the animal clinic again. And two, he was human.

He sat straight up, ran his hands over his face, his fingers through his hair. Human. No mistake. He must have Changed in his goddamn sleep, because he certainly hadn't done it on purpose. Had the dream brought it on somehow, or had the wolf called the Change? And just how the hell had he managed to get all the way back to the North Star Animal Hospital?

James struggled to his feet, feeling disoriented and strange, needing to get to the window and determine the time of day—of whatever the hell day it was—by the angle of the sun. He leaned a hand on the window frame to steady himself.

It was early morning, maybe six o'clock or so at this time of year. And considering just how far he'd run as a wolf when he'd left this place, he'd lost at least one day, maybe two. But that was a minor concern compared to other things. James gulped in the fresh dew-moistened air and took stock of his impossible situation.

Connor didn't seem to think that wolf and human personas could separate, but for James, the evidence was indisputable. And if Birkie was correct—and he had no doubt now that she was—then his wolf side had indeed recognized Jillian, sensed her, and come to her aid in the past.

And now the wolf was trying to maneuver James into complying with its current plan for survival, a plan that centered around Jillian.

James was dead set against the idea, yet there appeared to be limits to his choices. He could control his human side. The wolf, however, had become a wild card and was becoming bolder in its determination to take the lead. If James had no control over his wolfen side, could not order it to stay away from her, then Jillian was already in danger. Sooner or later the presence of a white wolf would interfere with her life in any number of ways. And such a large creature couldn't stay hidden forever. Eventually it would attract the attention of her fellow humans, and from there it was only a matter of time before someone either figured out the secret or sensed it. Birkie could discern a Changeling as surely as she could sense rain approaching—she couldn't be the only person with that gift.

Mate. Mine, the wolf had declared. But Jillian was a human woman, with human needs and wants. What if she went out on a date, what if she fell in love, what if she wanted to make a life with a human male? The thought rankled, brought a deep growl to James's throat even though he was in human form. He feared to think of what the wolf might do in the face of direct competition.

A mate. Even if he wanted such a thing, he didn't deserve it. Not after what had happened to Evelyn. Weary in body, heart, and soul, James sank onto a bale and dropped his head into his hands. The crushing weight of guilt on his shoulders was as familiar as the endless litany that echoed through his mind. *Should have known there was danger, should have been more alert, should never have left Evelyn alone. Should have been strong enough to walk away from her in the first place, should never have gotten involved with her.* His fault, all his fault, accusing him every time his human awareness surfaced within the wolf. Small wonder that he'd lived as a wolf, hunted and howled as a wolf, lived and breathed and existed solely as a wolf.

He wished he was in lupine form now. Being a wolf was easy. Too easy. It was certainly tempting to submerge himself beneath the wolf persona right now and not have to feel anything, think anything. *Shit*. Wasn't that exactly how he got into this impossible situation? He'd buried the man deep inside the animal, so deep that now the animal was determined to take over not only his life but Jillian's too.

He couldn't allow that. Nor could he allow Jillian to be harmed in any way. He had brought danger to Evelyn and their unborn child, danger and death. And he would bring the same to Jillian if he didn't find a way to stop the wolf within. But the only way he could think of was to remain human, and that he could not bear.

James pounded a fist into one of the heavy bales, knocked it flying off the top of the stack. Pounded another until it burst. And another. His heart was going to explode, *he* was going to explode. He beat upon the heavy, hard-packed bales, dozens upon dozens of them with all his Changeling strength, until his hands were bloody and not a single bale was left unbroken. He fell to his knees in the midst of the straw and howled, a long ululation from his very soul. Howled again. And again.

But he did not Change. He dared not. He couldn't trust the wolf, couldn't make it stay away from Jillian, therefore, *he would not be a wolf*. He would damn well walk out of this town—and her life—on two legs, if he could believe for one moment that the wolf would let things be, would give up on its quest to be near Jillian. But James knew now that wasn't going to happen. The first time he fell asleep, the wolf was likely to take over and make its way right back here.

Jesus Murphy. Looked like he was not only stuck with being human, but stuck with staying here.

"Fine," he said aloud, baring his teeth in defiance at whatever Fates insisted on screwing up his life. "If that's what has to happen, then fine." He felt anything but fine about it. Frustrated, pissed off, apprehensive and even—if he admitted it—pretty much scared shitless at the prospect of resuming a human life. But he wouldn't shy away from this decision. He would protect Jillian from the wolf and from anyone or anything else too. At all costs.

Chapter Fifteen

Connor hadn't been at the North Star Animal Hospital for a week. The tall vet had drafted Caroline for an annual trip to a number of small isolated communities further north. And that meant Birkie and Jillian had been running the clinic, and running, literally. Today had already included two cesareans (one cow, one dog), four pet spays (two dogs, one cat, one ferret), an overweight hamster, a snake with a skin condition, a goat with a broken leg, and a blur of vaccinations and check-ups.

As much as Jillian enjoyed the work, was stimulated and challenged by it, the sheer volume was something she had never experienced before. She couldn't imagine how on earth Connor had managed it on his own for such a long time. She wasn't certain how *she* had managed it in his absence, but fortunately she'd continued to sleep well. She blessed Birkie's name frequently for that. Although Jillian had been skeptical at first, the herbs seemed to be doing the trick. Even the dream catcher seemed to be working, since she couldn't remember a single dream. She smiled at that. The dream catcher's power probably lay in suggestion, but that was fine by her. Whatever worked.

However, she had to admit she was certainly tired now. A headache was throbbing behind her eyes, probably because she'd had nothing but coffee since breakfast. Come to think of it, there hadn't been any breakfast. As soon as the clock struck five, she had plans to go straight to her apartment and either eat or lie down. Maybe eat and lie down at the same time. The ancient Romans were said to have dined like that, so maybe she could too. Connor and Caroline would be back sometime tonight and would be at work in the morning. She only had to get through the rest of today. . . .

Jillian made her way to the front reception area to ask Birkie something but what was coming through the door made her forget all about it. A very small woman with blood-spattered jeans was dragging in the largest dog Jillian had ever seen, a Great Pyrenees. The giant breed was often used to protect livestock from predators—and this one's thick white fur was soaked and matted with blood. One of its ears was mostly torn off. Even injured, the dog looked formidable as it growled with lowered head and showed its sizable teeth.

The woman jerked the leash as they cleared the door. "Goddammit, quit that snarling this minute." She looked up from under a broad-brimmed hat, nodded at Birkie, then fixed bright black eyes on Jillian. "You'd be the new one. Name's Ruby. We had a little trouble with some coyotes. Cujo'd taken care of most of them by the time I got out there with the .22, but as you can see, the coyotes got a piece or two of him."

Jillian directed the pair to an examination room, and Ruby hauled on the leash like she was leading a recalcitrant steer. Cujo followed his mistress but glanced back at the vet and growled all the way down the hall, in spite of the trail of bright blood he was leaving.

"You can tell by the name that Ruby's a die-hard Stephen

King fan," explained Birkie. "Most of the time, Cujo's actually quite a friendly and loveable fellow. But he hates this
place. Some animals just get bad associations, no matter
how good we are to them. Last time he was here, he'd been
in a fight with a black bear and had the skin peeled off one
of his hindquarters. Connor had to roll it up like a big sock
and sew it back on. Time before that, one of his feet was
bitten clear through."

"Dog's a real warrior then."

"Has to be. Ruby runs the biggest sheep operation in
northern Alberta. And there's nothing a Pyrenees won't do
to protect his flock." Birkie stood up from her desk and
straightened her pristine lavender jacket. "Connor just
called to say he's still finishing up inspections at that new
bison processing plant. He'll be back tonight, but it'll be a
good six to eight hours at the very least. Caroline's with
him of course, so there's just you and me and Ruby. I figure if we all pile on Cujo, we might be able to get a shot
into him. But it'll have to be an elephant tranquilizer—that
boy doesn't go down easy."

Jillian took a deep breath and considered her options.
Although she appeared old enough to be someone's great
grandmother, Ruby was clearly tough as nails. Tough
enough to put a muzzle on her injured pet? Or hold it
down? The heavily muscled dog had to weigh in at over
200 pounds, bigger than even a St. Bernard and certainly a
lot heavier than Ruby. And although Birkie was adept at
restraining small animals, throwing an arm around this
beast promised to be a real rodeo.

Jillian ran both hands through her hair and thought out
loud. "I'm reluctant to give him a tranq or even a muscle
relaxant. He may be on his feet, but his eyes look shocky to
me, probably from blood loss. I wish we could wait for

Connor, but we've got to stop that bleeding. Plus, that ear's got to be stitched back together quick or we'll lose it," she said. "And if Cujo hasn't eaten us by then, every one of those bite wounds will have to be washed out and sewn up, or there'll be infection from hell."

She grabbed a large muzzle and walked quickly down the hall—sideways to avoid the blood—and entered the surgery. Ruby had both hands on the dog's collar and was trying to pull him into a sitting position, but he snarled and lunged at the vet the moment she appeared. The massive jaws snapped shut with a chilling ring, as Ruby swore like a construction worker and muscled the animal back a couple steps. He twisted free and ran to the other side of the steel table, where he crouched behind a chair, dwarfing it. There he continued to bare his teeth and growl, even at his owner.

"Just leave him be, Ruby. Move back away from him for now. He's in pain and he's pretty scared, plus I think he's in shock. Sometimes injured animals will lash out at their owners without meaning to. Birkie. . . ." Jillian knew the receptionist was close behind her. "I don't want you to come in here right now." Knowing her only hope lay in gaining the animal's cooperation, she stood still and spoke quietly to the dog. "Hey Cujo, you're not very happy to be here, and I don't blame you a bit. But you need a little help, so we're going to see what we can do for you." Slowly she began to move, intending to try to restrain the animal herself, when suddenly a tall, broad-shouldered man pushed roughly past her. For a moment she thought it was Connor—and then her brain registered the blond hair. "Hey, what the hell do you think you're doing?"

He shushed her with a backward wave. All his attention was on the dog. He didn't communicate with four-legged creatures in quite the same way as his brother—Connor could have whole conversations with animals if he wanted to—but James's Changeling abilities could easily quiet a dog, even a monster like this one. A few murmured words and a light touch was all it took before Cujo's lips relaxed back over his teeth, and the growling ceased. A muzzle was no longer necessary, but James knew the humans in the room would feel a whole lot better with one in place. Quickly he took a roll of heavy gauze from the wall and tethered the threatening jaws with a simple but effective figure eight, then lifted the dog to the stainless steel table. "Atta boy," whispered James and lightly placed a powerful hand on the animal's thick neck while sending soothing thoughts. Cujo lay quietly on the table as Jillian approached, remained still while she tended to the injured ear. Ruby talked incessantly about the sheep market while her dog was stitched up, but James paid little attention to the monologue. He was too busy wondering why Jillian was so angry. Fury radiated from her in waves.

In fact, Dr. Jillian Descharme didn't say a single word to him. Not until she was done, her patient was on his way home with his owner, and Birkie had left the building.

"Okay, what the hell did you think you were doing?" Her sea green eyes were bright with indignation as she wiped down the table with antibacterial spray. "I don't need untrained people jumping into dangerous situations like that."

James went over to the sink and washed his hands, even though they really didn't need it. Every movement was calm and deliberate, not just because he had to remember how to do this task—and the water felt strange, almost ticklish on his human skin—but because he was trying to measure out how to respond to Jillian when he didn't have a clue what the problem was. "Exactly right, doc. It was a very dangerous situation. The owner was in danger, and your receptionist. And so were you."

"I knew what I was doing. I'm not helpless, you know."

"I didn't say that. No one's accusing you of being help-less. But trying to handle everything yourself isn't necessary or smart—"

"What the hell do you know about what's necessary?" she snapped. "I have to handle stuff like this every day on my own. If I can't do the job, I have no business being here."

He glared back. Why the hell was she so upset? "The job doesn't require you to place yourself in harm's way."

"Dammit, I'm a licensed veterinarian—" she began but he cut her off.

"Yes, you are, and because you are, you know damn well that going into that situation alone was stupid. If it had been a poodle or a cocker spaniel, it might have been dif-ferent." James shook the towel out before putting it back on the rack, aware that he'd like nothing better than to shake Jillian. "But that animal outweighed you, was injured and in pain and looking to tear into you. And not one soul in that room, including you, doc, would have been able to stop it." The mental picture clutched at his gut.

"So you decided you should just waltz in and rescue us females?"

James's voice dropped lower, his eyes narrowed to steely blue slits. He stalked forward until he was nearly nose-to-nose with her, although he had to lean over to achieve that. "Don't you reduce this to gender shit. That just demeans both of us. I stepped in because I had the experience and the muscle to do what was needed in this particular situa-tion. So you could then do what you're skilled and experi-enced at. What I did is nothing against you, and if you think it is, then you're not as smart as I pegged you for."

She was spitting mad. James could see the rage radiating from Jillian like smoke from a wildfire. If looks could kill, he wouldn't be breathing. But there were other things in those glaring green eyes. Tiredness. *No, more like all-out exhaustion.* And pain. A headache? Suddenly concerned, he skimmed her cheek with the back of his knuckles—and caught her lightning fist in his hand an instant before she connected with his face. Caught the other fist too and held them both captive. Then James did something else completely reflexive. Still holding her hands, he bent his head and kissed that angry mouth.

For a split second he was certain she would either bite him or head-butt him. He could feel the outraged shock vibrate right through her; then something shifted subtly, changed. Whether it was in him or in her, or both, he didn't know, but there was a sudden spark of surprised recognition. The spark flared. He released her hands, and she didn't pull away. The kiss deepened, and they all but fell into each other. Her lips were both giving and demanding, and so were his. Hungry. Needing, then needing more. Neither of them was steady on their feet when they finally stepped back from each other.

"Why the hell did you do that?" Her voice was still angry but also a little shaky. Then he looked in her eyes and saw not anger but desire. Raw desire. The surprising power of it punched him in the gut a full three seconds before her fist did. By the time he got his wind back, Jillian was gone.

Jillian tried walking for an hour to distract herself, calm down. Then she shopped in every store along Main Street. She needed a giant economy package of work socks, didn't she? But even with her body still vibrating like a plucked string, tiredness and hunger won out. She had to find a place to sit down, refuel and regroup. She considered going to the Jersey Pub but remembered there was a baseball game on the big screen TV tonight, which would draw a large and boisterous crowd. Instead she headed over to the Finer Diner. Birkie had brought her there during her second day in Dunvegan, claiming it was the best place in town to eat. The little gas station and convenience store combo hadn't looked promising as a restaurant, but Jillian was a believer after that meal. Although she could sample much of the Finer Diner cuisine from the staff fridge anytime, microwaving a container just didn't equal the fresh-made experience.

She waved at the big man working the till as some teenagers purchased giant cups of soda and multiple bags of chips. Bill Watson was nearly as tall as Connor and built like a champion wrestler—which at one time he was—with a multitude of both tattoos and freckles covering his muscled arms. The backstreets of London and the outback of Australia blended in his voice, along with pure good humor. Deep and loud, his words boomed easily across the store to the red vinyl booth where Jillian had planted herself.

"Right then, lovey, no doubt you'll be looking for supper. The special is fish'n'chips, and Jessie's made her best-ever slaw to lie down wi' that."

"Sounds great." She leaned back and surveyed the store, glanced out the window at the row of businesses across the street and watched the gaggle of folks who stopped in front of the post office to chat or to sort their mail. It never failed to surprise her how much she enjoyed the little northern town and the people who lived here. There was a sense of community she'd never experienced before, even though she was more of an observer than a participant.

She certainly hadn't been just an observer when James kissed her. *That kiss* . . . Good God, she could still taste him. Jillian sighed a little in spite of herself. She remembered the way James had pulled her close, the feel of his hands running up and down her body, the incredible heat that radiated from him, that blond beard surprisingly soft against her face.

And then she remembered the way she'd plowed her fist into James's solid body before running like a rabbit. Her cheeks flamed. That had been dumb, just plain dumb, a reaction worthy of a school playground kiss. She could have just said *no thanks*, could have backed off, could have not kissed the man back in the first place—but she'd have to be made out of stone not to respond to James Macleod. Okay, maybe she could have kissed him and then said something supremely mature and dignified that would—what? Let him down easy? Discourage him? Was that what she really wanted?

Leaning her head on her hands, Jillian closed her eyes wearily. *Okay, I admit it, I'm attracted to him. But who wouldn't be?* She supposed she should probably apologize for hitting him. But having James pissed off at her was good insurance against a repeat of that kiss, and right now she wanted some insurance like that. Deep down, she was just a little afraid of being kissed like that again. Who knew what might happen? Something, anything. Everything.

She furrowed her brow and deliberately recalled the events that preceded the kiss. Like his lecture. And the way he'd arrogantly pushed her aside and taken over restraining the dog. Jillian tried so hard to find her edge, drum up some anger so she could ruthlessly douse the little fires his kiss had kindled. Couldn't do it. The truth was, James hadn't been arrogant, hadn't been showing off or trying to take

over anything. He'd been trying to keep her from being
badly mauled.

Oh, crap. As much as she hated to admit it, he'd been
right, totally, absolutely right. She'd been too tired to see
just how risky and *stupid*—he'd certainly picked the right
word there—she'd been to even think of touching that
monstrous dog without extra help. Her instructors back
east would be the first to give her an earful about "risk
management." Connor would have been within his rights
to fire her for endangering herself like that. His employee
insurance rates would have skyrocketed if anything had
gone wrong. And the dog could well have injured not only
her, but the other women in the room too. *Now I'll probably have to thank James or something.*

She sighed then. *Right after I apologize to him.* She'd been
rude. Snarky, bitchy rude. Sure, she was tired, she was hungry, she had a killer headache, she had all sorts of leftover
adrenaline in her system, but those things weren't James's
fault. The fact that he reminded her powerfully, simply by
existing, that she hadn't had sex in a long, long time—okay,
she could blame him for that one. But the rest, no.

However, in order to thank him or apologize or anything, she'd have to see him again. And how was she ever
going to look him in the face after that killer kiss? Especially when something inside her went liquid at the
thought of being wrapped in those powerful arms, held
tight against that hot, hot body.

She jumped as a steaming platter of fish and chips appeared in front of her. "Thanks," she managed. Bill winked
broadly and hurried back to the counter where a man was
waiting to pay for gas. At once she recognized the dark red
hair curling out from under the hat. Douglas Harrison. He
was looking right at her, but for a split second, she thought

he was going to walk out without acknowledging her. Then he seemed to think better of it and approached her table.

"Evening, Dr. Descharme."

"Jillian. How's the mare doing?"

"The foot's real good. The heat's out of it now, and she's not favoring it much. You did a good job with her."

"Thanks. I'm glad we could do something for her. She's got a great temperament."

"Yeah, she does, but Dad sure as hell doesn't these days. I wanted to apologize for his behavior."

"That's not your fault—or his. I didn't take any offense from it. Please don't apologize."

Douglas seemed to relax somewhat then. "He's not like that all the time, really. It's the damn Alzheimer's. He just gets these spells and goes off the deep end, doesn't recognize people."

"Or sees things that aren't there?" she ventured. "It must be very hard on you, on all of your family."

He nodded. "Some days are harder than others. Fortunately he still has some good days too, and that helps. Anyways, I don't want to interrupt your meal there."

"That's okay, I was just waiting for it to cool off a little." She had an idea. "Your dad mentioned werewolves, but he also said something about a white wolf with blue eyes. Do you know if he ever saw a real wolf or maybe a wolf-dog cross around here that matched that description? Something that might have given him the werewolf idea?"

Some people's skin turned pale when under stress. Others colored. Douglas turned a bright rose right to the roots of his auburn hair and looked so uncomfortable that Jillian was almost sorry she'd asked the question.

"Dad's lived here longer than either of us has been alive, built his cattle ranch in the early 20s by clearing away raw forest. I imagine he saw plenty of wolves in every color back then. Not now though. There's no wolves around the place now."

"You keep saying that but—"

"I've got to go. Thanks again for your work on our mare." He quickly walked out of the store.

Jillian watched him through the window, saw him get into a pickup and take off with a surprising squeal of tires. Nervous, she thought. The wolf thing made him nervous, as if he was scared of something. Why would that be? *And why are all the attractive men I meet so weird?* She was glad to find her food still hot and settled into eating, determined not to think about Douglas or James or any other members of the male species for the rest of the night.

Restless and edgy, James paced the parameters of Connor's farm. What he really wanted to do was Change and race through the sprawling fields and forest that comprised his brother's land. But he didn't trust the wolf, and so he was trying to work off his frustrations the slow way—as a human being on foot. He'd walked all the way here from the clinic. And now he'd walked most of the fence lines. So far, however, all the walking seemed to be simply aggravating him more.

He was sick to death of being human. His head was crammed with too much information, conflicting thoughts and multiple considerations, all underpinned with complex emotion. And over all, a new awareness of Jillian he'd rather not have.

Damn, the woman can kiss.

He sighed, swore. It had to be lust. Attraction, then lust. Hell, he hadn't had a woman in years. *Decades* to be correct, although he still struggled to accept the amount of time that had passed. It was perfectly normal to act on the attraction he felt for Jillian. But he had no right to what was normal, no right to encourage things between them. *Encourage, hell.* Although James had been out of the picture for thirty years, he was relatively certain that grabbing a woman he'd technically just met and kissing her senseless still wasn't the norm. Even more disconcerting was how much he wanted to do it again. And again. One of the most important lessons learned by every young Changeling was control. Discipline. Restraint. He'd never had a problem with it before, not in all his long life. Until now.

Now, both wolf and human nature appeared obsessed with Jillian Descharme. He was supposed to be protecting her, not seducing her. Obviously he'd lost not just his control but his mind somewhere along the line.

He shouldn't have kissed her, shouldn't have gone anywhere near her—what had he been thinking? James snorted. Thinking with his hormones most likely. It only made sense that a return to human form would bring human desires with it. Except his desires were for something more than sex, and that both confused and infuriated him. It was the wolf's fault, plainly. His wolf nature had introduced the notion of a relationship with Jillian, and now his human side seemed to be entertaining the idea.

Not that Jillian was encouraging things, however. She seemed to be pissed off at James every time he saw her. Of course, maybe he hadn't exactly caught her at her best. He tried to look at it from her point of view. He'd broken into her apartment in the night. Grabbed her in the loft. Run over her in the hallway. Small wonder she wasn't glad to see him when he tried to do something proactive like keep her from being eaten alive by a giant dog. But it still surprised him that she saw it as interfering. Maybe she liked to fight her own battles.

James considered that. She definitely had a warrior spirit. He'd glimpsed it that night in her apartment and admired it. There had been no screaming, no pleading, no fear at all in her—at least, no fear that she'd revealed. When she'd failed to deck James, she'd gone for a knife to gut him. Strange how that just increased her appeal.

A warrior spirit. She'd defied him in the loft when she had no hope of escaping, when she thought he meant her harm. *More than a warrior.* Because instead of fleeing when she had the chance, she'd paused and actually expressed concern for him. It stunned him, then and now. He'd knocked her flying in the hallway, and she hadn't complained, but again, there was concern for him in those sea green eyes. It had nearly undone him. James wiped a hand over his face, found himself sweating as he remembered helping her up, remembered those aching seconds when he couldn't make himself let go of her. When he very nearly kissed her.

Which made the kiss after the Cujo incident a whole lot less surprising. And the possibility of kissing Jillian Descharme again much more likely. How was he ever going to get out of her life and back to his own four-footed one? All he knew for sure was that the longer he stayed in human form, the more complicated his life seemed to get.

And what he was about to do would complicate it even further.

Chapter Sixteen

The doorbell rang, startling Connor into dropping the spoon into the soup he was stirring on the stove. He hadn't heard a car come in the lane and none of the dogs had barked. Only a Changeling could get to his home unannounced, and Zoey was in the city until tomorrow. Anyone else would have given him some mental warning. The heavy front door was wide open, letting the breeze come through the screen door. Whoever was there could easily have spoken to him, called out a greeting, even stuck their head inside. Something. Connor approached the doorway cautiously, silently, and looked out.

A man stood on the covered porch, looking out over the yard. The twilight silhouetted him, revealing only his shape and not his features, but it was enough. The powerful form definitely belonged to a Macleod. He was tall, like all of the Macleod brothers, broad of shoulder and heavily muscled. Only one of them, however, had the white-blond hair, visible even in the fading light, that tumbled almost to this man's collar and matched the pale close-cropped beard that followed his jaw.

James.

The man whirled. He recognized his brother and relaxed. A little.

Connor opened the door carefully, half-wondering if he was seeing things and half-afraid of scaring James off. Took a couple of steps outside. "You selling Girl Scout cookies or magazine subscriptions? What the hell are you doing ringing the doorbell like some stranger?" He searched his brother's face. The strong features, the intense eyes, were tempered with both knowledge and sorrow, but it was the face Connor had carried in his heart all these years. "God, James. I—" He couldn't finish for the emotions that squeezed his heart. He closed the distance between them and seized his brother in a rough embrace. *I never thought I'd see you again, not like this.* They held each other for a long moment then stood apart. Connor kept a hand on James's shoulder, feeling a little foolish yet unable to let go. "I'm glad you came."

James shook his head. "I'm . . . I'm not really sure what I'm doing here."

His brother's voice seemed a little deeper, a little rougher, but it was the voice Connor knew. He had to swallow hard, twice, before he could respond. "Doesn't matter. You can take your time, sort it out as you go along."

James waved an arm at the yard to change the subject. "Place looks good. Lots of potential."

"Place looks like hell." Connor snorted. "And as for potential, I've had it for over ten years now, and it's almost as run-down as when I took it over. I just don't get much time to work on it. A few years ago I hired people to come in and renovate the house, but it's a lot tougher to find someone to renovate a farm. Maybe you can give me some advice over supper." He held the door open. "Zoey's not here so I'm heating up some soup, got a couple loaves of Bill's cheese bread to go with it. You coming in to eat, or are you going to stand out here on the porch all night?"

"Guess I could help you with that soup."

The soup was stuck to the bottom of the pot but luckily hadn't burned yet. While they ate, Connor kept looking across the table. His brother James was actually sitting in his kitchen. It seemed normal and surreal at the same time. Connor made small talk about the farm, about the week he'd just spent up north with a mobile clinic, but towards the end of the meal, he just had to ask, "What made you come here in human skin?"

James was caught off guard by the question, seemed almost embarrassed. "I just thought about what you said, that's all. Made sense to give it a try."

"And?" Connor said expectantly.

"There's no 'and.'"

Connor rolled his eyes. "Don't bullshit me. I just phoned Birkie a while ago to get my messages. She said that *my brother* showed up today and assisted Jillian with a patient. Maybe you could elaborate?"

"Jillian was going to get hurt. They all were. I didn't get a chance to think about it. I was sound asleep in the damn loft and suddenly there was this overwhelming sense of danger. It was like being jolted awake with a cattle prod. I was down the ladder and in the room before I was even fully awake."

"Birkie mentioned it was a pretty dangerous situation. She was trying to figure out a way to use some of her mojo on the dog when you came in. Said she was damn glad to see you."

James shook his head. "Jillian was already in harm's way with nothing but a leather muzzle between her and—hey, you're not going to give her grief about this, are you?" The last words came out almost as a snarl.

Connor was surprised to see a glimpse of the white wolf

in the blatant warning that flashed across his brother's face, but he wasn't intimidated. "Damn right I will. She's a good vet, going to be a great one, but she doesn't have years of experience under her belt yet. I'm her boss and the senior vet, and that gives me the right to chew her out when necessary."

James got up without a word and went back out to the porch. Connor followed.

"So, that's quite a protective streak you've got going on there, bro."

"I know it."

"You're in human form because of Jillian." He made it a statement.

James leaned against a post. "Yeah. Wish I could give you a more noble reason, like I want to return to being a productive member of society, but that's not why I Changed. I won't lie about that." He turned and faced his brother. "The truth is, being human is the only thing I can think of to do, the only way to protect her. I can't control the wolf, so I can't be the wolf."

"For how long?"

"I don't know. As long as it takes, I guess, whatever it takes to make sure she's safe."

Connor thought James was mistaken about not having a noble reason. He could hear the determination in his brother's voice, see the absolute commitment to this path in his face. And just how uncomfortable this path was for him. Still, there were a lot of loose ends to this new plan. "And when you're certain she's safe, what then? You'll just go back to being a full-time wolf? Run on four legs for another thirty years?"

James swore in exasperation. "For Christ's sake, I've already gotten an earful from Birkie on the subject." He left the porch, stalked across the yard to the nearest corral. Rested his arms on the top rail and watched the horses within.

Connor watched the horses too, his horses, as their heads came up and they looked with curious eyes at the blond stranger leaning on the fence. He chuckled as they all trotted over to his brother. "I'll be damned," he said to himself. "Animals still act like puppies around you. You haven't lost your touch, bro." He watched the horses bumping each other, all trying to nuzzle James at the same time. Even the cranky old pinto, which didn't like people at all as a general rule, made an exception for him and was eagerly nosing in for a pat. "Small wonder you were able to deal with Ruby's monster dog." Again he wondered if James ever missed the land and the livestock he was so talented with.

Connor wanted nothing more than to leave things alone, take this time with his brother and just enjoy being with him. But there were things his brother needed to hear, and putting them off wouldn't make it easier. Even to say them was to risk alienating him. *Good Christ. Why do I get to be the one to do this?* His shoulders felt heavy as he crossed the yard to stand beside James, who waved a hand at the horses and sent them to the other side of the corral.

"Leave it alone, Connor."

"You have to listen."

"I don't have to listen to a goddamn thing. Leave it be."

"It's way too late, you know."

"Too late for you to shut the hell up?"

"Too late to just go back to being a wolf. You're so damn used to being an animal that you've forgotten the complex emotional world of human relationships. *Think*, for God's sake. You're on two legs, but you're still acting like a wolf, focused solely on one thing and that's Jillian. I agree that you need to look out for her, but there's a whole lot more you need to consider, other people you need to think about here."

"I haven't thought about anything yet." James faced his brother with both fury and frustration in his blue eyes. "I've been human for two damn days, and I've already had enough. You don't know what it's like. You don't know what the hell you're asking. I feel like my skin's missing and all the nerves are exposed. I just want to Change and—"

"Run away? That's been your answer to everything, hasn't it?" A fist lashed out in response, but Connor had expected it and spun neatly out of reach. Just barely. James had always been fast. "You can't run forever."

The follow-up blow connected solidly and split Connor's lip. With a growl that was more animal than human, he ducked his head and charged James. They grappled like boxers, like bears. Connor got a hand free and hammered his brother's ribs. James hooked a right into Connor's chin and followed it with an uppercut, staggering him. Before Connor could regain his balance, James tackled him, taking them both between the fence rails and into the corral. There they rolled together in the dirt, wrestling, punching, swearing. Connor was strong, but he'd never had his brother's skill as a fighter. In moments, James had straddled Connor and punched him solidly twice more. But just as James was drawing his fist back for a third time, a flash of light and a sudden explosion of electricity knocked him flying backward.

He came to about a dozen feet away, lying flat on his back in the dirt. A crackle of sparks still played in the air around him. James shook his head and blinked, hard, to clear his vision. And saw a very large wolf sitting beside him, watching him. The grinning animal was silver with a blanket of black over his shoulders—and James knew there was only one Changeling with that rare saddleback pattern. "No fair Changing in the middle of a fight, you cheating bastard." He said it without heat, however. Whatever anger he'd had before had been effectively blown away. Changing in close proximity to anyone wasn't recommended. It took energy to become the wolf, and an experienced Changeling automatically drew it not only from his own reserves but also from the earth, the air. The static build-up was immense. James remembered when he'd first learned that.

"Seems to me you pulled that little stunt when we were kids too." He'd been sitting on Connor then as well, and punching him in the face—God, were they ten? Twelve?—and Connor had Changed. The blast of static had thrown James a good twenty feet in a flurry of blue sparks.

Still seems to be the only way I can beat you. You didn't fly so far this time, though. Must have gained a few pounds.

"Get your smart ass over here and help me up, why don't you?" James struggled to his knees and just stayed there for a few moments. He was winded and a headache was starting to pound in the back of his head. At least he was still breathing. If he'd been human instead of Changeling, his heart might have stopped and he wouldn't be breathing at all.

A large hand appeared in his field of vision. James gripped it and let Connor pull him to his feet. "What the hell were we arguing about again?" He made his way to a fence post and gripped it hard to steady himself.

"I was telling you to quit running away."

"And I was telling you to back off, goddammit. I need a chance to think."

"You'd better think, and think hard, bro. You've been gone for *thirty years*. Three decades. Just how do you think the family is going to respond? Hell, how do you think Mom and Dad would react if they knew you were here, like this? Walking around in human form?"

James's irritation drained away abruptly. "What, our folks don't want me back?"

"No, James, they *do* want you back. You don't know how bad they want you back. They pray for it every day, every single day. They'll welcome you with open arms, just like all the rest of us will, believe me. What I'm saying is, don't fool around with their hearts."

"What are you talking about? You make it sound like I plan to hurt them or something."

"You're planning to be human for a little while, then disappear again. How do you think they'll feel? You can't just pop in and out of people's lives. It's not right." Connor ran a hand over his face and jammed it back in his pocket. "Good Christ, James, you've been *dead*. Maybe not physically, but for all intents and purposes, as far as your family is concerned, you've been dead for three decades. You can't come back from the dead and then disappear again."

Tentatively James let go of the fence post and straightened, stretched. He felt as if he'd been beaten with a sack of hammers. "Maybe I'd just better stay dead then."

"It's a little late for that. Think you can go back to being a wolf now and that'll fix everything? Because it sure as hell won't. Birkie's already seen you. Jillian's seen you. They know the family, they know the Watsons. Put it together."

Realization dawned. "The rest of the family is going to find out I was in human form," he said slowly as all the implications began to sink in. "I should never have Changed. I should have stayed a wolf," he said, half to himself. "I

should Change back now, before things get any more tangled."

"Which brings us right back to my original point, that
it's way too late for that. The family, the Pack, our friends—
hell, even Zoey will be devastated that she didn't get to see
you and I—shit, James, I don't want you to go." He paced
and waved a hand as he struggled for words. "Look, you did
what you had to do to survive when Evelyn died. You
Changed and you stayed a wolf for a long time. I get that, I
understand that, James. I didn't blame you for it, I never
blamed you.

"But then the years went by and you were still a wolf.
Decades went by, and that's what I have trouble understanding. Even for a Changeling, thirty years is one hell of
a long time."

"It didn't feel like a long time."

"Not to you. Not to you, but you ought to feel it from
this side. From the side of all the people you left behind to
miss you. Christ, you're my brother, James, and I miss you
every damn day of my life."

Douglas set the grocery bags on the kitchen table, a
shapeless heap of red and white plastic. There was milk and
other things that should go in the refrigerator, but they
could wait. What he wanted, needed, was in the brown
paper bag. He looked around, checked the coffeemaker,
smelled it. The coffee had been on too long, at that stage
where it was just this side of syrup, but at least it hadn't
burnt. It would be strong, but maybe he needed it strong
today. He poured two thirds of a cup, then drew the black-
labeled bottle from the bag, topped up his cup with the
amber liquid and drank it down greedily.

Better. Douglas felt his jangled nerves settle as the

warmth spread through him. Filled the cup again, half and half this time. *Why won't she leave things alone?* He liked the lady vet but she just had to bring up the goddamn white wolf. Okay, okay, so he'd panicked and lied when there was no real reason to lie. She was right, there were real wolves in the region. Lots of them, in fact. He wished that what Dr. Descharme suggested was true, that years ago Roderick Harrison had seen a genuine wolf or two or twenty that now inspired delusions of werewolves in his confused mind.

If wishes were horses . . . What he wished for most was that he hadn't seen the white wolf for himself. He wished he had never seen it become a tall blond man in the blink of an eye, or witnessed him discovering the woman on the floor. Douglas especially wished he had never heard that inhuman howl of unspeakable anguish. He had awakened twice this week in a sweat, with the howl ringing in his ears. Always, for the first few heart-pounding seconds at least, he was certain it was real and not in a dream. He poured another cup, mostly whiskey this time.

Werewolves. His father had never mentioned the subject again, at least not in his son's hearing. But the old man had still gone out at night, alone, sometimes. He always took his guns. He invited Douglas once, but he stayed in bed under the blankets with his eyes squeezed tight and pretended to be asleep. His father had made a disgusted noise and never asked him again. Thank God. Being an accessory to one murder was enough. Two, said the little voice inside. *Two murders, it was a double-murder. She was pregnant, just like Rosa. You watched your father do it, Dougie, watched him shoot her, kill her and her unborn child and you did* nothing.

He drank the cup quickly, hoping to drown out that little voice, but he kept thinking about Dr. Descharme's questions. Come to think of it, his father never said much about how he found out about the werewolves, only that he'd seen them often. Knew their habits, knew their secrets. But how? How did he know so much about them? And did he learn it before or after they killed his wife?

Filled with liquid courage, Douglas headed for his father's room. He stood in the doorway and watched his father snore. The old man had been wild for the rest of the night after the lady vet had driven away. But when morning came, he was remarkably clear-headed. He'd dressed, eaten, then saddled his horse. He rode out and checked over the livestock, inspected the fences, as if there wasn't a single thing wrong with him and never had been. Douglas wouldn't let him drive no matter what, not even an ATV in the pasture—and God, he hated the fights they had over that—but his dad's favorite horse was a sensible old mare who didn't put up with any nonsense. If his dad slipped into an Alzheimer's fog, the horse seemed to know. She simply brought him back to the house and stood there, waiting for someone to come out and get him.

Usually when Roderick Harrison had good days, he didn't have good nights. At best he would thrash in uneasy dreams, murmur unintelligible words. Sometimes he would wake up screaming that the wolf was coming, that the white devil was going to get him. Douglas would have to comfort his father like a small child.

But not lately. Last night the old man had slept peacefully without waking, and thanks be to Jesus, it looked like he would do so again. For a moment Douglas contemplated the drink in his hands, considered pouring it out. If his father was sleeping, he might be able to as well . . . but the drink was his insurance against dreams. He took a quick swallow, then another and headed down the hall to his room, taking the glass with him.

The moon was high, and James was still standing on the porch. He hadn't moved in an hour. Connor stood at the kitchen window, watching his brother and wondering for the hundredth time if he had done the right thing. He had argued hard for this decision, but it was James who had to make it. And he had. There would be no going back now.

Connor had called the family. Their parents, Ronan and Gwyn, were presently in Scotland, and one sister, Carlene, was in Wyoming. The rest lived here in Dunvegan and they were on their way.

He sensed the approach of Changelings in wolfen form, moving in swiftly from the southeast, heard the mental banter that hallmarked the twins, Culley and Devlin. He noted that their sister Kenzie was with them and knew that James heard them too and saw him stiffen. For a brief second Connor wondered if he'd pushed James too far, too fast. If he was going to Change or leave. Or both.

Quit worrying, Connor. Since when has anyone ever talked me into doing something I didn't want to do? I made the decision and I'll deal with it.

Connor's throat tightened and his eyes stung as James sat slowly, deliberately, on the top step and waited for his family to find him.

Chapter Seventeen

"The cow had a little problem, that's all. She threw a big calf. These things happen all the time with livestock. You're not a cattle rancher, so I don't expect you to understand."

Jillian folded her arms and glared up at the dark-haired man. Gerald Mountney Junior looked too well dressed to be a serious farmer. Although his tanned face was almost magazine-cover perfect, she could see something worse than cruelty behind it. Indifference. "I understand that the cow had a prolapsed uterus. And it's a hell of a lot more than a little problem when an animal in that condition doesn't receive timely medical attention. It's a wonder she isn't dead."

It was a veterinarian's nightmare. Sometimes after a cow gave birth, the powerful contractions would push part of the actual uterus outside of the body, where it was susceptible to both massive infection and injury. As the responding vet, it was up to Jillian to wrestle the swollen, discolored organ back into place and put in the stitches that would hold it there. It had been a long, difficult, miserable job with no guarantee that the creature would survive. Her arms felt like spaghetti and would likely be sore for days.

"'Medical attention' is what I'm paying *you* for." The

smile became a hard line, the black eyes narrowed and glit-
tered with anger. The smooth voice rose. "You just stick to
your cutting and sewing, and leave the opinions to an experienced cattleman." He began to push past her, but she
quickly stepped in front of him.

"If you're such an experienced cattleman, maybe you
could explain to me why you dumped the cow in one of
our corrals without telling anyone. And why you disappeared so we didn't even know whose animal it was when
we finally found it." Jillian met the man's eyes without a
flinch. "And every experienced cattleman I know hangs
around to give us a hand with their animal. They don't
drop it off like goddamn dry cleaning."

His face was far less attractive when it was flushed purple
with rage. "I don't know who the hell you think you are,
but you have no fucking idea who you're dealing with."

"I appear to be dealing with someone who shouldn't be
allowed to own animals. That cow should have been
brought in immediately, not a day later. Better yet, it should
have been a farm call. You should have called us to come
out. We could have fixed it on the spot so the animal didn't
have to go through the additional stress of being trans-
ported."

"That's the opinion of someone with a shiny new
diploma who thinks she's better than everyone else. It's
your word against mine."

"That's the opinion of a trained veterinarian. You'll find
it holds up well in court."

He took a quick step toward her and she braced herself,
brought her fists up to ready in a classic Tae Kwon Do
stance. Suddenly Mountney stopped dead, his eyes traveling upward and over her head. There was something else

besides temper in his face now. A flicker of fear? To her surprise, he backed up a step, then another. Tried to speak and couldn't seem to get anything out. Finally he spun on his expensive boot heel and stormed to his truck, a shiny club cab pickup in metal flake cherry. He spun gravel as he pulled out of the parking lot.

Jillian whipped around, thinking it was Connor behind her. "Hey, I had this under control. You didn't need to—"

She was struck speechless as she found herself face to face with James Macleod. More like face to chest, since he was so tall.

"You're right, you didn't need any help," he said. "But the man's a bully, and sometimes the best way to deal with a bully is to stack the odds against him. I figured if he saw he was outnumbered, he might take up a lot less of your valuable time."

The timbre of James's voice stroked something deep inside her. Her cheeks went hot as her body clenched then went liquid. *Get a grip, girl!* Her body ignored her, making her annoyed at herself and now twice as annoyed at James. She scowled up at him even as she ran a hand through her disordered hair. "Don't you have anything better to do than follow me around and interfere with my work?"

"I didn't interfere. Didn't say a single word."

Jillian narrowed her eyes at him, and he had the nerve to look innocent. It wasn't a look that suited his rugged features. "I'm not going to say thanks."

"'S not required. You didn't ask me for help."

"I didn't *need* help. What I need right now is to get back to work. Maybe if you had a job, you'd have a lot less time on your hands to spend meddling with mine." She saw the flash in his eyes as the dart hit home, and was feeling just petty enough to enjoy his irritation. Jillian knew she'd be mortified, even ashamed, later, but right now, she didn't want to be the only one frustrated and annoyed.

"As a matter of fact, doc, I'm here on business. I need a vet's signature so Birkie or Caroline can dispense some things on my list."

"What list?"

He shoved a sheaf of paper into her hands. "This list. It's for Connor's farm. And since I have some feed to load, I'll pick up these papers and the stuff later. Maybe you'll be in a better mood then, but I doubt it. I don't think I've seen you in a good humor yet. "

"I'm just fine until you show up." Dammit! Would he quit looking at her with those eyes? Who told him he could have such sexy eyes? "And don't think for a moment that I'm going to apologize for hitting you the other day."

"That's fine. I'm sure not apologizing for kissing you. Might do it again too. Consider yourself warned."

She stood with her mouth open as he walked away. And cursed herself for noticing how well those jeans hugged that muscled butt.

"I know it's close to closing, hon. But Connor's still out in the corral with that injured heifer, and I need to ask if you're up to seeing just one more appointment today." Birkie held up a file.

Although she had endless patience for the animals that needed her help, Jillian found it was often downright difficult to extend that patience to some of the owners. Especially the ones who came in near the end of the day. Still, it wasn't the animals' fault if their owners couldn't bring them in when Jillian was feeling more tolerant. James's comments about her mood sprang to mind, and she worked up a smile for her friend. It turned out to be a faint one, but it was a smile. "I'd be glad to. Not a wild elephant with a toothache, is it?"

"Nope, just a small dog. It's the owner that's wild."

Jillian didn't dare ask, just took the file marked "Pinky" and headed for the exam room. She was scanning Connor's notes when Charmaine Forrester breezed in. Or rather, her hair did.

Platinum curls were piled high atop the woman's head, where they tumbled down in a caricature of an outdated Nashville style. The fluffy cascade almost hid a tight black T-shirt and finally ended where rhinestone-studded jeans seemed painted over sharp narrow hips. Jillian found herself mentally calculating as to which weighed more, Charmaine or her garish hair.

As the young vet watched, fascinated, the woman pulled a shoulder bag from under her bleached tresses, drew out a silky mass of white and black hair and plunked it on the stainless steel table. There it coalesced into a purebred Shih Tzu.

"This must be Pinky," Jillian managed at last and automatically ran her hands over the dog's body. Thin, too thin. Female, and with the permanently enlarged teats of a creature who'd given birth in recent months and not for the first time. The dog's ankle-length coat was dull and falling out. Her eyes were dull as well. "What seems to be wrong with her?" she asked.

"Nothing's wrong with her," snapped Charmaine. "I just want to know if it took."

"If what took?"

"Well, the breeding of course." The woman looked at Jillian as if she was an idiot. "I paid two hundred bucks for Pinky to have an afternoon with a purebred stud, and I don't want to pay another two hundred if I don't have to. It's bad enough that it costs me forty dollars to see you to find out. Where's that good-looking Connor, anyway?"

Jillian ignored the question. "Normally we do a blood test to check for a hormone called relaxin, but this dog is obviously in no shape for breeding." She wished she'd had more time to read the file. "When was her last litter, and how many litters has she had?"

"Why she's had lots, because that's her job, to make cute little puppies. Isn't it, girlie-girl?" Charmaine hugged the dog to her and made smoochy noises at it. Pinky regarded Jillian with weary eyes.

She tried another tactic. "Guess you get a good price for those puppies, huh?"

"Six hundred dollars each, purebred, unregistered. If I get a real good stud and can register the puppies, I charge another three hundred." The woman bounced Pinky up and down. "She usually has six puppies too, and last time she had eight," she announced proudly.

Eight? Jillian imagined the tiny dog struggling to feed eight growing puppies. The nutritional demands of lactation called for high-quality food and lots of it, but even if Pinky was being fed like a champ—which she somehow doubted—the dog wasn't getting any real recovery time. She took a deep breath and sucked back her anger, remembering the words of one of her instructors: *Most pet owners who fail to care for their pets do so out of ignorance rather than malice.* There must be a persuasive argument that this client could respond to.

"Can you hurry it up with the blood test, doc? I've got a nail appointment."

So much for the educational approach. "A nail appointment? You're using your dog as a goddamn puppy machine and you're worried about a nail appointment?

"Hey, who the hell do you think you—"

Jillian cut her off. "This dog is exhausted. Do you get that? Completely and totally exhausted. Don't you care about her at all?"

"Don't you tell me I don't care about my girlie-girl. What the hell do you know?"

"I know that Pinky's practically skin and bones. She doesn't have the physical resources to produce a litter. And if you keep pushing her to breed, Pinky's going to die an early death, either during whelping or, if she survives that, from eclampsia when she tries to feed more pups."

Charmaine's face turned scarlet under her makeup and she clutched the dog to her, although whether to protect it or shield herself, Jillian couldn't guess. "How dare you say things like that to me! Pinky's been doing this for years. She's a . . . she's a *career mom* and she'll be just fine."

The argument gained both volume and intensity, and moved out into the empty waiting room until Charmaine Forrester finally whirled on her high-heeled boots and left in a huff, slamming the door so hard that the adoptions bulletin board fell from the wall in a flurry of papers, tacks, and photos.

Jillian stalked back down the hallway, clenching and unclenching her fists. It was some minutes before she was able to calm down. And a few more before she realized what an unprofessional ass she'd been to lose her temper like that. Arguing with a client, for God's sake. Sure, she'd confronted that Mountney character, but she'd kept her cool and reported him to the authorities afterward. But she'd actually yelled at Charmaine.

She didn't know where Caroline and Birkie were or what they must be thinking, but she was dead certain they'd heard it all. Connor might have heard it too, if he'd come in. *Crap. If he'd been three counties away, he'd still have heard it all.* Embarrassed color flamed bright along her cheekbones. *Crap, crap, crap.* She didn't want to lose her first real job because she couldn't control herself. *Could I have been more of an idiot?* What would her "Client Relations" instructor say? She'd done exactly what he had emphasized a vet should never do—gotten emotionally involved.

Jillian sank into a chair at the lunchroom table and laid her head on her arms. She should find Connor immediately and explain—no, not explain, there was no explanation, no excuse for her behavior. Apologize, that was what she should do first. Then resign. Maybe—

"Do you always beat yourself up like this?"

Jillian sat up quickly and scowled. Of all the people she'd rather not deal with right now, James was right at the top of her list. "What do you want?"

He pulled out the chair next to hers, flipped it around and straddled it with his arms resting on the back. "I want to know what's got you so upset."

She goggled at him. "You must be the only person in a two-mile radius who didn't hear me yelling at Charmaine Forrester. I could lose my job over this. I *should* lose my job."

"Your job's safe enough. If Connor fired his staff for getting exasperated with clients like that one, he'd have no one left to work for him. Including himself. By the way, Birkie says to thank you for saying a few things that she's been dying to say for years. She may start a fan club for you."

"I . . . oh, jeez, it was so damn unprofessional." Jillian

blew out a breath and ran a nervous hand through her hair, not realizing that it made it stick straight up in several places.

"No argument there. So tell me why you became a vet."

"What?"

"Tell me why you decided to become a vet. I want to know."

She eyed him suspiciously but his face seemed sincere enough. "I care about animals," she said, hesitating. *Oh, what the hell.* "Okay, so I love animals. I've been crazy about animals since I was a kid. But I respect them too. I like being around them and learning all that I can about them and from them." Her voice was clear and steady now. "I want to make things better for them whenever I can."

James nodded. "So wasn't that at the root of your argument with Charmaine? You didn't argue with her over her choice of hair color or her political persuasion. You wanted to make things better for that worn-out little dog."

"Yeah. Yeah, I guess that's what it boiled down to, but I probably just pissed off Charmaine."

"You sure did. Birkie says the woman'll have a terrific time telling the story to everyone she knows."

Jillian winced and put a hand to her forehead. "Great. Just great. She'll never come back, never take that poor dog to a vet again."

"It's not all bad. She's going to rehearse everything you said over and over to herself and everyone who'll listen. So some of it might sink in eventually. And out of everyone she tells, there's probably plenty of people who will agree with you, enough to sprinkle a little doubt in her mind."

"Plus she's one hell of a drama queen." Zoey Macleod was standing in the doorway. "If you knew Charmaine, you'd know she's addicted to drama, especially if it involves her. So she'll definitely continue to take Pinky to an animal clinic. Wanna guess which one?"

She hesitated, trying to read the answer in Zoey's freckled face. "Here?" she ventured.

"Without a single doubt. She couldn't resist the possibility of another scene. Know how I know that?"

Jillian studied her until the truth dawned on her. "Connor! *Connor* told her off?"

"Oh, you bet he did. Raised his voice on more than one occasion too. Ask Birkie about it sometime. And there've been a few other clients who have managed to push his buttons too. The point is that you can't care about animals and always keep your professional detachment in place. I'm not saying you shouldn't try—you don't want to start abusing clients—but there's always going to be a few who drive you absolutely crazy." She rolled her eyes. "Trust me on that. I had old Mick Kuchabsky in my office for an hour today, complaining and cussing about everything from the last week's editorial to the size of the print."

"Did you yell at him?"

"Eventually, but he's ninety-six and deaf as a post so it didn't faze him. I felt a little better though." Zoey winked and checked her watch. "Just stopped by to collect Connor—he should be cleaned up by now. We've got dinner at the Watsons' tonight, so I'll see you folks later."

"Thanks. Thanks a lot." The relief was like cool rain on a hot summer day. Jillian closed her eyes and just breathed it in for a long moment. Opened her eyes to see James looking at her with decided amusement in those impossibly blue eyes. It rankled for a moment, but then she reminded herself that he had been kind. Which was more than she had been the last time she'd seen him. "Guess I should say thanks to you too. I know you were trying to make me feel better."

"Don't know if I succeeded. You look pretty tired."

"It's been a long day. I just need a nap and I'll be fine." And sex, she needed sex too. Lots of sex. At this time of day she'd usually think only *food, shower, sleep*, but having James nearby was making her hormones hum. It was a shame his shirt was buttoned today. "I gave those papers to Birkie."

"I know, thanks for signing them. I just picked up the order from her."

He seemed to be looking at her very intently. Her own gaze traveled over his strong features and rested on his lips. She knew just what they tasted like, and a shiver raced down her spine. She wanted to taste them again. *I've got to get out of here.* "Good. Um, that's good. Glad I could help. See you." She had no choice but to be abrupt, not when she had to order her eyeballs to quit staring at the man, force her body to get up, and command her legs to carry her out of the room.

Her hormones protested loudly all the way to the livestock wing. She hung her stethoscope on the cattle stanchion, stripped off the lab coat and ran through several *hyungs* in her scrubs. *Right, left, hook, turn. Rhythm, power, control, balance.* Finally, drenched in sweat, she had to admit defeat. She had not achieved the calm she sought, hadn't even managed to vent much of her frustration. Sighing heavily, she trudged to her apartment and stood under the shower. Continued to stand there long after the hot water ran out.

Chapter Eighteen

Evenings were going to be the hardest, he knew that now. James could see the thumbnail shell of the moon sailing high and bright in the star-studded sky. The breeze whispered and called to him as he sat on the front steps of the cabin. The tendrils of air, ripe with forest scents, enticed him to give in, to leap away from his two-legged self and be one with the night. It was like entreating a parched man in a desert to leap into a cool oasis pool.

He gritted his teeth and turned away, determined to stay his set course and remain completely human. His wolf side was just too unpredictable. But God, it was hard to resist Changing and running free. Almost physically painful. *I wonder if addicts feel like this? Needing that one thing that gets them through another day, another hour.* James shoved those thoughts aside and tried to focus on something else.

Like his family. His brothers and sister had entered the yard as wolves, but they'd acted more like big dogs, leaping on him joyfully and knocking him flat. When they'd finally Changed, they'd hugged the breath out of him, couldn't stop touching and patting him all night as if to reassure themselves he was real. They talked all night too—or rather, his brothers and sister had talked. James found himself with very little to say. After all, what had he done over the past three decades that was worth talking about? His baby sister, Kenzie, had two doctorates. Two, for God's sake. Devlin was a published author. Culley ran a successful business.

And then Connor's wife had come in. Zoey. She was beautiful, he'd known that, he'd noticed her from a distance in her human form as she came and went from the farm, watched her with the Pack in her wolfen form too. But as a wolf himself, he'd never approached her, never talked to her, never known how smart or funny or kind she was, or how devoted to his brother. Connor had found his true mate, and they were as happy now as they appeared in the wedding photos on the living room wall.

Photos that included every member of the family but James Macleod. Not only had he not known about the wedding, he couldn't even remember what part of the country he'd been wandering at the time.

Rip Van Winkle. That was what Culley had called James. After the man in the old folk tale who went to sleep for many years, and awakened to find that life had gone on without him. Culley had meant it as a joke, and James had smiled at the time but inside, he was horrified by all that he'd missed.

Not only his family but the world itself had advanced in ways he hadn't expected. Culley's business was a prime example. It was *online* and he had tried to show it to James in Connor's home office. The computer hadn't remotely resembled the last one James had seen. And it was mind-boggling to learn that most people had one—or two or more—in their home as a matter of course. Devlin had one in his pocket for God's sake. There was no doubt that James had some real catching up to do in order to fit into the human world. He'd felt seriously overwhelmed, emotionally and mentally, by the time everyone went to bed near dawn.

Small wonder he'd chosen to sleep outside for a few hours, claiming he was too hot to remain in the house. Whether his siblings bought that excuse or not, James didn't know, but it was an immense relief to be out in the night air, away from all the little technological marvels that marked this new century. He'd rather have Changed, curled up in the nearby woods, but if he was going to be human, he had to learn to make do. The porch swings didn't look overly comfortable, but he found an old hammock between a couple of trees behind the house. And so he let himself be lulled into exhausted sleep by the soft susurrus of the breeze in the aspen leaves.

At least Connor had waited a couple days before springing his big idea on James. "I know you're still trying to adjust, bro, but you've got to have a reason to get up in the morning. You used to have your own ranch, used to enjoy it. Hell, you were damn good at it. I've never seen anyone with a gift like yours, and heaven knows my land could use that gift. The ground's just lying there fallow and wasted when it could be producing, but we both know that I'm never going to have time for it. Zoey loves the place but she's a city gal and running the newspaper keeps her busy enough." Connor waved his arm at the buildings, the fences. "Look at it, it's a mess. But it doesn't have to be. There's no reason the farm can't belong to both of us. Zoey and I talked about it and we're proposing a partnership. We'll put up the money and give you signing authority on all the farm accounts, if you'll just get this place whipped into shape."

In the end James had agreed to it, even though his gut was tight with fear, as if the whole thing was a monstrous trap, a ploy to keep him human, keep him here. It was an emotional reaction, he knew. He'd already made his decision to walk on two legs. But in truth, he hadn't given a thought to what he was going to do with his time. Protecting Jillian wasn't working out to a full-time job, especially since she didn't want him to defend her. Connor was right—again, which was getting just a little irritating—and so James found himself suddenly in charge of a very large, very rundown farm.

At his brother's invitation, James had taken up residence in an empty farmhouse. It had begun its life as a cabin for the hired man but had been added to over the years until now it was more like a sprawling lodge. The last person to live there had been his brother's late friend, Jim Neely. Old Jim had loved Connor's animals as if they were his own children, and there was nothing but good energy in and around the house. Good location too. Tucked back away into the trees on the opposite side of the farmyard from Connor's place, the house was invisible from every direction until you were almost standing in front of it.

But God, that first night indoors, in a bed . . . James had been disoriented, frightened in some primal way, like a child afraid of the dark. He didn't tell Connor, but that first night he had ended up sleeping outside on the porch. And the next night as well. No blankets, no pillow, just curled on the weathered boards like—

Like an animal. James made a disgusted sound. *Jesus, it's just a bed. I'll sleep in the damn thing.*

In less than an hour, James was back on the porch, sweating. He swore viciously, half at himself and half at the bed that terrified him, and waited for his head to clear and his heart rate to slow to normal. He tried to think rationally when what he really wanted to do was tear the offending piece of furniture into tiny shreds with his teeth. And wasn't *that* just another sign of his animal nature? Would his first impulses always be those of a wolf? "Okay, okay. Small steps then. Maybe I can't sleep in the goddamn bed just yet, but I don't have to sleep on the porch either."

He got up and went inside, just stood in the living room. So far, so good. Maybe he could sleep on the couch. Even a wolf would probably like sleeping on a couch. He remembered sprawling on Jillian's couch, wondered if it had been a good idea to startle her like that. Hell, that whole night hadn't been a good idea. Look what it had brought him to. Warring with his wolf side, trying to sleep indoors like a human being . . .

To be human or not to be human, that is the question. Culley had once paraphrased Hamlet when a wild game of four-legged rough-and-tumble gave the young Macleod boys a tough decision to make. Should they tell their mother about accidentally collapsing her line of clean laundry or stay in wolf form and run for the hills? It was over a century and a half ago, and they had laughed over that line many times since.

It didn't strike James as funny now. He no longer had the luxury of contemplating that question because Connor had been right. James couldn't just pop back into his family's lives, decide it wasn't working out, and vanish again. It would be cruel, and he was not a cruel man. He was only beginning to understand how much he had hurt his loved ones by disappearing the first time. He could never bring himself to do that to them again. Add to that the instinctive imperative to protect Jillian—if only from himself and his wolf nature—and James felt there was no other choice for him. He had to resume a human life.

Doesn't mean I have to like it. James stalked into the bedroom, kicked the offending bed, and grabbed a pillow and blanket. It had been simple to be human once, even enjoyable. He didn't remember having to struggle so damn much, didn't recall experiencing this level of frustration. And if it was simple once, it could be again.

He stretched out on the couch in the front room but couldn't relax. His eyes simply refused to close. His body wanted to curl up in a ball. He'd opened all the windows, but the room still felt stifling, even claustrophobic. At the clinic he'd managed to sleep in the loft, but it was wide open to the elements at one end, and the ceiling rafters were high above him. Burrowing into a pile of straw had been a whole lot more organic, more natural, than trying to get comfortable with a blanket and pillow. He thought wistfully of the hammock behind Connor's house. Maybe he should put up one of those in the yard. *Yeah, that'll work real well in the winter.* And the thought that he would still be human months from now was somehow depressing.

Jillian's probably sound asleep. An image popped into his head, and he let it linger: the small blond woman curled in her bed, her short hair sticking up in every direction, her delicate faery features, the pajamas with the silly frogs on them . . . He hoped she was sleeping better than he was. The last time he'd spoken to her at the clinic, she'd looked ready to drop, but then, she'd fought more than one battle that day.

That whole scene with Mountney, for instance. Jillian's body language had shown no fear as she faced down the arrogant bastard and traded verbal blows. There was passion in her voice, in her face, as she stood up for a neglected animal, a passion her body didn't seem big enough to hold. It lit her up like a prairie wildfire, leapt out and scorched her adversary. And the glorious blaze of her pulled at some-

thing in James as he watched. Pulled him now just remembering.

He had successfully resisted the powerful urge to charge
in and protect her. He'd learned enough about her to
know that Jillian didn't want to be defended, even though
Mountney was doing his best to bully her with threats. In
fact, she seemed to think an offer of help was some sort of
statement on her abilities. So James accorded her the respect he would give another Changeling and allowed her
to fight her own battle. But his wolf nature hadn't made it
easy. A low growl had crept into his throat, and his control
seemed balanced on a high, thin wire in a strong wind.
James knew then, *knew*, that if anything in the highly charged
scene shifted even slightly—if Jillian showed a moment's
uncertainty, if Mountney lifted a hand to strike her—the
wolf would have been at the man's throat in a heartbeat.

None of that had happened, thank God. James had par-
tially appeased the wolf by standing, simply standing behind Jillian and glaring over the top of her head at her
assailant as only a Changeling could glare. The guy had
backed down and left in a hurry, but Jillian definitely hadn't
appreciated what James had done. And she had no way of
appreciating what he *hadn't* done.

Later when she went head to head with that Forrester
woman, James was again fascinated by Jillian's passion. She
cared. She cared about the animals, she cared about her
ideals, and she even cared about him to a degree. The incident in the loft had shown him that. Not every woman
would risk asking a half-naked man if he needed anything,
especially after he'd just grabbed her and scared her almost
to death. *A warrior spirit and a compassionate heart.* Small
wonder he was mesmerized by her.

Which meant he'd have to be a hell of a lot more careful.

In the past, Jillian Descharme had left an impression on him, even as a wolf, that he couldn't shake. A connection he didn't understand but couldn't deny. But he had to stay in control, had to find a way to watch over her and keep his distance at the same time. It would be too easy, much too easy, to become involved with her, to encourage a relationship that would only place her in further jeopardy. His job was to protect her, even from himself.

Some protector I am. He couldn't even win a battle with a stupid bed, of all things. And he didn't seem to be gaining any ground with the damn couch either. In the end, James slept on the bare floor just inside the open door. It was a start.

Connor didn't see his older brother for days. The work around the farm was done as if by ghosts. The animals were fed and cared for, the tool shed tidied up, bales stacked and grain moved. Connor caught a rare glimpse of James as he was walking the far fields at sunup, kneeling now and again to run his hands through the soil. *Maybe I pushed him too hard about taking on the farm. Maybe it's too much too soon and he needs more time.*

Then one night he came home to a very different farm than he had left that morning. There were construction crews on the roofs of the buildings. Flatbed trucks of materials filled the lane. Heavy equipment vied for position in the corrals and smoke rose from burning piles of discarded fencing. The peace and quiet of the country had been replaced with a cacophony of power tools. He found a place to park his truck and walked into the heart of the chaos until he found James giving detailed instructions to a crew of electricians. Connor was intrigued. He waited until his brother finished, then tapped him on the shoulder. "Who are you and what have you done with my farm?"

"I'm your partner, and this farm needs to be brought back from the dead."

"Can't argue with that. It's needed serious work for a long time. How the hell did you find so much help? Looks like somebody kicked over an anthill."

"I discovered one thing that hasn't changed in thirty years—money still talks. I figured there's no point dragging all these projects out, so I offered hefty incentives to finish by the end of the month. Just in time, too. There isn't a roof that doesn't leak, and two of the equipment sheds are on the verge of collapse. There's no watering system for the stock, and the fuse box in the stable catches fire when you turn on a light."

Connor put his hands up as if surrendering. "I admit it, it was grim. I thought this place had a lot of potential, but if it was left in my hands, it would just revert back to the forest, like those ancient ruins you see in South America."

"You didn't do so bad. You got a contractor to come in and renovate the house at least. I hate to think what kind of shape *it* was in."

"Well, it had an air-conditioned roof that matched the barn, for one thing. Once we got that fixed, the contractor pointed out other things that should be done too. Remove the weasel family from the kitchen, the bee colony from the attic, and so forth. One thing led to another. I figure it's pretty much a new house now, but I like it. I imagine I'll like what you're doing when it's done too."

"I hope so. Look, if you and Zoey want anything done a certain way—"

Connor shook his head. "Nope. You go right ahead and do it, do anything, any way you see fit. Believe me, we'll be perfectly happy as silent partners." As he scanned the farm-yard, his gaze rested on three big shaggy beasts with long sweeping horns that hadn't been there the day before. "Christ, are those *Highlands?*" He knew full well they were, but it was so damn good to see them. He quickly blinked away the unexpected moisture from his eyes.

"Zoey told me about what happened to your livestock a couple years back, how they were all wiped out. I, uh . . . I figured it would be a good move to infuse some Highland Cattle genes into our Angus herd. You know, they have a good feed conversion ratio and they—"

Connor put a hand on his brother's shoulder. "You don't have to make excuses, bro. You did that for me, and I ap-preciate it, big time. I've really missed seeing those hairy critters around here." He was about to walk away, then turned back. "Almost forgot. Our multitalented Culley sent these over for you. It's your new ID."

James surveyed the little plastic cards his brother dumped in his hand. "Which one is the ID?"

"All of them. It's a collective term for the basics. Driver's license is probably your main one. Birth certificate—that's important. You'll have to memorize the new year, but the date and place are the same. Figured it would be less con-fusing for you."

"Seems to be a lot tougher to be a Changeling in the twenty-first century. Tougher to hide your age."

"You got that right." Connor rolled his eyes. It was a perennial problem for all of them. The lifespan of a Changeling was much longer than that of a human, and they aged very slowly. And that meant James couldn't use a single document from his previous life. Because according to them, he was seventy-five years old. Or dead. Either way, he had to start fresh. As Connor had. "Zoey says she can put a few gray streaks in my hair eventually, and Birkie has a little magic that will make me look older. I figure I've got maybe twenty to thirty years left here before I need to move on. I'm thinking I'll try Alaska next time. Mom and Dad want to go there too. Or Wyoming. Carlene says it's incredible."

"Mom and Dad still coming here to visit?"

"In the fall. They're leading a historical tour of the Highlands until late September. Then they have the rest of the year off, said they'd like to spend it here with us. You know, their first impulse was to drop everything and rush over here to see you. But they thought maybe that might be overwhelming, that they should give you a little more time to get your human feet under you." Connor watched his brother's face. Decided not to mention that holding off had been his idea, but he wasn't sure at that moment whom he had been protecting, his parents or his brother. "It cost them, James, let me tell you. They love you. We all do."

James nodded, then abruptly walked away. Connor let him go. *I know it costs you too, bro, just to be here in human skin. Please don't give up.*

He walked out of the bank with two new accounts, two more plastic cards, and a sheaf of papers and brochures. James's first impulse was to dump the paper into the nearest trash can, but Culley had cautioned him against doing exactly that. Thank God Culley was doing his bookkeeping, if it meant keeping track of this much crap.

James had to admit that Culley was doing a very good job of it, though. His youngest brother had showed him a

lengthy list of assets and investments waiting to be transferred into James's new accounts. Wealth accumulation was
relatively easy with a long lifespan, but still, James had been
shocked at the amounts.

He'd also been humbled. He'd never thought about all
the things his family had had to deal with, all the details
that had to be taken care of. They'd even had to bury Evelyn, sort her belongings, sort his belongings, sell off the
ranch, all without any help from him. As if he had died.
What had he put them through? Automatically he thought
about his parents again, and his throat tightened up. He
wanted to see them, badly, and dreaded the powerful emotions that were sure to come with it at the same time.
Maybe he'd be more comfortable, better able to handle
those emotions in a few months, when he'd had more
practice at being human. *Maybe pigs will fly. That's the whole
damn problem with being human. You always end up feeling
things you don't want to feel.* Nevertheless he wanted to see
his folks. He had no idea how he was going to apologize
for his thirty-year absence, but he was damn well going to
try.

The scary part was that he couldn't promise his family
anything, not a thing. He had no idea how long he could
stand to be human. All that held him to a two-legged existence was the overriding need to protect Jillian from his
own wolf. *As long as it takes. I'll do it as long as it takes.*

He'd hoped that just being human would be enough to
keep the wolf away from Jillian. God knew it wasn't
enough to keep her out of his mind. He caught himself
thinking about her countless times through the day, and at
night he dreamed about her frequently, often reliving that
kiss at the clinic. Sometimes dreaming beyond the kiss. . . .

When he awakened one night on the very verge of

Changing, he realized he'd have to find some other way to appease his alter ego. There was no doubt in his mind that if he'd finished the Change, the damn wolf would have headed straight to the clinic. To Jillian. *Maybe I need to give it what it wants.* Some of what it wants, he amended. If he dropped by the clinic in the morning, saw Jillian, would the wolf be satisfied?

He didn't know that once would be far from enough. And it didn't take long for Connor to notice either. His brother was waiting for him at the edge of the field when he finished seeding one night.

"Noticed you were at the clinic again today."

"Yeah, so?"

"So, seems like you're there a lot. Any special reason?"

"No big deal. Just checking on Jillian, that's all. Making sure she's okay."

"Every single day?"

"Look, I figure it keeps the damn wolf from looking in on her while I'm asleep. Just being proactive." It was true that James didn't trust his alter ego, but he wasn't about to mention how much he had come to look forward to going to the clinic. It wasn't something he admitted to himself. He never stayed long, a few minutes only. Enough to catch a glimpse of her. Sometimes to exchange a couple of words with her, hear her voice.

"Good Christ, James, it's pretty obvious to everyone that you like her a lot. Why the hell don't you ask her out? Come to think of it, if you're so damn concerned about her safety, it would be a lot easier to keep an eye on her— and the wolf—if you were in a relationship. Maybe you should think about that."

What? "Maybe you should mind your business. I'm not interested."

Connor's expression was smug. "Not interested. Sure. You must have mentioned her a half dozen times over supper last night. And at the clinic this morning I thought you were going to flatten Martin Bell when he asked where the little blond girl with the great ass was."

James flicked a murderous glance at the smirk on his older brother's face. Surely he hadn't mentioned Jillian that much. Connor was exaggerating, right? "Maybe I get tired of hearing jerks like Bell shoot off their mouths. So what?" And dammit, she did have a great little behind.

"So you're asking me to believe you're not the least little bit interested in Jillian Descharme? She's just a responsibility, someone you feel obligated to look out for, but nothing more?"

"I'm not asking you anything. Just leave it alone, Connor." It was all he could do to keep from shouting at his brother. Deep inside James was uncomfortably aware his anger was little more than a flimsy shield, and that pissed him off even more. He'd made a decision, goddammit! Decided it was best to stay away from Jillian, to resist the attraction he felt for her. Because in order to keep her safe, he could not have a future with Jillian Descharme.

He hadn't expected it to be so damn hard.

Jillian paused long enough from eating her triple-fudge mocha almond ice cream to down more aspirin. It wasn't her best choice, she supposed, but neither was letting her wrenched shoulder throb constantly. She'd delivered a 90-pound foal, and both her arms were now strained and bruised, while the shoulder hurt like hell. At least the mare came through the event just fine, and the foal was healthy and sound. Jillian might be sore, but she also had a sense of satisfaction that she wouldn't trade.

Birkie offered her a brown plastic bottle. "Chocolate syrup?"

"Does it come with a straw?"

They both giggled. The two were sitting on Jillian's couch with their feet propped comfortably on the sagging coffee table. The clinic usually closed at five, but thanks to a number of emergencies, they hadn't had a chance to shut the doors until nearly seven. Connor had headed home to Zoey, while Birkie and Jillian ate dinner in the staff room. They'd elected to have dessert—or "a sanity refill" as Birkie called it—in front of Jillian's tiny TV. There wasn't much to watch, but they were both too tired to care. Birkie picked a rerun of a gardening show and left the volume on low just for background chatter.

"I see James dropped by again," she said. "What did he have to talk about today?"

"Nothing really. We never seem to have much of a conversation. Besides I was, well—" Frankly, Jillian had been thinking about how much she'd like to jump James, but she wasn't about to say *that*. "I was really tired, and I left."

"Left?" Birkie snorted, leaned forward and pointed her spoon at the younger woman. "Honey, the moment you get too tired to spend time with a handsome man who's smitten with you, you are definitely working too hard. Sounds like we got you some days off just in the nick of time."

"I . . . you . . . he is *not* smitten with me. He doesn't even know me. And I don't even know him. And what kind of an archaic word is *smitten* anyway?"

"Ha. Smitten's a perfect word for someone who shows up here every single day."

"Oh, come on. Davis Jenkins is in here daily, and he's definitely not fond of any of us."

"Davis just likes to complain and drink up the free coffee in the waiting room while he does it. James Macleod, on the other hand, likes you quite a bit."

"Since when?"

"Oh, I'd say since all the way back to when Ruby brought Cujo in. You didn't see the way James was looking at you. I did, though. I stood in the doorway and watched him hold that dog. Ruby was talking a mile a minute about the price of lamb, but he wasn't listening to a word. His eyes were on you the whole time."

"He was probably just interested in what I was doing. More people than you might think like to watch stitching and surgery and all kinds of things like that. That's why reality TV is so popular."

"And that's why he was staring at your *face*?"

"He was not."

"Was too. Was today as well, when you were treating that pony that ran into a hornet's nest."

"Well, if he was, I didn't notice." She wasn't about to admit that it gave her a pleasant little flutter to know that he might have been looking at her. "The pony sure calmed down a lot when James came along, though. The owner wasn't any help at all."

"Don't forget how James hot-footed it out to the corral that time he saw Gerald Mountney Jr. giving you a bad time."

"I didn't need any help."

"Course not. But that's not the point. The point is that James was prepared to dive in and do whatever was necessary. He would have defended you if you'd wanted him to, you know."

"Yeah, I get that. It's a guy thing. So?"

"So he didn't. Because he also knew you didn't want

him to. That tells me he's thought about you and how you think, how you feel. Therefore he likes you. A lot."

Jillian narrowed her eyes at her friend. "Are you sure you're not a detective or something? Do you keep notes on all this stuff?"

"Just observant, hon. And even an old duck like me isn't going to turn down an opportunity to observe someone like James Macleod. Especially that mighty fine butt of his."

"Birkie!"

"Just stating a fact, hon." Birkie's grin was unrepentant. "Privilege just to *see* a butt like that. . . ."

Jillian poked fiercely at her ice cream with a tightly held spoon as she told herself she didn't give a damn about James's butt, the fact that she'd once wanted to compare it to the rest of his appealing physique notwithstanding. And for the five hundredth time she ruthlessly yanked her mind back from the sexy dream she'd had in the night about him. Much more of this and she was *so* going to order a shiny new vibrator off the Internet. Maybe that blue one . . .

"Come to think of it, seeing Mountney peel out of here with his forked tail between his legs was a close second," Birkie added. "But James's butt is still at the top of the list, don't you think?"

Jillian rolled her eyes. "Okay, okay, I admit it. James is hot, and I'm attracted. I don't know what difference it makes. Maybe he looks at me, maybe he even kind of likes me—maybe. But it's not like he's ever asked me out. We never really talk. We probably have nothing in common."

"Bah. I'll bet you have plenty in common. For one thing, both of you are very talented with animals. James has taken over Connor's farm for him, and you'd better believe that place is going to flourish from now on. He's already made a lot of changes."

"I heard something about that. I guess it's a good thing for Connor. He's so busy, I don't know how he ever had time for a farm."

Birkie carefully spooned a chocolate-covered almond out of her ice cream, savored it for a long moment. "Connor bought the place about ten or eleven years ago at an auction. He wanted to live out of town, and he liked the land. Big place and pretty too, backing right onto the Peace River. But you're right, he just hasn't had the time to make the farm produce. Really, the place is just a catchall for some of the unwanted animals he comes across in his practice."

"God knows there's too many of those."

"Amen. And we try to find homes for as many as we can, but when we can't, the creature generally finds its way to Connor's farm. He must have quite a menagerie by now."

"So James is managing the place for him?"

"Yup. More than a manager, though, he's a full partner in the operation. Moved into a house of his own out there too."

"Huh. Guess he's not homeless and jobless anymore." Jillian found herself unexpectedly relieved.

"Exactly. So when are you going out to visit the Macleod farm?"

"What? When Connor invites me, I guess. I'd say when James invites me, but I'll be old and gray before that happens."

Birkie made little tsk-tsking noises. "My dear, you have to be a lot more proactive if you ever expect to get to know James any better."

"I know that look. What you really mean is *devious*. I don't know if I'm that interested."

Her friend just looked at her.

"Okay, okay, I am. Just out of curiosity, mind you."

"Of course. So when do you want to visit James on his home turf?"

Jillian put up her hands. "I give up. You're the mastermind, you tell me."

"Well, it just so happens I have some plants and things for Connor. Maybe you could find time to do me a favor on your day off, make a little delivery?"

Chapter Nineteen

As a veterinarian, Jillian had been to countless farms. But she'd never assign the word *beautiful* to any of them. The Macleod farm was an exception. A long wooded lane led to a sprawling two-story house nestled in the trees. The old building had been made over into something that spoke of both history and comfort. The roofed porch that wrapped around two sides of the house had a charming assortment of mismatched chairs and rockers scattered about, and a couple of hanging swings. Pots of newly planted flowers sat in groups everywhere. Carefully tended beds of yellow daylilies and purple irises flanked the steps. The effect was one of invitation, of welcome.

She parked the truck in front of the steps, took Birkie's trays of plants to the porch and set them carefully in front of the door. She knew there was no one at the house. Connor was in surgery this afternoon. There was no sign of anyone else either. No sign of James, and that was a bit of a letdown, even if she knew he was likely busy. It was a sunny and pleasant day, however, and who could blame her if she decided to walk around a little?

Most farmyards were as clear-cut and visually barren as the fields beyond them but not here. Jillian counted five species of trees she knew and two she didn't in tall dense stands between every building. And every barn and shed was freshly painted in clean bright white with simple black trim to match the house. A refreshing change from the usual garish red barn paint most farmers favored, when they bothered to paint anything at all.

The buildings, although in good repair, looked to be of the same era as the house. The fencing, however, was a sharp contrast. No battered wood here, no patched and spliced wire. Instead, steel rails gleamed between steel posts, all in basic black. Jillian recognized the brand label as top of the line. No haphazard enclosures here either, but tidy, organized corrals and paddocks, linked in places by modern chutes. A clean and efficient operation yet far from sterile, Jillian thought. *Animals probably enjoy living here. God knows there're enough of them.* Dogs, cats, goats, chickens, and even a couple of outsized pigs seemed to have the run of the place. She couldn't help smiling as she recognized a few of the dogs, knew Connor had adopted them when their owners had requested euthanasia for reasons of convenience rather than mercy. They bounced over to her, swarmed her with affection. She laughed and tried to distribute petting and head rubs to all.

A sudden voice made her jump. "Looking for something?"

The dogs left her at once in favor of James. Jillian saw with interest that they didn't jump and leap but sat grinning at his feet. He gave them each a quick pat and turned his attention back to her. "What brings you out here?"

"Birkie sent some bedding plants over for Connor. I didn't know what to do with them."

"Where are they?"

"On the porch." She stood open-mouthed as he immediately strode across the yard in the direction of his brother's house. She walked quickly but was forced to break into a jog just to try to catch up. Jillian made it to the bottom of the steps just as James scooped up the trays from in front of the door.

"I'm sorry, should I have put them somewhere else?"

"Anywhere but with Connor. I don't know how anyone so gifted with animals can have such a black thumb when it comes to plants."

Jillian looked around at the abundance of flowers spilling out of pots and overflowing the garden on either side of the steps. "He seems to do all right with these."

James shook his head as he swept by her with the trays. "Zoey filled the pots while I cleaned up the garden. Connor had thistles the size of trees growing here."

"What kind of plants did Birkie give you?" She was trying to be pleasant but it was irritating to have to hurry to keep up again. She nearly ran into him when he stopped abruptly.

"You don't know them?"

"No. I studied zoology not botany. I can recognize a few things like the geraniums on the porch, but these have no flowers." She was surprised to see him—what? It wasn't a smile or a grin, but the ghost of each, a faint crook of one corner of his mouth. Still it had the effect of lightening his face, easing the fierce brow, although those blue Viking eyes were just as piercing. Jillian scanned the trays he was holding and pointed to a dark-leafed plant. "So what's this one here?"

In answer he pulled off a leaf and crushed it under her nose.

"Recognize it now?"

"It's familiar but I can't place it."

"Basil. Haven't you ever cooked with fresh basil?"

"I've never even cooked with the dried up stuff in the little jars. But I've eaten Birkie's homemade pizza so at least I know that I *like* basil." She pointed to another one. "What's this one that looks like tubular grass?"

"Chives."

"Are they all herbs?"

"Most of them. Connor is actually a decent cook when he has the time."

"Connor? *Our* Connor? The same man who gets so busy he forgets to eat? He must only cook about once a year then."

James chuckled at that and set off across the yard again. At a more leisurely pace.

"I have to say that this place looks terrific." Jillian was able to fall in step—almost. His legs were still a lot longer than hers. "I see a lot of farms, but this one really stands out. What do you produce here?"

"Nothing much yet. There's lots of preparation to be done before we raise anything."

"I'd love to hear about it." Then she had a brainwave that Birkie would be proud of. "Or I've got time for a tour if it's easier to show me."

He glanced at her as if to see if she was sincere, then stopped at a shed and tucked the plants inside. "These will be out of the sun here. I'll get them later."

The tour began with the closest corral, which contained three enormous Highland bulls. Their sweeping horns reminded Jillian of the Texas Longhorn of cowboy movie fame, but that's where the resemblance ended. Their shaggy fur and stocky build was more reminiscent of Ice Age oxen. It was a breed that Jillian hadn't encountered close up yet, and she got closer than expected as James led her right inside the corral with the creatures. They nosed their way over to him with an amiability she'd seldom seen in cattle, stood patiently as James scratched their foreheads under the fringe of long hair that hid their eyes. "Hardy beasts," he was saying. "Well suited to the kind of winter we get up here in northern Canada." He talked about their history, the pros and cons of using them as a beef-producing breed.

She thought at first that the bulls were unusually gentle, but the experience was repeated with each enclosure. Jillian began to understand that there was something unusual about James, not the animals. Did he have some sort of calming influence or aura, something that animals were able to sense? Was that why he had been able to restrain Cujo? And that poor pony that had been badly stung by a nest of hornets. It had been a frightened wreck. Until James came by. The animal had settled down immediately and allowed Jillian to treat it. *Too bad James couldn't calm the owner as well, but you can't have everything.*

Jillian glanced up at James as they walked among the corrals. He was relaxed, at home here. The warrior visage was softened, nearly nonexistent, as he spoke of his visions for the farm. He had a deep passion for what he was doing, she realized. Just as she felt a soul-deep fervor for veterinary medicine, James Macleod had an affinity for the earth. It was easy to listen to him. She'd never paid much attention to agriculture, outside of the health of livestock. Now she was getting a glimpse of how much farming was both an art and a science.

The horses in the far paddock spotted James and trotted over at once, just as every other creature here had done. With a start, Jillian realized she was more than a little envious of that. With the exception of dogs, most animals didn't run up to greet a person unless they were hoping for food.

Certainly livestock seldom showed interest when most farmers approached unless grain was involved. And animals definitely didn't run up to veterinarians. *Well, except for Poodle.* He always seemed pleased to be at the clinic, but the old Siamese cat was decidedly eccentric.

"You're like the Pied Piper," she blurted as a pig that must weigh close to 600 pounds ambled over to receive a scratch on the head from James.

"Why is that?"

"They all adore you. Look at the parade behind us, for heaven's sake." Jillian waved her free hand at the entourage that followed them. Dogs certainly, but also cats, goats, two pigs and an assortment of chickens and geese. "Why do they do that?"

James grinned. "Animals are excellent judges of character." And that was all the explanation he would give her.

Eventually they came to the edge of the farmyard, where the trees gave way to rolling green fields. "What have you planted here?" she asked. The plants were nothing like the orderly grain fields she'd expected. These were bushy with twisted, sprawling stems and an abundance of leaves.

"Green manure."

She wrinkled her nose. "What?"

"Seriously. Part of organic farming is to use natural methods to enrich the soil instead of chemical fertilizer. This is a field of alfalfa. It has very long roots that bring minerals up to the topsoil from deep in the earth. And it has the ability to take nitrogen from the air and put that into the soil too."

"Don't they make hay out of this stuff?"

"Most of the time, but alfalfa's a perennial and this field is several years old. Too old to make good hay. See how it's got a lot of stems? So instead of harvesting it, I'm going to wait another week and then plow it under while it's still green to enrich the soil even further. Voila, green manure."

"So there's no real manure involved?"

"No, it's just a slang term for growing a crop strictly as fertilizer. Although we do compost real manure to put back into the soil, but it'll be a year, maybe two before it's ready to use."

"It really means a lot to you to convert this farm to organic production."

Her hand was resting on his arm. He stared at it a moment then covered it with his own hand as if to keep it there. "It does. We don't have to destroy the land in order to persuade it to feed us. And I feel better eating food that was produced this way. Other people have other opinions of course."

Jillian looked up at him, studied his face. "You really believe in what you're doing, and I like that. I like the way you care about the land, and I like the way you care about the animals. I guess that means I like *you*."

She'd succeeded in surprising him, yet shouldn't he look pleased or happy or something? Maybe he wasn't as interested as Birkie thought he was. *Oh great, now he's frowning.* Maybe coming here was a huge mistake.

Or maybe not. James was still frowning, but his powerful hands had slid around her, gently gathering her in. He lowered his face to hers, eyes open as if to gauge her reaction. Jillian reached up to tangle her fingers in his white-blond hair and met his lips with her own. She poured herself into the kiss, felt the thrill of it vibrate through both of them. She felt reckless, exhilarated, as if she were leaping from a great height into a deep pool.

But the water wasn't still. Powerful currents rocked her, an ocean of sensation carried her along at dizzying speed.

Each time she tried to surface, James changed the angle of the kiss and pulled her under. His lips were hot over hers, soft but relentless. Jillian had one hand still fisted in James's hair, the other gripping his shoulder as he simply flowed into her system like the tide. She had tried to meet the kiss as she met everything else in her life, head on, trusting her own strength and mind and skill to prevail. But they were useless tools here. The tide was too powerful, the water too deep and fast, the inescapable pull of an undertow drawing her steadily towards the silky bottom. With James. She sighed and sank willingly into the nameless, sweet sea.

James felt her sigh shiver right through him, felt the subtle shift in her, a yielding. He wanted her, wanted to feel her skin against his, wanted to touch and to taste. The blood was pounding in his head and throbbing in his groin, as he ran his hands over her, held her tightly to him and ached to be closer still. His hand found its way under her blouse and cupped a teacup breast, felt the delicate nipple pressing into his palm through the silky bra. James shifted, trailed kisses along the angles of her face and down her throat.

Yes, yes, yes. With a start he realized he wasn't alone. The wolf was present and it was eager. Eager to have him claim Jillian fully.

No. With difficulty, James pulled back. God, he wanted nothing more than to continue what he was doing. But he wasn't about to give in to the wolf's plans for his life, or do something that might eventually endanger Jillian. And so he pulled back while he still could. He smoothed her blouse back into place and rubbed his hands up and down her upper arms. He was about to say he had work to do and she probably did too and maybe she should go—but those sea green eyes, still dreamy with arousal, were looking up at him. "Maybe we should continue our tour," he heard himself say.

"Maybe we should."

Her lips curved. They were still soft and full from kissing, and he very nearly bent his head to capture them again. But he could feel the wolf within and would not let it have its way. Dared not. If he kissed her again right now, he couldn't stop himself a second time. A horse nickered nearby, penetrating James's awareness, and James seized upon it like a life preserver. He tore his gaze away from those green eyes and looked out over the fields. If he didn't look at her, didn't fall into her eyes again, maybe he'd be okay. Still, he had to clear his throat twice to get his voice to work properly. "If you'd like to see some of the rest of the farm, we could go back and get the truck." His hands were still on her shoulders but he held her away from him. Not much—maybe an inch or two—but it gave him a chance to breathe. "Or we could ride. It's a good day for it. You like horses, right?"

"I love working with horses—but I don't know how to ride."

"What? You're kidding, right?" Genuinely shocked, he forgot his intentions and looked down at her.

Jillian shrugged. "I grew up in the city, so I was never really exposed to them. And then when I went to veterinary college, believe me, I was too busy learning about their inner workings to learn how to ride them. I always wanted to learn, though."

"No time like the present." He was relieved to find he could let go of her now. His brain was even starting to work—probably getting some blood flow again. James took a couple steps away and whistled shrilly, a four-note sound guaranteed to carry.

"What are you doing?"

"Calling Charlie."

"One of the horses? But aren't they in the corral?"

"Not for long."

Jillian started to say something, but James had a finger to his lips. Moments passed. With his Changeling hearing, the sounds of hoofbeats were immediately audible. But it didn't take long for Jillian to hear them, too. A pale horse with a riot of spots and speckles in his coat rounded the last shed and trotted toward them. An enormous gray draft horse and a trio of chubby ponies followed him. They milled around James like big dogs eager for play.

"Somebody knows how to open gates." Jillian chuckled.

But James didn't reply right away. He watched in fascination as she patted and stroked the glossy coats with both hands, grinning as velvet noses nuzzled her. The serious veterinarian was gone, and in her place was someone nearly bursting with childlike delight. She laughed out loud as the draft horse nudged her a little too hard with his massive nose and sent her skidding on her butt in the dirt.

James laughed then too and reached a hand for her. She expected him to pull her to her feet. Instead he picked her up and tossed her, wide-eyed, onto the back of the culprit.

"Omigod, he's huge. I'm going to get a nosebleed up here." But she didn't ask to get down. Her hands were already running over the dappled gray neck, winding through the silky white mane. "What's his name?"

"Toby. And he *is* huge. He's over eighteen hands high. I think his head alone weighs as much as you do." James eyed her speculatively. "Maybe a bit more."

She sniffed at that and leaned further over Toby's neck to pet him. "So does Charlie break out regularly?"

"Whenever we ask him to. Sometimes when we don't. Charlie can open every gate and door in the place, lets his friends out too sometimes as you can see."

"You must spend a lot of time rounding up animals."

"Nope. Charlie does that. He's an incredible cow-horse, best I've ever seen. More like a big sheep dog really." James scratched the Appaloosa behind the ears. "He can't carry much weight with those legs of his—see how the front ones bow out?—but he doesn't need to be ridden. He brings the cows in when we tell him to, or singles out the ones we need to work on, all on his own."

"But the other horses—"

"Will stay with him. He's not the biggest, but he's the herd leader and they don't stray. We're going to take our tour of the rest of the farm, and they'll all just follow us."

"They will?" That was as far as Jillian got before James suddenly vaulted up in one smooth cat-like motion and settled in close behind her, chuckling at her open-mouthed surprise. "Practice," he answered before she could ask. Although he knew there were few if any humans who could mount a horse of Toby's size without stirrups and from a standing start, no matter how much they practiced. Being a Changeling had some pretty good perks.

He waited for the next question as he nudged Toby forward. She didn't disappoint him. "Hold it, we don't have a bridle or reins or—"

"Don't need them, doc. Toby is used to being guided by legs alone."

"You're kidding."

"Nope. Ask Connor. He rides just like this all the time. So does Kenzie when she comes out to visit."

"Your sister does this?"

"Uh-huh. She's pretty good at it, been teaching Zoey too. I can teach you if you like. So you don't ride at all?" He was still surprised by that.

"Not a bit." She was accustomed to treating horses, not riding them, with both of her feet firmly on the ground. "I've sat on a horse inside a corral once or twice, but that's all."

"Well, then there'll be a whole bunch of things you won't have to unlearn."

Jillian surveyed her mount and ventured to lean over the side. "Toby is tall and broad and gray all over. Are you sure he isn't an elephant? I think I should take lessons on something a lot closer to the ground."

James laughed and brushed a kiss on top of her head, dared to nuzzle her wayward blond hair and enjoyed the scent of it. "You can try riding one of the ponies later if you want. For now, just pretend Toby is a tour bus and enjoy the ride." He wrapped an arm around her waist and nudged Toby into a brisk trot, chuckled as Jillian scrabbled to wind her hands into the horse's mane. "I won't let you fall, doc, I promise. Relax."

She glared back at him. "I'm perched on top of a tour bus with no visible means of control. It's a little tough to feel safe."

"Trust me."

"I'll try."

He smiled at the hesitation in her voice, then moved Toby into an easy gallop. "Wait, wait, *wait*," she squealed.

"I told you to trust me," he said with his lips near her ear.

"You didn't tell me you were going to go fast." She had a death grip on Toby's mane.

"Believe me, this is easier on you than a trot. See how you're not bouncing now?" He put his hands over hers. "Look, give me your hands. Let me hold them while you relax and feel how to move with the horse."

"You mean let go? Are you nuts?"

"I'm not hanging on to anything and I'm okay," he pointed out. "It's balance, Jillian. You know all about balance from whatever martial art it is that you practice."

"How did you know about that?"

"Your reflexes. And that power punch to the gut at the clinic. Not to mention that little battle in the loft we had—those little fists of yours really drill between the ribs. So what is it exactly that you practice?"

"Tae Kwon Do."

"Belt?"

"Blue with a red stripe. It's a little past intermediate. I'm hoping to test for red belt in the fall."

He nodded appreciatively. "Okay then, you know plenty about balance. So you can do this. Trust me and let go. Trust yourself." They were doing a large loping circle around the field now, with Charlie and the ponies following close behind. When Jillian still hesitated, James pressed his very best button. "You're not afraid, are you?"

Her fingers released the mane at once, and he had to stifle a laugh. Instead he held her hands, marveling anew at how small they were, seemingly too small to have knocked the wind from him after that first kiss in the clinic. He brushed his thumbs over the palms, then held her hands out from her sides. "Close your eyes, doc. Pretend Toby's a circus horse."

"I thought he was a tour bus."

"That's just his day job. Now he's a circus horse and we're the performers." James was surprised and pleased when she closed her eyes at once, when she lifted her hands free from his and held her arms straight out. He rested his hands lightly on her waist then and used his legs to direct Toby into intricate patterns and paces. Jillian never faltered. She had a natural grace, would make an excellent rider.

"It's kind of like flying," she said at last. "You were right about closing my eyes. It's amazing how not being able to see where I'm going actually helps me find my balance. Must be a Zen thing."

"Must be." He knew it was Jillian and not Zen that was affecting his own inner stability, however. She both knocked him off-balance and grounded him, simply by being near him. It was a volatile mix, and if he wasn't a lot more careful, he would fall.

Chapter Twenty

Jillian was catching on quickly. He could see her begin to anticipate the horse's movements. She could sense when Toby was turning and the direction, even feel when the pace was about to change. But through it all James was very aware of *her*. Her hips were wedged firmly into the vee of his legs, his thighs dwarfing hers. There was little space between her shapely little bottom and his groin. His hands tightened on her waist in spite of himself, although whether it was to hold her away or pull her closer, he couldn't say. The only thing he was certain of was that his jeans had become very uncomfortable.

"Why are you always so hot?" she asked suddenly.

"What?" He really should stop glancing down at her backside.

"Your body heat. You're always so warm."

"High metabolism." His voice came out thick. He needed a distraction, but his brain wasn't working again. "Family trait. Does it bother you?"

"No. No, it's kind of nice, actually. I like it."

She nestled back into him, making him fight to stifle a groan as his body reacted. God, she felt good. "You're doing really well, doc. Ready to try it on your own?"

"What? Wait!" She grabbed at his hands.

"I'm not leaving. I'm just going to move back a little and let go of you, okay? I'll still be right here. Put your hands up like before."

"All right." Jillian let her arms rise out from her body like wings. "I'm ready. I think."

James let go of her waist and eased back from her body, putting some welcome inches between his throbbing groin and her enticing little butt. The relief was enormous, but it slowly dawned on him that the distance between them was an illusion. The sun was low in the sky and cast golden lights into Jillian's hair. She was beautiful as she sat poised in front of him, moving as the horse moved. He could feel that she was in perfect synch with the horse now, beginning to instinctively shift her legs as well. And he could feel her enjoyment blossom into joy. For a few perfect moments she was in harmony with everything around her, and that harmony seemed to radiate from her and into him. He could hardly breathe, feeling her presence as if it was part of him. The curious connection seemed tangible—and transcendent.

James let the moment draw out as long as he dared, then reluctantly slowed Toby to a walk. Jillian opened her eyes and looked back at him, but he managed to dodge her gaze. He knew he couldn't muster a defense against those green eyes, not at the moment. Maybe not at all.

"Is he tired? Do we need to stop?" She lowered her hands, and James noted she now rested them on her legs instead of seeking Toby's mane again.

"It's a bit more exercise than he's used to, and he's carrying two of us. We're going to head down the coulee to the river. The horses can drink and the grass is good there."

"What the hell's a coulee?" She sounded if he had made up the word.

"City girl," he teased. "The coulees are the steep sandstone ravines that drop down to the river. They're eroded by rain and melt water, full of caves and fossils. Bears and cougars too."

"Really? Do you think we'll see any wildlife?"

"Well, it'll be twilight by the time we're done." And just what was he doing, he wondered, heading further away from the farm? The horses could be watered in their corrals just as easily, yet he couldn't bring himself to head back there yet. "Animals tend to move around more then, at dusk and at dawn. Maybe we'll get lucky and see some."

I hope so.

What? He lifted his head and regarded her. For a split second he was certain she hadn't spoken aloud. Then he shrugged it off. Imagination. Had to be. He couldn't even hear his own brothers' thoughts unless he was in wolf form.

Twilight had already come to the deep valley at the bottom of the coulees. The sky far above was gold fading to mauve, and the evening star was bright in the south. A faint breeze stirred the leaves of enormous trees, grown tall with ample water and rich soil. The river itself was smooth and glassy, reflecting the golden sky.

Jillian inhaled deeply, taking in the cool air, rich with scents. Water, earth, green and growing things. Abundant life. Forest primeval. She watched as ripples appeared here and there on the river, fish seeking insects. Swallows darted low along the water and ducks could be heard somewhere nearby. There was a timelessness here, she realized. It could be 2011 or 1811 or 1411, and look just the same.

"I guess that's why they call it the Peace River," she said aloud. "Despite being so big, it hardly looks like it's moving."

"Looks are deceiving. The locals call the river the *Mighty Peace*. It's calm on the surface but the water beneath is deep and moving very fast. A lot of swimmers misjudge it and end up caught in the powerful current. Some of them don't escape."

She was quiet for a long time after that. James was very much like the river. Calm and steady on the surface, but somehow she'd been drawn in and captured by the deep current beneath. Would she escape? And did she really want to?

All she'd known when she arrived at the farm was that she was tremendously attracted to this man. But when she'd decided to act on it, the results had been shocking. How could she have known a kiss could have such power? How could something as simple as the joining of lips flare all at once into a fusion of souls? And God, that sounded so corny. But it wasn't just any kiss. If James hadn't stepped back when he did . . . well, she wasn't sure she would have stopped him, and that was a little scary. He was still a stranger, wasn't he?

No. He might be a little strange at times maybe, but he was definitely not a stranger. She couldn't explain how she knew that, but she knew. That kiss had been less like the 'gee-I'm-physically-attracted-to-you' sort and more like the 'there-you-are-at-last' kind. Recognition, she decided. Almost reunion. The physical desire was strong, but she realized that wasn't the only force driving them. At least, it hadn't been the only force driving *her*.

If James wasn't a stranger, then what was he, exactly? She knew that she felt good around him, solid and grounded. Not less herself but somehow more. No one had ever made her feel quite like that.

"A dollar twenty-seven for your thoughts."

"What?" She blinked up at James.

"Your thoughts are worth a lot more than a penny, doc, but a dollar twenty-seven is all I have on me."

She stood perfectly still then, just looking at him. He could so easily pass for a Viking from another age. The pale blond hair, the close blond beard that accentuated the angles of his face rather than obscured them. The broad shoulders and tall, powerful build. The piercing blue eyes. The longer she looked at him, the more she realized that it was what was in the eyes that called out to her, pulled at her. His brow was often fierce and forbidding, and his eyes could be too. But in their bottomless blue depths there was more. Much more. Knowledge, pain, passion. And tenderness. This was a man who felt intensely, who would love deeply. She still didn't know everything about James Macleod, but Jillian knew she wanted to learn.

She simply stepped into him then, slid her arms up and around his neck, and tipped her face up to be kissed. She wasn't disappointed. His lips were hungry and so were hers. He demanded and she yielded. She demanded and he gave. Heat flared, raced over both of them like a brushfire over dry prairie grass, until skin and blood were alight.

James hiked her up until her legs circled his waist, supported her with a powerful arm while one hand slid under her shirt and palmed a breast, kneaded it as he traced her lips with his tongue. Jillian captured his tongue for a moment, drew it into her mouth with exquisite slowness, released it as he groaned deep in his throat. His hand on her breast became more demanding, his fingers teasing the nipple unbearably. His other hand cupped her bottom and squeezed it again and again until she began to move against him. Even through her clothes, it was electrifying to rub herself against his hard abdomen. A throbbing tension was growing low in her belly, a pleasurable restlessness building. She wanted more. She wanted the flame, the heat, she wanted to burn down in James's embrace. A hum vibrated in the back of her throat as she arched against his powerful body, as he shoved her shirt, her bra, up and out of the way. A moan broke free as he left her lips and bent his head to Jillian's naked breast.

He lapped and teased at it with his tongue, breathed hot on the nipple until she shivered with pleasure. Then without warning James set her feet on the ground, sank down himself until he was kneeling before her. He undid her jeans and kissed her belly, undid the bottom button of her shirt and lapped at her navel. He worked his way up until no buttons were left—and Jillian couldn't stand it anymore. She pulled off the shirt, then unhooked her bra. Tossed it. Wriggled off her jeans and kicked them away. Saw the punch of surprise and the flash of arousal in James's eyes. And reveled in the sensation of this man's strong hands on her bare skin. His mouth sealed again over a breast, hot and moist, drawing in the nipple, tugging at it. Began to suckle hard and strong. *Yes, oh yes.* Jillian held his head to her, fingers locked in his hair, her whole body shaking with waves of sensation. *God, yes.* James's calloused palm circled her belly where strange pulls and tugs deep within her core echoed the insistent tugging at her breast.

All that was left of the sun was a fading glimmer of color on the far horizon. The first stars were already making their appearance and the moon was on the rise. Here, among the trees, the shadows were blue and purple. Her skin was snow in the strange half light. But within, she was pure flame.

James pulled back a moment, shrugged out of his shirt. Stood and skimmed off his jeans. Jillian nearly moaned at the sight of his naked body. He was even more gorgeous than she had dreamed. Every muscle was powerful, defined. He was broad in the chest, in the shoulders, but there was an animal grace to his movements. Her gaze traveled appreciatively over his body and came to rest on his long, hard erection. Tentatively, she reached out a hand and ran her fingers over it. Her mouth curved as he hissed in his breath between his teeth, as she saw those powerful muscles quiver.

Smooth, so smooth. Kid leather over polished stone. She slid her hand over the rigid length of him and closed her fingers tightly, savoring the strength and hardness of it. And *hot*. James's body radiated heat but this was fire itself. Jillian's body clenched at the thought of just how that fiery shaft might feel deep inside her . . . and for a moment she had to fight to breathe.

She didn't see James move. She blinked and she was surrounded with his strength, with his heat, wrapped in those muscled arms and held close. Skin to skin, head to toe, as his shaft pressed and pulsed against her belly, as his big hands roved over her backside. Then just as suddenly he scooped her up and walked away with her through the trees and into a small clearing.

"It's a little softer here," he murmured and kissed her brow, her cheek, before easing her down. Jillian had expected grass but found herself lying on something surprisingly soft and spongy. She felt around her in surprise.

"It's just moss." James answered her unspoken question, then rested on his elbow beside her. He leaned over and took her lips before she could think of any more questions, ran a hand over the contours of her body, followed it with kisses over her breasts and belly, then palmed the moist curls between her legs.

She was restless and edgy now, needing, *needing*. And he knew. He ran his hand between her legs, long lazy strokes that reached all the way to her tailbone and back. He gradually kissed his way down until he was nestled between her legs, then lifted her hips in his large hands until he could rest her knees over his broad shoulders. He bent his head and ran his tongue along the delicate crease of her thigh, slowly, much too slowly. Jillian shuddered hard with the anticipation, every nerve shouting for James to hurry, please hurry, gasping for air as her heart pounded in her ears. She could just make out his face in the shadows, see him smile as he bent his mouth to her, sampled her, savored her, then drank her greedily.

A guttural cry burst from Jillian's throat. The sudden storm of pleasure had her gasping, made her body pitch and buck like a small boat caught in a rough sea. Sensation flooded her, swamped her with monstrous waves so racking and intense that she shook with the power of them. She exploded into the sky, into the sun, pulsing with a wave of heat that rippled outward until the very clouds were set afire.

When awareness returned, Jillian found herself lying beside James, looking into his Viking blue eyes. She blinked a few times to focus, feeling stunned but managing a shaky smile. He kissed her soundly, wrapping her up in his strong arms, anchoring her, keeping her from floating away. Safe.

"Wow." She didn't know what else to say, didn't trust her voice anyway. She wasn't too sure about the rest of her body either. *Languor.* That was the only word that seemed to fit the state her body was in, a deep luxuriant *languor*. Jillian was certain she was no longer lying on the bed of moss, but rather, was draped over it like an empty coat. Perhaps she had burned up after all, from the inside out. No bones left, just the hide.

"I feel like limp spaghetti," she blurted out.

James chuckled. "I think I liked 'wow' better."

She grinned and brushed his hair out of his eyes. Saw that those eyes had softened, filled with warmth and humor. She saw something else in them too. The fire was still raging.

James nuzzled her ear and took the lobe into his mouth, suckling it as he had her breast. A heated hand circled her breasts, her belly, nudged her legs apart and began to stroke her folds. The orgasm had left her intensely sensitive, and Jillian trembled beneath his touch, could hardly bear it. He murmured into her ear, tickling it with heated breath, and her entire body clenched and quivered. He pulled her closer, and Jillian felt his fiery hot erection pressed against her thigh. A finger slid inside her, explored as she moaned. Two fingers pressed deep, deeper. Her hips rose of their own accord, thrust hard against his strong hand but it wasn't enough. She was aching all over, edgy and wanting. *Needing* . . .

Jillian whimpered aloud when James took his hand away, but his muscled body was welcome as it moved over her. She welcomed the heat and the weight of him, welcomed his face over hers, framed by the starry sky. Welcomed his powerful legs nudging hers wider apart. And moaned with a kind of delicious exultation as he entered her. She felt herself slowly parting before the fiery heat, giving way, stretching to take the fire into herself until she had it all. It was bliss, luscious bliss, to be filled so completely. James paused there, eyes closed as if also savoring the sensation. He was still for a heartbeat, then two.

Then he began to move. The exquisite friction begot a deeply primal pleasure and Jillian became a wild thing, digging her fingers into the muscles of his buttocks, pulling him into her, thrusting her hips to meet his rhythm. She panted out a plea for more, *more*. A soundless vibration began to resonate within her, within him, as if a tidal wave of unimaginable proportions was bearing down on them.

Harder, faster, deeper. "Come with me, Jillian," he panted. "Come with me *now*."

Battered, wave-tossed, lost at sea, she heard his words above the thunder of her blood, the roaring in her ears, and instinctively linked her fingers with his. She arched to meet the strength of his body, the power of him as he filled her. As he both moved her and anchored her. As he was both storm and haven. They rode the cresting wave together, a pair of dolphins skimming above the powerful surf until the ocean suddenly fell away and they flew free.

Chapter Twenty-one

Birkie appeared at her elbow, arms folded. "Okay, something's seriously wrong here. Carlton Fuller's herd is sick because he was too cheap to vaccinate again, and you spent fifteen minutes explaining to him how that 'doesn't make good economic sense' instead of kicking his sorry ass from here to Winnipeg. Why?"

"Because it doesn't make sense from a business standpoint. If he—"

"I know that. What I want to know is—*why isn't he dead*?

Jillian looked baffled. "Well, I thought I'd try an educational approach . . ." She trailed off at her friend's expression.

"You, my dear, have either had a complete breakdown from overwork or you've finally gotten some serious nookie. Which is it?"

"Do we *have* to call it nookie?"

"We can call it whatever you like as long as you tell me about it."

"I'm not going to give you a play-by-play."

"I'll settle for details on events leading up to and immediately following. Your apartment after closing, I'll bring the chocolate."

"Deal."

*　*　*

He was the world's biggest idiot. What on earth had made him think that he was in control, even for a moment? The plan had been just to keep an eye on Jillian, satisfy himself with checking in on her at the clinic. Briefly, always briefly. Just long enough to assure himself—and the wolf within—that she was fine, that she was safe. And yeah, he could admit he looked forward to catching a glimpse of her or hearing her voice, sometimes watching her work or maybe saying hello. But that was all the contact he had permitted himself, all he had planned for. Not for one moment had James anticipated that she would show up at the farm.

Still, he could have avoided trouble if only he hadn't taken her riding, definitely if he had turned them back to the farm instead of heading down to the damn river, and most of all, if he'd just avoided looking in those big green eyes of hers. Sensible precautions that if taken, would have prevented what happened last night. Wouldn't they?

No. No, it would have only delayed the inevitable. The truth of that resonated uncomfortably within him. If he was honest with himself, he had never been in control, not since the first time he'd met her as a man, and certainly not since the first encounter he'd had with her as a wolf. Which meant he should have known, should have seen it coming. After all, he had admitted to himself long ago that he was attracted to Jillian. It was natural, it was normal, to be attracted. Even natural and normal to act on that attraction.

Like last night? Well, hell, he wasn't dead and it had been a long time since he'd been with a woman. He'd spent most of the morning trying to tell himself that was all it was. Except it wasn't all, not by a long shot, and he knew it. James couldn't even pretend that the wolf had anything to do with it, because his alter ego had all but disappeared after that first kiss. His mind had disappeared then too. Perhaps he could plead insanity. After all, he was still reeling from that kiss, even after everything that had followed. Jillian had looked up at him with those big sea green eyes and that faery face and it had been like a hard kick to the stomach. All the air had left his lungs, and James felt himself swimming in those eyes. Swimming and the water was oh, so deep. He had *had* to kiss her, had to more than he had to breathe. But she'd beaten him to it. She had fisted her hands in his hair and pulled his face to hers. There and then he drowned.

Small wonder his heart had galloped on ahead of his brain and developed feelings, strong ones. As much as he was struggling to rationalize the whole situation, his own words mocked him: *That's the whole damn problem with being human. You always end up feeling things you don't want to feel.* Only that was a lie too. He'd said things, thought things, felt things—and as much as he had told himself he didn't want to, he did. Very much.

He threw the spade he was carrying across the yard, launching it like a javelin with such force that the blade stuck into the barn wall about fifteen feet off the ground. He left it there and stalked away, wishing he could Change and race away into the forest.

Jesus Murphy! He had to get a grip. So *what* if he had feelings for her? He couldn't let that matter. All that mattered was what would be best for Jillian, how best to keep her safe. A relationship was completely out of the question. She was human and he had to remember that. Associating with a Changeling would only endanger her. What little contact she had now was probably too much. Sooner or later someone would notice. And Jillian would pay.

Bad enough that she was already going to be hurt—he'd

be stupid to think that last night hadn't meant something to her too—but at least she'd be alive. She was sure to hate him too, and rightfully so. Because not only could he never see her again, he couldn't even explain why.

She'd missed lunch again. Jillian finished with the goat in the corral and headed back into the clinic. She had just cut through the waiting room on her way to the kitchen when she spotted the large bouquet on Birkie's desk.

"These just came for you, hon." Her friend waggled her brows. "Pretty impressive choice of flowers too."

Jillian stared at them. She recognized the roses—but *what* roses. The large blooms were exquisite, creamy white and long-stemmed. But they were interspersed with tall plumes of tiny bell-like flowers, also white. And those shiny green leaves—"Is that holly?"

"It certainly is. Holly and white heather. Both of them symbolize a pledge of protection and defense."

"What?"

"It's the language of flowers, hon. Different flowers mean different things. This is a very strong message, a double message of protection."

"Protection of what?"

"Well, you of course. And the white roses, now those are just plain classy."

"Are they protecting me too?"

"No, silly. I'm going to have to loan you one of my books. White roses are always more powerful than red ones, you know. The white ones mean *'love always'* or *'pure love.'* Like I said, very classy, very unique. Aren't you going to read the card? Let me tell you, it took a pile of restraint to keep from running it out to you in the corral."

Jillian fingered the small envelope, noted it was sealed,

and tucked it in her pocket. "I think I'll read this privately first," she said and laughed when Birkie looked disappointed. "If it's G-rated, maybe I'll share."

"Oh, all right. Can I at least keep the flowers on my desk a while?"

"Of course. They'd be wasted sitting in my apartment all afternoon. I'll come and get them at closing time."

A pledge of protection. That seemed a little medieval, but maybe James was just trying to be romantic. Or maybe he didn't know any more about the so-called language of flowers than she did. But the white roses. . . . Those were romantic in any language. Jillian hurried to the lunchroom, hoping for a few more moments between patients. She tried to open the envelope in a civilized fashion but in the end, she ripped it. The picture on the face of the card was simple, trees in a forest. She smiled, thinking of when she'd last been in a forest . . . then she opened it and her smile disappeared. She was still standing there staring at what James had written when Birkie came in to announce the next patient. Jillian handed her the card without a word and headed to the examining room.

Jillian. You're a beautiful woman but it would be best if we didn't see each other anymore. I'm sorry.

"Well, Jesus, Mary, and Joseph. Best, he says. Best for *who*?" Birkie shook her head, blinked hard until her eyes cleared. "Isn't that just like a man? Trying so hard to protect the one you love that it ends up hurting both of you." She sighed and stashed the flowers in the supply room until closing. Then she quietly took them to the dumpster and dropped them in.

James was drill-seeding the back quarter section of land. Most farmers used herbicides to kill off all existing plants before putting in a crop, but there would be no chemicals used on Macleod land. He'd studied the latest techniques and decided to go with a no-tillage policy as well. That meant seeding the fields without plowing them, leaving the existing plant cover to hoard moisture and shelter top-soil from the powerful west winds. It would take time, plenty of it, but James was determined to steer the farm to organic production.

It would take a lot of work too, but that was fine with him. In fact, the more work, the better. Right now, work was the only thing keeping him sane. Usually the land was soothing to his spirit, the soil enlivening. But not now and not for the last three weeks. Even from the cab of the tall tractor, he should have been able to feel a unique closeness to the earth but lately he'd just felt empty, hollowed out and aching. The deep peace and satisfaction he usually found in green and growing things was missing, and in its place was desolation.

James told himself repeatedly that he'd done the right thing by walking out of Jillian's life. He should never have let things go so far in the first place. Should never have kissed her, should never have held her—but he couldn't seem to bring himself to regret it. God, that night together, tangled on the forest floor. Whenever he closed his eyes he still heard her heart hammering behind her teacup breasts, still saw downy curls glinting gold between her slim legs.

Everything had changed. *She* had changed. He had looked at her with human eyes for the first time while she slept in her apartment. That little frown on her fine features had immediately evoked a storybook picture of a cranky faery. But that night in the forest, the cuteness disappeared. The silvered light had revealed something downright ethereal, profound. Even regal. Not Tinkerbell but

Titania herself. It was in the angles of Jillian's face, in her sea green eyes, in her wild cap of hair. In her narrow frame that seemed far too small to hold the blazing passions that drove her. In her skin that was so much fairer than even his own, so amazingly soft over compact muscle. Every night in his dreams he ran his hands over her body, delighting in the lines of it, the colors and textures, even as he breathed in the enticing scent of her, as his heart thrilled to the sound of her voice, her laughter. And every morning he had to remind himself that for Jillian's sake the dream had to remain a dream.

The sun was down, but the darkness didn't matter to James. The tractor had powerful headlights and his night vision was acute. He could easily finish this field tonight. Maybe the one on the south side as well. Whatever would keep him busy enough to stay awake was fine with him. James just didn't feel up to having another dream of any kind. Besides, when he was awake, it was easier to control the wolf within. Relatively easier. Since James had ended things with Jillian, the wolf had been increasingly surly, miserable, short-tempered and likely to snap at anyone. *Just like my human self.* He didn't know how long he could keep a leash on the wolf, knew that it would find its way back to Jillian sooner or later. Maybe he should leave town. The wolf would have a tough time interfering with Jillian's life if James was in, say, outer Mongolia.

When the fuel gauge beeped a warning, he geared down and brought the tractor to a standstill, switched off the seeder. There was a fuel tank and a pump on the back of his truck, but he'd left it parked under the trees on the far side of the field. That was okay, he could use the walk. Maybe it would clear his head.

Stars were appearing and he could just see the full moon

above the trees. It was glowing yellow like a Japanese lantern, but it would lose color as it climbed. James rubbed his hands over his face and opened the cab door of the tractor, let the breeze pour through, scented the air, let himself breathe deeply and rest, relax, just for a moment—

—*suddenly he was the wolf, racing through a shadowy forest under a velvet sky bright with stars. He had to go faster, had to reach her, had to help her. Followed the river until it flowed through a city, until game trails gave way to manmade trails. Followed them until he caught the scent of violence and fear, hate and hopelessness. Followed until he caught sight of the upraised pipe. Of the brutal hands that held it. Of the man intent on destroying the life that fluttered in the slight figure crumpled on the ground beneath him.*

The Change overtook him without warning. James cried out in shock and surprise, then his human voice was strangled off abruptly by the shift in form. His human mind had time for a only single thought as he leapt down from the tractor. *Jillian.* He had to get to Jillian.

The great wolf ran full out across the field, belly close to the ground, claws digging into the clay soil, tail a white plume touched with the moon's golden light.

Chapter Twenty-two

The calf was a big one, even for its large-boned breed, weighing almost as much as she did. Bloody to the armpits, her coveralls soaked with amniotic fluid, Jillian dragged the creature out of the three-foot long incision in its mother's side. The cow, blissfully unaware of that incision due to the contents of a large syringe carefully inserted between two of its vertebrae, was looking around in mild interest. She blinked in surprise as the vet slipped in the wet straw and went down under 110 pounds of wriggling Charolais calf.

"It's okay, baby, it's okay, we'll get you out." Jillian fought her way to her knees, deftly stripped the sac from around the calf's golden face, reached into its mouth to pull its tongue forward and clear the throat. And laughed when her fingers were seized and sucked with gusto.

Grabbing a towel, she rubbed vigorously to dry the calf, grunted as she hauled the newborn over to where the cow could nose it. For a moment the veterinarian looked on in satisfaction as the mother licked her newborn, memorizing the scent, cementing the bond between them. Animal bonds, Jillian knew, tended to be unshakeable. *Not like humans.* Sighing, she unwrapped a fresh surgical pack—the contents of the first had fallen into the wet straw—and began the long process of closing up.

The full moon was more than halfway across the sky when Jillian drove away from the Murdock's farm. She had the heat on full blast and she'd taken off her coveralls, but her clothes were wet through. Her teeth chattered as she fumbled with a radio station. Most farmers would at least have offered her some coffee or something. But then, every farmer she knew would have come out to the barn and pitched in. She had hoped for that kind of help when she couldn't reach Caroline. Jillian had thought about asking Connor for help. After all, it wasn't *his* fault his brother was a jerk. But she just didn't feel up to seeing any of the Macleod clan tonight. And so she had taken the calving call alone, even though the farm was in a remote location, nearly two hours away.

At least both cow and calf were fine. Jed Murdock hadn't been pleased that Jillian had shown up instead of Connor, but he wouldn't be able to complain about her work. And maybe a hefty bill for the extra hours she'd spent would encourage the Murdocks to be a little more helpful next time.

Not that she minded being busy. It was harder for unwelcome thoughts to creep into her awareness when she was focused on work. That was why she had thrown herself into every task she could find at the clinic, why she was even making up tasks. Birkie had eyed Jillian with concern when she'd restacked the hay bales in the livestock area, but she didn't care. It was better than thinking about how much she ached inside, how much James Macleod had hurt her. Except for the card that came with the flowers, she hadn't heard from him. No letters, no phone calls. And certainly no face-to-face communication. After being at the clinic every single day, he hadn't come by even once for three solid weeks. *Pretty hard not to read* that *message.* She would never have picked him for the one-night stand type, but then, how much did she really know about him? It was her own fault for getting too involved too soon, for letting her hormones off the leash way too early. The fact that her heart had led the way didn't bear thinking about.

And so Jillian was determined not to think about anything. Her plan was to keep busy, so busy that the thoughts wouldn't stand a chance of getting through, so busy that she simply fell into bed late each night and was asleep before she hit the pillow. The system had worked just fine for the past three weeks. But now she was worn right out, and for the first time she wondered how long she could keep this up.

There was certainly no shortage of tasks to keep her busy tonight, even though it was well after midnight. The instruments still needed to be unpacked, washed, and sterilized. The surgical drapings and her wet coveralls had to be put in the washing machine and soaked. And she was already so damn tired. Her eyelids fluttered down, once, twice. . . .

Jillian jerked her head up just as the cab of the truck was flooded with light. There was another vehicle behind her with its brights on. She squinted as it rapidly closed the distance between them. From the height of those blinding headlights, she judged it to be a truck. A car's beams wouldn't have filled her pickup cab so thoroughly. Sound flooded in as well. Though her windows were closed, she could hear the high-pitched thrum of a powerful engine and the brain-beating bass of a massive stereo system. It had to be kids. How did they stand to be inside that? She could feel the vibration of whatever music they were playing in her teeth, for God's sake.

Jillian prayed the driver would switch to low beams soon. She peered through half-closed eyes at her side mirror. It was indeed a tall pickup truck, but it was weaving back and forth, fishtailing on the gravel road. "Great, they're fooling around or drunk. Probably both." Jillian was suddenly uncomfortable about being alone and wondering where she'd stashed her cell phone when a row of dull orange spots appeared like eyes on the other truck's roof. Jillian made out the rack of hunters' floodlights just as they powered on.

Dammit! Jillian slapped at the rearview mirror, flipping its face to the ceiling. "Stupid asses!" She cursed vehemently as white light shot back at her from the side mirrors, the dashboard glass, everywhere. Pain stabbed her tired eyes. She cupped a hand around her brow as a flimsy shield and tried to focus on the road ahead. The light was bright . . . and getting brighter. She wanted to slow down. She'd been under the fifty miles per hour speed limit for the gravel road, but not by much. She touched her brakes lightly, once, twice, hoping the other truck was paying attention and wouldn't run into her.

A bright yellow diamond flashed into view on her right, dazzlingly bright in the other truck's lights. She squinted at the highway sign and deciphered its symbols: *a hill with a steep grade*. She realized at once where she was. At the bottom of the hill would be the narrow steel bridge that spanned Little Burnt Creek. If the other truck was going to pass her, it would have to do it soon. She prayed it *would* pass. Her nerves were already rubbed raw by the assault of light and sound.

Suddenly the headlights swung away to her left, leaving her in abrupt darkness and temporarily blind.

She took her foot off the gas pedal as her eyes fought to

adjust and her unknown antagonist thundered by, bass pounding so loud it hurt Jillian's ears and stabbed at her brain, vibrated in her very bones. "Stop it! Stop it!" she yelled, unable to even hear herself. The vehicle passed her in a blast of impossible noise and a rattle of gravel, hurtling down the hill. She caught a glimpse of a large red pickup with shiny chrome roll bars before the darkness swallowed it. The mind-numbing bass faded into the distance and was finally gone.

Shaken and disoriented, Jillian pulled the truck to the shoulder of the road. It wasn't there. There was nothing under the right front wheel as she tried in vain to steer the still-rolling truck back to solid ground. Suddenly there was a sickening lurch as the rear passenger wheel dropped over the road's edge as well. The truck teetered on the crumbling brink, and she realized she couldn't make it back onto the road. Jillian steered instead for the deep ditch, trying to take it at an angle so the truck wouldn't tip. But then the ditch itself dipped and disappeared into darkness. The brakes couldn't stop the momentum of the heavy truck as it hurtled down the steep embankment through a stand of brush.

Thick branches slapped at the windshield, cracked it. Books and packages on the seat flew up and struck her as the vehicle lurched and bounced crazily. She saw the dark surface of a creek in her headlights, then glittering plumes of water all around her as she struggled to steer through it. A roaring filled her ears, her brain. There was no time to hope that the water wasn't too deep, to pray that the engine would keep going. And no time at all to react as the darkness in front of her suddenly resolved itself into a tree. It was the last picture in her mind as something enormous punched her full in the face.

Awareness faded then rushed back like a tidal surge. Heavy folds of white material swamped her, and Jillian screamed as she tried to bat it away. The air was thick with dust, choking her. Finally her brain kicked in and she realized she was fighting with the air bag.

Her whole body jellied in relief, and she was grateful she was already sitting down. For several minutes Jillian just sat there with her hands gripping the wheel. She took a deep breath that sent her into a coughing fit. When it abated, she hit the button to roll down the window and leaned forward to rest her head on the steering column and let the cool air wash over her until her heart stopped hammering. Until she felt steady. Steadier. Well, almost steady.

Looking around, she assessed the situation. Truck. Tree. Water. She was half in and half out of the shallow creek, the front of the truck resting against a large poplar on the opposite bank. The hood didn't look bashed in from here. Maybe the vehicle was still drivable. Maybe she could walk the truck out in four-wheel drive. But first she'd have to lock the hubs on the front axle by hand. *Note to self: Next time, pick a vehicle you can shift into four-wheel drive from the inside.* Jillian popped the shoulder belt and spent a few minutes fumbling behind the seat for a flashlight. It was hard work. Her body was sore and her face felt like she'd tried to stop a train with it. One of her hands didn't seem to work very well. She cursed repeatedly as new pains flashed here and there, as her feet kept getting tangled in the deflated air bag. There seemed to be enough of the sagging white material to make a goddamn hot air balloon.

She kicked free of it and paused to catch her breath. "Okay, then, I'm okay. Everything's okay. Let's get it done." Jillian swung open the door, saw it skim the surface of the water but didn't hesitate to jump down. She gasped at the iciness of the water, as the fast current both shoved and pulled at her. It had to be mountain runoff—it felt like it came straight off a glacier. Reaching for the door with one hand and gripping the flashlight with the other, she took a step forward. And discovered too late that the bottom of the creek was slick with mud and algae.

Without warning, her feet flew out from under her, plunging her beneath the icy water. The current immediately dragged her along the bottom. Panicked, Jillian clawed and flailed at the dark surface—the creek couldn't have been more than three feet deep—but there was something in her way, something she kept banging her head and body against, that kept her submerged. Her lungs were screaming, her mind was screaming as she fought blindly for her life.

Then something grasped her arm, gripped it tight. She fought that too, but it was strong and towed her along the icy bottom, then up into the blessed, blessed air. A moment later she was on her hands and knees on dry ground, coughing and choking and puking up water.

It took a little while before she became aware that someone had an arm around her waist, supporting her, pounding her back. Jillian gulped in air in huge, ragged breaths and collapsed, her strength utterly spent. Powerful arms encircled her, lifted her, cradled her in warmth.

"It's okay, doc, you're okay now. It's over, just breathe now, baby. Just breathe."

With a jolt she realized she was sobbing like a child. Embarrassed, she scrubbed a hand over her face and yelped when both her hand and face protested the contact. Opening her eyes, she found herself face-to-face with a Viking.

"What the hell are *you* doing here?"

Chapter Twenty-three

Her voice was strangled and raw—not to mention annoyed—but it sounded terrific to him. Carefully he pushed her dripping blond hair away from her face, brushed the water from around her wide green eyes. "Jesus, doc, you scared the hell out of me. The next time you want to go diving for pearls, take some equipment."

"I . . . I couldn't get out, I couldn't get out of the water, something was holding me under." She tried to push him away but started coughing again. When she regained her breath, she simply sagged against him, exhausted.

He wrapped his arms tightly around her. He was as wet as she was, but he could at least share his naturally high body heat. "You were underneath the truck, doc. The water's up to the running boards, and you must have kept trying to come up under the chassis." Christ, she must have been terrified. It had certainly terrified *him*. In wolfen form he'd raced full out, crossing the miles as the crow flies, utilizing all the speed a Changeling was capable of— and then some. Not knowing what was wrong, only that there was danger and he must *hurry*. The compulsion whipped him mercilessly, drove him to a near-impossible pace until his heart was ready to burst. Just as it was the night he'd raced to Evelyn's side. Past and present had blurred in James's mind as he ran. Fear that he might be too late had clamped icy jaws around his throat, making it harder to breathe even as his lungs burned for air.

Fortunately, the connection the wolf had with Jillian had led him straight to her. James had caught her scent as he crested the hill, followed the wide swath of freshly broken brush leading down the ditch and into the creek. He spotted the truck when he was halfway down the slope, was relieved to see Jillian open the door. Then relief turned to horror as she stepped out into the water and slipped beneath it. He Changed as he leapt into the creek, splashed and skidded on his hands and knees in the dark icy water, while he felt around frantically for something, anything, he could grab.

With a start, James realized he was shaking almost as much as Jillian. He pulled her even closer, tucked her head under his chin and simply held on. Grateful he was sitting down, grateful to have her gathered in his lap and wrapped tight against him. Safe. He drew her scent into his lungs, again and again, each time holding it there, close to his heart. He listened to her breathing, listened to her heart beating, the rhythms of life, *her* life. He rubbed his cheek over her wet hair as powerful emotions shook him to the core. Dear God, he had been in time. *He had been in time.*

James radiated his Changeling body heat to warm her as much as he could. Finally, when their shaking had subsided and both of them were steadier, he relaxed his hold on her, but not before he brushed his lips over her brow, her head. The sudden taste and tang of blood jolted him, reminded him that Jillian might be alive but she needed more than affection to stay that way. "Keep this on, okay?" His jacket was wet but he wrapped it snugly around her just the same. At least it had some residual warmth in it, and it would keep the breeze off her until he found something drier. "I'll be right back."

He waded out to the truck. A check of the ignition revealed that the battery was dead. So was the radio. There was a cell phone on the floor but it was in pieces. James took a quick look around the cab for anything else useful, then made his way to the back of the truck. Here he had more luck. The canopy had kept the cargo dry, and he had no trouble finding matches and supplies, for which he blessed his brother's name. There was no shortage of blankets and clothing either, the preparations of a vet who had made too many farm calls in bad weather.

There was dead willow along the bank and James worked fast to gather an armful and coax a fire into life. The flames gobbled the twigs and dried grass greedily, moved on to the larger bits of wood without a pause. He set a duffel bag on the ground beside Jillian and knelt to study her in the firelight. The orange glow should have lent color to her face but she was paper-white. Trickles of blood had emerged from her hairline, merged into a single rivulet that ran steadily down the side of her face. Her green eyes were wide, too wide, the pupils dilated even though she was looking straight at the flames. Not good, not good at all, he thought. "Take your clothes off."

"What?" She looked startled.

James opened the bag and rifled through it. "You've got to get out of those wet things right now."

"What for? Why can't you just take me home?"

"I don't have a vehicle with me, Jillian." *Please, God, don't let her ask any questions. I can't exactly say I ran here.* He rushed on before she could say anything. "Your truck is out of commission, and we're a hell of a long way from town. The radio's out. I don't have a cell phone, and yours is broken. We could be here a while, so you need to be warm and dry. Step one is to take off those wet clothes."

As she opened her mouth to protest, James simply picked her up and placed her on her feet. Steadied her. "You don't get a choice here, Jillian. You're not thinking straight. Hypothermia is dangerous, and I'm betting you've got a concussion as well."

He had removed his jacket from her shoulders, taken off her jacket and was starting on her shirt when her temper flared and she backed up a step, fists clenched.

"Don't touch me." Jillian flung the words at him like stones. "Just don't. I don't know what kind of privileges you think you have, but undressing me isn't one of them."

That momentary flicker in her eyes, anger mixed with something very like humiliation, cut him to the core. Guilt roughened his voice. "This isn't the time, Jillian. You want to go a few rounds with me, fine, you can have all the free swings you want later. Right now we need to take care of you."

"I can take care of myself just fine, thank you."

He didn't want to fight with her. He raised his hands in a conciliatory gesture, praying he wasn't making a mistake. "Suit yourself. But if you're not peeled out of those soggy clothes in five minutes, I'll do it whether you want me to or not." He meant it. Her eyes flashed but her anger was a bonus—it would keep her adrenaline up, and God knew she needed it. "You've almost died once tonight, doc, and I'm not about to let you try for twice." He yanked out a big flannel shirt, some jeans, and a wool blanket, and placed them on top of the bag for her. He pulled out an outfit for himself and stalked to the other side of the fire, keeping his back turned to give her some privacy. Besides, if he didn't look at her, maybe he could concentrate. He had to keep trying to contact Connor or some other member of the Pack. It was a long shot, literally, to succeed at mind speech over such a distance. But there was little traffic on this road, even less at this time of night, and it was miles to the nearest farm to get help. True, he could Change again and cover the distance on four feet, but he would have to leave Jillian alone—and that he didn't dare do.

Suddenly he felt a connection. It was odd—as if his mental call were a fish and someone was reeling it in. That someone couldn't be a Changeling, the energy was different. *Birkie!*

Chapter Twenty-four

Jillian kept an eye on James. At first it was to guard the privacy she'd insisted on, but unexpectedly she found herself staring. The campfire glow highlighted his powerful build, the angles of his face. Even naked, he looked like a warrior, and it annoyed her that she found that so appealing, that it played on some sensitive primal nerve within her. That she flat-out wanted him. . . .

She forced herself to look away then. How *could* she still want James Macleod after he'd slept with her, then ditched her? It's just a physical thing, she told herself sternly, a knee-jerk reaction she had no control over. But who knew the desire would be so strong? And worse, that her heart would be tangled up in it as well? Because here it was three weeks later, and she was still missing him. They hadn't even dated, didn't even have a relationship to speak of, and yet she missed him constantly. And just as constantly she told herself that it was silly infatuation, that she needed to get out more, she needed to meet more people, she needed a hobby, she needed to date more. She watched James zipping up his jeans on the other side of the fire and wished she had the nerve to walk over and *unzip* them. Her core clenched hard. See, she told herself. Just plain old physical attraction. So why did her heart feel like it had a hole in it?

"I must have hit my head," she muttered under her breath. After all, her head did hurt an awful lot. So did everything else, for that matter. Jillian's stomach muscles were sore inside and out from retching up water, and her ribs felt bruised from trying to expel the fluid from her lungs. There was a bright fiery pain starting to make itself known in her arm, her hands. James had said she was under the truck. That was ridiculous. She didn't remember getting out of the truck. And where did all the water come from? There were headlights, lots of lights, blinding her . . . but she found she could remember nothing else.

She forgot all about James then too. Her hands were numb and sore at the same time—which she couldn't understand—and her body was cold and awkward. Except her arm, which was on fire. Her teeth chattered uncontrollably as she fought with wet fabric. She cursed the buttons as they defied her efforts. Her anger gave way to frustration, and then nearly to tears. She couldn't think, she was so damned tired, and her fingers would not obey her. Jillian was only mildly surprised when her legs suddenly gave out. Barely noticed when strong arms caught her before she hit the ground.

"I think I must have slipped," she murmured. Something was fluttering at her cheek, patting it lightly. She tried to brush it away but her arm hurt.

"Come on, doc, I know you're tired but you need to stay awake for a while. Wake up for me, Jillian."

"Quit it. Go away," she moaned and turned her head away, but a large hand cupped her cheek.

"Jillian! Wake up *now*."

"What the hell are you doing?" Her voice was raspy. She tried to sit up and a tight groan of pain escaped her.

"Easy there, doc. You passed out. My fault. I didn't realize how bad you were hurt." Gently James helped her into a more upright position. "Just take it easy for a few minutes, okay?"

"Yeah, okay." She was too tired and sore to argue, too confused to think. It all took energy, and she didn't seem to have any. Jillian let herself lean back against him, was surprised that his body heat seemed to be flowing right into her. There was a fire at her feet, but there was almost as much warmth radiating from James. In spite of all the pains that were competing for her attention, she felt almost cozy in this big Viking's lap.

Those warm and cozy feelings were short-lived as the Viking proceeded to inspect her scalp. "Ow, dammit!"

"Got a couple of cuts here that might need stitches. You're bleeding quite a bit, but head wounds always do. My younger brother Devlin cut his head open when we were little and I thought he was going to die, there was so much blood everywhere. Scared me. But two stitches were all it needed. He turned around and walloped me with a stick not twenty minutes later so I needed three stitches myself. Luckily Mom was pretty good at it."

"You are *not* going to stitch—" Jillian fought with the blanket to get an arm free. Although her temper lent her a few drops of adrenaline, the blanket nearly won. She was surprised to find her right arm bandaged and splinted from palm to elbow, surprised too to find her hands battered and bleeding, knuckles and nails fairly singing with pain. Was even more startled to find she was naked under the blanket. "Where the hell are my clothes, you goddamn pervert? I'm sure I told you not to touch me."

"You certainly did, so I guess your short-term memory's intact. Saves me from having to ask you what day it is and all that shit. Maybe the concussion isn't too bad."

"I don't have a concussion. And I want my clothes back, right now." She wrenched her head away from his probing fingers. "You're *not* stitching anything."

"Settle down before you hurt yourself more. I wouldn't think of taking a needle and thread to you, doc. Connor's got plenty of adhesive closures in the first-aid kit."

She struggled anyway. "I don't care. Just let go of me. I want my clothes and I want you to leave me alone." She'd made it out of his lap, trying to clutch the blanket around her with her battered fingers and stand up at the same time. If only she wasn't so damn dizzy. Suddenly James was in front of her, his powerful hands on her shoulders. Jillian's temper flared, thinking he was trying to restrain her. Then a glimmer of sense kicked in, and she realized he was actually holding her up.

"Easy there, doc. You almost passed out again."

"I did not." She said it without heat however. She didn't have the energy left to argue and breathe at the same time.

"Jesus Murphy, woman," he muttered and steadied her as she sat heavily on the ground. James grabbed a corner of the blanket and tucked it more firmly around her. He sat back on his heels and waited until she glared up at him. "Look, Jillian, help's coming, but it's going to take a while for it to get here. I know I'm not your first choice of rescuer right now, but you're stuck with me. You're mad as hell, and you've got damn good reason to be, but now isn't the time to fight about it. You're injured."

"I'm fine."

"That so? Guess I splinted your wrist for nothing then. And what about this?" He pressed his finger on her left collarbone, and she yelped in spite of herself.

"That hurt, you bastard."

"It ought to. You're purple from chin to shoulder on that

side. I'd be surprised if it's not broken too. You get into a fight with someone?"

"No, why—ow!" She tried to swat his hand away from where he was carefully poking at her cheekbone.

"I'm certain your face was a different shape when I last saw you. I'd say there's some swelling going on here. Definitely a lot of bruising."

"Goddamn air bag went off in the truck," she muttered, wishing he'd stop staring at her.

His eyebrows shot up. "The air bag did that? I thought they were supposed to protect people, not beat them up." James reached for the top of her head then, and she flinched before he'd even made contact. He withdrew his hand without touching her. "Okay, enough with the show and tell. I was just going to point out that your head's cut in at least two different places, possibly three. Worse than that, I have to say I don't like the way you're coherent one minute and confused the next. You're a doctor for God's sake. You *know* you're injured. At the very least we need to stop the bleeding. Now will you *please* let me help you?"

She frowned. Wavered. "What about my clothes?"

"I'll get you some clothes, doc, I promise. Truce?"

She nodded and the sudden movement made her head throb viciously. She could see the sense in what James had said—a hot trickle down the side of her face told her she was bleeding—but she dared not let any truce continue for one minute longer than necessary. She needed to be mad, needed her anger. Various parts of her body throbbed with pain—but it was nothing compared to the growing pain in her heart. She couldn't explain to James that to be so close to him, able to see him and feel him and touch him, was turning into slow torture. She wouldn't tell him how much he had hurt her, what a disappointment it was to know that he didn't want her.

"I'm going to put some butterfly closures on these cuts, just to stop the bleeding until we can turn you over to a professional. Okay?"

"Okay. Don't forget my clothes."

"I won't forget." James knelt beside her and began gently blotting the cuts on her head with gauze. "These are bleeding pretty freely, but there's a lot of gunk in your hair."

"Gunk? Is that a technical term?"

"Debris. Flotsam. Leaves and mud plus God only knows what kind of bacteria live in that creek. There's a lot of runoff right now from rain in the hills, and that means the water is full of all kinds of garbage from upstream. You don't need some damn infection on top of everything else, so I'd like to use some peroxide here. Okay with you?"

"Hey, I'm already a blonde so it can't hurt." Tilting her head back made her horribly dizzy, and Jillian was grateful for the steady supporting hand that cupped the back of her neck. She stifled a groan as the cold stinging liquid fizzed on her scalp.

James continued to work on the area until he was satisfied the adhesive closures would stick. Once he'd patched up her scalp, he turned his attention to her hands. She held them out in front of her, prepared to be stoic again. But a loud yelp escaped her when he poured the peroxide over her cuts and scrapes.

"Sorry, doc."

"My head didn't hurt like this," she hissed through gritted teeth. Her hands trembled as the fiery liquid bubbled and foamed, but she kept them outstretched so James could work on them.

"Your head just had a couple of cuts. It wasn't scraped all to hell." His touch was light as he bandaged the worst of the damage. He paid particular attention to carefully wrapping the ends of her fingers that had split nails. "We don't want you to snag these on anything or they're going to hurt a lot more."

"I don't understand what happened to my hands. I don't remember them being in this condition." She'd always kept her nails trimmed as short as possible. How could they possibly have gotten so horribly broken?

James finished another fingertip, started wrapping the next. "I imagine you did this on the underside of the truck."

"The truck? I—omigod." For a horrifying moment she was under the water again, struggling in the icy darkness with the unyielding thing that held her under. Terrified as she tried to claw her way through it—

"Stay with me, doc."

"What?" The nightmare dissolved, and she was sitting on the ground, dry ground. There was a fire at her back and a Viking was putting things into a first-aid box. The box looked ridiculously tiny next to his big hands, but his movements were competent and sure. Then the Viking looked at her with blue, blue eyes. He frowned and gripped her chin with his fingers, forcing her to pay attention.

"Jillian, you're scaring the hell out of me. Breathe."

Startled, she complied. Breathed in and out several times until her head cleared. And relaxed a little as she surveyed her wrist, her fingers. Although she was a medical professional, Jillian hated being doctored herself. But she had to admit, grudgingly, that this man was pretty good at it. "I'm surprised you're not a veterinarian like Connor," she blurted at last.

"Me? Too much of a farmer at heart. I'd rather raise animals than patch them up all day long. But you end up having to learn some of this stuff because a vet's not always handy. Neither is a doctor."

"Well, thanks for patching me up. And I guess I should thank you for not letting me drown."

"I'm just glad I was in time."

He got up, rather abruptly she thought, and checked the fire. As if he suddenly didn't want to look at her. Jillian felt her face heat and pain stabbed her heart again. She sighed and tried to change the subject. "How did you get all the way out here, anyway? You said you didn't have a car."

James didn't answer. Just as she decided to repeat the question, he knelt by the duffle bag and started rifling through it. "I promised you some clothes, doc. Let's see what we can do."

By the time help arrived, Jillian was dressed. Sort of. All the clothing in the duffle bag belonged to Connor. The jeans were far too large to be of any real use, so she ignored them. The thick flannel shirt hung just past her knees once she had struggled into it. She'd been forced to let James fasten the buttons and roll the sleeves while she fumed. Her wrist was throbbing and her usually slender fingers felt as thick and ungainly as bananas, useless for anything requiring fine motor skills. She tried to put socks on herself but soon threw them down, swearing.

"Here, let me." James picked up the big pair of woolen socks and eased them onto her as if she was a child. They went up to her knees, meeting the shirt. He pulled a sling from the first-aid kit and arranged her arm more comfortably, then tucked the blanket back around her just as Connor and Zoey drove up with Birkie.

Chapter Twenty-five

There was no hospital in Dunvegan, and the entire medical clinic would have fit into the livestock wing of the North Star Animal Hospital. In the cramped waiting room, James voiced his opinion that maybe Jillian should be taken to the city for proper treatment, but Birkie just patted his hand and smiled.

"Lowen and Beverly Miller are excellent doctors. I've known them for years."

Connor looked around from behind Zoey, who was sitting in his lap. "Give yourself some credit for being a pretty good medic yourself, James. They took an X-ray of Jillian's wrist and decided to plaster right over what you'd already done. Lowen said he couldn't improve on how well those bones were set."

James said nothing, just kept watching the door, feeling his patience wearing thin with waiting. He wanted to see Jillian. Period. He knew she was all right, yet he needed to see for himself, see that she was alive and well. It could be a long time before he got his fill of seeing her, of hearing her talk. Hell, of listening to her breathe. It had been close, much too close. The entire drive to Dunvegan he'd been thinking about what could have happened, and thanked the heavens over and over that he had been in time.

When the doctors emerged, they didn't have a chance to say a word before James was out of his chair and in the doorway of the treatment room. Jillian was sitting in a chair, dressed in green hospital scrubs and booties.

"New duds?"

"Yeah, they loaned me a set to go home in. I think I like the blue ones we've got at the clinic better."

"I don't know. These kind of bring out your eyes." They did, too. Her short blond hair stuck out in all directions; her faery features were obscured by bruising and swelling. James would bet money that she'd have two shiners by the next day, and still those sea-green eyes arrested him.

"Ha. I think I'd have to wear red to bring out my eyes at the moment."

"Jillian, we need to talk." He wasn't sure what he was going to say, how he was going to explain, but he knew he had to make a start somewhere.

"No." She shook her head carefully but kept a hand on it as if to brace it for the movement. "No, we don't. Please. I really do appreciate what you did for me tonight. Thanks for the underwater rescue and the first aid." She waved her cast at him. "The doctors say you're a natural. Guess you have another career to fall back on if you get tired of farming."

"Guess so. Look Jillian, I'm sorry that I—"

"*Don't.* I mean it." The light tone vanished from her voice, and her delicate mouth was set in a straight line.

Jesus Murphy, what am I doing? "I should have thought. It's not a good time. I'll wait a couple days until you've had a chance to rest. But I have things I need to say to you."

"No, James. You already said them. You're not interested and that's that. I don't want you to feel sorry for me and think you should hang around."

"It's not like that."

"No? Let me tell you what it's *not* going to be like. It seems to be very trendy to have sex and then just be friends, but I'm not wired that way. So let's just say a nice, clean goodbye, okay? End of story. And as for tonight, thanks again for what you did for me, but I have other people to help me now." She rose and headed for the door. Waited with folded arms for him to move out of the way. "I'm really tired, James, and I'm going home with Birkie now."

"I'll call you." He felt like the ground was crumbling away from under his feet.

"I don't want you to. Goodnight."

"But—" She had already brushed past him and gone out into the waiting room. Head reeling, James watched Zoey wrap a blanket around her and Connor offered an arm for support. With Birkie leading the way, the four of them headed out the door, and he followed.

"You coming, James?" Connor called over his shoulder. "We're just going to drop these gals off and then head home."

No. No thanks. He used mind speech because a hand seemed to have tightened around his throat. Jillian was alive. She was all right. And she was dismissing him.

The truck headed south on the main street. James turned and walked north. He could feel the wolf stirring within. The further he walked, the more restless, almost anxious the wolf became. *Stop it, you dumb animal. She doesn't want us. Get the picture?* The wolf settled reluctantly, and James could almost swear he heard it whimper. Hell, he felt like whimpering too. *This is wrong, this is all wrong. Shit!*

He reached the edge of town and kept walking until the paved road gave way to gravel. The thumbnail moon was out, a silver scythe in a field of stars. Farms became forest, and soon James left the roadway and entered the trees. He paused beneath a giant spruce, breathing in the rich scents of the woods at night. And called the Change to take him.

He had almost forgotten what it was like to Change on purpose, to be both wolf and man, aware and in control, to lope through the forest in his lupine form, liberated, exhilarated. He nosed along a game trail, picked up the spoor of deer and gave chase until he had brought down an old doe. He feasted on the hot, fresh meat, replenished his starved cells, fueled his rapid metabolism. Drank deep from a cold mountain-fed stream.

The sheer freedom should have brought him joy, but James's heart was a lead weight in his chest. He thought about heading back to Connor's farm. Instead, he made his way to Elk Point. On a great slab of stone overlooking the river valley, he laid his head on his paws with a very human sigh. He had no idea how to get Jillian to listen to him. Nor did he have any idea what he wanted to say to her if he could. All he could think was that it was over between them, that he had ended the relationship almost before it had begun. He should be glad for that, shouldn't he? She would be much better off without him, safer. *I didn't want to endanger her, didn't want her to become a target by hanging around with a Changeling. Looks like I got my goddamn wish.*

But how would he watch over her, protect her, when she didn't even want him around? And how would he be able to see her and not want her?

The moon dipped lower in the sky. The white wolf pointed his long muzzle toward it and howled, a long mournful drawn-out note that carried across the entire valley, echoing off the cliffs across the river. His battered heart found expression but not solace in the song, and he howled and howled again until all the real wolves in the area were compelled to join him.

Dawn gilded the eastern horizon when James finally walked up the long lane of the Macleod farm, his boots crunching in the gravel. He still didn't trust his wolfen self to stay away from Jillian so he'd returned to human form when he'd left Elk Point. He'd hoped that the lengthy walk on two legs would help him think things through, but he had only come to the same conclusion as before. He had completely ruined things with Jillian and wished he hadn't. Wished there had been some other way . . .

Heavy-hearted, he walked past the trees in front of Connor's house. Past the barns and the sheds and the corrals to the house, his house now, hidden in a thick stand of mixed poplar and spruce on the south side of the property. James closed the door behind him, still very much aware of the action. He wondered if someday he'd walk in and shut the door without even thinking about it. Would he ever be that comfortable in his human skin again?

It was cool but not cold in the house—it was June after all—but he built a fire anyway. Just for the ambience he supposed. *There's a real human attribute. One point for me.* In truth, he couldn't care less about how human he was, just as long as the damn wolf wasn't in control. That was all that really mattered, wasn't it? James sat heavily on the couch and stared at the fire for a long time, willing himself not to fall asleep. The very last thing he wanted to do was dream of Jillian again.

When the fire finally burned down to ashes and went out, James dreamed not of Jillian, but of Evelyn.

He was on his hands and knees weeding Connor's sprawling front garden. And suddenly she was next to him, planting tiny new bulbs among the tall purple irises and sprays of golden daylilies. In the arbitrary reality of dreams, it seemed completely normal for her to be there. Of course she was there. Where else would Evelyn be?

"What are you doing?" she asked him.

"Gardening."

"No, silly. What are you doing about Jillian?"

"Nothing. I ended it."

"Did she want to end it?"

"She does now."

"But she didn't before?"

"I never asked her."

"That's not very fair, James," she chided gently. "You haven't even given her a chance."

"I can't give her a chance. It's too dangerous."

"Dangerous for who, James?"

"Something could happen to her. Someone might find out what I am and then she'd be a target."

"You don't want what happened to me to happen to her."

"Not to her, not to anyone. I can't do that to someone again, Evie. Not again."

"You've always had that overactive sense of responsibility. Remember how I used to tease you about that?" She planted the last bulb and laid her hand over his. "What happened to me wasn't your fault, James. It was never your fault."

"I should have protected you. I should have been stronger, I should never—"

"Never have fallen in love with me? Never have tried to make a life with me?"

His heart twisted painfully within him. "At least you'd still be alive."

"Maybe. And maybe not. A million things could happen

to any one of us on any given day. If I had been hit by a bus or struck by lightning, would you shoulder the responsibility for that too?"

He didn't know how to answer.

"Are you sorry you loved me?"

"What? God, no. I . . . Evelyn, you were the most wonderful thing that ever happened to me."

"But when I died, it was the worst thing that ever happened to you. Maybe you would have been better off never knowing me."

"No." His voice was firm with conviction. "No, I can't be sorry for that, I can't wish that. We didn't have very long together, but every moment meant something to me."

She smiled at him then, that beautiful beaming smile of hers that seemed lit from within. "Well, silly, I'm not sorry for loving you, either. Think about that. And think about Jillian again. I like her. And you like her too."

"Jesus, Evelyn."

She laughed at his discomfort. "If you love Jillian, it doesn't take anything away from me, you know. I wish you'd give her a chance, give yourself a chance."

He shook his head. "I won't put her in harm's way like that."

"You keep saying that. You think that someone might hurt her because of what you are."

He nodded, then frowned when she shook her head.

"You haven't considered that Jillian spends a lot of time with Changelings already. She works for Connor, lives in his clinic, represents him every time she goes on a farm call, is associated with him by the entire community," Evelyn explained carefully as if to a child. "Not only that, she sat with Culley and Devlin at the Jersey Pub one night, and went shopping with Kenzie only last week. She eats at the

Finer Diner regularly, and Bill and Jessie invited her to their home. It seems to me that whether you're in her life or not, James, she's already surrounded by Changelings."

It had never even crossed his mind. How could he not have noticed, how could he have been so stupid? Someone could be out there, watching Jillian, homing in on her. Suddenly a new thought occurred to him, a way to head off the danger. "Evelyn, tell me who it was. Tell me who—" *Shot you. Murdered you.* He couldn't make himself say it aloud.

"I don't know everything, James. Only the things that are important."

"This *is* important." He hadn't seen the intruders. Didn't know if there were a dozen or only one. He couldn't even guess at a suspect. Neither could anyone else. The fire effectively destroyed any evidence the police might have used, and heavy rain washed away any trail so that even a Changeling could not follow. But what about Evelyn—had she seen, had she known? "This is *goddamn* important."

"Not as much as you think, hon. Vengeance won't bring you peace."

"I was thinking more of a preemptive strike. That'll bring me plenty of peace."

She shook her head. "Try mercy instead."

Mercy. James was appalled by the notion. How could she say such a—

She pointed to the ground. "Do you know what I've planted here?"

"Evelyn, please." He didn't want to talk about gardening, but her expression was serious. Reluctantly, he recalled the tiny bulbs she'd been working with. "Um, crocuses?"

"Lily of the valley. Lots and lots of it. Tell me what you think of that."

For her sake, he tried. "I guess those will look nice here, but it's already mid-summer. It'll take a long time before these little bulbs really take hold, maybe another year before there are any blossoms." James considered. "Connor will like it, though. Lord knows he needs flowers that come up by themselves. I just don't understand how he can be so great with animals and so terrible with plants. Zoey, now, there's hope for her but she's busy—"

"It's not for Connor and Zoey, hon. I planted these especially for you. Don't you know what it means? You used to know a lot about flowers and their language. You said your grandmother taught you."

"She did." In fact, he had used that long-ago knowledge to compose the bouquet for Jillian. He searched his mind and came up blank. "I can't seem to remember this one."

"Lily of the valley means the "return of happiness." That's why I picked it for you, James. It's time. Your time."

"Evelyn, I—"

He awakened then, to find the morning sun gilding the stones on the cold fireplace and his face wet. *God. Dear God.* He felt off-balance, both comforted and shaken. Part of him wanted to linger in the glow of the dream, and the other part wanted to get to work on something, anything, that would ground him. Eventually the desire for solid reality won out, and James forced himself to get up and get moving.

Still, the effects of the dream lingered. Frequently throughout the day, he found himself having to run a sleeve over his eyes. It had been so good, so damn good to see Evelyn, to see her whole and smiling. To see her long dark hair glinting in the sunshine, see her in her favorite gardening clothes—faded jeans and one of his shirts with the sleeves rolled up a half dozen times. A smudge of dirt on her face and laughter in her dark eyes. Just hearing her voice had eased something inside him.

Later, when the initial glow had worn off, he remembered that she'd spoken about Jillian and a terrible suspicion formed. *Please don't let my wolf have anything to do with this.* That's all he needed was to have his furry alter ego try to further its goals by invading his dreams, by planting images of the one person he was most likely to listen to. It couldn't do that, could it? What if the comforting dream, in which Evelyn was so vital and alive, was tainted? Fixed? Nothing more than lupine propaganda?

Christ, I'm getting paranoid. He *was* the wolf and the wolf was him. Still, his animal side had acted on its own more than once, and there was no denying it was totally devoted to Jillian. Maybe his wolfen self was really his own subconscious—and the dream just a product of his own desires.

And maybe he was losing his goddamn mind . . .

Luckily there was no lack of farmwork to bury himself in, no shortage of tasks big and small to occupy his time and his thoughts. He spent most of the day plowing under the entire section of old alfalfa to enrich the soil, and had passed Connor's house only briefly. Hadn't noticed anything different. But late in the afternoon, after he brought grain to the horses in the front paddock, he caught a glimpse of something *white* in the gardens flanking Connor's steps. Mounds of white, low to the ground, almost like snow heaped amongst the sword-like iris leaves and the clusters of yellow daylilies. *What the hell?* Furious that his black-thumbed brother had carelessly dumped something on the garden, James stalked over to see—and the empty feed buckets dropped from his hands.

Lily of the valley was everywhere. Barely eight inches

tall, the tiny white bells on delicate stems massed above broad emerald leaves, crowding between the irises and the daylilies, spilling out of the garden in such abundance that the little plants were even coming up through the cracks in the walkway, pushing through the gravel driveway, marching across the lawn. Lily of the valley was a spring flower and preferred shade—yet the miniature plants sat in the hot June sun looking fresh and dewy, as out of place as roses in a desert.

Stunned, James sank to his knees between the forgotten buckets. He had worked the soil between the neglected daylilies and irises by hand, knew for a fact, *knew*, there were no other bulbs of any kind in the garden. He had weeded only two days ago. The rich dark earth had been bare when he was done. There had been nothing there, nothing at all.

Evelyn.

He remained motionless for a long time, not daring to move, hardly daring to breathe, in case the beautiful apparition vanished. It wasn't until a breeze picked up and wafted among the diminuitive blossoms, making them bob and sway, that James ventured to touch one. He could feel the tiny stalk with its bell-like blooms, cool and fresh. Real. Suddenly he leaned into the flowers, gathering a great armful of them. Clutching them to his chest, he bent his head and inhaled great lungfuls of the scent again and again. He crushed handfuls of the delicate bells to his face where their essence mingled with tears. The delicate sweet scent seemed to wrap itself around his aching heart like a healing balm, bringing a powerful peace.

James sat amid the blossoms for a long, long time. Calm. Clearheaded. And thankful beyond all words. Thankful for the affirmation of his dream, grateful to have seen Evelyn whole and happy. Thankful to know that his rebellious wolfen side could not possibly have conjured this.

A return to happiness. Evelyn said she had chosen these flowers to convey that message to him. As he contemplated that, a number of ideas suddenly fell together in ordered sequence like tumblers in a lock about to open. James thought of the wolf, *his* wolf, and its efforts to embrace survival whether he wanted to live or not. Remembered Birkie's words, that survival meant going on with life in all ways. Recalled Connor's certainty that it was too late to turn back, to turn away from being human. James had been so angry, so frustrated with all of them. So resistant to everyone and everything.

Worst of all, he had resisted the one person, right in front of him, who had been courageous enough to move forward with her life and make something of it after a terrible and traumatic ordeal. Jillian was not just surviving, but thriving. How could he do less? *A return to happiness.* James knew suddenly, clearly, that it was time for him to fully return to life and embrace all that it meant.

He had to find Jillian, had to find a way to undo the damage he'd done.

"The doctor said four weeks of rest. You've barely had one."

"I can't see myself missing four weeks of work. That's too much."

"That's the verdict, hon. You heard it yourself after the CAT scan." Birkie put a fragrant cup of herbal tea on the bedside table. "Nothing but a lot of rest is going to improve that noggin of yours. And even when you start to get better, any overexertion is going to bring the symptoms back full force."

Jillian sighed. "I know the drill. I've had a concussion before, a few years ago. From the attack."

"And you also know that having a concussion before is exactly why you can't expect to bounce back in a couple of days from this one."

"It's just so darn hard to do nothing. Lying here, lying still, my mind works just fine. I feel fine and think I should get up and do something."

"You are doing something—you're whining." Birkie grinned. "First time in over a week. That tells me you're starting to heal. But you were paper-white and sweating after the ride over here yesterday. I'm still not convinced you should have left my place just yet."

Jillian had had her own doubts about her decision. She'd traveled by ambulance to the city for the CAT scan, sleeping through most of the ride there and back. A little dizzy, a little headache, but not too bad. After that, she'd expected riding over to the clinic in Birkie's truck would be a snap, but she hadn't taken into account the fact that she would be sitting up. The dizziness and nausea were so intense, she'd had to close her eyes most of the way. And once at the clinic, she'd been forced to head straight to her bed to sleep it off. "You've been wonderful to me, but I really wanted to be here. It's home now."

"Well, I understand that a person needs to be in their own familiar surroundings with their own stuff. And at least I can look in on you while I'm here during the day. I admit I worry about you at night, though."

"All I'm going to do is snore, I promise. You won't be missing anything but having to wait on me."

"Ha. There was a real burden. You didn't need any watching after that first night, and you slept most of the whole first week. It's not like you demanded heated towels and chocolates on your pillow."

"Chocolates on my pillow was an option? I wish I'd known."

"Drink your tea, hon, and we'll see about the chocolate. By the way, I've been putting your mail on the table. You have quite a stack built up."

"Bless you and thank you. I'd forgotten all about it. Although I imagine it's mostly bills." Jillian sat up carefully. Sipped at the tea. "You know what really bothers me? I still can't figure out how I managed to get a stupid concussion. Believe me, the air bag went off. I didn't hit anything."

"Maybe not, but the air bag certainly hit you. You know, I'll bet you drive with your hands high on the wheel, don't you?"

"What?"

"Say, about two and ten o'clock. Add to that the fact that you're on the short side like me. Bang, the air bag goes off and the impact probably drove your wrist right to your head. Broke the wrist, nearly cracked the skull."

"Have you been watching reruns of CSI again?"

"You bet. But the Millers said so too. And we found out later that there was a recall notice for that particular year and model of truck because the air bag was discovered to be too powerful. Let me tell you, Connor had that truck over to the dealership the next day to have that bag ripped out and replaced. He feels terrible that this happened to you."

"I'm sure being hit by the air bag was better than hitting the tree. I should feel bad about Connor's truck. I must have banged it up pretty good."

"James says you banged yourself up pretty good on the undercarriage. Lowen says that could account for the concussion as well, plus you've got nine stitches in three places to show for it."

"Nine? Huh, I thought I counted seven." She fingered gingerly through her hair.

"You can count again this afternoon when Bev comes by to take them out."

Jillian closed her eyes and eased back down on the bed. The urge to get up and do something had abruptly passed. Not only was all her energy gone, but she couldn't even remember what it was like to have any. Her collarbone was throbbing again too, but she reminded herself to be thankful it was just bruised and not broken. Although it was tough to remember that when pain woke her in the night. "I feel really bad that Connor's going to be shorthanded."

"You're the one that's shorthanded. That cast still itching?"

Jillian surveyed her wrist and its fluorescent-pink casing. "Nope, not today. At least not yet."

"Good. Don't worry about Connor, he'll be just fine. He managed for several years before you showed up. Ran full tilt, but managed. Besides, it won't hurt for him to gain a renewed appreciation for you. We're finished with calving season until January rolls around, so that takes a lot of the pressure off. And James has been riding along to assist with big projects like herd checks and such. Speaking of James, he asked about you again this morning. He still wants to see you."

Jillian knew he had phoned Birkie's house at least once a day, sometimes twice. What was it going to take for him to get the message? And how long could she hold out? She opened her eyes and looked at her friend. "I don't want to see him, Birkie. I just can't. It's hard enough to be firm about this, you don't know how hard it is."

"I think I have a pretty good idea, hon." She sat on the edge of the bed and seemed to consider something. "You know, I haven't said anything to you before, but perhaps I should have. James cares about you a lot, much more than you know. Much more than he knows, I suspect."

Jillian automatically shook her head and was instantly sorry. She froze in place until the wave of nausea subsided and the pounding in her skull faded. "I gotta quit doing that," she squeaked.

"Here, let me help you with the tea. It'll help settle things."

The tea soothed her stomach immediately, which didn't surprise her. Birkie's concoctions were always effective, although Jillian had given up asking what was in them. The older woman rattled off Latin plant names as easily as if they were ordinary baking ingredients.

"James will be back you know, hon. He's not a man to give up once he knows what he wants."

"And you think he wants me." She didn't dare entertain the notion that it might be true. She had closed that particular door, locked it and piled mental furniture against it. Didn't want to open it again. "Dammit, he dumped me, Birkie, dumped me and didn't even tell me why. It hurt a helluva lot. It still hurts. Why would I want to give him the chance to do that again?"

"Men are funny creatures. They do the most ridiculous things sometimes for the most noble of reasons. He might have been trying to let you go because he believed it would be better for you, even though he wanted you very much. Being protective."

Jillian stared. "You've got to be kidding. *Protective?* What is this, the Middle Ages? No wonder he sent such a strange bunch of flowers to do his talking for him." Her voice rose enough to send nail-like spikes of pain through her head, but the surge of anger wouldn't let her stop. "And protect me from what? I should have been protected from *him*. Why didn't he tell me to my face that he didn't want a relationship? And he sure could have mentioned it before I slept with him." She swore then, both from fury and pain. "If James really had some stupid archaic notion of protecting me, he could have brought up his concerns and discussed them with me so I could make my own damn decision." Jillian sank back on the bed, utterly spent and unable to tell which hurt more, her heart or her head. Her stomach roiled treacherously.

"Easy there, hon, it's all true. Every word of it. Now don't you think you'd feel better if you told him exactly what you just told me?"

Yeah. Yeah, she probably would. She'd tried to be firm and reasonable at the doctors' office. Even with her heart in tatters, she'd tried to walk away—okay, more like limp away—with some dignity. It was obvious now that it wasn't going to be enough. James refused to stay away. Still, she was far from ready for a confrontation. "Can't it wait until I'm vertical? I might want to punch him out and I just can't manage a proper Tae Kwon Do position lying down."

"You just let me know when you're ready. I'll try to hold him off until then, but I confess it hasn't been easy for me to shoo him away. He's hurting too."

"*He's* hurting? What did I ever do to *him*?" Jillian narrowed her eyes at her friend. "What is it you know that I don't? Has he been talking to you?"

"Not a single blessed word, hon. Haven't even seen his handsome face except the night of the accident. However, what I know is that James is a complicated man. There's a tender heart behind the thorny exterior. Things haven't been easy for him since his wife died."

Died? Jillian was silent for a long moment. "You said he had been married but I just assumed he was divorced. She died—that's so awful. Why didn't you tell me that before?"

"I guess because it was awful. Maybe I hoped it would come up when you and James were talking, that maybe he would say something and I wouldn't have to. Foolish of me, I know. But Evelyn was my niece, you see, and well, I guess I prefer to remember the happier things."

"Oh Birkie, I'm so sorry."

The older woman leaned over and squeezed Jillian's hand. "Thanks for that. Actually, I think you would have liked Evelyn. You remind me of her in some ways. It happened several years ago now, and most of us have made peace with it as best we could. Except James, that is. He still blames himself for it."

"Why? How . . . how did she die?"

"Murdered. Shot by an intruder in her own house. She was pregnant."

Jillian swallowed hard. There were no words for such an enormous tragedy, the terrible waste of a life, of two lives. And what had the loss done to James?

Birkie continued as if she had heard Jillian's thoughts. "James feels it's his fault for not being there. He was out moving cattle and arrived home to find her."

My God. "But how could he think it's his fault? He couldn't have known, couldn't have anticipated. Nobody expects something like that to happen, especially not in their own home. Did they . . . did they catch the murderer?"

"No." The older woman shook her head. "James was

shot too, when he entered the house. Didn't see who it was. Whoever did it walked away. And I think that made it even worse, for all of us."

Jillian understood that all too well. The men who'd attacked her had never been found either. It had taken a lot of counseling, a lot of hard work, to create some kind of closure when closure could not naturally be found. Eventually she had discovered a measure of peace within herself, but there would always be moments that had to be managed, like that flashback on the trail below Elk Point. She found herself wondering what it was like to be James. Were there moments that still haunted him?

Chapter Twenty-six

Douglas didn't know what to make of his father's sudden improvement, but he was grateful for it. The morning after the episode with the lady vet, Roderick Harrison had awakened in his right mind—and stayed there. He hadn't had an episode since. No dementia, no loss of memory, no cognitive lapses. Nothing. The doctors were extremely impressed, although baffled. Some chalked it up to the new medication. The Alzheimer's seemed to be in some kind of remission, so much so that other doctors questioned the original diagnosis. No one looking at the old man would guess that the mere month before he had mistaken his only son for a hired hand.

Roderick slid easily back into the routine of overseeing the ranch. He spent increasing amounts of time with old Varley Smith, the ranch manager, which wasn't surprising—they'd been friends for as long as Douglas could remember. His father even went to a cattle auction, winning a good-looking group of replacement heifers. He celebrated by joining Varley and a few of the hands at the Shamrock Bar, a place he hadn't gone into in years. Not since the Alzheimer's had begun to take hold. "I'll look out for him," Varley had whispered to Douglas before they drove off. And he had, as Douglas knew he would. They'd returned after midnight with Roderick only pleasantly drunk. The next day, he was in a sterling mood, eating a full breakfast with gusto and hurrying out to take delivery of the heifers he'd bought.

Normal. Ordinary. Everything just as it had always been before Roderick's mind had begun to play tricks on him. The full moon came and went, and the wild episodes that so often accompanied it failed to materialize. Roderick remained himself. Douglas didn't know how long this would last, but he was grateful for the respite. Especially since the mental frenzy that once so frequently gripped his father seemed to have migrated into his own brain. Even Jack Daniels hadn't been able to keep it at bay. White wolves chased Douglas in his dreams, stalked him from behind hay bales and outbuildings during the day. He'd nearly screamed aloud yesterday afternoon when he caught a glimpse of something white moving behind the house. Turned out to be just sheets on the clothesline, put there by the housekeeper. Douglas had been so unnerved, he'd spent the rest of the day drinking himself into a stupor in his room. Slept like the dead.

There was sunlight streaming in his window when he finally woke, and the clock on the nightstand said 8:39. His father would have something to say about that, no doubt. Roderick would have been up, dressed, had his coffee and checked the livestock by six. Still, Douglas didn't particularly care. His brain felt somewhat fuzzy but he wasn't on edge. Was relaxed for the first time in days. He drank a tumbler of Jack Daniels before he got out of bed to make sure he stayed in that mellow frame of mind. By the time he had a shower and dressed, he felt so bombproof that if a dozen wolves suddenly parachuted into the front yard, he doubted he'd be able to raise an eyebrow. He negotiated the route to the kitchen, just as Varley burst in the back door.

"Rod's gone."

"What?" No, no, he was feeling too good for this. Much too good. "Gone where?"

"I don't know. He took my pickup."

"Well, maybe he just felt like going for a ride. He was okay this morning, right?" He willed Varley to say yes.

"Well, yeah." Varley seemed to relax a little. "Yeah, he was just fine when I saw him earlier. Sorry to panic, Dougie. I guess I'm not used to him driving, not since we had to take the keys away from him last year. He's probably just headed into town."

It made sense. His father used to like to drive into Spirit River a couple times a week just to get the mail if nothing else. "Maybe you could take my vehicle and check. If I go, he'll just think I'm nursemaiding him and get all pissy. I really hate to spoil it if he's enjoying himself." Douglas was pleased with that last little brainwave. In reality, he didn't feel up to facing the bright sunlight out there, never mind his father.

"Good point, good point. I'll see if I can catch up to him, maybe talk him into going to the Diamond for coffee and pie. We used to go there a lot, give the waitresses a hard time." Varley winked. "Don't worry, Dougie, I'll find him and ride herd on him without him knowing it. Let you know how it goes."

Douglas was relieved when the ranch manager left, more relieved when he squinted through the window and saw his own pickup heading down the lane to the highway. He wondered if he should have another drink or just go back to bed. Maybe both. With his father in Spirit River, and Varley looking after him, Douglas could count on having the rest of the day to relax. He felt his mood lift at the prospect, and suddenly he felt like making some eggs, no, an omelet. A Spanish omelet, by God, with a steak on the side. He whistled as he searched the fridge for ingredients.

Roderick Harrison had often used his pickup truck as a blind. If a hunter was patient enough, waited long enough, his quarry would come to regard the vehicle as part of the landscape and ignore it. He'd shot many a coyote, sometimes a deer, from the open window while parked downwind near the edge of the timber that covered the northern section of his ranch. The method would earn him a hefty fine anywhere else, but it was perfectly legal on his own land.

The blind principle worked equally well when he wasn't hunting, just wanting to observe. It was a good way to watch testy mother cows with new calves, or get a count of the elk herd that sometimes wandered into the south quarter to steal hay.

He wasn't observing cattle or elk this time. Roderick had angled Varley's truck to give himself a clear view of his target, just a few hundred yards away. In addition, he'd parked the pickup between two rusted-out trucks in the shade of an abandoned building, a near-perfect location for reconnaissance. He had a sleeping bag with him and enough food for two days, but he wasn't going to need it. Within the first couple of hours, Roderick was able to confirm what he had suspected since Dr. Descharme's visit to his ranch.

There was a werewolf at the North Star Animal Hospital.

"The auras give them away every damn time," he murmured as he watched a tall dark-haired man leave the building again. There were other people in the parking lot, but their auras were thin and pale, almost watery by comparison. Light yellow mostly, misty white or green. One old farmer would probably have been horrified to learn his aura was pastel pink. But the tall man's aura was that vivid blue found at the heart of a lightning bolt. It radiated from him, pulsed with energy like a live thing. Dr. Connor Macleod was definitely a werewolf. But to Roderick's amazement, the veterinarian wasn't the only one. By the end of the day, five more werewolves had come and gone, two females and three males.

The old man had seen enough. He was just reaching for the ignition key when another arrival caught his eye. A big man, tall like the vet, but more powerfully built. And blond. Roderick stared, focusing and refocusing the lenses of his binoculars, his bowels turning to ice water. "It can't be. Jesus God, it just can't be."

James Macleod had come back from the dead.

The lab tests said *wolf*.

Jillian stared at the papers in her hand and let the rest of the mail slide to the floor. The DNA results on the white hair samples revealed pure, unadulterated wolf. Jillian's theories of a wolf-dog hybrid vanished like a soap bubble, and she was left with the uncomfortable knowledge that a genuine *Canis Lupus* had somehow found its way into her apartment.

Maybe she shouldn't have been so insistent about leaving Birkie's house.

She reread the letter that Ian Craddock had enclosed with the results. He complimented her on the quality of samples she had sent for testing. Yet, although the DNA was unquestionably one hundred percent wolf, his lab had been completely unable to determine which sub-species it belonged to. Despite its pure white coloration, which would seem to indicate perhaps an arctic wolf, the genetic material most closely matched the gray wolf. *But not completely.* Craddock said he had given her a hefty discount on the large bill because of this, although she suspected it was actually because she had been a favored student. But whatever her former teacher's reasoning for the reduction, she was too distracted to enjoy the economic good news.

She'd met a wild wolf. But why would it approach her, why would it be so affectionate—and protective? She supposed it could have been raised by humans, might have learned to look at humans as pack members. But if she saw it again, she'd have to remind herself that it was wild, and wild things always reverted to their true nature. Didn't they? Animal handlers the world over concurred that to assume a wild animal was tame was not only disrespectful of the animal but also downright dangerous.

But it was *her* wolf, her friend. The one who had saved her. When she thought of the attack now, it wasn't the pain and terror she remembered most. It was the shining white shape that emerged from the darkness and chased the men away. A massive wolf, its snowy fur stroked by starlight, a creature so beautiful that she was certain she was dreaming. Until it licked her face.

The wolf had lain beside her and kept her warm. She had thought she was going to die and was so grateful not to be alone. She remembered that she had started crying then, and the wolf had lapped away her tears. It had whined in its throat, and there was near-human expression in its vivid blue eyes. *It was sad for me. It cared, I know that it cared about me.* The results from a DNA test, or any other test, wouldn't change her certainty of that.

I guess that's my answer. I've never been afraid of the wolf before, and I'm not going to start now. Maybe I won't run outside looking for it, and maybe I'd prefer it didn't visit me in my apartment, but if I see it again, I'm not going to be afraid.

So far, though, the wolf hadn't returned. Not inside the clinic, and nowhere else that Jillian was aware of. But the creature knew where she lived. Did it wander around outside at night? Had it watched over her as she came and went on farm calls and errands, when she came home late from visiting with Birkie? Or had it gone on its way—wherever that was? Maybe it had. After all, it hadn't shown up when she had the accident. Had James scared it off?

The last time she'd seen the wolf, it was lying on her couch, and what it was doing there remained a mystery. It was the same night that James surprised her in her apartment, and she could only conclude that he must have left a door open somewhere. Jillian couldn't imagine any other way that the great white wolf had gained entry to the building. And how had it gotten out?

"I feel like I'm missing something." Did James know about the white wolf? Had he seen it? Come to think of it, the wolf had reentered her life at roughly the same time she'd met James. Was that coincidence—or connection? She really should ask James about it, see what he knew, but that could be difficult when she didn't want to talk to the man, didn't want to see him ever again.

The phone rang as if on cue.

"Jillian, we need to talk," James began.

"Whatever happened to 'hi, how are you?'"

"You keep hanging up, so now I'm cutting to the chase. Look, I have things to say to you."

If she was honest with herself, she wanted to hear them. She really did. But she didn't dare. "We already had this conversation, James. I don't think it's a good idea to repeat it."

"I think it's—"

"Goodnight, James." She put the receiver down. It was simple self-defense, she reasoned with herself. So why did she feel so guilty? Suddenly she banged her fist on the phone. "Damn it!" She hadn't asked him about the wolf.

Annoyed, she picked up the mail from the floor. It had taken her three days to get around to looking at it. She had barely opened half the envelopes, but she'd had enough for one day. She piled it back on the table next to a stack of overdue wolf mythology books. She sighed. She hated to ask Birkie or Zoey to take them to the library—her friends already did so much for her—maybe she could ask Caroline instead? The young veterinary assistant often stopped by to ask if there was anything Jillian needed.

"Energy. What I really need is energy. Isn't there someplace I can order some? Have it delivered like pizza?" Sudden fatigue had Jillian sliding into a chair, feeling like the gravity in the room had increased fourfold. It was frustrating, but she was learning to relax and wait for her energy to return, to have faith that it would return. It might take a few minutes or a few hours, but after a little rest, her energy would come back. If nothing else, having a concussion was a lesson in patience. Whether she wanted more patience or not. Jillian sighed, pulled a book from the stack and began turning pages. An hour later, she was still there, engrossed in werewolf legends from France and Spain.

When she finally looked up, dusk had given way to night. She stood and stretched—very slowly and carefully—then made her way to the fridge where a quick check of the freezer revealed an appalling lack of ice cream. No problem. There was some in the staff lunchroom, and maybe some pudding or custard as well. Her stomach was touchy these days, favoring bland and easy-to-eat items. The ongoing nausea had frightened her at first. But the doctors had been thorough in their follow-up exams, determining that the queasy stomach was linked to the dizziness she could naturally expect as she recovered, not to something scary like a blood clot on the brain.

Jillian pulled her comfy old bathrobe around her shoulders and headed down the hallway. It had been a hot day and the shadows on the tile floor were deep and cool. Easy on the eyes, too. She could imagine the headlines: *Mole woman subsists on ice cream. Gains 500 pounds in the dark.* Well maybe not. She'd noticed the past couple of days that her jeans were loose around the middle. *Mole woman discovers new wonder diet—concussion and ice cream.*

Just as she neared the kitchen, there was movement at the end of the dark hall. She blinked and held her breath as a large pale object resolved itself into a canine shape. An enormous canine shape, but no dog moved with such supple grace. It was the white wolf—and it was heading in the opposite direction. She held her breath as she watched, and even at this distance, even in the shadows, she could see the orchestrated movement of muscle under the snowy coat. *Omigod.* How long had the wolf been here? Although it surely must have been lingering outside her door, it seemed unaware that she was now in the hallway. She took a step forward in spite of herself as the animal disappeared around a corner. It was in the livestock wing.

Jillian hesitated only a moment. Then she was hurrying—gingerly, and with a hand trailing the wall to steady herself—down the hall as fast as her condition would permit. She rounded the corner and regained sight of the wolf just as it bounded silently to the top of the bales she'd stacked against the far wall. It leapt across an impossible distance to land neatly inside the loft door. Sheer surprise kept her frozen for an entire second. And then she was running for the ladder. At least she intended to run. The best she could manage was an embarrassing sort of rapid shuffle. Breathing hard, she clambered awkwardly up the ladder, favoring the arm with the cast on it and trying to be quiet all at the same time.

Dizzy from the effort, Jillian topped the rungs and peered into the loft. It was easy to spot the wolf, even in the dark. It would have no trouble spotting her either, but luckily it wasn't looking in her direction. She was trying to catch her breath and decide what to do next when she became aware of a fine vibration running through the metal ladder rungs under her hands, her feet. Her eyebrows rose as she began to feel it in her teeth too. The vibration was subtle, not an earth tremor but finer, as if the ladder was being bombarded with sound. But there was no sound. . . .

She glanced up to see if the wolf had also noticed, and was astonished to see the massive animal begin to shimmer like a mirage. Its snowy fur gleamed with strange bluish light. A breeze picked up, swirling bits of straw and dust into a lazy vortex around the creature. Jillian could feel the cool, dry air on her face now, and with it came the tang of ozone. Her skin tingled, the hairs lifted on the back of her neck. Through it all, the wolf stood perfectly still, even when blue sparks danced in the air around it. Suddenly the animal vanished completely. In its place stood a tall, powerful man. The breeze stopped, as did the vibration. The last of the sparks sizzled into the straw and winked out. And Jillian stared, open-mouthed, as James Macleod shook himself, stretched, then walked over to the window at the far end of the loft.

She struggled in vain to make sense of what her eyes were telling her. Then backed slowly down the ladder, praying James would not hear her. If it *was* James. When she reached the floor, she half-stumbled, looking over her shoulder as she walked. Thank God that she was still in her slippers—while her footfalls were clumsy, they were at least silent. She hoped. Which was more than she could say for her heart. It was pounding loudly in her chest, so loud that she could hear it herself. Jillian drew air in great shaky gulps that threatened to become hiccups until she was forced to stuff the sleeve of her bathrobe over her mouth to suppress the sound. Nausea and dizziness from the exertion nearly overwhelmed her. She paused to lean on the wall frequently for support as she made her unsteady way back to her apartment.

Chapter Twenty-seven

Something was sparkling as Jillian opened her eyes. Blinking, she realized the morning sun had caught the little crystals in the dream catcher. Or was it afternoon sun? She had no idea what time it was and didn't feel well enough to care. Jillian lay in bed and watched the light bounce around the wall in bright colors. Amber, green, purple, red, blue. *Blue.* Blue sparkles, blue *sparks.* There had been blue sparks last night when the white wolf turned into James Macleod.

That had been one wild and crazy hallucination. She knew it couldn't have been a dream, at least not completely—she had only to look over at the furniture stacked in front of her door. The dresser, the table, even the magazine rack. And how dumb was that? The last weighed, what? Two pounds, maybe three? But she'd been desperate for anything she could get her hands on, anything that might keep out whatever she thought she had seen in the loft. And when the adrenaline had finally subsided, she'd paid heavily for the overexertion. She'd spent half the night in the bathroom throwing up and the other half trying to rally the strength to get to her bed.

She was still paying for the night's activity. She felt drained, ill. A headache maintained a steady throb just behind her eyes. And it didn't help to know that she'd brought it on herself. "I have a moderate to serious concussion. Birkie told me not to overdo it, Connor told me not to overdo it, Lowen and Bev both told me not to overdo it, even the clinician who ran the CAT scan told me not to overdo it," she lectured herself. "So what do I do? Go running around the clinic in the dark. Of course I saw weird things."

One niggling question remained, however. Was everything she saw a hallucination? The DNA tests on the white hair from her couch had proven not only that a white wolf existed but that it had been inside her apartment. Had the wolf found its way back into the clinic last night? Had she followed a real wolf or a dream wolf? But if it was a real wolf she followed, why did the event suddenly turn into complete fantasy? And at what point?

That leap, for instance. Jillian worked it out in her head. The livestock area was huge, and the span between the stacked bales and the loft door had to be at least thirty-five feet, maybe more. No wolf could jump that. A tiger might, she supposed, but even a big cat would have to work at it. A wolf? No chance. Therefore what she saw in the livestock wing could be no more real than what she saw in the loft.

"Duh! What did I expect after racing down the hallway? And I can't believe I climbed up that stupid ladder. I'm lucky I didn't pass out and fall." And as for the wolf turning into James, that was no stretch of the imagination. She had just talked to him, was just thinking about him, and then she had read all those stupid stories. "Therefore, none of it was real. I didn't see the wolf in the hallway, I just thought I did." She didn't much like the idea of seeing things, though. She got up carefully and headed to the bathroom, stared at herself in the mirror. Her reflection looked more tired than usual, disheveled, but not particularly crazy. At least she didn't seem to be foaming at the mouth or rolling her eyes back in her head. "Lycanthropy. Werewolves." She tried out the words, watched for changes in the mirror. Saw none. "Guess I'm still sane, even if I'm seeing things. Well, mostly sane." Her head pounded while she brushed her teeth, and she decided to forego a shower. For a moment she thought about breakfast, but her stomach refused to discuss the subject unless it involved something creamy and frozen.

By the time she climbed back into bed, she was resigned to staying there for the rest of the day. Jillian hoped Birkie would stop by in the afternoon. It would be good to have a friend to talk to, although she might not mention that part about the ladder. *Please God, let her bring ice cream.* She moaned aloud as she remembered all the stuff piled in front of her door. "Dear God, skip the ice cream. Please let her bring a forklift."

Roderick Harrison was just as Douglas remembered him. Just as devoted to the Pine Point Ranch as ever. Just as hardworking and active as always. Just as bullheaded and bossy too. But gradually it became apparent that Roderick was also as fixated as ever on something Douglas would rather forget.

It began as a stray comment over dinner. "Wolf tracks in the northwest pasture, Dougie. We've got to keep an eye on the stock."

It probably didn't mean anything more than that, Douglas told himself sternly, but still, his stomach clenched and he found himself unable to finish the meal. When he retreated to his room, it took a tall glass of Jack Daniels to help him calm down. More to ensure he didn't dream that night.

It was mid-morning before Douglas finally made his way downstairs again. He was on his way to the kitchen, intent on putting something gentle in his stomach, maybe poached eggs and toast. Maybe just toast. Something to soak up the acid so he could have a drink to start the day.

"Dad?" He was startled to find his father still in the house. Shouldn't he be out riding the goddamn range or something? Roderick didn't appear to notice him though. He was standing in the living room, staring at the collection of family photos on the stone mantel. There was still a photo of Douglas's mother there, a tall, pretty woman, her hair dark red and wavy just like her son's. Douglas had always liked the picture but now wished he'd followed his instincts months ago and put it away. He took a careful step backward, then another, hoping to exit the room, but it was too late.

"Corena was a good woman." Roderick continued to stare at her photo. He was still as stone with his hands at his sides, but they were clenched hard enough to make the veins stand out. "It wasn't her fault, not really. Damn werewolves, they laid claim to her. I fought to keep her with me, but they claimed her and in the end, they got her. I should never have listened to her. I should've shot every damn one of them when I had the chance. She'd still be alive if I'd done that."

"Dad, I—"

"They're back, you know. We didn't finish the job and now they're back."

"Goddammit, Dad, give it up already," Douglas burst out. The fleeting thought crossed his mind that if he'd had that drink, he would have been mellow enough to keep his mouth shut, but maybe he'd been silent too long, much too long. "I'm sick of hearing about your fucking werewolves. You already shot two people that I know of, and God only knows how many others." He was shouting now.

Roderick roared back. "I was protecting this family. I tried to protect your mother, even after she had you, and then I tried to protect you, too."

"Protect me? You took a fourteen-year-old kid along to commit a fucking *murder*. What kind of protection was that?" Douglas paused and sucked in air. It was enough time for something his father had said to sink in. "What do you mean, *even after she had me*?"

"I raised you as my own. I didn't ask any questions. We couldn't have kids and God help me, I wanted a son, someone I could leave the ranch to."

He stared at his father for several seconds. Jesus, Mary, and Joseph, the man must be having a relapse. He walked over and took his father's arm, and when he spoke, it was with a lowered voice. "Dad, it's me, Douglas. Your son. And I have a sister, remember? Rosa."

"We adopted Rosa. Corena had a young niece out east that got herself in trouble, so we took on the baby, pretended she was ours. It was easy enough, she had red hair like your mother. No one was ever supposed to know. Even Rosa doesn't know. Then a few years later your mother came up pregnant with you." Roderick shook his head from side to side, still staring at the photo. "It was a damn hard pill to swallow. God, I didn't talk to her, couldn't even look at her. But after you were born, I thought maybe we could work things out."

Douglas let go of his father's arm then. This wasn't sounding like a recurrence of the Alzheimer's, not at all. In fact, it didn't sound like any episode his father had ever had. "What are you saying here? That I'm not your son? Are you trying to make me believe my mother was a cheat?"

"It wasn't her fault, not really. It was the damn were-wolves. She couldn't help herself, couldn't resist them." The old man turned and faced his son, his eyes sad but steady. "We had an argument one night, and she went out. I found out later that she'd met some of them wolf people in a bar, started hanging around with them behind my back every chance she got. I didn't know then just how evil they were but I knew it would end badly."

"What? *What?*" Douglas sank into a chair then, his legs rubbery and his heart beating against his ribs like an animal trying to escape a cage. It was possible that his father had slipped into some bizarre hallucination, some new neurosis. Not just possible, but plausible. Maybe an aneurysm, a stroke? Yet Rod appeared calm, his color good and his breathing steady. His words were clear, distinguishable. Douglas looked for some clue in his father's eyes, some subtle tip-off that Rod had regressed or fallen prey to some new ailment. He found none. "What the fuck are you saying?"

"She left us for one of them, Dougie. She left us to *become* one of them. She wanted to take you with her, make you one of them too, but I couldn't let her do that." He turned back to the photo and spoke more to himself than Douglas. "I couldn't let her."

"Don't hang up." He'd given up on any kind of traditional greeting. A couple dozen calls in a week had netted him nothing more than the click of the receiver on Jillian's end. "We need to talk."

"Please stop calling me."

The connection went dead. Again. James swore and nearly threw the cell phone out the window of the tractor cab, but at the last moment jammed it into his shirt pocket instead. He'd gotten the phone from Culley the day after the accident, resolving to be more prepared to protect Jillian in the future. After all, what if Birkie hadn't tuned in to his mental calls for help? What would he have done? Yet the cell phone sure wasn't helping him much now. Culley had regaled James with a mind-numbing array of available models and features. But what he really needed was a phone that could say the right words for him, words that would persuade Jillian to listen.

Were there any? Her fine features made her look faery-like, but Jillian Descharme was tough and strong and smart. He couldn't blame her for shutting him out. He'd been a complete moron and he'd hurt her. It was unforgivable, and yet he had to find a way to persuade her to give him a chance. Somehow.

He'd tried going in person. So far, knocking on her door hadn't yielded any better results than calling her. After the first time, the door no longer opened. She was ignoring him, and while that normally would have pissed him off, he was having a hard time holding onto his anger for more than a moment. In fact, what he felt was lonely. Sad. He missed her, so much so that he'd gone out running as the wolf a few nights ago. Initially he'd intended to distract himself, but instead, he ended up at the clinic. He'd lain outside her door for a very long time, with his head on his paws. Knowing she'd embrace the wolf if she saw it, but wanting her to welcome the man.

He hadn't Changed since.

James made a point of talking with Connor and Birkie frequently. He always started out with farm topics—*Any clinic suppliers offer organic products? Anyone got Angus heifers for sale right now?*—and then eventually worked in questions about Jillian. *How's her progress, how's she coping?* He could see in their eyes that neither Birkie nor his brother was fooled by his casual act, but thankfully they played along and didn't ask questions or, worse yet, offer sympathy.

He was pleased to learn that Jillian was up and around, and active again, although it concerned him that her version of being active meant walking the perimeter of the clinic's ten-acre property. Birkie had assured him that Jillian stopped to rest frequently, but James knew full well the small blond woman would push herself to go the distance, every day, no matter how crappy she felt. She was already campaigning to return to work, but Connor hadn't relented yet. James could well imagine that frustrated her—after all, she lived and slept and breathed her work—but privately he sided with his brother. Birkie had let slip, however, that she and Caroline were passing Jillian small projects, not so much because they needed the help but to keep Jillian from going stir-crazy and to help her feel connected to the work she loved.

He could relate to that. Wasn't he doing almost the same thing? Making up excuses to go to the clinic, seeking small tidbits of information just so he could keep from going crazy, so he could feel some kind of connection to the woman he loved?

The shadows were long when he finally finished in the fields. He shut down the equipment and climbed down from the tractor, deciding to leave it where it stood. He was a long way from the main farmyard but he wanted to stretch his legs. And think. The scent of alfalfa and earth rose to meet him as he walked across the fields. The sun was low in the sky and golden—and James thought immediately of how it had glinted in Jillian's hair. Automatically he looked over toward the forested coulees and remembered his night with her. There had been passion, but the experience had also touched him deep inside; some essence of Jillian had moved him. And the next day he had ruined everything.

Ah, hell. He had to try again. And this time he'd damn well camp out on her doorstep. If he could just persuade her to listen. He didn't dare think past that.

Chapter Twenty-eight

I can't believe I've done this again. What was I thinking? She should have known better, definitely should have known better. But she had been so tired of lying around. Birkie had left for the day, and Jillian had just wanted to get a little exercise, stretch her muscles, just plain move. Except for the minor relapse the night she'd followed an imaginary white wolf, she was making tremendous progress. Her wrist had healed quickly, and the itchy cast was finally gone. The concussion was healing too, and she actually had bursts of energy at times. Small bursts, but enough to give her hope that life would get back to normal eventually. She was walking every day, but she had other muscles that needed a workout. The doctors had encouraged her to engage in mild activity, but maybe martial arts weren't quite mild enough.

The result was that she was lying on the concrete floor of the livestock wing, weak, dizzy, and trying desperately not to throw up. The floor was still soaked from being hosed down earlier, but then, she hadn't expected to be lying on it. Especially not in an exercise bra and spandex bike shorts. She curled into a fetal position as she began to shiver, yet her head spun horribly every time she tried to get up. Could she possibly feel any worse?

"Jillian!" James was suddenly kneeling beside her. "Christ, are you all right? What happened?"

For one fraction of a second, Jillian's heart thrilled traitorously at the sound of his voice. Then her brain kicked in, and her spirits sank like a lead weight in a pond. Things were, indeed, worse. *Of all the gin joints in all the world. . . .*

He was feeling her forehead, and she swatted at his hand. She swore as the sudden movement nearly caused the nausea to break free.

"Talk to me, dammit, tell me where you're hurt," he ordered, grabbing her flailing hand and checking her pulse.

"I'm trying not to puke, that's what's wrong," she said through gritted teeth. "Leave me alone."

"No. Now what happened?"

She drew a long shaky breath. Two. "I was doing a few simple exercises, running through some basic Tae Kwon Do sequences. I just overdid it, that's all. Got a little dizzy. I'll be fine."

"*Overdid it.* You mean you pushed yourself too hard. Dammit, it hasn't even been a month yet since the accident. And here I thought you were a pretty good doctor."

"Well, so I'm a lousy patient, okay? I feel stupid enough without an audience, thank you. Now go away—*Stop!* Stop that!" He had slid his hands beneath her and turned her into him, was carefully gathering her up. "Put me down, you jerk."

"You're right, you are a lousy patient. But you can't stay here on this cold, wet floor. Your teeth are chattering, for Christ's sake."

"Oh God, please put me down, I'm going to—" She did. Again and again, even when it seemed there couldn't possibly be anything left. Through it all, James held her steady. Warmth surrounded her, calming and soothing her until the terrible nausea subsided. Jillian lay limp and exhausted in James's arms, certain that there was nothing left of her but a thin outer shell. "I told you I was gonna puke."

"So you did. Better now?"

"A little maybe. God, I made such a mess. Get any on you?"

"Naw. Missed us both. And I'm sure this room has seen worse messes than this. I'll hose it down later." He eased her around so her head was resting on his shoulder. Held perfectly still for a moment, to give her dizziness a chance to pass. "Let's get you to bed."

"No." She gripped his shirt as he began heading for the door. "Don't move. What if I throw up again?"

"Well, if you do, you do. We're both washable. But you need to lie down."

Unable to muster an argument to that, Jillian just closed her eyes tight and gritted her teeth in anticipation of the trip. Was surprised at how smoothly he moved, how little motion she felt. Instead, her senses were almost totally preoccupied with the dependable strength of his muscled arms. Even the scent of his shirt, his scent, calmed her. She relaxed in spite of herself, and her eyes stayed closed.

I missed you. I'm so glad you came back. Jillian stroked the great animal's head, ran a hand over the long white fur, marveled at the silky texture of it. *The doctors kept trying to tell me you weren't real, that my mind made you up. But I knew you existed, that you were real. I knew it inside. I knew it.* She knew this feeling too—there was nothing like it. Radiant warmth emanated from the giant wolf, like the physical heat from a glowing campfire infused with a reassuring emotional warmth. Smiling, she opened her eyes—

—and found herself looking at a broad heavily muscled chest. Slowly she lifted her gaze to a shadowed but familiar face. Stared at the overlong white-blond hair her fingers were presently stroking. What the hell was James Macleod doing here? What was *she* doing here? His brilliant blue eyes were closed, his breathing deep and regular.

Stunned, Jillian yanked her hand back just as it started to shake and hastily tried to tuck her arm beside her. It wasn't possible though, not with the man's powerful arms wrapped around her. She could feel his big hands on her back, gentle, protective. The heat from his body was soothing, like basking in front of an open fire. The unique scent of him surrounded her. She couldn't breathe without inhaling the intoxicating blend of powerful male and something else, something both familiar and wild. She puzzled it out until she realized it was the forest she smelled. No, more specifically, the forest at night . . .

This is crazy. I'm dreaming, right? I dreamed about the wolf and now I'm dreaming about this man. Somebody please tell me I'm dreaming. She was in her own bed, she could figure that much out. The light from the clinic's parking lot shed an amber glow through the window blinds, brushed the shadows in the room with bronze. A hundred thoughts whirled through her head and none of them made any sense. Especially when the wolf-dream was so fresh in her mind, the pleasant emotions lingering, her body comfortable, her heart content.

The contentment was the most baffling thing of all. Why wasn't she hollering the place down? She should be furious, shouldn't she? She'd been trying so *damn* hard to never see James again and here he was. In the flesh. Very hot sexy male flesh. It was getting hard to breathe, not because he was holding her tightly, but because she couldn't help being aroused. *Thank God he's only naked to the waist.* Her body was definitely on James's side, her heart was on his side. All she had left with which to resist James Macleod was her brain and it was starting to fog over, too.

"Feeling better?"

God, his eyes were so blue, even in the dim light. "Yes. No. What the hell are you doing in my bed, Macleod?"

"You were ice-cold and white as a sheet. You needed to get warm. It was this or build a bonfire with your couch."

"Okay, well, I'm fine now. Thanks. You can go home."

"I'm not leaving until I think you're fine. And then, not until we talk."

"No talking. No way. No fair." Jillian shoved at him, struggled out of his arms, and lurched out of bed, feeling as graceful as Frankenstein's monster. Dizziness rose in a wave, with nausea close behind it, but she choked them both down as she turned to face James. And immediately lost her breath. Did he have to look so damn sexy? He was resting on his elbow, looking at her with those intense Viking eyes. The over-long hair, the close-cropped beard, even the crinkling of hair on his broad chest gleamed gold in the amber light. She wanted him, badly, wanted to touch him and smell him and taste him. Her whole body clenched. Hard. Which only added to her aggravation.

"Jeez, will you settle down? You're going to make yourself sick again. I only wanted you to hear my side of the story."

She latched on to her anger as if to a life raft. "Your side? Look here, James Macleod; you have no right to ask me to listen to anything. Besides that, I can't discuss a relationship right now. I can't think about it, I can't focus on it. I have no time right now to think about you and me. I'm concentrating on trying to get better—"

"Bullshit!"

"What?" She gaped at him. She hadn't seen him move,

yet he was standing in front of her, looming over her, his features as fierce as they were sexy.

"I said *bullshit*. Right now, all you've got is time to think. Days and days of time to think. So don't stand there and try to tell me you haven't been thinking about you and me. I just want to make sure you have all the facts before you decide to write me off."

"Write *you* off? You're the one who disappeared without a single damn word after our one and only night together." Anger set her pacing to the other side of the small apartment, anger layered over hurt. The fact that she still hurt ticked her off even more, and she wrapped herself in fury as if it was protective armor.

"I didn't leave without a word. I sent flowers and a card letting you know."

"Letting me know what, exactly?" Her head was pounding and her stomach was sending warning signals, but raw emotion superseded all. "That you were too cowardly to tell me to my face that you didn't want me?"

"That I love you."

What? The nerve of the man. She whirled, about to tell him what he could do with such an outrageous statement. But the sudden movement was the last straw for her sensitive stomach. She paled and her knees turned to Jell-O. "Omigod—"

She retched painfully, but her stomach was long since empty. It seemed to take forever for the nausea to subside this time. When it did, her head cleared as well, and Jillian found herself kneeling over a wastebasket, supported by James's powerful arms. She had no idea how she got there.

"Done now?"

"Yeah. Yeah, I think so." She shivered a little, then settled back against him. "God, I'm sorry."

"For what? I should be sorry for upsetting you, and I am. But I meant what I said. I love you." He picked her up gently and set her on the bed. Went into the kitchen and rummaged in the fridge until he found a can of lemon pop. He brought her a tall glass of it with ice and sat beside her.

Jillian sipped the pop gratefully, but suspected it was going to take a lot more than that to revive her. She felt worn out both physically and emotionally. She really didn't want to have this conversation right now, but they seemed to be having it just the same. It just wasn't fair. "Look, I don't understand at all. How can you possibly love me when you ditched me like that?"

"I admit it wasn't my best decision. I just didn't think I'd be very good for you."

She was stunned. Had Birkie been right? Had protective male logic been behind James's actions? "Well, you did make me puke twice, so maybe there's something to that notion. Not to mention knocking me down in the hallway, scaring me to death in the loft. Oh, and breaking into my apartment. Yeah, you're probably standing at about negative twenty on the good-for-Jillian scale."

He had the grace to look sheepish. Standing with both hands in the pockets of his jeans, James unexpectedly re-minded Jillian of a small boy who had broken a neighbor's window. She hurried on to make her point before she lost her resolve completely. "But all that aside, you can just drop any misguided male notions about trying to protect me. It's my damn decision to make as to whether or not I want to risk hanging around with you."

"Okay."

"That's it? That's all I get? Just 'okay'?"

For a split second he looked blank, then he put a hand to

his head. "Christ, I'm missing my cue to apologize, aren't I? I am sorry, really, *really* sorry. Sorry for all the stupid things I did and sorry for not saying I was sorry sooner. Sorry that I'm not better at being human—I mean, I'm sorry I'm not better at relationships."

That's a lot of sorries. Jillian had the feeling this man didn't offer apologies lightly either. "I guess I'll have to forgive you." She offered him a smile, hoping to see an answering one but none appeared.

"So are we . . . are we back together then?"

She handed him the empty glass and sighed deeply. "That was forgiveness, James, not necessarily reinstatement. And I don't know how we can get 'back together' when we hardly had more than a day's worth of a relationship to start with."

"You know there was more than that. A lot more. It was important from the start."

"Maybe so, but you can't ask me to make hugely important relationship decisions right now."

"Why not?"

She saw something like worry flicker over his face, but she wasn't going to make it one bit easier for him. "Duh! Because I'm tired and I'm sick. Because I might throw up again, and if you keep pressuring me, I'll make certain I do it all over you. I'm going to have a shower, a long one. And then I'm going to bed. I want to feel a whole lot better before we continue this intense conversation. So you can damn well wait till tomorrow to discuss you and me any further."

"Fair enough. I'll wait." He folded his arms. "But I'm waiting right here."

"God, you're pushy, Macleod." She said it without heat, however. Instead, she ran a hand over her face and through her hair. Sighed again. It just wasn't fair to have a bare-chested Viking right in front of her and not feel well enough to jump him. She was certain that if he was in her bed, there would be sex. Great sex. Lengthy terrific sex. But she was also certain that even brief and mediocre sex would finish her off. And besides, she hadn't even made a decision about James yet. Not exactly. Well, not officially. Certainly not one that she was ready to share with him just yet. Oh hell, she knew what her decision was, she just wanted him to suffer a little. "Fine, take the couch."

"I'd rather bunk with you. You might get cold again." He surveyed her carefully. "I promise I won't take it as a decision."

His words caused a delicious tingle to travel up her spine, but that wasn't why she found she couldn't refuse him. There was something in those blue, blue eyes, some raw vulnerability she didn't understand. And then she did. He needed her to accept this, accept him at this moment, even if she decided to send him packing tomorrow. Her head was swimming and it wasn't from the concussion. "I'm . . . I'm . . . I'm going to have a shower now. But no funny stuff when I get out, mister. I need some uninter-rupted sleep."

She tried to sound firm. Assertive. In charge. But James's mouth curved into a subtle smile just then, and her heart did an amazing double half gainer of Olympic quality. She rushed to the bathroom before it showed on her face.

The hot water loosened a little of her tension, but not much. She was in love with James Macleod, and she was both exhilarated and appalled. *I hardly know him. Okay, I kind of do, but I want to know him a whole lot better. Will he let me? He's so . . .* She tried to think of the right word. Prickly at times. Reserved. No, more like guarded. Yet

James had been anything but guarded that day at the farm. And that night in the forest. . . . She sighed and tore her thoughts away from that avenue. For now. Instead, she remembered the things that Birkie had told her, the tragedy that James had endured. Surely that would make anyone a little prickly and reserved. And maybe hesitant about another relationship. She wondered if she was up for the challenge of building a relationship with James, then decided she must be. After all, he hadn't exactly shown her his best side, and here she was in love with him anyway. Life was just never what you expected.

She found a fresh pair of pajamas, her favorite flannels with the little frogs. Dried her hair. Brushed her teeth. And resolved that if there was going to be a relationship, then there were going to be a few rules.

Her mental list of rules evaporated like water droplets on a hot griddle when she came out of the bathroom. James was already in her bed, resting on his elbow and holding the quilt open so she could get in. *Omigod, he's naked.* She remembered their night in the forest together all too well, and it wasn't nausea that sent her stomach plummeting to her feet like a carnival ride. She switched the light off almost in self-defense and took a couple of deep breaths before crawling into bed. She deliberately faced away from him, but he simply curled his muscled body around her. The familiar heat enveloped her and that amazing sense of safety, of well-being. A big hand began to glide up and down her back. "I said no funny stuff." Her voice sounded squeaky. So much for being assertive.

"I agree, no funny stuff tonight, but you've got enough tension here to string a piano. You'll never get a good rest when you're all knotted up like this."

She was about to argue when the big hand moved again

and suddenly she couldn't say a word. The strong fingers were surprisingly gentle as they knowingly worked their way up and down her spine, her neck, her lower back, that tight spot between her shoulders. James located and massaged every knot as if they glowed in the dark and he could see them, untie them. She felt herself relaxing in subtle stages, drifting downward. She felt his lips brush the back of her neck just before sleep claimed her.

James snapped awake, both his human and wolf sides fully alert. The small figure curled next to him was moaning restlessly, the blankets kicked aside.

"Shhh baby, wake up. You're dreaming." He gave her shoulder a gentle shake, and felt her body shudder, then relax. He pulled the covers back over her, curled his body close, and slid an arm around her. He thought she was asleep—until she covered his big hand with her smaller one and squeezed it. There was no reason for the wild joy that whipped through him. No reason for the dizzying thrill that followed as she turned and opened one eye, a mere glimmer of green, and focused on him. No reason for the elation that sang along his nerves as she whispered his name.

Right then and there James decided he didn't give a tinker's damn about reasons. All the misery of the past few weeks had slid away during the night even as the tight fist of pain around his heart had eased. Love washed over him like a midsummer thunderstorm, sudden, wild, and fierce. Cleansing and bright. And in its wake, peace.

He kissed the top of her head and nuzzled her hair. Breathed in the unique mix of berry shampoo and essence of Jillian. Wondered if he needed to be on guard—after all, he'd Changed in his sleep recently. As tough as this small woman was, she was human. Changing too close to her could send her flying with enough force to break bones. Yet he knew his wolfen side was completely devoted to Jillian. He had to trust that the wolf would do nothing to endanger her.

What he really needed to worry about was how to tell her about his wolfen side. How would he bring it up? And when? *Say, Jillian, did I mention I was a Changeling?* He remembered telling Evelyn for the first time. She'd laughed at him, refused to take him seriously. He'd had to tell her over and over, and finally show her, before she believed him. But she hadn't been afraid.

Jillian wouldn't be afraid either, he thought, once she knew the truth. But it was much too soon to tell her. Definitely too soon. He wanted to give the relationship some time to grow and strengthen before he revealed his secret. He was confident she would be able to handle it, would eventually embrace the truth with all the wonder and curiosity that she brought to her work with animals.

But it was one thing for her to accept the existence of Changelings, and another to decide to be one. Would Jillian want to enter his world fully? It would be her choice. He would love her no matter what. He put the thoughts away, shelved them in some mental corner for another time. It was too soon to be thinking about such things. For now, he just wanted to savor this unique contentment, this peace.

Chapter Twenty-nine

Jillian automatically slapped the alarm into silence. The clock read 6:00 A.M., but it was Sunday. She didn't have to get up. Of course, she hadn't had to get up for a long time, but she was naturally a morning person, and she liked the routine. *If you sleep in, you miss things.* Like the scents of dew-laden fields drifting in the open window. Like naked men in her bed. James was facing the window, but she could hear him breathing deep and steady. Felt the heat radiate from his skin. He was on top of the blankets, and she allowed her eyes to rove over his body, study the shapes of muscle, the lines and angles of his powerful frame. He looked delicious. Tingling warmth blossomed low in her core and she fantasized about kissing every square inch of James Macleod.

God, she felt good. Better than she had in days and days. True, she hadn't moved yet, but for this one moment in time nothing hurt. Not her head and not her heart. But as for doing all the things she'd like to do to the mouth-watering male next to her, she doubted she would have the stamina. *Damn.* For now she'd have to make do with planning out her moves for when she was back to normal, when she wouldn't have to hesitate to—

"Ready to go waterskiing?"

She laughed and James rolled over, his movements smooth and easy. Almost catlike. He kissed her forehead and rubbed noses with her. "Good morning, sunshine." Then those startling blue eyes were looking into hers, and forming thoughts became very difficult.

"I think you're the second biggest surprise in my life," she blurted.

His eyebrows went up. "Second? I'll have to try harder."

"No, no, I mean, among the major cosmic events in my life, you're second. You would have been first, but there's this wolf—"

"A wolf took first place away from me?" He looked amused.

"Maybe I should start at the beginning. No, wait, let me think. I'm going to brush my teeth and think, and then I want to tell you some things."

She took her time in the bathroom. Last night's shower had made her hair dry in strange wisps and curls, and she fought to tame it. It was harder to pull her thoughts together, though. She was going to tell James about the white wolf—and she was nervous. What if he didn't believe her? At best, she would feel ridiculous. At worst, it could end a very promising relationship. How could she be with someone who would dismiss something so important to her? Because the white wolf *was* important to her. The creature had not only saved her life all those years ago, but it had been an important factor in her recovery. And in her eventual choice of profession. What role it played now, she didn't know, but it was still very much a part of her life. Even if she didn't understand it.

When Jillian came out, she found James brewing coffee in her tiny kitchen. He had pulled on his jeans, but they were rakishly unbuttoned. She swallowed, hard, and forced her eyes to look somewhere else. Anywhere else . . . Finally she grabbed James's hand and steered him to the table. "I have some things I want to tell you, things that are important to me. Will you listen?"

"Of course I will."

"I mean, *really* listen. All the way to the end and no falling asleep from boredom."

"Honey, you could read the phone book to me and still have all of my attention. Whatever it is, if it's important to you, it's important to me."

She seriously doubted the phone book thing, but not that he would listen. And so she told him. About the attack, about the enormous white wolf that saved her. About the effect the wolf had had on her life, about the reunion she'd had with it—or one like it—since she'd arrived in Dunvegan. About the DNA tests and her efforts to learn more about the wolf. Even about the myths and legends she'd been reading and the dreams she'd had lately. All of it. Every detail.

She took a deep breath then, not sure of what to do now. She had to give James credit for paying attention as he'd said he would. His intense gaze had never left her face, his coffee sat untouched. But she couldn't read his expression and that worried her.

Finally he reached across the table and took her hand. "You've had some very unique experiences. But the wolf didn't save you—"

"I see." Disappointment shot through her like broken glass. "I guess it all sounded pretty fantastic. I don't know why I thought you might believe me."

"No! No, the wolf is real. There are plenty of wolves that live in this area. And there's a white one, too."

"You've seen it?" She narrowed her eyes at him. He'd

better not be trying to appease her by making this up. "A huge one with unusual eyes?"

"Yes, I've seen it. Many times."

"Prove it."

"It's . . . it's pure white but not an albino. No black hairs on the ear tips, but it has a black nose, black claws. Not just big, but a lot bigger than a normal wolf. You're not imagining it, honey."

She took a deep breath, suddenly aware she'd been holding it, and her eyes filled with tears. "So you do believe me."

"Well, why wouldn't I? Even if I hadn't seen the wolf for myself, I'd still believe you."

"I just . . . it's just that, my head. . . ." She stammered into silence.

"I get it. You have a brain injury—"

"It's just a concussion." Technically a concussion *was* a brain injury, but calling it that made it sound so much worse.

"—so you expect people to question your grip on reality. Maybe you're questioning your grip on it, too."

She rested her chin in her hand. "I guess maybe I am. That hallucination last week really threw me. I mean, thinking that I saw the wolf turn into you. How crazy is that? I've been a little worried about my sanity since. I know I have the DNA results, but emotionally, I guess I still needed some reassurance that the wolf is real. *Really* real."

"It's living, breathing real." He smiled at her then. "Big. White. Blue eyes. *Really* real."

"Thanks for that."

"But it didn't save you."

"What?"

"That's what I was trying to say. The white wolf is real, it came to you and it chased the bad guys away. But it didn't save you, Jillian. You did that yourself. Sure, you thought of the wolf a lot. But what you did was pick something to hang on to, to build with. If it hadn't been the wolf, you would have found something else to use. *You're* the one that climbed up out of hell. You did it yourself, Jillian. You're the strongest person I've ever known." His grip on her hand tightened as he looked at the table for a long moment, then back at her. "I wish I could say I'd been like that. When Evelyn died, I wanted to die too. And I sort of did. I withdrew from everything and everyone. I thought I was protecting them. I mean, after all, loving me had gotten Evelyn killed—" He held up a hand as Jillian started to protest. "No, it's true. But I think I just might have been protecting myself all this time, too."

"Maybe you needed to."

"Maybe. But I don't need to now. And I don't want to now. I see you and I see not just someone I love, but someone I want to be like."

"You know, giving me a swelled head just can't be good for my concussion."

He kissed her hand then, and held it to his cheek for a moment. Then looked at her with a thoughtful expression. "You know, some people would envy you the personal encounters you've had with a wolf, the connection you seem to have with it. Others might have a more negative outlook."

"They might think I'm crazy? Hey, been there."

"Oh no, they'll believe you. But throughout history wolves have often been associated with evil. Here you are with an up close and personal relationship with a wolf and that makes you evil too, at least in some people's eyes."

"Evil? You're kidding. This is the twenty-first century—how can people believe that?"

"Evil exists. What do you call the men who attacked you?"

She was quiet then. *Evil.* "Okay, you're right, there's definitely human evil. But wolves? That seems pretty extreme."

"There are some extreme people in this world. I'd want to be careful who I tell about this."

"I guess you're right." She thought of Douglas Harrison's father, how he'd raved about the *big white devil* and warned her to run. But he was ill. No one would take him seriously, would they? "Fortunately, I haven't taken out any ads in the newspaper. You and Birkie are the only ones who know about the wolf. I've been meaning to talk to Connor about it, but it seems every time I see him, we're both busy."

"It wouldn't hurt to tell Connor. But otherwise, let's keep it to ourselves."

She nodded. "That makes sense. Besides, it's kind of special, this thing with the wolf. I don't want to tell everybody in the whole world. It'll spoil the magic, somehow. Maybe I'm afraid too, that if I talk about it too much, the wolf will stop coming to see me."

"I don't think so. I think the wolf will keep visiting for a long time to come." He sounded dead certain.

"I don't want to be greedy. It's so wonderful that the wolf came to me at all, and to have gotten to see it again . . . Well, there are no words. I'll never understand why it picked me, though. Why it would come here, come to me, of all people."

There was a long pause. "Wolves are intelligent creatures." He cleared his throat, seemed to be measuring his words. "They're sensitive. Curious. I imagine a wolf can feel the good energy from a place, a person."

"But it's a wild animal."

"Doesn't matter. Are you afraid of it?"

She didn't have to think about that. "Logically I ought to be. Anyone with sense would be. But no, I'm not and I can't exactly say why. I guess that sounds pretty dumb."

"No. You're intelligent and sensitive too. I'm pretty sure you would know if the animal meant you harm. And I'm also certain that you're not going to act like a tourist with a bear and try to feed it marshmallows out of your hand."

"Well . . ." She recalled her encounter on the trail below Elk Point. Even a tourist wouldn't be crazy enough to hug a wolf, and she decided not to mention that little lapse of judgment. "I think a wolf would prefer dog biscuits, or maybe bacon."

He laughed then, leaned over the table and kissed her. Sat back and put his hands behind his head. "So you want to create a wildlife center?"

The muscles had shifted in that broad Viking chest, and Jillian couldn't help being fascinated. James would have no trouble using one of those heavy broadswords from a museum . . . or carrying her away. . . .

"Hello? Wildlife center?" He was grinning as if he knew exactly what she'd been thinking.

"It's the next step for me." She hoped her face hadn't gone red. She focused her eyes firmly on James's face. Although that was pretty distracting too. "A wildlife center, I mean. I want to specialize in wildlife rehabilitation, especially wolves."

"Connor's mentioned there's a need for one in this region. But I thought he treated plenty of wild creatures in his clinic. Seems like there's always a fawn or two, or some kind of bird there. What would your center do?"

"We can give initial treatment here, but government policy dictates that the animals have to be shipped immediately to a certified recovery center. The nearest one is hundreds of miles away, and the travel subjects the animal to a great deal of stress. Plus there aren't enough rehab centers to fill the need so too many animals end up euthanized that might have been saved." She rose and dumped the old pot of coffee, made fresh. "I'd like to change that. If I had more experience under my belt, I could write up a proposal, apply for a grant. Maybe some of the local people would be interested, maybe volunteer some services to help get it off the ground."

"You'd need a place for it, though. Some land."

She slid a cup toward James and sat down with her own. "That'll be the tough part. A wildlife rehab center takes a lot of space, and you have to own the land or have a ninety-nine-year lease on crown land before you can apply for the grants. There are all kinds of rules and regs." She sighed. "I know it's a big dream. It's going to take a lot of time and money to make it come true. But someday."

"I have some land."

Jillian shook her head. "You have a farm. For farming."

"I also have land. I own a fair chunk of the river valley. That's not zoned for agriculture. Why couldn't we use that? We could start building anytime."

"But . . . but you, why would, we aren't. . . ."

"You said I was the second biggest surprise in your life. Well, you're the number one biggest surprise in mine, and I'm not letting you out of my sight again. I figure a big project like a wildlife center should keep you here for a long, long time. Maybe give me enough time to talk you into building a life with me, too."

"A life?" Jillian floundered, her heart bumping against her ribs. She was dizzy but not from the concussion. "I mean, we like each other and all but. . . ."

He chuckled as he came around the table, leaned his face close to hers, nuzzled her cheek. He brushed her lips with his, making her breath hitch suddenly. "I think there's a lot more than 'like' between us, Jillian Descharme, and we both know it. A *lot* more. And I want to give you more. I want you to take more. Starting right now." He pulled her from the chair, kissed her long and slow and deep until she sighed into his mouth. He steered her to the bed and laid her on top of the blankets, followed her down. "I want to make love to you, and I want you to just lie here and feel it. Don't move, just feel, okay? Nothing else."

She frowned up at him. "It's the concussion, isn't it? I don't want you to make love to me if you think I'm an invalid."

"Uh-uh, it's not like that." He kissed her again, slower. "Naturally I'd refrain from acrobatics for now, but if I was afraid of hurting you, we wouldn't be doing this at all." He had her attention now. Trailed his fingers along her face. "I need this from you, Jillian. I don't know how to explain it, I just need you to *feel*. Feel me touching you, feel my skin next to yours, feel me inside of you." His voice changed, thickened. The words came out so low and deep that she could feel them vibrating within her. "Feel *me*. I want you to feel me, Jillian." *And want me. Accept me. All of me.*

Those last words resonated within her head, almost seemed to originate there. She could swear he hadn't moved his lips. But he was moving them now, placing soft, sensual kisses along her brow, over her eyelids, her temple. His mouth was hot against her skin, soothing and arousing at the same time. Her breath caught in her throat as he suckled her earlobe, nibbled along the line of her jaw, and outlined her lips with the tip of his tongue.

She was already dizzy and dazzled by the time he slid his mouth over hers. His lips enticed, persuaded, coaxed, with a relentless tenderness. She didn't notice that the buttons of her pajamas had been carefully undone, the material pushed aside, until he pulled her closer, skin to heated skin. She stretched catlike, instinctively basking in the delicious glowing heat. Melted before it. Her heart pounded in her ears and a delicious shiver began at the base of her spine.

Still kissing her, he rolled so that she was on top. She shrugged out of her pajama top and pressed herself against him again, luxuriated in the sensation of her nipples against his hot skin, rubbed them over the crinkling of hair on his broad chest until they stood out and her breasts felt tight, aching. Needing. Until she had to shimmy up and present them to be kissed. She moaned long and low as James obliged. His big powerful hands roved over her back, the rough palms rasping deliciously over her skin and helping her to shimmy out of the rest of the pajamas. James cupped her bottom, kneaded and squeezed, even as he continued to lavish attention on her breasts, building her excitement to a fever pitch. She wanted, needed, had to have. She could feel his hard erection straining upward against his jeans and rocked her hips, rubbed herself against the bulging material. She reached down for the zipper, but he caught her hand and kissed it, rolled her neatly onto her back. "Yes, oh yes," she breathed. "Now. Now, now, now."

"Not yet," he said. "Later, later, later."

She groaned, reaching for his zipper again, but he

dodged, grabbing her hand, then seizing the other as well. She tried to arch her back, strained to rub herself against him but there was no relief from the wildness she felt, from the frantic need. She turned her face away from his inflaming kisses. "Stop teasing."

He kissed her again, but softly. Soothingly. "I'm not teasing you, sweetheart. I have an itinerary."

"An *itinerary*? That's for travelers."

"A very strict itinerary. And I *am* traveling. Watch me." He kissed his way rapidly from her throat to her navel, then continued his kisses down her belly.

James nuzzled her mound, inhaled deeply. Her scent was unique, delightful, enticing. It called to him to taste. She cried out and came hard at the first stroke of his tongue, sending a jolt of excitement through him. Quickly he unzipped his jeans and slid them down before he strangled. Then bent his head to her again, pressed his palms on the insides of her thighs, holding her in place as she arched and bucked. He lapped at the delicious downy folds, moaning deep in his throat as they opened to him, revealed the tender pearl hidden away. Gently he surrounded it with his lips, drew it into his mouth. Licked and suckled it softly, felt it tighten like Jillian's rose nipples. Her gasps and cries of pleasure poured fuel on the fire in his own body.

But this time was for her. He changed tactics then, made long strokes with his tongue, darting it inside her, then laving up and over her tiny bud. Plunge and stroke. Plunge and stroke. Build the glorious tension within her.

It was building in him too. Her excitement was feeding his and his body craved release. But what he craved more was the expression of things he couldn't put into words. The release he needed most was of unnamable feelings that were suddenly crowding his heart. He could only *show* Jillian, let his touch give voice to what he couldn't say. He wanted so much to give and give to this woman, touch her body until he touched her soul.

Orgasm rippled through her, this one soft and long and sweet. He rose then, and was instantly dazzled by the sight of her. The morning sunlight had splashed across her translucent skin, gilding her delicate breasts and turning her sea green eyes to emerald. She arched her hips upward to meet him as he buried himself in her, joined with her in the bright clear light.

James was more aware of his dual nature than he had ever been. As a man, his heart was close to bursting with a powerful mixture of joy and tenderness, with the rightness of the moment. As a wolf, instinct older than time sang in his veins, exulting in the taking of a mate. The knowledge that it was for life welled up from his very soul, carried him higher and higher until he tumbled into the heart of the sun.

Chapter Thirty

The sun was going down and Roderick Harrison's dinner was still being kept warm in a tinfoil cocoon in the oven. Douglas was unconcerned. His father could be fixing fences on the far side of the sprawling ranch. Could be tending a cow with a problem, or searching for a calf. Could be in town having a beer or two and losing a game of pool to Varley. The Alzheimer's continued to be in some sort of remission, and his father had simply resumed his old life.

Must be fucking nice, Douglas thought bitterly. Meanwhile his own life had been turned completely inside out. And no amount of Jack Daniels could stop his father's words from replaying in his mind. *She left us for one of them. She left us to* become *one of them.*

His mother had loved a werewolf. He didn't doubt their existence, he couldn't, not after what he'd seen when he was fourteen. And he didn't doubt that his father hated werewolves, certainly wouldn't declare that his own wife had been with one unless it was true. Roderick had never uttered such a thing even when the Alzheimer's was particularly bad. Nor had he ever once said Douglas wasn't his son. Oh sure, he'd looked straight at him and not recognized him, even mistook him for an employee on several occasions. But there was a big difference between that and saying he didn't have a son at all.

So whose son was he? Did having a werewolf father make him a werewolf too? Would he know? He stared at the photo on the mantel, at the smiling woman with curly auburn hair. His hair. He shared that feature with her, shared the amber brown eyes and the shape of the face, even the damn freckles. What had he inherited from his unknown father? A talent for howling at the moon? Tearing out the throats of deer?

He ran a hand over his face, rubbed his eyes as if trying to erase that particular vision. Knowing Roderick Harrison, Douglas found it hard to blame his mother for having an affair. But why the hell couldn't she have chosen a human lover? At least he'd only have to wonder who he was, not what he was.

The coffee pot shook in his hand, scattering droplets. Finally he set it down and gripped the edge of the counter to steady himself. He yawned hugely, helplessly, until he thought his head would split in two. In spite of all the drinking he'd done recently, he'd slept poorly. Every time he nodded off, he'd dreamed of wolves. Only he wasn't being chased by them.

He was running with them.

He jerked when the phone rang, swore as he grabbed the receiver. Varley was on the other end.

"Your dad there, Dougie?"

"No."

"You know where he is?"

"Not a clue." Frankly he'd flat-out avoided the old man since that little revelation in the living room. Didn't know if he simply never wanted to see his father again or just not right now. Douglas had questions, lots of questions—but would the answers be worse than not knowing? And could he trust an answer from his father? His *stepfather*, he amended quickly.

"Look, two of the rifles are missing from my place. Your father's favorites, the Browning and the Remington. Some boxes of cartridges. He say anything to you about hunting?"

Dad's got a gun? Douglas forced his voice to be calm. "Not really. Said he found wolf tracks in the north section a few days ago but never mentioned anything about going after them."

"Shit." Varley was silent for a long moment until Douglas wondered if he'd hung up. "Shitfire. I know Rod's doing really well and all, but I just don't like the idea of him wandering around with a goddamn gun. Christ on crutches, Dougie. We both know he could have a relapse at any time, but he could also have an accident just because he's old and he's by himself."

"You're right." He said what he was expected to say then, although he didn't feel like it. "I'll go look for him."

"Good man. I'm going to get a couple of the guys to help me check the woods on the other side of the north pasture. Keep me posted, okay?"

"You got it. Thanks for the call." Douglas put the phone down carefully, his pulse pounding in his ears. "Thanks for the call, my ass!" Every instinct he possessed told him that his worst nightmare had just come true. Roderick Harrison wasn't hunting wolves at all.

He was hunting werewolves.

The sound of the back door slamming made him jump. He was even more surprised when his father came through the kitchen door and laid a quarter of venison on the counter with a flourish.

"Got a nice young buck, down along the line of spruce in the south pasture. Thought it was about time we had some game on the table. Varley around?"

"He's out looking for you. North section by the woods. He was . . . figuring you might need a hand with whatever you got," Douglas lied a little. He heard his father's words, saw the deer—but it didn't feel right, something was off. "You can call him on his cell."

Rod was in a buoyant mood as he picked up the phone. He arranged for Varley to swing by the house and pick him up, called for another hand to set up the table and the meat saw in the machine shed. Argued amiably over whether to do sausage or hamburger after they cut off some steaks, whether to use plastic wrap or butcher's paper.

Within a few minutes, Douglas was left standing alone in the kitchen staring at the bloody spot on the counter. Rod had taken the quarter with him to trim down and package.

All normal. All ordinary. Everything just as it had always been. Except Douglas's gut said it wasn't. He sighed and poured half a cup of coffee, topped it up with the Jack Daniels he had stashed in the bottom cupboard. Considered drinking it.

Then poured it down the sink.

"It's brilliant." Connor spread out the sketches on the table in the lunchroom. "The design isn't just great, it's absolutely brilliant. Jillian drew these?"

"She did." There was pride in James's voice. "This is her dream, and she's been designing it for years in her head. I just encouraged her to put it on paper."

"She has an amazing grasp of how wild animals think, what they need to feel secure. Look at how there are no corners, no hard angles. It's—what's the word I'm looking for?—organic, flowing. I've never seen anything like it. You didn't help?"

"A couple small tweaks, just recommendations really. She did it all, created something incredible."

She's done more than that. She's worked a miracle. Connor shielded his thoughts as he looked at his brother. James was relaxed, easy in his own skin. His human skin. And happy. Connor had to look back a lot of years to remember his brother happy.

And as for Jillian, well, she seemed to be floating on air. Glowing since he'd finally consented to let her résumé work part-time. Officially at least. He knew full well she'd been doing little things for Birkie and Caroline when he wasn't looking, everything from running lab tests to updating files. At first Connor tried to talk Jillian into manning the reception area for half days. She was so horrified by the prospect that he had relented at once. What had he been thinking? Jillian was too good a veterinarian to be tied to a desk. Instead, he relegated the small animal surgeries to her. Besides, considering some of the customers that came through the front door, surgery was probably a lot less stressful for her.

Jillian appeared in the doorway just then, still dressed in her greens. Connor watched as James swept her under his arm and kissed the top of her head. Both of them smiled and Connor's eyes moistened unexpectedly. "Finished in surgery already?" he managed.

"There were only a couple of spays today. And I removed a lump from Poodle's leg."

"That old Siamese? Good God, he must have used up eight and three-quarters of his nine lives by now." Connor shook his head.

"Poodle?" James looked baffled.

"It's his name," explained Jillian. "Kind of like the old Mr. Magoo cartoons. Remember his cat was named Bowser?"

"I thought that was because he couldn't see it was a cat. Maybe Mrs. Malkinson has the same problem."

Birkie joined the conversation from the hallway. "Enid Malkinson can identify a finch in a bush at a hundred yards. She wanted a poodle for her birthday one year, but her husband gave her a kitten instead."

"And the rest is history," said Connor. "A lot of history actually. That was what, two husbands and three decades ago? Poodle's a genuine antique."

"Speaking of antiques, bossman, I've got a couple of overdue accounts I need you to look at." Birkie headed back to the front.

"I hate numbers," Connor grumbled but followed her.

Jillian could still hear the sound of retreating footsteps when James began placing soft tender kisses on her throat, her ear, along her jaw. He took her mouth slowly and sweetly until she lost her breath and had to pull back, one hand planted on his chest to keep him at bay. "You make me dizzy."

"I could make you more than that. Let's go back to your apartment." He leaned in to kiss her again, but she dodged and fled to the other side of the table, laughing. She spotted the sketches.

"Hey, these are mine."

"I was showing Connor the design for the center. He thinks it's great."

"He's okay with the location? What about Zoey? Is it too close to their farm?"

"We own the farm together, and no, he doesn't think it's too close and I'm sure Zoey will agree when she sees the plans. We already owned the section of river valley that borders the farm. But I bought this land adjacent to it not long ago, thought it might come in handy." He grinned then. "And see? It already has."

"You have great powers of prediction."

"I can predict more. I can predict that you're going to move in with me today."

"You predicted that yesterday and it didn't happen."

"But that was then and this is now. Come home with me."

She shook her head. "I want a little more time. I'm thrilled to be working, even a little. I *need* to be working. But my energy doesn't last, and I'm just as thrilled to be able to be home in bed in thirty seconds flat. Plus I don't have to cook a single thing. I swear Bill and Jessie have doubled the amount of food they stock this fridge with."

"Feed a concussion, starve a fever?" He circled the table and slid his arms around her, planting a tender kiss on her forehead. "I admit, you look tired out, honey. Wish I could kiss your concussion better for you."

"It *is* getting better. It just takes time."

"I shouldn't be so impatient. It's just that I want you with me, want to get started on that life together."

She sat in the chair he pulled out for her, was silent for a long moment. "I think we've started already."

"Well, I spend the night here."

"No, more than that. I mean . . . James, I'm pregnant."

Stunned, he knelt awkwardly in front of her and took her hands, his eyes searching her face.

"I'm sorry, I'm really sorry, James, I don't know how it happened—well I know *how* it happened—but I take the pill for God's sake. I've never missed taking it, never. Not once." She put her hands to her head. "I tested twice to be sure, yesterday and today, but it's positive. I'm just so sorry."

He placed a finger over her lips. "Stop right there. Stop

saying you're sorry; you've got nothing to be sorry about. You didn't do this. I should be apologizing to you."

"I guess *we* did it, really. Both of us together."

"Okay. When did we do it? I mean, how long?"

"It has to have been the very first time we were together. In the forest. I thought I was late because of the accident, thought maybe the concussion had, you know, thrown off my system or some darn thing, but . . . oh, I never expected this."

"Well, it's a surprise, but as surprises go, it's a pretty great one."

"What?"

He wrapped his arms around her, pulled her down into his lap and kissed her hair, her brow, her cheeks. "It's great. Wonderful. Fantastic. Terrific. Um . . . I can't even think of enough words, but it's definitely great."

She grabbed his face then, made him look at her. "You're *happy* about it?"

"Didn't you hear what I just said? Hell, yes, I'm happy about it." He pulled back a little to look at her. "What about you? Are you okay with this?"

"Well, like you said, it's a surprise. A big one. I . . . I don't know how I feel yet. I need some time to wrap my head around it, and I need to figure out how to fit it in with being a veterinarian."

He pointed a stern finger at her. "No steer wrestling."

"Definitely no steer wrestling. I'll have to modify a lot of my activities. And see, I just don't know how that'll impact my job."

"Jeez, you're worried about your job? You belong here. You've had a concussion for weeks and the clinic didn't fall down. Everyone pulled together, and you're doing what you can. You did, what, three surgeries this morning?"

"Yeah, but they were just little ones. There's an end to a concussion. I get better and people don't have to take up slack for me, everything's back to normal. At least, that's what's supposed to happen."

"Pregnancy's not a permanent condition, honey."

"No, but being a parent is."

"You wouldn't be the first veterinarian with a family." James tucked her head under his chin, breathed in the smell of her hair. "There's going to be challenges, but we'll figure it out as we go. Why don't we start by getting married?"

"You don't have to marry me."

"What the hell did you think I was planning to do? Haven't you heard anything I've said about building a life together? Haven't I pestered you every day for two weeks to move in with me?"

"It's not the same—"

"Jillian." He lifted her chin with a finger until her eyes met his. "I'm sorry if I haven't been clear enough. You shouldn't have a single moment of concern as to my feelings or my intentions. I love you. I'm not easy to love or to live with, but I'm just selfish enough to want to marry you anyway. I want to live with you in a home in the country and build a wildlife center and fill it up with deer and wolves and foxes and owls."

"Moose, too. Sometimes we get moose."

"And *especially* moose. Am I being clear enough now?"

"I think maybe I'm starting to get the picture."

He took her lips, softly, gently. Kissed her until she moaned low in her throat. "Is that a *yes* I hear?"

"Mmmmm—yes. Hey! Stop!"

He had scooped her up and was heading down the hall. "First things first. You're tired, you need to lie down. I'll bet you haven't had breakfast either, and it's already time for lunch."

"You're going to be a real pain about this, aren't you?"

He paused in front of her door until she reached down and opened it. Swung her inside. "You bet. I'm going to make your life miserable, and I'm going to begin by making you something to eat." He set her carefully on the edge of the bed, stood back and looked at her with concern. "I should have asked. Are you feeling okay? Are you sick or anything?"

"I'm not throwing up in the mornings. Although I have to wonder how much of the nausea I've had since the accident was due to the concussion and how much was because I'm pregnant." She covered her lips with her fingers on that last word. "God, I'm not used to saying that yet. It feels weird. Kind of scary. Okay, a lot scary. This is really going to change my life."

"*Our* life," he corrected and sat beside her, gathered her under one arm. "But we'll be okay. It's sooner than we might have planned, but what's that plaque on Birkie's desk say? The one with the John Lennon quote on it."

"*Life is what happens to you while you're busy making other plans.*"

"See? This is unexpected, but that doesn't mean it's not a good thing." He kissed the top of her head. "A wonderful thing. We'll raise this child right in the midst of all those animals we rescue. Not to mention we've already got three ponies and a dozen dogs for him on the farm. That's a pretty good life for a kid, don't you think?"

She hugged him tightly then, unable to speak, and held on for a long time.

Chapter Thirty-one

"I'm moving to the country, I'm getting married, and I'm having a baby," Jillian told her reflection in the mirror. She saw a young woman with short but unruly blond hair, green eyes, and fine features. The same woman she saw in the mirror every day, but somehow she was different now. "Wow, that's a lot of changes. And not necessarily in that order either."

Connor had called James for help in dehorning a pen of cattle. She'd napped while he was gone, not because he wanted her to but because she couldn't help it. She did tire easily. She'd chalked it up to the concussion until this week when yet another period failed to appear. That was when she got Caroline to drive her downtown to one of the pharmacies. She'd loaded up a shopping basket with tons of things she didn't need, just so she could bury two pregnancy test kits in the bottom of it. She thanked her lucky stars—if she had any—that she got a young cashier who didn't know who she was, and that Caroline didn't come back before everything was paid for and bagged.

She'd tested the minute she got back to her apartment. The strip turned blue. She'd heard that sometimes the strip was hard to read, but no, this was definitely blue. Jillian spent the rest of the day and half the night trying to think of non-pregnant reasons why she was testing positive. She waited until James left for the farm early that morning and tested again. Blue.

She certainly hadn't planned on blurting the news to James at lunchtime, but it had worked out just fine. *He* was just fine, which was the amazing part. Or maybe not so amazing, considering the kind of man he was. Like Birkie had said, James was a complicated man with a tender and loving heart. Just last week, Jillian found him cuddling a couple of orphan puppies in the back room. He tried to claim they were cold and he was just warming them up, but she didn't buy it. So it wasn't too hard to picture his big powerful hands holding a tiny baby. It wasn't hard to imagine him with a child either, not after he'd spent twenty minutes in the clinic's waiting room letting an 8-year-old girl show him her pet iguana. James would be a great dad.

But what about her? She'd never thought much about the whole parenting thing. Her entire focus had been on getting through all the years of study and classes and practicums to become a vet. *I would have thought about kids eventually. I like kids almost as much as animals.* It was dealing with adults that could be difficult. She'd often wished the patients she treated didn't have owners attached. Unless it was a child. She got along just fine with the kids who brought their pets to the clinic. She'd probably be okay with this whole baby thing too, if she ever got used to the idea.

Jillian puttered around the apartment, discovered the kitchen garbage can was overflowing, and decided to take it out before it walked away on its own. James was probably still helping Connor. She glanced around for him, but as she passed the livestock wing, she noticed that the cattle pen was empty and the floor had already been hosed down. She checked her watch and noted that the clinic had closed several minutes ago. Maybe James had gone back to the farm for something. No matter, he'd turn up eventually.

She squinted as she approached the back door and tried to shade her eyes. The late afternoon sun was glaring through the window, reflecting off the white tile floor and the pale walls of the hallway. It was a relief to step outside. It was bright out here too, but at least the light was coming from only one direction. Blinking, Jillian headed for the trees at the back of the parking lot where the bin was set up. It was a hot day and the shade was welcome by the time she tossed in her bag, but with the aroma of *eau de dumpster* hanging heavy in the air, she didn't want to linger. Resigning herself to re-crossing the wide expanse of sunlit pavement, Jillian turned. And stopped dead.

Roderick Harrison was pointing a rifle at her.

"What the hell are you doing? Put that down!" Jillian demanded, sounding a lot braver than she felt. She was deliberately assertive, sensing it would be a mistake to act like a victim. The man wasn't wild-eyed and raving like the last time she'd seen him, but there was an intensity to him that would have been scary even without the weapon. She clenched her fists, automatically looking for some way to engage him, but he was well out of her reach. Besides, her martial arts training covered only attackers with hand weapons. A rifle could kill from a distance.

"I told you to run while you could. Told you to get away, but you wouldn't listen. I can see the blue, you know."

"The blue what?" It was good that he was talking. Maybe she could keep him talking. *Please God, let someone see me out here.* She thought about screaming for help, but that didn't seem like a good idea, not with the gun aimed at her midsection. She could be dead long before anyone heard her.

"The aura. You all have it. The whole damn nest of you." He spat on the pavement without taking his eyes off her. "Corena would never have left if it wasn't for you. She'd still be alive. She'd still be with *me*."

"Who's Corena?"

"You know damn well who she is. You all know each other. And no one's allowed to leave the pack, are they? Goddamn fucking werewolves. You're just like the goddamn mafia, you gotta have control, gotta have order. She tried to leave, and you killed her."

She should have guessed this was about werewolves. She tried to play along, sound calm and reasonable. "I'm sorry to hear you lost someone. But I'm sure nobody here had anything to do with it."

"I've seen that big white devil here, seen his whole pack here. This is goddamn werewolf headquarters."

He had seen the white wolf. That was the reason behind this. But what was the right thing to say? He'd expect her to deny it. *Acceptance. Validate what he's witnessed.* "It's true that the wolf has been here. The white wolf is a frequent visitor to our clinic."

It surprised him. He seemed to consider for a few seconds, studied her through narrowed eyes. "And the others?"

She drew a blank then. "What others? I've only seen one wolf."

"Kept you for himself then. Kept you away from the others. I should have known when I saw his aura all over you. He's going to change you, and keep you. Breed up a whole new pack." He pointed at her belly with the gun. "Already started."

A shiver ran through her. This was too weird, much too

weird. How the hell did this guy know she was pregnant? She hadn't known herself until—Forget that, she ordered herself. *Focus on what to say now. How do I talk my way out of this? How do you reason with a crazy person?* "But I'm not a werewolf myself."

"That's only a matter of time." He raised the rifle, aiming at her head.

Oh Jesus. Think "Corena wouldn't want you to do this."

"I let her talk me out of it once. I should never have listened." His finger was on the trigger. "Liars and deceivers. That's what you are, all of you. Pretending to be human, but underneath you're all teeth and claws, just waiting for a chance to use them."

Jillian jolted at the sound of glass breaking from the direction of the clinic. Harrison glanced behind him, and she used the distraction to dive to one side. She landed hard, scrambled up ready to run, when an unearthly howl, a blood-freezing battle cry, held her in place. An enormous white wolf, *her* wolf, was racing toward them, glittering shards of broken glass still flying from its coat. The sun glinted off its bared teeth as it leapt for her assailant. And Harrison swung to meet the attack. "No, don't!" she screamed.

The explosion hurt her ears, deafened her. Wolf and man hit the ground together, rolled. The rifle skittered to the pavement. Then the white wolf lay still. Blood soaked its snowy white fur and pooled in the sun.

Her ears still ringing, Jillian couldn't think, could only react. She ran to the wolf, scrambled to find a pulse. "Stay with me, stay with me," she chanted, over and over, as she put pressure on the terrible wound in an effort to stop the bleeding. Only when Roderick sat up and started looking around for his weapon did she remember him. "You bastard! You goddamn *bastard!*" He was between her and the gun. If he reached it, she was dead and so was the wolf. She had no choice but to let go.

Jillian launched herself on top of her assailant, punching and kicking, screaming for someone to help her at the top of her lungs. It was more like wrestling than the kind of fighting she practiced, but she knew how to put power behind her punches. She managed to drill him solidly with a quick succession of blows, although a vulnerable spot was hard to come by from this position and she hadn't quite regained all of her strength after the accident. Harrison reeled, then rallied, surprising her with a powerful backhand. With his greater weight behind it, the blow knocked her flying. She landed on the pavement next to the wolf, rolled nimbly to her hands and knees. Dizziness had her pausing for a second, only a scant second, but it was long enough to hear the bolt of a rifle being slid back.

She looked up fast, fully expecting to be shot, but nothing was pointed at her. Douglas Harrison had a rifle trained on his father.

"Put it down, Dad."

Roderick had just closed his fingers around the stock of his own weapon. He spun around on his knees at his son's voice, his rifle in his hands. Beyond him, Jillian could see Connor emerge from the clinic at a dead run, then stop still when he saw the situation. She could hear sirens in the distance. Someone had called the RCMP. Could she make a break for it now—or would running set Roderick off? The man was still armed. Still crazy, unpredictable. And seemed more irritated than worried that his son was trying to stop him. Meanwhile, the wolf lay beside her, bleeding. If she left now, he would die.

Quickly Jillian kicked off her shoe and peeled off a sock

with one hand, folded it into a makeshift compress and
mashed it into the gaping exit wound. She pressed the heel
of her palm against it tight and held it, searched through
the bloody fur with her other fingers for a pressure point,
an artery. Something, anything, she could press to stem the
supply of blood. She glanced up, saw that Connor had
edged closer to the scene. Bill Watson was with him. She
also saw that Roderick was on his feet now, rifle at the
ready.

"They're werewolves! Every damn one of them!" Roderick was saying. "Thanks to you, we didn't finish this
white bastard off that night, and now look. There's a whole
fucking nest of them. Someone's got to make a stand.
Someone's got to stop them."

"No, Dad," said Douglas, never relaxing his grip on the
rifle. "Someone has to stop *you*. I was too young and too
scared to stand up and stop you before, but not this time.
Put the gun down."

"Want me to believe you'll actually *use* that? You couldn't
pull the trigger that night when there was a werewolf right
in front of your face. I told you to shoot. I told you, and
you just stood there sniveling." Roderick spat on the pavement. "Think I don't know you haven't picked up a gun
since? All you can pick up now is a glass. You couldn't
shoot me if you tried." He pointed his rifle then, not at
Douglas, but at Jillian.

"I mean it, Dad."

"It's still the best strategy. You know that killing these
two creatures will draw the rest out. There's a couple over
there already." Roderick nodded his head toward the
clinic. "More will come. We could get rid of the whole
bunch at once if you helped me."

"I won't let you do this again. Put it down, Dad."

Roderick ignored him, sighted on his target. There was a twin explosion of sound. And the old man was on the ground, his hands wrapped around his leg and a look of incredulity on his face. His own shot had gone wild, and his rifle had tumbled to the pavement. He made a wild reach for it, and Douglas fired again, placing the shot between his father's fingers and the fallen gun. Roderick snatched his hand back as if it was burned and glared at his son. "You don't understand. They won't let you walk away. You'll pay for letting these creatures go. They'll make you pay."

Douglas simply walked over and kicked the rifle across the parking lot, threw his own after it. "Pay what? I've already paid for the ones you killed. Paid and paid, my whole life. I'm telling the story to the authorities as soon as they get here."

"You called the damn cops on me?" Roderick's face turned purple with rage. "I raised you like a son. Even after your mother ran off, I raised you like my own son."

"She didn't run off," Douglas said quietly. "And the werewolves didn't kill her, either, did they? I talked to Rosa and we figured it out. Maybe you didn't mean it, maybe it was an accident. But afterward you had to make up a story you could live with. It's too bad more people had to die just to feed your fantasy."

"It's not a fucking fantasy. They're werewolves, every last one of them. I'd never have hurt her if they hadn't kept luring her away. It's their fault." Roderick pointed a shaking finger at Douglas. "Their fault that I . . . that I. . . ." He was silent then, holding his leg and rocking back and forth. He didn't look at Douglas again.

Bill had already knelt by Jillian's side. He threw a beefy tattooed arm around her shoulders and gave her a surprisingly gentle squeeze. "Are you okay, lovey?"

Connor was feeling the wolf's head as if searching for a fever, and closed his eyes for a long moment. "He's there, but barely," he pronounced. "We've got to take him inside." He didn't even glance at Jillian, just gave instructions. "Bill and I will carry him, and you keep your hand right where it is." He didn't wait for an answer. She had to move fast to stay in position as the men slid their hands under the wolf's body and lifted.

Sergeant Fitzpatrick and two of his officers ran by them as the trio made their way slowly toward the clinic with the injured wolf. Jillian glanced back only once. Roderick was still on the ground, hunched over and clutching his leg. He seemed shrunken. Defeated. One officer was kneeling in front of him, talking into a radio, requesting an ambulance. Another was gathering up the rifles from the pavement. Douglas stood with his arms folded, talking with Fitz. Everything seemed under control.

Jillian wished she had things under control. They were moving slowly and carefully, yet the crumpled sock she was using to put pressure on the wound was soaked through. She called for them to stop so she could kick off her other shoe and utilize that sock too. She folded it, packed it on top of the first sock and held it down tight. "Okay, I'm ready."

"No you're not," said Bill. "You've got bare feet now." He looked at Jillian and jerked his head toward the back entrance to the clinic, the one she had used only a short time ago. There was a sea of glass glittering on the pavement. The door itself was not only missing its window but was leaning outward and hanging askew, one of its hinges broken. It looked as if something had exploded through it . . . "And we're not bloody likely to fit through that door all together-like."

Connor considered. "We'll go in the truck bay and through the livestock wing. But we've got to move faster."

In the truck bay they were met by Culley and Devlin, who took over carrying the wolf while Connor ran ahead to the Small Animal Surgery. Bill offered to take Jillian's place but she shook her head. She was using both hands and dared not move either of them, not yet.

They laid the wolf on the biggest table in the surgery. It would have been on the small side for Cujo, Ruby Ferguson's ill-tempered dog. The wolf's body covered the stainless steel surface completely, his broad head hung over one end, and his long legs draped limply over the side.

Connor had a wheeled tray of sterile instruments laid out. He came around and stood by Jillian. "Okay, let's see what we've got."

Gingerly, she removed the socks, unrecognizable now. They were just wet red wads, little distinguishable from the damaged tissue itself, surrounded by blood-soaked fur. She sucked in her breath as she took a good clinical look at the wound. It was *huge*. Jillian didn't know what kind of gun Roderick had used, only that while the entrance wound was relatively small, the exit wound was a gaping hole. As far as she could tell, parts of the shoulder had been blasted clean away, bone, hide and all. Connor darted straight into the gory mess with fine instruments, seeking to clamp the blood vessels. Jillian blotted the welling blood with gauze pads, then started an IV.

They worked together, taking turns stitching the terrible mess as best they could. Connor's sister, Kenzie, had slipped into the room somewhere along the line and proved herself a capable nurse, keeping both vets supplied with whatever they needed. Jillian checked the vital signs frequently.

The wolf was still alive, but barely. Finally she took Connor's arm.

"This isn't going to work. The damage is just too great. There's no way to fix it."

He didn't look at her, just continued to work. "We're fixing it."

"But there's so much missing. The socket's gone, the attachments for the muscles. This animal is going to be permanently crippled and in pain, even if it survives. It'll have to live in captivity for the rest of its life."

Connor appeared to ignore her. She became aware then that not just Kenzie was in the room, but Culley and Devlin. Bill and Jessie were in the hallway, looking in. They weren't paying attention to her. In fact, no one appeared to have heard her. All eyes were on the wolf.

What was going on here? She'd never seen them all together in the same room, and none of them had been in this room. Had they all been here visiting at the clinic when the situation erupted? Everyone seemed so intense, as if it was a family member in a hospital emergency room. Was she not the only one the wolf had visited? Maybe all of them knew about the wolf, had a relationship with it just like she did. After all, James seemed to be familiar with it . . . And just where *was* James? She hadn't had a moment to notice before, but his absence now seemed very odd. If all his family and friends were here, if it was important to them, it would be important to him as well. And surely someone had called him to mention that a lunatic had held her at gunpoint. If he couldn't get here, he would have phoned, wouldn't he? Of course he would. Likely had, several times, but she'd been a little busy. And who knew if anyone was answering the phones? It was long after hours and Birkie was safely home. He's probably on his way right now, she thought. He'd be mad as hell that he hadn't been there to protect her and even madder that he couldn't get through to her.

"I need you, here." She knew Connor was talking to her. "Right here, your hands are smaller." She turned her attention back to the wolf, took another turn putting fine stitches in a seemingly futile effort to reassemble what wasn't there.

Connor lifted the lips of the wolf. The gums were pale, almost white. Connor swore, ripped open a drawer and rummaged through it. Pulled the wrapper off some transfusion tubing. There was an IV insert at both ends and a squeeze pump in the center. It was used to take blood directly from donor to recipient. It made perfect sense to Jillian. What Connor said next did not. "Devlin, you're up first."

What the hell? She stopped what she was doing and watched incredulously as Devlin pulled off his shirt, as Connor swabbed the inside of his elbow. "Wait! What are you doing?"

"We need blood. He's fading fast."

"Connor, have you lost your mind? You can't give human blood to a wolf. Are you *that* tired? You'll kill him."

All eyes were on her then, and it was uncomfortable. Their expressions seemed a bizarre mix of patience and pity, as if she were a small child who had just said something embarrassing. She automatically dismissed the odd impression as ridiculous. "There're no bags of canine blood left in the fridge until the supply truck gets here tomorrow—that amputation on the Great Dane took all we had. We could check with Sergeant Fitz if he's still here, ask if we could use his big Shepherd. Or Dalin Boyd has a Rottie and he lives just down the road. Maybe both."

Connor rubbed a hand over his face. "There are things

here you don't understand and there's no time to explain them."

"I understand that donor and recipient have to be genetically close."

"Trust me, Devlin's close. In fact, he's a perfect match. We've done this before." He stopped talking to her, and instead, instructed Devlin to hop up and sit on the counter by the sink. "We need some height here or it won't flow properly. Hold your arm like this. That's right."

What? *What?* Jillian stood open-mouthed, her bloodied hands arrested in mid-stitch. "You can't do this! I care about this wolf very much. I don't think we can save it, but I'm damn well not going to let you experiment on it."

Connor inserted the IV into Devlin's arm, taped it down. "I care about this wolf more than you know. I need you to either trust me or leave."

Bill came up behind her and put a huge hand on her shoulder, and Jillian was immensely relieved. "Tell him, Bill, something's wrong with him. Stop him. Make him understand."

"There's a lot you don't know about this creature, lovey. And a lot you do know. It's not really a wolf, you see.

"It's James."

Chapter Thirty-two

The sun came up. It was almost a surprise, considering the whole world had gone insane the night before. At least her world had. Jillian hadn't slept, but lay on her bed with a pounding headache that had nothing to do with the fading remnants of her concussion, and everything to do with launching herself at Connor when he tried to put the IV into the wolf's leg. She'd gone in swinging, determined to save the white wolf, and suddenly everyone was holding her; she was the one being dragged from the room. She'd struggled and screamed until her chin connected with someone's elbow. She hadn't knocked herself out, but it had stunned her. Long enough for them to barricade the surgery door against her.

She'd shouted and banged on the door to no avail. She ran to her apartment and phoned Birkie but there was no answer. She called the RCMP, the SPCA, and any other authority in the area she could think of. It wasn't office hours for anyone but the police, but she knew the individuals, found their home numbers in the phone book. Called long distance and got her old genetics instructor, Ian Craddock, out of bed. Told them all what her boss was doing and every one of them had the same reaction—they laughed. Connor's reputation was far too solid for someone like her to shake in any kind of a hurry, especially with such a bizarre story. If only James were here. He'd believe her. He'd make his brother see sense too, would save the wolf.

Would have. Past tense. If he'd only been here. Hours had gone by now.

The wolf, her wolf, the beautiful white wolf that had saved her life and shown her such affection, that had come to symbolize hope and all things good, had just saved her life a second time—this time at the cost of its own. If it survived the surgery—which was doubtful—it wouldn't have survived the cross-species transfusion. And there wasn't a single blessed thing she could do to change that. Grief welled up and spilled out, and she cried as she hadn't in years, cried even harder that James wasn't there to hold her. She had no idea where he was, only that she needed him. Her world had been turned inside out, and the only place it could ever make sense again was in his arms.

Where was he? She thought for sure he'd show up in the night. Or call.

Damned if she wanted to ask any of his family where he was. Or his friends. If what Bill had said was meant to be some sort of weird comic relief, not only had it fallen flat, it was in bad taste. Yet no one had said a word. Was it some sort of strange family joke? What kind of reaction had they been hoping for? It made no sense. *They* made no sense. She thought she'd gotten to know these people a little, thought they liked her. She had liked them a great deal, felt affection and acceptance from them. She'd started to feel that she could belong here. And now James was missing and his family and friends had somehow turned on her.

There was a knock at the door. "Jillian? Jillian, honey, can I come in?"

"Birkie!" Jillian hurried to the door, pushed away the table and chairs she'd angrily shoved in front of it. That hadn't served any purpose except to retaliate in kind— they'd blockaded her from the surgery? Fine, she'd make sure they couldn't get in here. Except no one had tried to get in. No one had come at all until now. *Not even James.* She nearly pulled Birkie into the room, hugged her thoroughly, cried some more although she thought she'd finished.

"There, there, hon, everything's going to be fine."

"Oh, it's *not* fine. Nothing's fine! The wolf is dead, my beautiful wolf. You didn't see what Connor was doing, you don't know—"

Birkie patted her arm. "Your wolf is still alive, hon. And reasonably stable too. They've got him recovering in the livestock wing—"

Jillian bolted for the door. She was prepared to take on anyone or anything that got in her way, but she encountered no one. The doorway to the livestock wing was wide open. The wolf had been bedded down in very human fashion, resting on a wide mattress and covered by blankets. Jillian stopped her headlong flight at the sight, approached slowly, almost hesitantly. Was it real? The rise and fall of the blankets was faint, difficult to discern. It looked like the wolf was breathing, but was that just what she wanted to see? She knelt and listened to the animal's muzzle, fingered an eyelid open with her gentle but shaking hand, and her heart caught at the sight of the familiar blue eye, rejoiced when the pupil shrank with the sudden light. She couldn't help herself. She placed a hand on each side of the animal's broad skull, touched its forehead with her own. And sobbed out her relief.

It was some moments before she could sit back, several

more before she caught her breath and quit hiccupping
and sniffling. She wiped her face on her shirt and perched
on the edge of the mattress, hugging her knees and rocking
a little. Peace was here. The world had gone berserk but
peace was here with the wolf, just like always. After yesterday, she wasn't sure where she belonged anymore. Except
here, with the wolf. Watching over him the way he had
watched over her.

"So how bad is it, bossman?"

"The glass for the back door will be here this afternoon.
The contractor says he'll have to replace the entire doorframe, but it'll all be done by the end of the day so we can
lock up tonight." Connor rested his elbows on the top rail
of the clinic corral. Sighed. "Good Christ, he kept asking
what happened to tear out the steel hinges like that. I had
to lie through my teeth and tell him a steer escaped from
the livestock wing and rammed through it."

"Well, you could hardly tell him that your brother went
through it. But that's not what I was asking about. I want to
know how bad things are with Jillian. Culley says things
got a little tense around here."

"Jesus, Birkie, that's the understatement of the century. It
was a tough surgery, an impossible surgery. I was trying so
hard to forget it was James because I couldn't afford the
distraction. Well, I forgot all right, and I also forgot I had a
non-changeling in the room. She thought I was trying to
kill him."

"Well, you have to give her credit for determination.
You wouldn't believe how many phone messages you've
gotten this morning from agencies and people she called to
try to stop you."

He groaned. "I have a lot of those on my cell too. Thank

God I know most of these folks. I'll have to call them all back eventually, although I don't know what to say. They already think she must have a screw loose—except her teacher, he wanted to know what I'd done to her—and it's not fair to her to agree with them. But I can't tell them the truth either." He rubbed his hands over his face, held them there for a minute. "God, Birkie, I can't believe this is happening. What are the chances of James getting shot again? It's even the same damn shoulder. And Fitzpatrick took me aside this morning and told me this is the same murdering bastard that shot James before."

"And killed our Evelyn. Yes, Fitz came by and told me. The son confirmed it."

"The whole thing is just uncanny, it's twisted, it's . . . it's just damn fucking wrong, is what it is."

"It's a chance for things to turn out right this time."

He groaned. "Fat chance of that."

"You're worried for James and Jillian both, aren't you?"

"Christ, yes! He's hurt bad. If he makes it—"

"He'll make it, Connor." Birkie's voice was firm.

"You haven't seen the damage. It's going to be weeks— maybe months—before he'll be able to Change. And what kind of hell will that be for her? Not knowing where he is. Not hearing from him. No matter what excuse we made up, it wouldn't account for it. If he was called away to visit a sick aunt, I would be too. And he could still phone. In fact, if he was in a coma in Timbuktu and couldn't phone, someone would still notify us and she'd be on the next plane."

"So what are we going to do, bossman?"

He wiped his face on his sleeve. Sighed heavily. "I don't know what to do. No idea. She loves him and what is she supposed to think except that he's taken off? And you know what the worst thing is? She's pregnant. James told me yesterday, had only just learned it himself."

"I thought she was. Her aura's been different for a while now. I felt a bit guilty but there was no way to warn her that human birth control methods are usually ineffective against Changeling males. She still thinks James is human."

"Which brings us to a very human problem. As far as Jillian knows, James went missing on the same damn day he found out she's expecting." He rested his arms on the top rail again, laid his forehead on them. "What's that going to look like?"

"Like he didn't want the baby—or her."

"What else could she think? Never mind the fact that she doesn't deserve that kind of heartbreak and stress. When he finally shows up, what's he going to say? What's the damage going to be to their relationship? And what's the damage going to be to James if he loses their relationship?"

"You're thinking too far ahead, Connor."

"Like hell I am. James loves her. I wasn't sure he could, wasn't sure he'd let himself, but he *loves* her. He's happy—you've seen him with Jillian."

"He's come a long way."

"We all prayed that James would come back to us, Birkie. Thirty damn years we prayed he'd come back. I'm scared shitless he'll go back to being a wolf and . . . and. . . ."

"You don't want to let him go." Birkie put a hand on his back as he buried his face in his arms.

"I can't let him go. I can't. He's my brother. We only just got him back."

"Well, there's only one thing to do then."

"What?"

"We have to tell her the truth."

Connor laughed harshly without looking up. "Oh, that'll work well. Bill already tried that. And besides, she doesn't trust any of us, not after this, and she especially doesn't trust me. She won't let me within a hundred yards of her."

"She trusts *me*. And maybe she won't let you near her in human form, but there's another option."

"You're kidding." He dropped his hands and turned to stare at her. "You must be."

"Desperate times call for desperate actions, hon."

At the sound of Birkie's voice, Jillian sat up and ran a hand through her hair. She'd been lying down, half on, half off the mattress, her face next to the white wolf's.

"I'm sorry, dear, were you sleeping?"

"No. No, just resting." She reached up and accepted a hug from the older woman, scooted over so Birkie could sit on the edge of the mattress. "I'm sorry I took off, I just—"

"You just had to see your wolf, I understand that." Her friend smiled at her, patted her arm. "You didn't know he was still with us. Sounds like he's a hero too."

"Yeah. Yeah, he saved my life. Again." Jillian felt herself tear up once more. Was it pregnancy hormones that had her blubbering at the drop of a hat? She felt like she'd cried more in two days than she had in her whole life. Sighing, she rubbed her eyes with the heel of her hand, then related yesterday's events in the parking lot. She was thankful anew for the fact that she could tell her friend anything. Sure, there was a very real white wolf lying right there, but Birkie had believed her from the beginning.

"The wolf loves you a lot, hon. He was there for you, protected you."

"I tried to protect him too, but everyone got so weird.

Birkie, they even threw me out of surgery! God, I wish James had been here to help me." Her eyes filled again, and she swiped at them irritably. "In fact, I just don't understand why he's not here now. Do you know where he is?"

Birkie took her hand, squeezed it. "Well now, yes I do, but it's going to take some explaining."

"Where—"

"Are we friends, Jillian? Do you trust me?"

"Well, yes, of course. Did something happen to James? Is he all right?" Her eyes widened suddenly. "He left again, didn't he? I told him I was pregnant and . . . and. . . ." She couldn't finish.

"And I've never seen a man so thrilled. I am too, by the way. We all are. Of course James didn't leave."

"Then where the hell is he? Look, please stop being mysterious and just tell me straight out."

Birkie shook her head. "Honey, I need to ask for your patience. I'll tell you absolutely everything, I promise, but I need a promise from you that you'll hear me out, that you'll listen with an open mind and an open heart. Can you do that?"

"I'm not liking this." Jillian had never seen her friend so serious. "But okay, I'll try."

"Last night Connor was doing something you didn't understand."

"Ha! Doesn't take much understanding. Blood's not generic, you can't mix species. That's elemental enough for a third-grader."

"Ordinarily that's true. If your wolf was an ordinary wolf. But he's not."

Jillian frowned, put a hand on the animal's head. "The DNA test said he's a wolf. I showed it to you."

"And exactly what kind of wolf did it say he was?"

"Well, that was inconclusive, but he's still a wolf."

"What if I told you he wasn't? Better yet, what if I showed you he wasn't?" Birkie turned and whistled softly.

Jillian was about to reply but her voice suddenly caught in her throat. An enormous wolf had appeared in the doorway. It filled the doorframe for a long moment, then stepped cautiously into the room at Birkie's beckoning wave.

"Birkie!" she managed to whisper as she grabbed her friend's arm and held it tightly. "It's as big as my wolf. My God, there's more than one."

"Oh yes. Quite a few, actually. These two are brothers."

Jillian goggled briefly at her friend, but had to turn her eyes back to the newcomer. It turned slightly, and she could see the silvery pelt was marked with a blanket of black over the shoulders—a saddleback pattern that was rare in wolves. Birkie extended a hand to it, and the huge creature trotted over immediately to lie at their feet. Jillian swallowed hard, opened her mouth to speak, closed it again.

"Here, you can pet him if you want to. He's mostly tame." Birkie rubbed the dark wolf behind the ears.

Jillian reached over to offer a hand to the handsome creature when she got a good look at its eyes. They weren't green but gray. Pale gray. For an instant she felt she was on the verge of remembering something. Then whatever it was eluded her, leaving her strangely disappointed. "He has really unusual eyes for a wolf," she managed.

"Yes, he does. So does your wolf, doesn't he?"

"Well, yes. It's one of the things that I can't explain. Wolves don't have blue eyes. Yellow eyes, brown, sometimes green. But not blue. And not gray either. It's like a whole new subspecies." The wolf touched its nose to Jillian's hand, licked her fingers, then bumped its head under them to be petted. "He seems to be just as friendly as my wolf, too." She sighed, shook off her fascination with the new animal and turned to her friend. "This is one hell of a secret you've been keeping. Why? Why didn't you tell me about this? After everything I confided in you about the white wolf, you couldn't mention you already knew about him, that you had a wolf, too?"

"Oh, he's not my wolf, hon, he's a friend. They're both good friends. And because of that, I wasn't free to tell you about them. I told you once that I keep confidences and I do." Birkie spoke to the dark wolf then. "I think you'd better show her now."

The wolf rose and trotted a few yards away.

"What does this have to do with James? Where is he?" Suddenly Jillian's scalp prickled strangely. She touched her hair and was surprised to find it standing straight up. She ran a hand through it, felt it crackle and snap with static. "What the—" She looked at Birkie. Her friend's hair was always perfectly styled, but there were stray hairs unwinding themselves now, and all of them were drifting upward.

A cold draft gusted through the room, and a shiver ran through Jillian from neck to tailbone. She glanced around for the source but the windows were closed and only a hallway lay beyond the door. The loft door was high above and behind her, but the breeze wasn't coming from there. It was coming from—

The dark wolf. Tiny bits of straw and hay were eddying around the floor, slowly at first, then faster. They swirled about the wolf, and blue sparks snapped and popped in the air. *I've seen all this before. But that was—*

Without any warning, the big animal was gone and in its

place stood Connor Macleod. He looked just as he usually did, with his denim shirt and torn jeans, and his hands resting in the pockets of a rumpled lab coat. The breeze died away. A few blue sparks crackled in the air, fell to the concrete and went out.

Stunned, Jillian felt as if her brain had winked out as well, as if a fuse had blown. Her mind was blank for a long moment, then it was suddenly bombarded with an avalanche of thoughts and ideas, all coming together at once. Bill's words. The vision in the loft. The wolf in her apartment. The stories she had read, the legends she had studied. *Brothers*, Birkie had said, the dark wolf and the white wolf. Gray eyes—and *blue*.

She put her hands to her head, held on tight as it threatened to explode. Then the thoughts converged, neatly, like streams feeding into a river. They merged, melded, flowed smoothly and effortlessly into a whole. Jillian put her hands down, drew a deep breath. Another. Put her shaking hand on the white wolf's broad forehead, stroked it gently, let calmness and peace fill her until she was steady and could open her eyes.

"Are you okay?" It was Connor. Birkie was looking at her, too.

"Is that a trick question? A wolf just turned into my boss right in front of me, my boyfriend turns out to be a wolf I've known for years, and I'm supposed to be okay?" Jillian laughed a little, ran her hand through her hair. "Actually, a lot of things make sense now, and that's what scares me. It's a good thing to be worried about being crazy, though, isn't it? Like if you think you might be insane, you're really not?"

"You're not crazy, not at all." Birkie slid an arm around

her and squeezed. "In fact, you're doing just great, honey. Give yourself some time. It's a lot to take in, a lot to get used to."

Jillian shook her head in wonder. "Oh God, it feels like I woke up on another planet. A few moments ago, were-wolves lived only in movies and books. Now they're real. And I can barely believe I said that." She looked up at Connor. "You were using Devlin's blood last night because he's a werewolf, too, isn't he?"

"A Changeling, yes. Our whole family. Bill and Jessie. Fitzpatrick. A few others."

"Fitzpatrick? Sergeant Fitzpatrick? You're telling me that the head of our local RCMP detachment is a werewolf?" Although why that should be any more shocking than the rest, she didn't know.

"Changeling," Connor corrected. "Yes, Fitz is a Changeling just like the rest of us."

"Changeling." She tried out the word. "Well, at least it sounds a little less Hollywood than *werewolf*." Jillian turned to Birkie then. "Is everyone in town a Changeling? Are you a Changeling too?"

Birkie smiled and shook her head.

"Well, that's a relief. I was starting to feel like the only human left." Jillian looked down at the wolf as she stroked its ears. The blanket was rising and falling steadily now; she didn't have to strain to see if he was breathing. *He. The wolf. James.* Cold fear abruptly squeezed her heart. "I think . . . I think I'd rather believe that James left me than believe that he's lying here hurt like this. Is he going to be okay?"

"I can't promise anything," said Connor. He checked the white wolf's vitals, then laid a hand on her shoulder. "I wish I could, but you're a vet. You saw the damage for yourself, and you can guess that James isn't out of the woods yet. Ask me again in forty-eight hours, ask me when he wakes up. He's stable right now; we're all hoping and praying he stays that way."

He was right. As a vet, it was exactly the prognosis she'd give, but it still hit her hard. The wolf could die, and she'd already shed plenty of tears at the thought of losing her lupine friend. But to never see James again . . . *Dear God.* She shoved the terrifying thoughts to the back of her mind, slammed the door on them tight. Tried to focus outside herself. Thought about Connor—what had it been like to have to operate on a family member?

A family member. Jillian thought of the others who had been in the operating room, and realized she wasn't the only one scared to death.

Chapter Thirty-three

His hand on the white wolf's broad forehead, Connor's eyes were closed. He sat perfectly still as if listening. Long minutes passed before he finally looked up. "I can't reach him. I've tried and tried since this happened, but I can't seem to connect with him."

At Jillian's puzzled expression, Birkie leaned over and whispered, "Telepathy, dear. Most Changelings can talk to each other in their minds."

"Of course they can." Jillian felt as if she'd just slipped a few notches further down the proverbial rabbit hole. *Can they fly, too?*

Connor continued. "James may need help finding his way back to us. If you talk to him, it could help."

"You mean he's in a coma?"

"Not in human terms. He's not only inside the wolf's body, but he could be locked in the wolf persona as well," said Connor. "For all intents and purposes, he is a wolf. And James needs to be reminded he's human. It's the human side we need to connect with. He'll listen to you. You've got a powerful connection to both the wolf and the man."

"What do I say?"

"Anything at all," Birkie explained. "The sound of your

voice might give him something to latch onto. Like a life-
line."

"And then he'll wake up? Will he be himself, I mean,
will he be human then?"

"No. But just waking up would be a hell of a lot of
progress," said Connor. He looked like he was about to say
more, but shook his head and abruptly left the room.

Birkie hugged Jillian. "I imagine you'd like a little time
to yourself, honey. We've dumped a lot of information on
you. I'll bring you some lunch in a while, answer more
questions if you have them. I imagine you'll have a lot. Are
you okay for now?"

"Yeah, I'm mostly fine. Thanks." She put on a brave face,
managed a smile even as emotions surged through her. But
as soon as Birkie left, the tears began to fall and this time
she didn't try to stop them. Some were out of relief, and
some were out of fear. Eventually they slowed enough to
let her find her voice. "They tell me you're in there somewhere, James," she said to the wolf, stroking its ears, its face.
"I'm scared to believe it and scared because I *am* believing
it. I need you to come back to me and help me understand
it all. I'm pretty lousy at asking for help, James, but I'm asking now. Come back to me and help me sort this out, because I'm worried I've gone crazy. I'm scared the
concussion has hurt something in my head and I'm delu-
sional. Or maybe being pregnant has affected my brain."
The tears started again, and she knotted her hand in the
wolf's thick mane, held onto it as if she was dangling from
a cliff and it was the only thing left to hang onto.

"What I'm most afraid of is that you're gone. You know
I love you, James, but you don't know how much. *I* didn't
know how much. And I'm so scared it's too late and I
won't get to tell you face-to-face just how much you mean

to me. I really want to build that life with you. Come back to me."

Deep within the wolf, a faint awareness stirred. James struggled against the thick gray haze that seemed to blanket his mind. Pain was on the other side of the fog, searingly bright, waiting to stab at him. And he was tired, more tired than he'd ever thought possible. Exhaustion pressed down on him like a weight. A stray thought surfaced that he must be still alive. Surely he couldn't be this damn tired if he was dead.

Someone was talking to him. A woman. He should know her, she was important. Green eyes. He knew she had green eyes, so he should know who she was, shouldn't he? He worried at the puzzle for a few moments, then let it be. Just listened to the soothing, pleasant voice, felt it stroke his mind with familiar fingers. Listened until the dull waves of oblivion began to pull him under again.

No. He couldn't let himself fade out, he had to find this woman. Somehow, everything would be all right if he could just find her . . . if he could just find. . . . *Jillian! I've got to get to Jillian!*

Memories flooded back like an inrushing tide. James had been in the clinic's lunchroom, putting together a meal for two. He'd had his head in the fridge when the most god-awful fear had gripped him by the throat. Fear for *her.* He raced for the apartment but she wasn't there, wasn't anywhere. The sense of danger screamed along every nerve he had; the wolf within snapped and snarled. *The wolf will know where she is. It always knows where she is.* Instantly he'd called the Change, given the wolf its head. And the wolf had wheeled and raced for the back door with all the power and speed at its command, hurled itself through the narrow window in an explosion of metal and glass.

He'd barely touched the pavement when James caught sight of the gun trained on the woman he loved. His heart stuttered for a single beat. And then he bounded across the heated pavement, leapt with bared fangs. . . .

Then what? He wasn't quite sure what happened after that. He'd been injured, probably shot, but it didn't matter. What mattered was that he must have been in time, James and his wolf together, they must have been in time to save Jillian. She was alive, he could hear her, sense her, feel her, right here next to him. She was all right. And the child within her, his child, must be all right too. Safe. All safe. James relaxed into the wonder of it, his heart satisfied, peaceful. He focused contentedly on Jillian's voice, listened to her words.

"—please come back to me, James. I miss you and I'm so confused. They tell me you're in there somewhere but I can't feel you. I need you to come back and explain all this to me, make it make sense—"

Wait! I'm right here. He had never heard Jillian sound so lost, so sad. Not since the wolf had found her on the trail all those years ago. With a start, James realized he was in wolf form now too. He shouldn't be, he should have Changed—unless he couldn't. *Just how bad am I hurt?* He turned inward then, felt carefully along the edges of his awareness where gray fog hid the bright lines of pain. Followed those lines to their source and discovered his shoulder to be all but missing. *Again?* Good Christ, it had taken months to recover last time and this wound felt even worse. But he hadn't been trying then, couldn't have cared less if he lived or died last time. Now, he not only wanted to heal, he wanted to be human again. He had to get to Jillian, had to reach her, talk to her. Hold her. *Especially* hold her. But there would be no Changing with this kind of injury. A Changeling had considerable regenerative powers, but they could be accessed only in wolfen form. Not only that, his lupine side would not permit him to Change. Period. The wolf was devoted to James's survival and all energy would be funneled into healing.

Meanwhile, Jillian needed him, and here he was lying down on the job.

Not for long, he decided. If the only way he could comfort the woman he loved was by licking her face and wagging his tail, he was damn well going to do that much. Slowly, tentatively, James began the long agonizing climb through the haze toward consciousness.

The full moon silvered the rocks on Elk Point, touched the tips of the trees with sterling. Not to be outdone, the stars blazed overhead in a deep velvet blue canopy. Jillian wrapped her arms around her knees and allowed herself, just for a moment, to forget everything except the vivid beauty of the night. She drank it, breathed it, drew it into her lungs as if she couldn't get enough, drew it into her soul. There was a harmony here that spoke to her deeply, that she had missed in the past few years in the eastern city. Missed without even knowing what it was she was missing. The work at the clinic fed her mind. The northern countryside was unexpectedly feeding her spirit, comforting it.

Coming here seemed to be good for the white wolf too. She looked down at the magnificent animal stretched out on a rock beside her, his snowy coat glowing in the moonlight. *James. James is in there.* She reminded herself of that often, although her wolf still felt like, well, a wolf. The massive creature might have eyes that were the same shade of Viking blue as James's eyes—but she couldn't see James behind them. Her throat tightened with grief even though James wasn't dead. At least, everyone said he wasn't dead, that he was right there inside the wolf. But she couldn't feel him there.

Blue eyes looked up at her, and the wolf nudged her arm with its nose. Jillian complied, putting an arm around his neck so he could lay his massive head in her lap. *There won't be much room for that soon.* She wondered if the wolf knew about the baby. She wondered if James remembered the baby, or her, or anything at all. Was he thinking as a wolf or as a man?

I should be grateful he's alive at all. I should just be glad for that. After surgery, it had been four whole days before the wolf awakened. Four long, terrible days when she didn't know if he would live or die, if she would lose both her beloved wolf and the man she loved. She had watched over him, night and day. And on the fifth day, she had awakened to a large pink tongue licking her face.

Things had been better then. She talked to the wolf endlessly as she cared for him, although she still couldn't think of him as James. The handsome creature seemed to pay attention to every word, was even more affectionate than before. Sometimes she heard its voice in her mind, reassuring her that she wasn't alone. But it was never more than a few stunted words, it wasn't really James's voice—did the wolf have its own personality, separate from the man?—and it didn't diminish the pain of missing James. She still felt a great calm when she was near the wolf, but there was sadness underneath, an ache that never went away no matter how hard she fought it.

While he could offer no guesses as to when her James

might return, Connor had been right about the incredible regenerative powers of Changelings. The white wolf's shoulder was largely intact now, healed from the inside out. The gaping wound had closed over recently, but not before Jillian saw that fresh bone and joint and tendon had replaced the broken and the missing.

Exercise was the best medicine then. Small amounts at first, slow circles around the clinic before and after closing time, until the injured leg would bear the creature's weight. Then longer walks outside. Always at night of course. The presence of a giant white wolf at the North Star Animal Hospital would raise eyebrows if not alarms. Lately, as the wolf's limp became less pronounced, Jillian had been driving out to the riverside trails below Elk Point. It was still a covert operation. The wolf hid under a blanket in the back of the truck, and they could go only at night. Occasionally Connor had accompanied them, sometimes Birkie. But most nights she preferred to walk alone with the white wolf. And every night she wished she was walking with James.

She swiped at her eyes with her sleeve. *This whole werewolf thing is really getting on my nerves.* For a human being, she thought she'd been pretty damn patient, accepting of the impossible, understanding of the bizarre. She'd seen not just Connor but the other members of his family Change into wolves several times now, had met all the members of the Pack and gotten to know their stories. It had been fascinating at first, especially to a veterinarian. But right now she was just a woman who needed her man's arms around her. And she had no idea when that would happen—or if.

"Damn," she sniffled. It was getting much too easy to feel sorry for herself. She pushed the sadness back, imagined packing it into a box and mailing it to Antarctica. It didn't really work, nothing worked, but it distracted her a bit. After all, James wasn't dead. He was alive somewhere, and she should be glad for that. She was determined to try to stay positive, both for herself and the baby. But it was harder every day.

The wolf nudged her arm, sat up next to her, dwarfing her. She leaned against the thick soft fur, felt the wolf's tongue on her forehead. He pushed her again with his nose, leapt down from the rock and trotted away. Perhaps he was getting a drink. The wolf was often restless lately, a good sign that he was recovering fully.

Jillian watched the moon's reflection glimmer in the river below. The night was warm and dry, and she considered sleeping right here in the circle of stones. She'd be warm enough next to the wolf, and certainly safe.

Without warning, a blast of wind surged out of nowhere, whipped leaves around her, chilled her. She yanked the edges of her jacket together, but the icy current of air had already ceased. *What on earth was that? Wind sheer? A micro burst?*

She glanced up at the stars and froze. One seemed to be moving, falling—and suddenly she realized it wasn't a star at all, but a spark. A tiny blue spark. It drifted down and landed on the rock beside her, sizzled the edge of a dry leaf and winked out.

"Jillian."

She whipped around to see James standing in the stone circle. Her heart caught in her throat and she began shaking. "Are you real?" she managed at last.

In answer, he opened his arms and she ran to him.

"You're alive, oh God, you're alive, you're back, you're here, omigod please tell me you're really here," she sobbed out as she was enfolded in the familiar strength, the heat.

She breathed him in, smelled him, tasted him with frantic kisses, ran her hands over every part of him she could reach.

His big hands were moving too, running over Jillian's body, through her hair, cupping her face so he could cover it with kisses, thumb away the tears. "God, honey, don't. It's all right," he murmured, tucking her head under his chin and wrapping his arms around her tightly, rocking her. "It's all right now."

She couldn't settle, couldn't relax. Her entire body was alight with raw, instinctive need and she struggled to get her hands under his shirt. "Just touch me, oh God, James, please touch me. I need you, I need—" Words failed as urgency overpowered her. She had to get to his skin, had to press her skin to his. *Had to.* Some primeval switch had been thrown, and she might die or implode if she didn't get these damn clothes out of her way.

The wildness infected him too. James's lips became hungry on hers, and the offending clothes disappeared rapidly. Hands flew, his and hers, in frenzied need, to touch, to grasp, to glide over trembling flesh. Lips left hot trails of rapid, desperate kisses. Hearts beat with a primal need to be in one skin. They tumbled to their knees, still entwined around each other. He bore her backward and paused, about to thrust into her, and touched her belly with a question in his eyes.

"It's all right," she whispered. Jillian gasped as he filled her, as he reared back and filled her again and again. Oh, *yes*. This was exactly what she wanted, what she craved. *Yes, yes, yes* . . .

She clung to him with arms and legs, breathed his name into his mouth and rose to meet him. It felt so good, so damn good as his much larger body moved over hers, into hers. He overwhelmed her with heat and strength, yet she wanted it. Wanted him, heart and soul and body. All the worry and fear and loneliness of the past few months slid away as she called for him to bring her. They peaked together, and on the long, slow drift back to earth, she felt the world right itself.

James stirred reluctantly and found himself facedown in the sand, half on Jillian, half off, but probably still too heavy for her. Sense rushed in then and quickly he raised himself on his elbows and looked at her. There were tears on her face. "Oh Christ, I've hurt you." He sat up at once, scooped her into his lap, wiped the tears with his knuckles as he scanned her body frantically. "I'm sorry, I didn't mean to be so rough, it's just . . . I just . . . and the baby. I was worried about the baby, but—"

She put her fingers over his mouth. "Relax. The baby's fine. I'm fine. Everything's fine."

"But—"

"*But* I totally loved it. *But* I'm happy." Her eyes were dreamy, delighted as she looked at him. "You didn't hurt me, so quit with the sorries, okay? The doctor said that sex wouldn't bother the baby in the least."

"Really?"

"I promise. Here, check for yourself." She pulled his big hand over her stomach, rested her hands over it. "See?"

Her belly was sweetly rounded, just beginning to bloom. Had he lost more time than he thought? "Um, just how long have I been MIA?"

"About three months or so."

Jesus. He hugged her to him then, kissed her forehead. "I'm sorry to have left you on your own for so long."

"If you say you're sorry again, I'll have to hit you. Yes, I missed you like crazy, I was scared and worried, and I had to take everyone's word for it that you were still alive. And why was that? Because you saved my life. Because I needed you and you came. Don't be sorry for that." Her voice gentled then and she cupped his face with her hands. "We've both been through a lot. Let's just focus on the now, okay? I just want to spend a lot of time enjoying you."

In answer, he kissed her long and deep and slow, rubbed her tummy in lazy circles—and froze.

"What? What's wrong now?"

"Shhh—nothing. Here, move this way." James sat up straighter, pulled her into the vee of his long legs with her back against him. Kissed her temple to distract her as he reached his hands around her, all senses alert. He sought a spot low on her belly, skimmed his hands back and forth over the warm skin like a caress. And suddenly there it was. Life. Carefully he sought to discern, to sense, to sort the shimmering vibrations he felt into—

Two. James's heart skipped a beat as he realized there were *two.* No mistake. The delicate sensations fluttered beneath his hands and in his mind like faery wings. Joy and wonder surged through him, and he began to laugh.

"What's so funny? Did the baby move? I didn't feel anything."

James only laughed harder, the sound full and rich and deep, booming through the stone circle and echoing across the valley. That little frown appeared between Jillian's brows and still he couldn't stop the laughter. Finally, he flopped weakly back on the sand.

Jillian found her sweater, blotted his face with the sleeve. "Are you okay? Are you done now?"

"Yeah. Yeah, I think so." For God's sake, he was practically wheezing. And his sides ached, but oh, it felt so good.

"Are you going to let me in on the joke or was that just post-wolf hysterics?"

"There's no joke, honey. We're gonna need two cribs."

She goggled. "What?"

"Twins, we're having twins."

"We are *not*."

"Trust me, there's two in there." He watched her struggle to come up with an argument, shook his head at her. "Sorry but Changelings can tell. Have you ever seen Connor use that fancy new ultrasound at the clinic?"

"Of course I—well, I don't see him do a lot of things," she said defensively. "We're both busy." Her face changed suddenly and she grabbed his arms. "This isn't some cute little way of telling me we're having a litter, is it? How could I have been so dumb? The baby's a Changeling isn't it? I've been so worried about you that I didn't even think—"

He nearly burst out laughing again at the alarm on her face, but wisely decided to choke it back. "Twins don't constitute a litter, honey."

She didn't look reassured. "You think this is funny, but I've never seen any werewolf children. No one in your family has any kids except some sister I've never met."

"Carlene. In Wyoming," he supplied. "She has three."

"Whatever. For all I know they're all running around on four legs."

"Only when they want to. No, wait!" She was trying to move away from him, but he caught her and pulled her firmly back into his lap. "I'm sorry, I can see I'm not taking this seriously enough. You deserve a straight answer. My brothers and sisters and I are all Changelings but we started out like normal human children. Looked like them, acted like them, played and fought and laughed and cried like them. No pointed ears, no fangs, and no fur. No eating of raw meat. Definitely no tails."

"You're sure?"

"Cross my heart."

"Really sure?"

He waved a hand at the circle of stones around them. "Elk Point is a sacred place. I couldn't tell a lie here even if I wanted to."

"The baby's fine?"

"Babies," he corrected. "Yes, they're just fine. In fact, they're wonderful and so are you."

She placed her hands over his where they rested warm on her belly. Her fingers were trembling. "Oh God, James, it's all so much. We're going to have a family. We're going to be parents. I'm going to be—"

"My wife. And a brilliant partner at the North Star Animal Hospital. And the director of an innovative new wildlife rehabilitation center. And the most beautiful mother on the planet." He moved his hands up to cup her breasts, nuzzled over her hair to plant kisses on the sensitive nape beneath. "You're going to be busy, honey. I think we'd better do this again while we can still fit it on your calendar."

"Do what?" she laughed, although he could tell she knew.

In answer he simply cradled her against him and sought her lips. And loved her slowly, sweetly, thoroughly.

Epilogue

The October day was a gem. Warm, bright sun and cool, pleasant air. Perfect, James thought, for the official opening of the Northern Lights Wildlife Center. He surveyed the crowd assembled in the middle of the new complex, noted the TV news crew and the dignitaries with no small sense of pride as Jillian Macleod stepped down off the podium amid a long clatter of applause. She'd been a bundle of nerves for days, rewriting her speech constantly. But when the time came, she'd set the speech aside and simply talked to the audience about what animals meant to her, and how grateful she was to work with them. It was perfect. *She* was perfect.

He shifted the toddler dozing on his shoulder, wondered if Culley still had her brother. Or maybe Devlin had stolen Hunter by now. There was fierce competition for the twins among James's siblings, and he counted himself lucky to have gotten a turn to hold even one of his children. He planted a kiss on little Hailey's forehead, breathed in the soft smell of her hair. The twins were almost two now and their very existence amazed him. He imagined he'd still feel that way when they were twenty.

He lost sight of Jillian as the crowd milled about, inspecting the facility. Among them, he knew, were fellow veterinarians, zoo directors, and representatives from other wildlife centers across the continent. James couldn't resist putting his Changeling senses to good use and listened in on bits of conversation, picked up their surprised and approving comments on his wife's innovative design. He recognized plenty of local people as well, clients from the clinic, farmers and ranchers from the area. Jillian had gained quite a following.

He saw Douglas Harrison, acknowledged him with a nod. After the arrest of Roderick, James had learned there were more victims than he knew—and realized Douglas was one of them. He'd asked Fitzpatrick to arrange a meeting. "I don't imagine I can ever forgive what happened to Evelyn, but I do know it's not your fault," James had said to Douglas. "You were a kid, you weren't responsible for what your father did. You couldn't have stopped him either. I wish he hadn't done it, but I wish just as much that you hadn't seen it." He'd left it at that. Fitz kept him updated, let him know that Douglas was doing well. Roderick on the other hand would be spending his remaining years in a psychiatric ward rather than prison. The man's mental state had deteriorated rapidly when police unearthed Corena Harrison's sad remains in the wooded area of his ranch.

Finally the crowd seemed to be thinning. James wondered how long it would be before he saw his wife again when suddenly she appeared in front of him. He kissed her soundly, then scooped an arm around her to pull her closer and kissed her again. "You were great up there. I liked what you said, and I think everyone else did too. Did you finish your tour already?"

"I gave a couple of interviews and then Zoey handed out press releases. Connor took over the tour for me." She plucked the child from him and settled her on one hip. Hailey stretched, grinning sleepily at her father. "Birkie wants to take her home now. She and Kenzie are watching them both tonight."

Tonight. The night of the full moon. Jillian's left hand was bandaged and he reached for it, intending to inspect the bite wound beneath the gauze, but she yanked it away. "It's still fine since the last time you looked at it. I'm a vet, trust me."

He settled for grabbing her other hand, held it firmly. "You're feeling all right?"

"Never better," she said lightly and turned to walk away but he didn't let go.

"I mean it, Jillian. It's your first Change." They'd talked about it for months. She'd made her decision to join his world fully—yet only by biting her could he give her that gift. It was the hardest thing he'd ever done. And now, with her first Change imminent, he was the one needing reassurance.

"Are you trying to scare me? You weren't this nervous when Hunter and Hailey were being born. I got through that and I'll get through this, and you know that both Zoey and Jessie have been coaching me." She stood on her tiptoes and kissed his cheek. "Okay, I'm nervous, too. But all my life I've dreamed of understanding animals better. This is more than I ever imagined possible, and I want it, James. I want all of it. I want the wolf and I want *you*."

He held her, just held her, for a long moment until Hailey became restless. He tickled her and she squealed, breaking the bubble of tension within him.

"You know," Jillian stage-whispered, "if you let me give this child away, we could have a couple of hours to ourselves before dark."

He let go of her immediately. Jillian laughed as she walked a few steps, then thought of something and returned.

"Are you going to the house, hon? Could you please put this in some water?" She pulled open her lab coat to reveal a carefully rolled-up paper napkin protruding from the inner pocket. "Someone left it on the podium for me." She gave him a long lingering kiss, filled with the reassurance James needed—and a promise for later that he was looking forward to collecting.

He watched as Jillian and Hailey bounced away across the complex. Saw them meet up with Birkie and Kenzie. Culley and Devlin were playing with Hunter—and James didn't need Changeling ears to hear Hunter's delighted yells. He chuckled and looked down at the napkin Jillian had placed in his hand. Unrolled it carefully to reveal a tiny stalk of lily of the valley that didn't seem to know how out of season it was.

A return to happiness. He looked again at his family. Knowing more than happiness. Knowing joy.

Good girls should NEVER CRY WOLF.
But who wants to be good?
Be sure to pick up Cynthia Eden's latest novel, out now!

Lucas didn't take the woman back to his house on Bry-
ton Road. The place was probably still crawling with
cops and reporters, and he didn't feel like dealing with all
that crap.

He called his first in command, Piers Stratus, to let him
know that he was out of jail and to tell him that there were
two unwanted coyotes in town.

The woman—Sarah—didn't speak while he drove. He
could feel the waves of tension rolling off her, shaking her
body.

She was scared. She'd done a fair job of hiding her fear
back at the police station and then at the park, at first anyway. But as the darkness had fallen, he'd seen the fear.
Smelled it.

Sarah had known she was being hunted.

He pushed a button on his remote. The wrought-iron
gates before him opened and revealed the curving drive
that led to his second LA home. In the hills, it gave him a
great view of the city below, and that view let him know
when company was coming, long before any unexpected
guests arrived.

When the gate shut behind him, he saw Sarah sag

slightly, settling back into her seat. The scent of her fear finally eased.

Like most of his kind, he usually enjoyed the smell of fear. But he didn't . . . like the scent on her.

He much preferred the softer scent, like vanilla cream, that he could all but taste as it clung to her skin. Perhaps he would get a taste, later.

With a flick of his wrist, he killed the ignition. The house was right in front of them. Two stories. Long, tall windows.

And, hopefully, no more dead bodies waited on the steps here.

He eased out of the car, stretching slowly. Then he walked around and opened the door for Sarah. As any man would, Lucas admired the pale flash of thigh when her skirt crept up. And he wondered just what secrets the lovely lady was keeping from him.

"We're going in to talk." An order. He wanted to know everything, starting with why the dead human had been at *his place.*

She gave a quick nod. "Okay, I—"

A wolf bounded out of the house. A flash of black fur. Golden eyes. Teeth.

Shit. It wasn't safe for the kid. Not until he found out what was going on—

The wolf ran to him. Tossed back his head and howled.

Sarah laughed softly.

Laughed.

His stare shot to her just in time to catch the smile on her lips. His hand lifted, and almost helplessly, he traced that smile with his fingertips.

Her breath caught.

Lucas ignored the tightening in his gut. "Shouldn't you be

afraid?" After the coyotes, he'd expected her to flinch away from any other shifters. And Jordan was one big wolf, with claws and teeth that could easily rip a woman like Sarah apart.

She looked back at the wolf who watched them. "He's so young, little more than a kid. One who is glad you're—"

No.

Understanding dawned, fast and brutal in his mind. *I'm more than human.* She'd told him that, he just hadn't understood exactly *what* she was. Until now.

His hands locked around her arms and Lucas pulled her up against him. Nose to nose, close enough so that he could see the dark gold glimmering in the depths of her green eyes. "Jordan, get the hell out of here." He gave the order to his brother without ever looking away from her.

The wolf growled.

"Go!"

The young wolf pushed against his leg—*letting me know he's pissed, 'cause Jordan hates when I boss his ass*—and then the wolf backed away.

"Now for you, sweetheart." His fingers tightened. "Why don't we just go back to that part about you not being human?"

Her lips parted. She had nice lips—sexy and plump. He shouldn't be noticing them, not then, but he couldn't help himself. He noticed everything about her. The gold hoops in her dainty ears. The streaks of gold buried deep in her dark hair. The lotion she'd rubbed on her body—that vanilla scent was driving him wild.

He was turned on, achingly hard, for a woman he barely knew. Not normally a big deal. He had a more than healthy sex drive. Most shifters did. The animal inside liked to play.

But Sarah . . . he didn't *trust* her, not for a minute, and he didn't usually have sex with women he didn't trust. A man could be vulnerable to attack when he was fucking.

"You know what I am, Lucas," she said and shrugged, the move both careless and fake because he knew that she cared, too much.

"*Tell me.*" Her mouth was so close. He could still taste her. That kiss earlier had just been a tease.

Try MISTRESS OF THE STORM,
the third in Terri Brisbin's sensual trilogy, out now!

Every possible space in the hall of Duntulm Keep was filled. Many of those who owned land in the surrounding areas attended the early autumn feast hosted by Davin to meet the men from Orkney and take their measure. Though invited to sit at table with him, Duncan declined Davin's invitation, choosing to sit away from the guests so he could observe them. It seemed the fires of hell had left his sense of curiosity intact when they burned away all the rest, so he listened and learned much about the visitors from the north.

Greeted as cousins, they were related to Davin through the marriage of their grandparents or some other ancestor, and the welcome he gave was warm. Foodstuffs and ale were plentiful and everyone ate and drank their fill. Ornolf placed a bowl and cup before Duncan, bothering him every so often so he would eat and drink. The smoke grew thick as the fires burned lower, offering heat but not much light. The torches and rushlights added what they could, but Duncan could see clearly through the dimness and the haze.

It was a strange effect he'd noticed the last few months, and served him well in his attempts to watch and learn. He was studying the similarities in appearance between Davin and the one called Ragnar when the woman arrived. The room suddenly grew brighter and the chatter lessened as though everyone wanted to see her at once.

Nothing she wore was ostentatious, but the cut of her gown drew every man's eyes to her body. He could not identify the material of it, but it draped her curves as though painted over her flesh instead of being a garment. Duncan noticed the tightened nipples of her very full breasts as the gown molded to them and the way it fell into the junction of her thighs. When she turned to sit down, he and every other man noted the way it hugged her arse, flowing into the indentation of the cleft and outlining her strong legs. Watching her move in it, he did not have to imagine what her body was like—he could see it.

He let his gaze wander over her, waiting for her to be seated so he could see her face.

Something he had not felt in months coursed through him in the moment their eyes met. A heat, a need, a wanting made him ache. Her eyes widened as though she knew her effect, but she looked away when someone spoke her name.

Isabel.

Who was she?

What was she?

How could she cause him to feel the blood heating and rushing through his body when he'd thought himself empty of such things? Duncan shifted in his chair and continued to watch as the attention of those gathered began to drift back to the honored guests. But he realized every man eventually turned back to watch Isabel.

She'd gathered and arranged her hair in a way that made her look well bedded. Its black waves accentuated every move she made and framed the creaminess of her skin perfectly. It was her mouth that sent waves of heat through him; her lips were bow-shaped and red as though well kissed. The blush in her cheeks added to the display—one he could tell was orchestrated carefully for its effect. Tearing his gaze from her, Duncan looked at the people she had followed into the feast.

Strange.

The man and younger woman she'd walked behind had taken seats much closer to their host, while she remained farther away. Was she the girl's maid? Neither of the women resembled the man in any way for he was as light as they were dark in hair and eye coloring. Duncan thought the women might be related based on the frequent glances they shared, cousins probably, though mayhap even sisters.

But, if sisters, why did they so clearly separate themselves at table?

The meal continued and Duncan resumed his perusal, watching her as she ate the food placed before her, and as she spoke to others, seeming to watch every move made by the man with whom she'd entered. It was only when she lifted her chin, gazed up at the ceiling of the chamber and closed her eyes that Duncan realized he'd seen her before. Searching his memory, he finally remembered where and when.

In the early hours just as the sun rose, when unable to sleep, he would walk the battlements of the keep, gazing down at the sea and the village outside the walls. Several times in the last months he'd noticed her leaving the keep just before dawn, and walking to the south beach.

With nothing more than curiosity to keep his attention, Duncan would watch as she took off her clothes and flung herself into the water. Her practice was the same each time he'd watched—dipping twice under the surface of the water and scrubbing her skin as she did. Then she would plunge down and remain in the freezing waters until he thought she'd perished. He remembered several times when he began counting how long she stayed under the water, wondering if she would rise from it at all.

Over the months he'd witnessed her behavior, the changes within him making any tension he felt as he counted out the seconds lessen—until he'd watched in complete disinterest, no matter how much he knew he should be concerned.

Watching the way she tilted her head, he was reminded of the way she looked up at the sun as she walked, sometimes struggling, out of the waves. In the earlier times he'd seen her, he'd thought she might be a selkie or water spirit. But, lately, he observed her actions from an emotional and physical distance—until she lowered her head and gazed at him through her lashes.

That heat seared him again, letting him feel things he'd not felt in months. Was she a selkie risen from the sea or some otherworldly creature capable of giving him back all he'd lost? His moments of disinterested watchfulness were over, for his body and his soul knew she was more than she appeared, and his mind knew he must discover her secrets and their link to his own. Standing, his feet moved before he could think on what words to say or what he wanted. All he knew was that he wanted . . . her.

Don't miss DEAD ALERT by Bianca D'Arc,
Coming next month . . .

Fort Bragg, North Carolina

"I've got a special project for you, Sam." The comman-der, a former Navy SEAL named Matt Sykes, began talking before Sam was through the door to Matt's private office. "Sit down and shut the door."

Sam sat in a wooden chair across the cluttered desk from his commanding officer. Lt. Sam Archer, US Army Green Beret, was currently assigned to a top secret, mixed team of Special Forces soldiers and elite scientists. There were also a few others from different organizations, including one for-mer cop and a CIA black ops guy. It was an extremely spe-cialized group, recruited to work on a classified project of the highest order.

"I understand you're a pilot." Matt flipped through a file as he spoke.

"Yes, sir." Sam could have said more but he didn't doubt Matt had access to every last bit of Sam's file, even the top secret parts. He had probably known before even sending for him that Sam could fly anything with wings. Another member of his old unit was a blade pilot who flew all kinds of choppers, but fixed wing aircraft were Sam's specialty.

"How do you like the idea of going undercover as a charter pilot?"

"Sir?" Sam sat forward in the chair, intrigued.

"The name of a certain charter airline keeps popping up." Matt put down the file and faced Sam as his gaze hardened. "Too often for my comfort. Ever heard of a company called Praxis Air?"

"Can't say that I have."

"It's a small outfit, based out of Wichita—at least that's where they repair and maintain their aircraft in a company-owned hangar. They have branch offices at most of the major airports and cater mostly to an elite business clientele. They do the odd private cargo flight and who knows what else. They keep their business very hush-hush, *providing the ultimate in privacy for their corporate clients,* or so their brochure advertises." Matt pushed a glossy tri-fold across the desk toward Sam.

"Looks pretty slick."

"That they are," Matt agreed. "So slick that even John Petit, with his multitude of CIA connections, can't get a bead on exactly what they've been up to of late. I've been piecing together bits here and there. Admiral Chester, the traitor, accepted more than a few free flights from them in the past few months, as did Ensign Bartles, who it turns out, was killed in a Praxis Air jet that crashed the night we took down Dr. Rodriguez and his friends. She wasn't listed on the manifest and only the pilot was claimed by the company, but on a hunch I asked a friend on the National Transportation Safety Board to allow us to do some DNA testing. Sure enough, we found remnants of Beverly Bartles' DNA at the crash site, though her body had to have been moved sometime prior to the NTSB getting there. The locals were either paid off or preempted. Either option is troubling, to say the least."

"You think they're mixed up with our undead friends?" They were still seeking members of the science team that had created the formula that killed and then turned its victims into the walking dead. Nobody had figured out exactly how they were traveling so freely around the country when they were on every watch list possible.

"It's a very real possibility. Which is why I want to send you in undercover. I don't need to remind you, time is of the essence. We have a narrow window to stuff this genie back into its bottle. The longer this goes on, the more likely it is the technology will be sold to the highest bidder and then, God help us."

Sam shivered. The idea of the zombie technology in the hands of a hostile government or psycho terrorists—especially after seeing what he'd seen of these past months—was unthinkable.

"If my going undercover will help end this, I'm your man." He'd do anything to stop the contagion from killing any more people.

Sam opened the flyer and noted the different kinds of jets the company offered. The majority of the planes looked like Lear 35's in different configurations. Some were equipped for cargo. Some had all the bells and whistles any corporate executive could wish for and a few were basically miniature luxury liners set up for spoiled celebrities and their friends.

"I'd hoped you'd say that. I've arranged a little extra training for you at Flight Safety in Houston. They've got Level D flight simulators that have full motion and full visual. They can give you the Type Rating you'll need on your license to work for Praxis Air legitimately."

"I've been to Flight Safety before. It's a good outfit." Sam put the brochure back on Matt's desk.

"We'll give you a suitable job history and cover, which you will commit to memory. You'll also have regular check-ins while in the field, but for the most part you'll be on your own. I want you to discover who, if any, of their personnel are involved and to what extent." Matt paused briefly before continuing. "Just to be clear, this isn't a regular job I'm asking you to do, Sam. It's not even close to what you signed on for when we were assigned as zombie hunters. I won't order you to do this. It's a total immersion mission. Chances are, there will be no immediate backup if you get into trouble. You'll be completely on your own most of the time."

"Understood, sir. I'm still up for it. I like a challenge."

Matt cracked a smile. "I hear that. And I appreciate the enthusiasm. Here's the preliminary packet to get you started." He handed a bulging envelope across the desk. "We'll get the rest set up while you're in flight training. It'll be ready by the time you are. You leave tomorrow for Houston."

"Yes, sir." Sam stood, hearing the tone of dismissal in the commander's voice.

"You can call this whole thing off up until the end of your flight training. After that, wheels will have been set in motion and can't be easily stopped. If you change your mind, let me know as soon as possible."

"Thank you, sir." Unspoken was the certainty that Sam wouldn't be changing his mind any time soon.